HMS SUBMISSION

Christopher gasped. His first kiss! It was messier than he'd imagined it would be: wet and awkward and clumsy and the most wonderful thing he'd ever experienced. The crotch of his trousers grew tighter, chafing his swollen prick as Willicombe's tongue continued to explore his mouth. Christopher's shaking hands slid down the rough work-shirt and gripped the solid flesh of Willicombe's bare buttocks.

Breaking the kiss, Christopher slipped a hand beneath the underfootman's sandpapery chin and tilted his face upwards.

Willicombe's eyes were closed.

'I want to lie with you, Willicombe.' The words were out before he could stop them. 'I want to lie naked with you, as you lay with Elsa. I want to rut with you as the deer in the forest rut.'

HMS SUBMISSION

Jack Gordon

First published in Great Britain in 1998 by
Idol
an imprint of Virgin Publishing Ltd
Thames Wharf Studios,
Rainville Road, London W6 9HT

ISBN 0 352 33301 4

Cover photograph © i2i Images

Typeset by SetSystems Ltd, Saffron Walden, Essex
Printed and bound in Great Britain by
Mackays of Chatham PLC

SAFER SEX GUIDELINES

These books are sexual fantasies – in real life, everyone needs to think about safe sex.

While there have been major advances in the drug treatments for people with HIV and AIDS, there is still no cure for AIDS or a vaccine against HIV. Safe sex is still the only way of being sure of avoiding HIV sexually.

HIV can only be transmitted through blood, come and vaginal fluids (but no other body fluids) passing from one person (with HIV) into another person's bloodstream. It cannot get through healthy, undamaged skin. The only real risk of HIV is through anal sex without a condom – this accounts for almost all HIV transmissions between men.

Being safe
Even if you don't come inside someone, there is still a risk to both partners from blood (tiny cuts in the arse) and pre-come. Using strong condoms and water-based lubricant greatly reduces the risk of HIV. However, condoms can break or slip off, so:
* Make sure that condoms are stored away from hot or damp places.
* Check the expiry date – condoms have a limited life.
* Gently squeeze the air out of the tip.
* Check the condom is put on the right way up and unroll it down the erect cock.
* Use plenty of water-based lubricant (lube), up the arse and on the condom.
* While fucking, check occasionally to see the condom is still in one piece (you could also add more lube).

* When you withdraw, hold the condom tight to your cock as you pull out.
* Never re-use a condom or use the same condom with more than one person.
* If you're not used to condoms you might practise putting them on.
* Sex toys like dildos and plugs are safe. But if you're sharing them use a new condom each time or wash the toys well.

For the safest sex, make sure you use the strongest condoms, such as Durex Ultra Strong, Mates Super Strong, HT Specials and Rubberstuffers packs. Condoms are free in many STD (Sexually Transmitted Disease) clinics (sometimes called GUM clinics) and from many gay bars. It's also essential to use lots of water-based lube such as KY, Wet Stuff, Slik or Liquid Silk. Never use come as a lubricant.

Oral sex
Compared with fucking, sucking someone's cock is far safer. Swallowing come does not necessarily mean that HIV gets absorbed into the bloodstream. While a tiny fraction of cases of HIV infection have been linked to sucking, we know the risk is minimal. But certain factors increase the risk:
* Letting someone come in your mouth
* Throat infections such as gonorrhoea
* If you have cuts, sores or infections in your mouth and throat

So what is safe?
There are so many things you can do which are absolutely safe: wanking each other; rubbing your cocks against one another; kissing, sucking and licking all over the body; rimming – to name but a few.

If you're finding safe sex difficult, call a helpline or speak to someone you feel you can trust for support. The Terrence Higgins Trust Helpline, which is open from noon to 10pm every day, can be reached on 0171 242 1010.

Or, if you're in the United States, you can ring the Center for Disease Control toll free on 1 800 458 5231.

Prologue

M ick slipped an arm around the silken-scarfed neck and pushed the figure into the alley.

The man tripped, began to struggle. He opened his mouth.

Mick pressed the edge of the knife against a smooth throat, half-steering, half-dragging the figure onward.

Beneath the sharp blade, a prominent Adam's apple bobbed. A gasp hissed from surprised lips and resounded in the night air.

It was already too much. Mick seized a flailing arm. 'One shout, my lord –' twisting a finely boned wrist upwards, he held it firmly against the man's back and increased the pressure of the knife '– and, by God, it will be the last sound to leave your mouth!'

The struggles ceased.

Mick tightened his grip. 'I'm glad you value that voice of yours, my lord – and, to be sure, a fine voice it is too.' He glanced around once, scanning the narrow alley. It was now well after midnight and their surroundings were dark and secluded. Thrusting the well-dressed figure against a wall, Mick released the wrist but kept the knife at the fellow's throat.

The man stumbled a second time.

Mick caught him, before those beautifully cut clothes became smeared with muck and grime. 'Up you come, my lord.' Using the knife, he manoeuvred the rigid figure around to face him.

High above the alley, a shard of moonlight illuminated a pale, apprehensive face. 'You will hang from the gallows at Newgate for this!' The deep voice trembled, cutting the feet from under brave words.

'I do not think so, my fine friend.' Mick pressed the edge of the blade beneath the strong chin and tilted the face upwards into the moonlight.

Younger than he'd thought, when he'd first spotted him back in the alehouse: a gentleman in search of opium or another of London's illicit pleasures. Barely thirty, but tall and broadly built. It was their closeness in size which had drawn Mick's attention. He focused on the fine down of blond fuzz above a quivering lip, exerting a little more pressure beneath the whiskerless chin.

Another gasp left the full mouth. 'I have money.' Panic had now replaced the bold taunt. 'Take it – please take it!'

Mick cocked his head. 'Sure I know you have money, my lord –' his free hand fingered the rich brocade of the man's frockcoat, slipping under the silken tassels of a necktie and flicking them upwards '– and other things of value.' The hand wandered down six silver buttons, pausing at the top of well-fitting silk breeches. As he brushed a palm lower, the strong face paled under the moon's yellow glow. 'Take your clothes off!'

The pale skin blanched further. 'I – I, er –'

Mick's laugh was deep and good-natured. 'And be quick about it!' Still laughing softly, he plucked the three-cornered hat from the carefully coiffured head and fingered the long feather which sprouted from the brim. With a flourish, he placed it jauntily on top of his own tangled locks, where it perched at a rakish angle. Removing the knife from the man's throat, Mick sheathed the blade. His other hand left more reluctantly. Ever vigilant, he glanced over his shoulder then moved back, blocking any means of escape from the alley with his bulk.

The well-cut frockcoat came first. Hauling off his own, sadly ragged garment, Mick threw it on the filthy ground and carefully placed the man's finer jacket on top of it, feeling the money-pouch heavy in the inside pocket: a welcome bonus. The ruffled shirt, with its delicate cuffs of lace came next, then hand-tooled buckle shoes, hose and breeches of the best Irish linen.

Mick wrenched off his coarse undershirt and tossed it over his shoulder, where it landed in a pool of sewage. Worn, threadbare pantaloons joined the undershirt. He wore no underwear or socks, and the ripe unwashed smell of his strongly masculine body drifted up into his nostrils.

Standing naked except for the three-cornered hat, Mick watched the man hesitate at the rich cotton galligaskins which were all that stood between his vulnerable body and the cool night air. Aware of a familiar stirring in his groin, Mick pushed the thought away: this was business. 'Don't worry, my lord – one prettier than you awaits my company tomorrow.' He sank to a crouch, gripped the waistband of the man's undergarment and tugged.

Then stared.

As the loose underpants bagged around pale, quivering knees, another paleness drooped tantalisingly downwards from a bristling blond bush.

The man's member was limp with fear, draped in a heavy coat of ruffled skin which fell in folds over the hidden head. But even flaccid its length and girth almost took Mick's breath away. Six inches. Hard, it had the potential for at least ten, if the foreskin ruffles were anything to go by. He whistled long and low. 'And what have we here, my lord?'

Hanging tight behind the large member, the man's artistocratic balls shrank further.

Mick's eyes travelled up from the thick cock to a scarlet face.

The man raised shaking fingers to a frowning mouth.

'To be sure, this is a most unexpected gift.' Mick reached out a hand and wrapped his fist around the shaft.

The man bit into clenched knuckles. A low moan escaped quivering lips. Involuntarily, the member twitched against a rough palm.

Mick chuckled. 'So it wasn't merely laudanum which brought you down to the docks.' He held his fingers loosely around the length, savouring the way the man's cock flinched in his hand with every whispered truth.

The responding moan was lower this time.

'You were watching the longshoremen, my lord . . .' Mick's own groin tingled. The man's reply came in a twitch against his fingers. 'You were watching them drink, their strong, work-stretched muscles relaxing in the oil lamps of the alehouse as they caroused with the serving wenches.' He could feel the man's breath on his face, sour with porter and fear. Mick inhaled another smell from the pungent groin inches from his eyes. 'What were you thinking while you watched, my lord?'

A sharp intake of breath mirrored a sharp twitch against his palm. The cock stretched another inch – in girth and length.

'Did you wish it was yourself, seated upon that docker's knee, his toiled-hardened hands running all over your body?'

'No, no –'

Mick grinned as the man's staff thickened in his grip. 'Were you imagining that burly longshoreman's cock jutting up through his hide breeches and rubbing against your leg while he whispered lusty words into your ear?'

'No, no – I –'

'Oh yes, my lord.' The thick hair on his chest rose in the night air. 'That is exactly what was going through your mind. Maybe you have arranged a tryst with one of the seamen? Is that where you were skulking off to, when I pushed your good self into this dank, dirty alley?' Mick stared up at the anguished face.

The man's silence spoke volumes. As did the steady thickening against Mick's fingers.

Mick tightened his grip, feeling the skin stretch from corrugation into silk. 'Another rough rogue is waiting somewhere out there – waiting to slake his lust with you.' He ran his thumb over the engorging head of the man's prick as it burrowed through the heavy layer of foreskin.

The aristocrat groaned.

Mick grinned. Between his own, well-muscled thighs, another prick was pushing its way up his stomach. The grin slipped from lips which parted in a corresponding longing: it had been a good few days, and he had to admit the man was tempting.

But he had what he wanted. Further lingering in the area would be a risk.

The stout length of flesh pulsed against his palm and made its presence felt in the hurried debate.

Mick glanced once over his shoulder, then rose to his feet. 'Well, since you have been kind enough to donate your fine clothes to my worthy cause, it is only right that I give you something in return, my lord.' Fist tightening on the man's staff, he steered the shaking figure into the darkest recesses of the alley and fell to his knees.

One hand still gripping the knife, Mick pressed his face into the man's warm groin. As he sucked the first four inches of aristocratic prick into his mouth, the three-cornered hat slipped from his tangled hair.

Mick ignored it: mud would brush off. Flicking with his tongue, he eased another inch of meat between his lips.

The length twitched, engorging further.

Mick groaned as the man's prick swelled in his mouth. His hand released the shaft and moved to the tight bollocks. A sheen of sweat slicked their taut, hairy surface. Cupping the heavy sacks, he rubbed the root of the man's cock with his thumb and moved forward. Teeth sheathed behind widening lips, Mick bore down until his nose was buried in wiry blond hair and the man's entire length entered his mouth.

A sound, half-sigh, half-whimper drifted down from the face above.

Mick barely heard the man's pleasure. Blood pounded in his ears. Other blood was rushing to swell and stretch the cock further. The large head pushed past Mick's soft palate and into the top of his throat.

He fought the gag reflex, breathing heavily through his nose against convulsive swallows.

Two feet above, the whimpers lowered in tone and became grunts of satisfaction as Mick's throat caressed the prick.

The scent of lavender water filled his head, barely disguising the ranker, manly odour of the man's arousal. A tiny drop of anticipation dampened the edges of Mick's slit in response to the smell. Jutting up from between his own legs, his own cock flinched as Mick dragged the salty man odour deep into his lungs and tried not to choke.

His throat slowly relaxed. Every other muscle in his body was tensed and enflamed. Kneeling there in the alley, Mick waited until his victim's prick lay fully erect along his tongue. Then he tightened his lips around the root and slowly raised his head.

He could taste the arousal now, which leaked freely from the tip. Savouring every inch of flesh, Mick flicked his tongue over the tiny slit and continued to draw his lips up the solid shaft to the velvet head.

The low grunt from the man pinned to the wall replaced the sound of blood pounding in Mick's ears. Hips thrust towards him, following the movement of his lips.

Mick paused, flicked again.

Another grunt. Another thrust of pale, lavender-scented hips.

Then a hand on the back of his head, pushing his face back down.

In a lightning movement, Mick unsheathed the knife. A fraction of a second later, his arm arced above his head and he was pressing the razor-sharp edge against what he hoped was the man's throat.

Breath hissed through clenched teeth.

Then the hand on his head removed itself.

Mick kept the blade there and continued to draw his mouth up nine flexing inches.

Now they both had something to fear. Mick grinned around the rim of the cock's large head, then raised his eyes.

In the moonlight, his captive's knees were bent. Head lowered in the direction of his captor, the man's wig was askew and the aristocratic face was a mask of terror and barely concealed desire.

Rolling his tongue over the velvet glans, Mick removed the blade from the man's throat and hooked the tip beneath the powdered locks. The wig landed somewhere to his left.

Mick stared into dilated pupils, his tongue continuing to stroke the sensitive glans.

The man's fists were clenched. Desire and need rendered every sinew rigid.

Never breaking the gaze, Mick eased his lips out then up and over the helmet-shaped head.

'No – no – no – no –' Wigless, the man's shorn, spiky skull shook from side to side.

Mick cradled the large head on his bottom lip, gently grazing the tender underside with unsheathed teeth.

'No – no – please –'

Brushing his navel, Mick's own shaft bucked and twitched. Thick stomach hair was damp with expectation, and a tightening in his swollen bollocks made him gasp.

'No – please –'

A shaking hand lowered itself, twining fingers into Mick's long dark locks.

'Please don't stop –'

Mick dropped the knife. Hands gripping the man's goose-fleshed arse-cheeks, he pushed his mouth back down the quivering shaft.

The cock filled his mouth. Above him, the aristocrat's words were replaced by a series of low moans, which grew to low, grunting gasps as Mick dragged his lips up and down the man's stout staff. Pulling the fellow closer, his hands slipped between the man's thighs, fingering the heavy ball-sac in rhythm with the strokes of his mouth.

Expertly manicured hands tightened in his hair. The cock flexed along his tongue. Breathing rapidly, Mick felt the tension ripple up from deep inside the fellow.

Then the hot seed hit the back of his throat in a thick wad.

Slumping back, Mick opened his throat further and clasped the aristocrat to his face.

The spunk trickled down his gullet. He barely tasted it, amidst the heaves and shudders of its owner.

In the distance, vague voices drifted through the night, just as Mick's own release built in his balls.

Pulling himself away, he jumped to his feet. The naked aristocrat slid down the wall, limp and drained.

Mick listened, grinning at the exhausted figure.

The voices were getting closer.

Grabbing the heap of purloined clothes and his knife, he seized the man's chin with his other hand. 'Thank you, sir.' He lightly kissed the parted lips. Then Mick stuck the three-cornered hat on his head and bounded from the alley.

One

———

'Charge your glasses, ladies and gentlemen. Christopher and Violet!'
'Christopher and Violet!'

The sound of clinking crystal and congratulatory salutes rang in his ears. At his father's side, Christopher managed a wan smile. Gathered in a semi-circle around them, his own and Lady Violet Marlborough's relatives were applauding. Several of the ladies looked a little envious – as did a good few male guests. He stared at his betrothed's plump, comely face.

Lady Violet coyly hid her rosy lips behind a fluttering fan. From beneath long, thick lashes, her large brown eyes sent another, all too clear message.

Christopher squirmed inside his tight-fitting frockcoat and focused on the sparkling diamond tiara nestling pertly within his betrothed's hair. The Marlboroughs could trace their rich lineage back to Norman nobility: anything they hadn't inherited they could buy – including, they presumed, a suitable fiancé for their youngest daughter.

'Now, if I may be permitted to say a few words –'

Good-natured laughs of scepticism greeted his father's request.

Christopher sighed, impatiently smoothing invisible creases from his starched white shirt: down from Oxford a mere three weeks and already his family were cluttering up his time with social niceties. His research into the poetry of Geoffrey Chaucer lay waiting in the library.

Lady Violet fluttered her fan. The sparkling hair decoration reflected light from a large chandelier. Christopher blinked.

Those ancient papers and intricate manuscripts called to him in a way Lady Violet had so far failed to do, on any of their three previous meetings. His was a scholar's life: books were his long-term companions. He had few friends and certainly no need of a wife.

A paternal palm patted his shoulder. Viscount Fitzgibbon's voice cut through his musings: 'My son is indeed a fortunate young man to have secured such a jewel.'

Christopher's hands curled into fists of discomfort. He managed another apology of a smile. The announcement of their betrothal had been a sudden, hurried affair, surprising everyone – himself included.

As Viscount Fitzgibbons droned on, his son and heir looked beyond Lady Violet's immaculately coiffured ringlets and tried to rein in his impatience.

The crowded ballroom was filled with exquisitely attired people he didn't know and whose acquaintance he had no desire to make. Above the elaborately scupltured wigs and hair adornments, Christopher Fitzgibbons' gaze moved along row upon row of other, sombre-faced Fitzgibbons.

Captured for ever in frowning oils, the family gallery scowled disapprovingly down on him.

His father: recently retired from the navy, after an illustrious career which had begun as a midshipman to Captain Cook and ended fighting shoulder-to-shoulder with Admiral Nelson.

His grandfather, who had opened up the East Indies route and secured valuable trade for his king and country.

His great-grandfather, second officer on board one of the first British vessels to round the horn of the great Dark Continent.

A lineage stretching all the way back to the first Fitzgibbons, who had travelled with Drake to the New World and received his viscount-ship for services to Her Majesty Good Queen Bess.

Christopher shivered: the mere smell of the sea made him ill. The very thought of ships drained the colour from his aristocratic, finely chiselled features. He tore his gaze away from his ancestors' stoical scrutiny.

In the background, the present viscount continued to extol the virtues of Lady Violet, his flattery bordering on the bawdy.

Christopher cringed. Moving his gaze over the top of his guests' heads to the newly commissioned oil of Cook's *Discovery*, he caught the sparkling eyes of Willicombe, the new underfootman, stationed at the far door.

The man smiled impishly, then winked.

Startled by the servant's audacity, Christopher dragged his eyes away. A sudden heat drenched his body.

'Now please take your partners for a polka.' Viscount Fitzgibbons' hearty voice cut through Christopher's confused thoughts.

Before the blush had a chance to reach his cheeks, he was grabbed by his betrothed and pulled into the dance. Gazing at Lady Violet's ample bosom, Christopher could only hope his flushed face would be attributed to anticipation of the approaching nuptials.

'Do you know the Marquess of Sligo, my love?'

Christopher looked blankly at his fiancée, still trying to recover his breath from the last dance. 'Er, I don't believe I have had the pleasure.' He scanned the group of young men who buzzed attentively about Lady Violet like bees around a honeypot. Most of his betrothed's friends were strangers to him. Christopher wiped his sweating face with a linen handkerchief. Introductions had already been made to five of the dandies, but their names had passed over his head.

'Michael McGuire at your service, sir.' The words were tinged with just the hint of an Irish brogue.

Christopher stared at the tall, broadly built figure who bowed then extended a hand. The voice was bassily powerful, and the straightforward offering of a fist made a pleasant change from the flouncing extravagances of the rest of Violet's fawning entourage. He gripped the man's fingers and immediately felt his own crushed in an iron grip.

'You are a lucky fellow, sir.'

Violet giggled and hid her mouth behind her fan.

Christopher smiled and tried to drag his hand free.

The grip increased in power. 'Lady Marlborough is a more lovely flower than any which grow in the poppy fields of Ireland.'

The discomfort in his fingers was growing. He tried to make them smaller, in order that they take up less space in the man's broad palm.

Violet was giggling again.

The dark eyes twinkled. 'Indeed, there are many more delights in England's green and pleasant lands than I thought.'

Christopher was sure he could feel the fine bones in his hand start to crumble. Transfixed by smouldering pupils, he detected something behind the words, something which caused him more discomfort than his crushed knuckles. With all the strength he could gather, he wrenched his hand free. 'Thank you!' His voice unusually was shrill.

One of the dandies sniggered. In the background, the orchestra struck up a quadrille.

Beneath his tight-fitting jacket, Christopher was sweating profusely. The pain in his tired feet eclipsed the throbbing in his crushed fingers. The beginnings of a headache pulsed at his temples. If he had to dance another step his legs were sure to give out. Red-faced, Christopher groped for further pleasantries as he nursed his damaged fingers. 'What brings you to England, my lord?'

Ignoring his question, the tall man turned to the Lady Violet and bowed. 'Would you do me the honour – if the Honourable Christopher has no objection?'

Over a broad shoulder, twinkling eyes regarded him with some amusement.

Christopher flapped his damaged hand and winced. 'Please do.'

His fiancée's eyes barely registered Christopher's permission. She fluttered her fan. 'It would be my pleasure, my lord.'

As he watched the man lead a still-giggling Lady Violet towards the centre of the room, whispered words from the dandies seeped into his ears. Relief at his narrow escape from further exertions overcame any sense of irritation. Christopher quickly scanned the room.

His father was deep in conversation with Lord Marlborough.

His mother was smiling with a group of ancient dowagers.

Music and the sound of light feet filling his ears, Christopher slipped unnoticed from the crowded ballroom.

His father had locked the library, and securing the key without drawing attention to his absence from the celebrations was not an option.

'Checking on the deer, sir?'

Strolling through the grounds of Fitzgibbons Manor in an attempt to clear his mind, Christopher jumped at the breathless voice behind. He turned.

A pair of eyes shone impishly through the twilight.

Christopher shook his blond head. 'Just walking.'

'Fine night for it.' Willicombe rubbed his large, callused hands together enthusiastically. 'Mind if I walk with you, sir?'

In truth, Christopher was slightly annoyed at the intrusion, but he was too tired to protest. 'Not at all.' The rugged face of the Marquess of Sligo hovered in his mind, taunting him.

Willicombe fell in step at his side. 'She's very beautiful.'

Christopher paused, staring at the man.

'Your betrothed.' The curly head nodded respectfully. 'If you don't mind me saying so, sir.'

Christopher almost smiled. 'I don't mind – and yes, she is lovely.' He walked on.

'And popular.'

A frown descended over Christopher's fine features. 'Yes, very popular. I'm a lucky fellow.' He repeated to himself what everyone had been telling him all night.

'Don't worry – it's just nerves, sir.'

'Nerves?' The muscles in his stomach tightened.

'Yes, sir – we all get them the first time, so to speak.'

Christopher sneaked a glance at his unexpectedly insightful, if forward, companion. About his own age, Willicombe was new in his father's employ. On his arrival from Oxford, Christopher had noticed the boyish-faced underfootman, noted the strong muscles beneath the sleeves of the man's well-fitting blue livery as he'd lifted the heavy boxes of books down from the carriage as though hefting mere feathers.

Tonight he had changed out of his uniform and was casually dressed in rough work-shirt and breeches. A scarlet kerchief was jauntily knotted around his unshaven neck.

'Yes, you're probably right.' Christopher suddenly wondered why he felt more at ease with this rough creature than he did with any of the guests back in his father's ballroom.

Side by side, they ambled along a narrow path in silence.

From what his mother and his own eyes had told him, Christopher knew at least three parlourmaids and the scullery-girl had already fallen under the boyish footman's spell, giggling and whispering whenever Willicombe was in the vicinity. He stared at the brightly coloured neckerchief and wondered if it was some lover's token. The idea made him vaguely uncomfortable and he wrenched his eyes away, concentrating on the increasingly dim path ahead and the solid tramp of Willicombe's hobnailed boots.

Somewhere in the distance, a bird-call soared through the dusk.
'Nightjar.'

Christopher paused, turned.

Willicombe was staring up into the trees.

A different bird replied to the first.

'Thrush –' the man cocked a curly head towards the sound '– singing to his mate.'

Then a hoot. Christopher smiled, recognising the unmistakable call of a night hunter. 'An owl?'

An expression of surprise broke over Willicombe's boyish features. 'Aye, sir – tawny owl. Are you interested in birds?' Dark eyes examined his.

The smile froze on Christopher's face. A sudden warmth flooded his cheeks, although evening's chill was settling fast with the night. He looked away from the curious gaze, fumbling for words. Abruptly, nature took pity on his confusion and a veritable twilight chorus broke out in the foliage above their heads.

Willicombe laughed and named them all, pointing upwards.

Transfixed by the rich, West Country voice, Christopher barely heard a word. He stared at the side of the underfootman's rosy-cheeked face. The man was badly in need of a shave, and dark bristles edged the heavy jawline in darker shadow.

'April, sir.' Willicombe laughed.

The sound dragged Christopher's eyes away from the object of his scrutiny.

His dazed look was registered and misinterpreted.

The laugh grew coarser. 'Spring – the sap rises in all God's creatures, sir.'

Christopher watched in horror as the man gripped the ample bulge in the front of his hopsack work-breeches.

Then another sound rose over the call of the birds: a harsh, guttural snort, accompanied by a dull clang.

Christopher jumped, scanning the thicket in sudden panic.

'They've started, sir.' An edge of excitement tinged the words. 'Come on!' Willicombe swerved off the path and began to creep through a particularly densely packed group of trees.

A louder snort from somewhere beyond the thicket made Christopher hesitate, eyes fixed to the slowly receding seat of the underfootman's rough breeches. Then another clash of antlers pulled him from reverie and he found himself following.

★

'You dance like an angel, my lady.' Mick smiled, twirling her into another turn.

'I am not your lady, my lord.' The response was teasingly coquettish.

His smile broadened as he took in the rising flush in her powdered cheek. He quickly replaced it with an exaggerated sigh. 'Sadly, I have been beaten to that honour.' His mind recalled the slim, strangely uncomfortable youth whose long fingers had almost turned to clay in his grip. 'And by a mere boy, at that.' He twirled her again, brushing her ear as she twisted past him. 'You need a man, Lady Marlborough.'

'Foo!' Violet tossed her head haughtily, hiding a titter behind a flourished fan. 'I believe you have the devil in you, my lord.'

And I believe you want my devil in you, my blue-blooded temptress! With a deft flick of his wrist, Mick spun the tiny-waisted woman away from him, in accordance with the quadrille, and took another partner.

As Violet linked arms with man after man, he watched with satisfaction as her elaborately jewelled head turned time and time again to find him. Suppressing a smile, Mick looked away and threw himself into the dance, lavishing compliments on a succession of adoring ladies.

He knew Lady Violet's type: they only wanted what they couldn't have, and the more they couldn't have it the more they wanted it. For the rest of the evening he found other delights with which to occupy himself, making sure he was poised to embark on another polka or minuet with yet another blooming virgin whenever Lady Violet managed to inveigle her way into his vicinity.

She was indeed a spirited filly, and using her own haughtiness to break her was amusing. Mick almost envied the slim, awkward youth his place in her marriage bed, after he had taken what he intended to take.

In the throes of another mazurka, he couldn't help wondering where the Honourable Christopher had vanished to.

When Christopher emerged breathless from the copse, pulling twigs from his hair, Willicombe was leaning against the large trunk of a fallen tree. In the clearing ahead, two huge, dappled stags stood feet apart, heads lowered. An impressive crown of horn sprouted upwards from each skull. A little away, a doe was casually nibbling bark from a sapling.

The dark curly head turned, index finger pressed silently to full lips.

Christopher crept forward.

One stag pawed the ground, snorting steaming streams of aggression which condensed in the cooling air.

Then both animals charged. The sound of their tangling, clashing antlers resounded in Christopher's ears. Then a whisper:

'They're fighting over who gets to mount her, sir – see?'

Unused to such language, Christopher recoiled, just as one of the stags twisted its heavy head lower, forcing itself and its opponent up on to two legs. Christopher stared at two other fully stretched members which jutted out from between fuzzy hindquarters, mirroring an unwelcome twitch in the crotch of his own well-fitting hose.

His gaze was registered. Willicombe's low, awe-filled voice filtered through the clank of antler and the snorts of frustration:

'Can you smell them, sir? Smell their lust?'

Night scents drifted into his nostrils, above a darker, muskier odour. The unfamiliar aroma penetrated deep into his lungs and made his head spin. Christopher watched the beasts disengage then charge again. Whispered words continued to seep into his ears:

'She's not really interested, sir – it's nothing to her which one of those strong beasts shoots his seed inside her: they will both father fine fawns and she knows it.'

Christopher's gaze flicked to where the doe was still grazing quietly. When he looked back to the duel, the stag on the right had gained an advantage and was pushing the other towards a clump of bushes.

'I've watched this happen over and over again, sir – it's as if this is the part the beasts enjoy most.'

Eyes straying back to the engorged lengths of fuzzy-based flesh between both animals' hind legs, Christopher gasped as the victor lowered the about-to-be vanquished to its finely formed knees.

The defeated stag slumped forward. A new sound burst forth from flaring nostrils, low and primal. It struck a note in his own body, trembling into his bones and striking at the very heart of him. His legs felt weak.

'Seems to me they'd do it, even if she wasn't around, sir – it's in their blood, part of the good Lord's design.' The West Country voice was hoarse.

Over the sound of defeated snorting, Christopher could smell Willicombe's breath, mixing with the faintly mossy scent of the underfootman's hair. His head spun. Through half-focused eyes, he watched the vanquished suitor gallop to the edge of the clearing as the victor approached the doe. Christopher felt the casual weight of Willicombe's arm around his shoulder. His body shuddered and the twitch in his crotch grew to a burning itch, but he couldn't move away. The voice was wet on his ear:

'Look at the beast's John Thomas, sir – isn't it magnificent?'

Willicombe's head rested against his. The closeness of the man's body sent shivers of discomfort over his clammy skin. Christopher's heart pounded, almost obliterating a new sound from the remaining stag. His gaze was fixed on the ritual in front of him.

The majestic animal was again on hind legs, front limbs balanced on the back of the submissive doe.

Christopher's lips parted in a sigh. He was unable to drag his eyes from the stout length of moist pink flesh which jutted against the doe's haunches. Beneath his tight-fitting jacket, a trickle of sweat made its way from his armpit, prickling against his skin and dampening his undershirt.

Three yards in front, the doe was silent as her victorious lover rutted noisily inside her.

Christopher tried to close his eyes. Couldn't.

'He's giving it to her good, sir – giving it to her the way she likes it.' Willicombe's voice was breathy and gruff.

The words and their delivery raised the hair on the back of Christopher's neck. Several feet below, the burning in his loins was about to erupt.

As the coarse mating continued, the arm around his shoulder tightened. Then a strong grip was pulling him round and Willicombe's rough fingers were tugging at the front of baggy breeches.

'I must go, Lady Marlborough.'

In another part of Fitzgibbons Manor's sprawling grounds, Mick stood up and turned away from a powdered, concerned face.

'Not on my account, I hope.'

'How can I stay? How can I bear to be in your company when you are promised to another?' He stared into the darkness. Plump fingers tentatively touched his arm.

'Oh, Michael –'

He pulled away, as if burnt. 'Don't torture me further, Violet. I am a broken man.'

Less tentative fingers regripped. 'I had no idea your feelings ran so deep.'

He spun round. 'Do you think me one of your mincing bucks, who change their affiliations as often as their spangled hose?' Anger flashed across his face. He pressed a clenched fist against his chest, as if trying to hold together the pieces of his broken heart. 'I am a passionate man, Violet — with a passionate man's needs. I do not give my devotion lightly or easily.' From amidst her carefully arranged ringlets, a sparkling ruby winked at him. 'And if that devotion is not reciprocated, I will not press my suit.' He focused on the rosy jewel and wiped his eyes.

A plump finger stroked his cheek. 'I am a passionate woman, Michael — Christopher is my father's choice, not mine.' A moue of distaste twitched the rosebud mouth. 'There is little appeal in bookish virgins for a woman of my appetites.'

He tried to hide his surprise as she moved closer, taking his hand and raising the voluminous skirts of her crinoline.

'At least be honest, Michael McGuire.' Lady Violet steered his fingers between layers of petticoat, a lusty smile playing around her lips. 'You are about as interested in marriage and devotion as I am.' She guided him up, then lower.

His palm felt the warm swell of her curved belly. As his fingers slipped lower and he pulled her backwards into the shrubbery, Mick stifled a chuckle and wondered if young Christopher knew what lay ahead of him.

Two

C hristopher couldn't move.

Willicombe hauled his semi-erect member free of its hopsack prison, gripping the root. 'There's another fine beast for you, sir.'

In the dying light, Christopher stared at the stiff member. In contrast to the underfootman's tanned fingers, the man's John Thomas was pale. It curved upwards from a thick bush of curly black hair, flexing to the right.

'A match for anything those stags can produce, eh, sir?' Tightening thumb and knuckles, Willicombe waggled the heavy length of flesh.

It beckoned to Christopher like a giant, swollen finger. He took a step back. Willicombe's other arm remained around his shoulder, preventing any further retreat.

In the background, the rough grunts of rutting deer filled his ears. Beneath his well-fitting linen hose, Christopher's crotch was hot and sticky. The realisation brought a hot flush to his pale cheeks.

Willicombe continued to waggle his cock, arching his back and causing the turgid length to bounce off his stomach. With each slap of flesh on fabric, the member lengthened, swelling a little more. The underfootman gasped. 'He prefers the night air, sir.' The words were low, punctuated by other animal grunts. 'John Thomas likes to get out and about, feel the spring breeze on his back.'

Christopher watched, awestruck, as the man released his shoulder and leant back against the tree, stroking himself.

'See, sir?' Willicombe's member had a coat of ruffled skin, which was slowly stretching. Under the man's practised caress, a large, pink head pushed its way from beneath the pale collar. 'He likes it.' The voice was hoarse.

Christopher's mouth was dry. His arms hung limp by his sides. Something fizzed in his ears. His brain wouldn't work. The hot sticky feeling in his groin was joined by an increasing discomfort. Every available drop of blood in his veins was fleeing downwards, galloping into the staff which pushed against the front of his hose.

Willicombe murmured, 'John Thomas likes to watch the stags, sir –'

Abruptly, Christopher found himself staring at the baggy seat of Willicombe's breeches as the man turned back to refocus on the clearing.

'– he likes to think about the tightness of the doe's quim –'

Another sound joined the rutting – the rasp of flesh-on-flesh and the creasing of the sleeve of Willicombe's work-shirt as the man stroked himself more urgently.

'– and the feel of her haunches against his belly.'

Christopher's feet had taken root. He couldn't move, couldn't speak. He stared at the back of the underfootman's curly head while another, velvety head made its presence felt against the waistband of his hose.

Willicombe planted hobnailed boots more widely apart. The rustle of his clothing increased in speed.

A sound was gathering in Christopher's lungs, half scream of horror, half howl of desire. He opened his mouth. Nothing came out. Then, moving of its own accord, his right hand found the front of the linen breeches and he was rubbing himself through the finely woven fabric.

The underfootman continued to stare at the deer.

Christopher's eyes followed the gaze.

Great streams of exertion burst forth from the male beast's flaring nostrils.

A new smell drifted into his nose: saltier and warmer. And closer. Christopher staggered towards Willicombe's hunched outline. Over the tensed shoulder, he could see the man's John Thomas was now a glistening mast of wet flesh, moistened by the clear sticky liquid which oozed from the tiny slit in the bulbous head.

Then the curly head turned. Dark eyes sparkled through the gloom.

Christopher stared at the underfootman's face.

Willicombe's features were contorted. The full lips pulled back into a parody of a smile. Beneath, air hissed through clenched teeth. The man was hauling on his member, each wrench mirrored by a twist on his boyish face.

Christopher's palm pressed more firmly against the curved outline in his own hose.

Behind them, a loud snort of release from the four-legged beast shattered the moment and heralded a parallel gasp.

As Willicombe lurched backwards, clutching the head of his twitching cock, Christopher turned and stumbled into the undergrowth.

'What, no library tonight?'

He was creeping, scarlet-faced, up the back stairs to his chamber when his father's voice boomed like a cannon behind him. Christopher stiffened, turned.

Viscount Fitzgibbons regarded him with a broad smile. 'I wonder what has taken your mind from your precious studies?' One steely eye winked knowingly.

Blood flew to his cheeks.

Viscount Fitzgibbons placed a broad palm on his shoulder and patted. 'A little discretion would not go amiss, my boy: Lady Violet's absence from the ball drew comment, as did your own.' A bawdy grin split the weatherbeaten face. His father plucked the last of the twigs from Christopher's frockcoat and shook it to the floor. 'You may be betrothed, but decorum must be observed.' A note of sternness had entered his voice.

Christopher flattened himself against the wall of the stairwell. At six foot three inches, his father was at least six inches taller than himself, a difference made all the greater by the man's ramrod, naval bearing. His father loomed over him. Christopher inched away.

Then the stern note vanished, replaced by what sounded like pride. 'I'm glad to see there is some red blood in those veins of yours, after all!'

The hand moved from his shoulder and slapped his back, almost knocking Christopher off his feet.

'A chip off the old block, my boy.' Viscount Fitzgibbon's hearty laugh resounded in his ears. 'You'll have little time for books after tonight, I'll wager.'

'Yes, Father. Good night, Father.' As he made his way up the stairs, some distant part of Christopher's addled brain wondered where and with whom Lady Violet had passed the latter half of their betrothal celebrations.

★

Inside the carriage which bore the Marlborough coat-of-arms, the Marquess of Sligo wiped the last traces of Lady Violet from his lips with an embroidered handkerchief while the lady herself readjusted the voluminous skirts of her crinoline.

'And I cannot persuade you to stay for the rest of the season?' The words were tinged with regret and the breathiness of recently spent passion.

He raised her plump hand to his mouth and kissed it. 'A ship leaves tonight – you know it is better for both of us if I am on it.'

Spaniel eyes gazed up through thick lashes. The Lady Violet's eyes filled with tears. 'But –'

'No buts, my sweet.' He kissed each nail, starting with the pinkie and working over to the index finger. The taste of his own body lingered on her skin. 'I will not ruin your life, and that is what would happen if we remain in the same country.' He lowered his eyes and hid a smile.

'At least let me give you something small to remember me by.'

'I have no need of mere trinkets.' The Marquess of Sligo released her hand and lightly gripped her pert chin. 'I will carry you in my heart across the seas – the memory of our brief time together will stay with me always.'

'Please, Michael –' Her hands moved to behind her neck, unfastening the slender chain then holding out it and the tiny, silver flower which hung from its links. 'I would like you to have this.'

He shook his head: the ornament was worth pennies, if that. 'Our love is above mere possessions, my beauty.' His eyes brushed the dark, ringleted locks in which a sizeable ruby no longer glittered. 'Oh! You have lost your hair decoration – it must have fallen when we were –' He broke off, the words falling into a knowing smile.

The memory brought a flush to her cheeks. She returned the smile, then tossed her head petulantly. 'Never mind that.' Plump fingers pressed the tiny silver violet into his, closing broad knuckles over the keepsake. 'Tell me you won't forget me – ever!'

He almost grinned at the arrogance of the woman! One quim was very much like another, although this one's appetite for Irish cock had been remarkable in its voracity. The Marquess of Sligo sighed theatrically. 'If you insist, my sweet – although the memory of your sweet kisses is the only memento I need.' He slipped the cheap trinket into the pocket of his frockcoat, where it nestled beside the large ruby and two rings she had yet to miss.

Her dark ringlets rested on his shoulder as the sound of hooves thundered onwards towards the docks. 'Perhaps I could visit your estate, sometime.'

He pulled her to him and kissed the top of her head. 'Yes, my beauty, perhaps you could.' Experience had taught him protestations would arouse suspicion.

They nestled in a comfortable silence for the rest of the journey, her mind full of their wild time in the shrubbery, his on the future.

When the coachman halted at the docks, the Marquess of Sligo got out, then turned.

She was at the window, cleavage glinting beneath the drape of her cape.

He smiled, bowed. 'Goodbye, my lady – and thank you.'

'Adieu, sweet Michael – write to me!'

He nodded. 'As soon as my feet touch Irish soil, the pen will spring to my hand.'

With a final bow, he turned back to the large schooner. The vessel's rigging clicked in a midnight breeze. As he walked towards the gangway, his ears strained for the sound of departing hooves. When none came, he waved briefly over his shoulder before sauntering up the gangplank and onto the deck.

Still no hooves.

Glancing around, he saw the ship was deserted: the crew would still be ashore, slaking their thirst in the pubs and brothels of nearby Deptford. On silent feet, he slipped behind a heap of rope and headed for the stairs which led below. He ducked down in the shadow of a barrel of pitch.

Eventually, the clack of departing hooves.

The Marquess of Sligo waited until they disappeared from earshot, then sprang from his hiding place and jauntily made his way back down the gangplank in the direction of the nearest alehouse.

As he walked along the dockside whistling softly, he tossed the tiny silver violet into the murky waters of the Thames.

In his candlelit chamber, Christopher undressed hurriedly, tearing the clothes from his body. He seized the ewer of water, tipped its contents into the washing-bowl and doused his burning face.

Why did he feel like this?

Was he ill?

Perhaps he had fallen prey to some fever.

Water ran down his finely chiselled features. Christopher shivered, grabbed the washing-cloth and began to scrub at his body.

Each rub of the rough flannel sent flickers of flame over his already hot skin.

Christopher frowned. He rinsed the wash-cloth and wiped his left armpit. The smell of his sweat mixed with another, muskier odour.

The frown twisted into a scowl of distaste. Raising his eyes, he caught a glimpse of himself in the mirror. Christopher stared.

A pale, gangling body stared back at him. Narrow shoulders. Thin arms. A smooth, hairless chest barely worthy of the name, tapering into a slim, girlish waist.

Christopher looked away, scrubbing more vigorously at his right armpit. His body held little appeal for him. He was a scholar, concerned with more cerebral matters. This husk of skin and bone, flesh and muscle was a mere scabbard for the rapier that was his mind.

A smile crept onto his face. He had a fine mind – everyone at Oxford said so. It was a mind capable of much thought and exact analysis. He could cut his way through swathes of documentation, slashing away for hours until he located the precise nub of information for which he searched.

Christopher rinsed the flannel and dragged its rough surface over his stomach.

His professors had great hopes for him. When his thesis on the semantic influence of John Dunbar on the work of Geoffrey Chaucer was complete, its publication would bring him great glory in the academic world.

He moved the wash-cloth lower. A frisson of something neither pleasant nor unpleasant shimmered over his body. Christopher looked down.

Sprouting from a blond bush of hair, the shaft of his semi-erect member jutted mockingly up at him.

Christopher recoiled in horror. With a shaking hand, he swatted the errant length with the wash-cloth.

The frisson increased in intensity, making him gasp. His staff seemed to take the gesture as a challenge, flexing outwards to meet the attack.

Lowering his head, he swatted again.

The responding shiver of pleasure made his knees tremble. Christopher bit back a cry and tried to pull himself together.

Bodies were nasty, uncouth things. Urges were something to be borne and overcome. He'd had feelings like this before, when studying particularly bawdy passages in The Wife of Bath's tale. If he ignored them, they usually went away. Christopher closed his eyes and continued to wash himself, carefully avoiding any further contact with the groin area.

As he soaped and rubbed at the inside of his thighs, he pushed his mind onwards. Now that he had put in an appearance at the first ball of the season, he should be able to beg off most future occasions. A couple of sticky passages in The Miller's Tale were proving problematic, and if he could just devote a few extra hours –

Bending lower to scrub behind his knees, something warm and solid poked him in the stomach.

His eyes shot open. Christopher stared at the droplet of moisture which had seeped from his slit, adhering the crown of this unwanted arousal to the skin of his stomach. Unable to look away, he watched the globule stretch into a fine thread of mucus as gravity pulled his cock outwards. Lengthened into near invisibility, the silken fibre suddenly snapped.

Christopher reeled backwards. Disgust flared sour in his mouth. He bumped into the washing-stand, sending the bowl and its contents crashing wetly to the floor, soaking his bare feet.

An image thrust itself into his brain, over the sound of breaking porcelain – an image of Willicombe's rough fist, moving up and down the underfootman's stout staff and smearing the rod of flesh with the same sticky liquid.

Stifling a sob, he leapt into bed, blew out the candle and pulled the covers over his head. His heart pounded in his ears. The image refused to leave his mind.

As he curled on to his side and drew up goose-fleshed legs, Christopher Fitzgibbons wondered why a mind so adept at unravelling the intricacies of Geoffrey Chaucer's poetry was defeated by the workings of his own body.

'What'll you have, my boy – porter? Brandy?' Viscount Fitzgibbons raised a broad hand and gestured to a passing serving lad. 'Put some colour in those cheeks!'

Christopher shifted uncomfortably in the large, padded armchair. No library – again! He sighed. No sooner had he staggered from his chambers, having slept badly, than his father had insisted he accompany him to London on business. Six valuable studying hours had already been wasted, traipsing around the Corn Exchange, while Viscount

Fitzgibbons gossiped and haggled with other, hearty landowners over bushels of grain. Christopher sighed again, glancing around at the wood-panelled walls of the Admiralty Club. Finally, even his father was forced to pause for refreshment.

'What can I get you, my lords?' The serving lad was stockily built. He smiled deferentially at Christopher.

A large glass of water was uppermost in his mind. Christopher leant forward and opened his mouth.

'Two rums – and be quick about it!'

His father's voice boomed in his ears. Christopher closed his mouth.

'Yes, my lord, right away.' The serving lad retreated, bowing furiously.

Christopher sat back in his chair: rum made him nauseous and went straight to his head. He was already feeling queasy from the smoke from half a dozen clay pipes. His father regarded him with a slightly regretful smile.

'Ah, I miss all this.'

Glancing at the huddled groups of uniformed and non-uniformed men who were taking loudly and knocking back great quantities of drink, Christopher's lips curled with distaste.

'It's not just the sea which gets into your blood, my boy – it's the whole way of life. The company, the camaraderie: there are no better men on earth than the men of His Majesty's navy.'

Christopher managed a weak smile and wiped his mouth with a lace handkerchief. His father talked on.

'It's a pity you have chosen not to carry on our family's great tradition and serve your time before the mast, Christopher.' A bawdy leer replaced the disappointment. 'But you have your work cut out for you with another mast, eh, my boy?'

Christopher shuddered as his father's palm landed heavily on his shoulder.

'The Lady Violet returned a message saying she was indisposed today when your mother called to invite her to tea.' Viscount Fitzgibbon's craggy face creased with innuendo. 'I trust you will be more gentle with your betrothed in the future, you sly pup!'

His father's raucous laugh resounded in the crowded room and brought several stares. Christopher sank bank, trying to merge with the leather upholstery.

'Your rum, my lords.' The serving lad placed two pewter tankards on the table in front of them.

'About time!' Viscount Fitzgibbons gripped the curved handle and downed the drink in one, then tossed two silver coins at the deferential boy. 'Another!'

'Yes, sir – right away, sir.' The stocky waiter grabbed the money and scuttled off.

Christopher eyed his tankard warily.

'They serve the best Jamaica rum in London, here.' His father wiped broad knuckles across his still-leering mouth. 'Drink up, my son.' He pushed the tankard closer to Christopher's elegant hand. 'Put hairs on your chest and fire in your belly, that will.' The knowing leer intensified. 'Or maybe you have enough fire there already?'

Christopher had no idea what was wrong with Lady Violet and didn't really care. But his father's comments were making him distinctly uncomfortable. He snatched the drinking vessel and raised it to his lips.

The first sip burnt like acid.

The second created a searing ball of flame inside his mouth.

The third rendered his throat numb. Christopher drained the tankard and replaced it on the table.

'Good lad! That's heritage for you – not a sniff of the sea and you can still drink like a sailor.' His father thumped the table. 'Another rum for my son here!'

Liquid fire hit Christopher's stomach. He gasped, suppressing a cough. Heat ignited his digestive juices and sent tongues of flame back up his gullet. His eyes watered.

'Fitzgibbons? I thought it was you, you old sea-dog!'

Through blurring vision, Christopher attempted to focus on the source of the tobacco-hoarsened voice. His father was on his feet, shaking hands with a gnarled giant of a man.

'Josiah Rock! Have they not fed you to the fishes yet?'

'Davy Jones's locker still awaits me, Fitzgibbons! I heard you'd become a landlubber, though.'

The fire in Christopher's throat had reached his face.

'This is my son, just back from an encounter with that Spanish knave, El Niño – Orlando, this is ex-Admiral Fitzgibbons, one of the worst sailors His Majesty ever had the misfortune to employ.' Christopher managed to focus on a slender, drawn-looking young man in a midshipman's uniform who was shaking hands with his father.

'So the Rock spawned a pebble?' Viscount Fitzgibbon's voice was getting louder. The gravelly words made Christopher's head hurt.

'It's a pleasure to meet you, lad.'

'The pleasure is mine, Admiral.'

The two sailors floated before his eyes. Christopher blinked and they merged back into one. Then a hand hauled him to his feet.

'Christopher, I am honoured to introduce Captain Josiah Rock and his son, Midshipman Orlando Rock.'

He stuck out a hand and felt it pumped vigorously twice. A third face floated somewhere in the background, a face which was vaguely familiar.

'And you, sir – I don't think I've had the pleasure?'

'Michael Montrose, Duke of Connemara at your service, Admiral Fitzgibbons.' The man shaded his left eye in salute.

'Ah, another naval man.' Viscount Fitzgibbons returned the salute.

'Aye, Admiral – that has been my honour. First officer aboard HMS *Determined*.'

His father beamed. 'I am a mere viscount since I resigned my commission, your grace.'

'Ah, but once a sailor, always a sailor, Admiral.'

This hint of Irish brogue struck a note deep in Christopher's rum-soaked brain. He stared at the tall, darkly handsome man.

'And is this your son?'

Three

For a few seconds, Mick's nerve wavered slightly.

Hand extended, the wan, blond youth swayed in front of him. 'Christopher Fitzgibbons, your grace.' The words were slurred.

'At your service, sir.' Mick seized limp fingers and suppressed a frown. The Admiralty Club was the last place he'd expected to encounter this bookish fellow. What was he doing here, amongst the cream of His Majesty's naval society? His fingers tightened around the warm knuckles and he thought fleetingly of last night. Staring into the youth's drunken eyes, he saw no sign of recognition. But it was still risky. Quickly recovering himself, Mick squeezed one last time, then bowed and released the hand.

Behind him, the two old duffers were regaling each other with tales of seagoing prowess.

Mick watched the blond youth stagger backwards and collapse into the leathered armchair, where he wiped his flushed face with an already damp handkerchief. Seizing the opportunity, he draped a brotherly arm around Orlando Rock's broad shoulders and lowered his voice. 'What say you and I take our leave and find somewhere quieter?'

'My father has invited you to dine with us.' Within the grey, drawn face, small, deep-set eyes flicked uncertainly to where Josiah Rock and Viscount Fitzgibbons were ordering more rum. 'Perhaps we should –'

'They'll be here for the remainder of the day, to be sure.' Mick blithely waved away any protestations: it was a shame he would not be able to see the lavishly furnished interior of Rock Hall, but there would be other times. 'We can dine later.'

The deep-set eyes continued to flick. 'I should really –'

'Come with me.' Mick moved his lips closer to a pink ear. 'I know a small alehouse where no one knows us.' He summoned every weapon in his vast arsenal of persuasion into his rich, lilting voice. 'Where we can talk quietly and discreetly.' Out of the corner of his eye, he noticed Christopher Fitzgibbons had fallen into a drunken slumber. Perhaps escape would not prove necessary after all. Then Orlando's soft voice was brushing his own ear:

'I would like that, your grace.'

'But be on your guard against pickpockets, my friend – where we are going is rather an uncouth area.' Moving his hand from the braided shoulder, Mick led the way through a now-carousing crowd towards the door.

He slipped the buxom landlady three silver pieces as soon as they entered, then steered the naval officer to his usual table in a dark corner.

Three glasses of porter later, the drawn face had begun to loosen up. As had those thin, previously tight lips.

'Have you ever been shipwrecked, your grace?'

'Michael, please –' He stared at the fine covering of black hair which peeked from beneath the man's starched white cuff. 'No – thankfully, every vessel I have served on returned to port intact.'

Orlando raised the tankard and took a deep draught. 'Yes, be thankful indeed, Michael. Seven days and nights adrift on a tiny raft.' Midshipman Rock lowered the tankard. His handsome face was pale. 'No food, no water – three of my men dived overboard after the first day, sure their chances in the water were better.'

Mick stared.

Orlando had none of his father's bluster and bonhomie. His voice was quiet and emotionless. 'We passed their lifeless bodies on the third day. Food for the gulls – or the sharks.'

Mick examined the sombre, finely featured face for signs of inebriation. As the man stared soberly into his tankard, he risked a glance at his pocketwatch: buxom Rosie would not hold the room upstairs indefinitely, and he was running out of money. 'But you were rescued, my friend.' He reached across the table between them and rested a hand on a sloping shoulder.

The deep-set eyes darted up from contemplation of the dregs of porter. 'Only partly, Michael – in truth, a greater portion of Midshipman Orlando Rock was left back on that raft, to die with my men.'

Mick frowned and hoped it wasn't the part which was taking his interest at present; if so, this was going to be more difficult than he'd thought. He already knew, from casual questions dropped in the right ears and silver slipped into eager palms, that Orlando Rock, first-born of Josiah Rock, was quite the rake about town between voyages, free with both his favours and his money. But there was other talk: talk of how the rugged young Rock had become withdrawn and moody, spurning both male and female company since his ship's fateful encounter with the infamous Spanish brigand El Niño and the ensuing shipwreck.

Impatience made him bold. Moving his hand from the shoulder braid, Mick pushed an errant lock from Orlando's face. 'I too am a man of the world, my friend – I know what men can become when deprived of the civilising influences of naval order.'

A flicker of interest stirred within the deep-set eyes.

Mick seized it with both hands. 'I have seen dreadful things – things which set me apart from society. We are two of a kind, Orlando – let us help each other.' Gently, he tucked a lock of hair behind the man's ear and raised him to his feet. His voice was low. 'Tell me your pain, my friend – but not here.' He raised his eyes to the oak-beamed ceiling then focused on the strained face, wondering which particular vice this man had been introduced to, at the resourceful hands of El Niño.

Orlando's nod was brief but unmistakable. As they made their way to the rough wooden staircase at the end of the polished bar, so was the hard outline in the front of his naval pantaloons.

Whatever Midshipman Rock had lost on board that raft, it wasn't his desire for the bodies of men.

No sooner had Mick turned the key in the lock than he was grabbed in a powerful embrace.

With one hand, Orlando tore at the brass buttons of his midshipman's jacket while the other gripped the back of Mick's neck and pulled him into a lusty kiss.

The man's mouth was hot and urgent. Mick returned the pressure, thrusting his tongue deep between Orlando's lips and tugging at his own clothes. Frockcoat and waistcoat were thrown on to the floor, the latter ripping in his haste. As he attempted to free himself of his knee-breeches, an engorged groin rubbed itself against his, forcing him back and pinning him against the wall.

Mick moaned, feeling the naked outline of the other's excitement strong against his own. His tongue twined with Orlando's. He sucked the man's saliva into his mouth, feeding on the warm, porter-flavoured liquid. Bare-chested, they ground against each other, the thick hair of Mick's pectorals rasping over the smooth mounds of Orlando's flesh.

Pulling his belt free from the waistband of his knee-breeches, Mick tried again to lower the garment.

Orlando broke the kiss, panting and breathless. 'Keep them on.' A sheen of spit and sweat glistened on the man's closely barbered upper lip.

Mick stood motionless as the now-naked midshipman fell to his knees in front of him and began to nuzzle the bulge which was rapidly filling the crotch area. He gasped.

Orlando's shoulders were broad and tanned from those days on the raft. Long sinewy muscle flexed in his forearms. Eager hands slipped behind Mick and clutched the cheeks of his arse.

The heavy leather belt hung loose in Mick's grip. He stared at the man's skin, rendered a glowing copper by the candle's flickering light and noticed the faint but unmistakable marks of the lash which decorated the tawny flesh.

Orlando pulled Mick closer, tonguing and mouthing his hardening cock through the worsted fabric. The harsh pant of laboured breathing filled Mick's ears. A smile crept on to his face. Tangling his fingers in the man's increasingly damp hair he pushed Orlando's face roughly into his groin and ground his stretching length against muttering lips. As a moan of satisfaction joined the rasping sounds, Mick's eyes flicked to the heap of discarded clothing and the tooled leather money-pouch which sat amidst tangles of naval uniform.

The smile spread to a grin.

Strong hands slipped from his arse-cheeks on to the backs of well-muscled legs.

Mick returned his gaze to the frantic man at his feet, and the lash scores.

El Niño had obviously marked this midshipman inside and out, before scuppering the man's vessel and setting him adrift on the high seas.

Raising his right hand above his head, Mick coiled the length of leather around his fist, then parted his thighs and thrust forward with his hips. His other hand dragged Orlando's face from his now-drenched prick and positioned it at his stomach. He gripped the back of the warm neck.

A howl of disappointment sprang from the man's lips.

Then Mick bent his knees, drew his arm back further and brought the broad belt down hard on glistening shoulders.

Orlando's howl sank to a low moan.

Mick drew back his arm and let the leather fall again.

And again.

With each kiss of the belt, a groan of satisfaction met his ears. Three feet below, other signs of pleasure dripped from Orlando's flexing cock and landed wetly between Mick's buckle-shoes.

Long, rectangular welts raised themselves on the broad back, each red slash outlined in a ridge of white.

Mick felt his prick swell further. He was no expert in these matters, which he knew required a more practised hand, but the mere action of his right arm seemed to be having the desired effect. And he could learn. Suddenly, the money-pouch shrank to a mere trifle. If Midshipman Rock was prepared to compensate him for expenses, Mick could see the beginnings of a mutually beneficial arrangement here.

Beneath his other hand, Orlando's neck was now sweating profusely. Mick continued to deliver heavy strokes to the strong shoulders and back until his own body was slick with exertion.

Orlando's head moved over Mick's tensed abdomen. He tried to return his mouth to the ridge of pulsing flesh within his punisher's knee-breeches.

Mick laughed, as he knew El Niño would have laughed at this cowering, cringing gentleman. Tightening his grip on the damp neck, he pushed his willing prisoner on to all fours and launched a more violent attack on the man's firm buttocks.

Orlando screamed and tried to get away.

'Oh no you don't!' Trusting Rosie the landlady to show her usual discretion, Mick stepped back. He released the neck and replaced his hand with his foot in its buckled shoe.

Orlando's face hit the rough wood of the floor with a thud. Breath exploded from his lungs and his firm buttocks pointed ceilingwards.

Mick increased the pressure of his foot and watched prime midshipman's rump push itself towards him. Focusing on the dark crevice between the cheeks of the man's pink-striped arse, Mick rained a heavy volley of strokes on to the quivering flesh.

Orlando writhed under his foot.

Mick continued to lash the tawny flesh. His own body flushed with exertion. Breathing heavily, oxygen rushed to his brain, charging his blood until it pulsed throughout his body. Sweat dripped into his eyes. He wiped his forehead with the sleeve of his shirt and noticed the fabric was already soaking. Mick frowned, bringing the belt down time and time again on increasingly scarlet skin.

Orlando met each blow eagerly, thrusting his firm arse up towards it. The low-hanging hairiness of the man's full bollocks swung between splayed thighs.

The heavy sac quivered and flinched with each lick of the belt. Punctuating the blows, the wet slap of cock-flesh on belly-flesh filled the small room.

'Your foot.' The words were wrenched from Orlando's lips.

Mick frowned, mid-swing of the belt: was the weight of the heavy, buckled footwear too much on the back of the man's neck? He raised his shoe.

In seconds, Orlando had twisted around and was now cradling the mud-smeared sole in large hands. 'Use me, Michael –' Midshipman Rock stroked the stiff leather, then eased off the shoe and kissed stockinged toes lovingly '– use me with your foot.'

Then his ankle was released and Orlando was once more on all fours, holding his firm, wealed buttocks apart.

Mick's eyes widened. He glanced from the small, spasming orifice to his own broad, square-toed appendage. 'My friend, are you sure?'

The response was low, heavy with desire. 'As sure as I was that the lick of your belt would free me from my pain.' Orlando turned his head, gazing over his shoulder with huge, swollen pupils. 'Now finish what you have started.'

Mick paused then unlocked the door and took the stairs two at a time. Flexing and unflexing his aching right arm, he couldn't help envying El Niño his stamina: the brigand had certainly taught Midshipman Rock a few exotic lessons in endurance.

Rosie stared at him blankly as he rushed into her kitchen in search of the dish of the day. Now minus his breeches and clad only in underwear, Mick applied a liberal smear of goose-grease to his right foot. The fat was still warm and thickly viscous. A shiver of eroticism swept over his body as the heavy slime squidged between his toes and slipped over the high instep.

Ankles gripped, Orlando lay on his blistering back, strong, densely haired thighs raised above his head. 'Use me quickly – and use me hard!' The man's previously hoarse voice was now a pleading whisper.

Dipping his fist again into the jar of goose-grease, Mick slathered the rich fat over both hands and knelt between Orlando's spread legs. The actual mechanics of the man's request were still a little beyond him, but he was accustomed to fathoming out the details of a job as he worked.

Orlando's pucker was a crinkled rosette of anticipation. The orifice clenched and unclenched under Mick's gaze. The musky scent of Orlando's need rose up over the greasy stench of the goose-fat, hot and masculine and urgent. Mick leant forward, nudging the man's low-hanging bollocks aside. Then a gasp brushed his ears and the spasming hole gaped ajar as he eased one then two fingers inside the midshipman's body.

Muscle resisted at first, then gripped the three-fingered invader in a tight vice. Mick massaged slowly and thoroughly, fighting resistance.

Whatever had happened on board El Niño's vessel or the raft, it had not happened often: Orlando's arse was as tight as a virgin's quim. Forehead furrowed with effort, Mick curled his fingers upwards.

The movement was answered by a series of anguished moans.

He continued the motion, stretching and loosening the entrance to the man's body. Mick's cock was now fully hard inside his lawn underwear and tented the soft fabric like the mast of a great ship. Pushing on past the first and second knuckle, he rested his face against the side of a hairy, quivering thigh and waited for his own breath to steady.

Orlando's rectum was hot and surprisingly moist. Walls of muscle massaged his fingers, slicking the skin with sweat-grease.

Mick wiggled his near-crushed digits in an attempt to stimulate sensation in the tips.

A gasp flew from beyond the splayed thighs. Then Orlando was bearing down on to his hand, trying to suck more of Mick inside.

Bracing his other arm on the rough, wooden floor, Mick slowly began to separate his three fingers.

Orlando groaned.

Four inches inside the midshipman's body, the tips of grease-slimed digits gradually eased apart. Mick's brow was creased in concentration. The side of his second and fourth fingers pressed into the flexing sinew of the walls of Orlando's arse. Moving back into a crouch, Mick closed his fingers and pressed them heavily into the right side of the warm, fleshy tunnel. He brought his other hand into play, easing the thumb then forefinger of his left hand just beyond the man's arse-lips.

Orlando grunted. The hairy thighs slid from his grasp and fell either side of Mick's broad shoulders. 'Use me – please use me!' The midshipman's voice was low and guttural.

Mick's cock took another leap. He pressed with his thumbs, widening the elastic pucker. Orlando's words resounded in his ears over the soft, wet sounds of his intrusion into the man's body. Hard, male muscle parted to embrace the stretching digits. The hole was gaping now, pleading with him to fill it as Orlando's mouth pleaded in parallel. Then his goose-greased foot was slipping under him and his arse hit the floor.

Instinctively, Mick gripped the midshipman's quivering thighs for support.

Too late.

His right leg was propelled forward and before he could stop himself he sprawled backwards while his foot thrust itself between Orlando's arse-cheeks.

The responding grunt of pained satisfaction tore through his surprise. Using the man's legs for leverage, Mick hauled himself on to elbows.

A vice was tightening around his right foot, just below the toes. The pressure made him gasp. As he stared between the midshipman's trembling thighs, Mick blinked at the finely stretched arse-lips which now trembled at the bottom of his instep.

Raising himself up, his foot slid further in.

Orlando's eyes were closed. Sweat soaked the dark hair. His face was a crumpled map of pleasure.

Staggering on to one leg, Mick stared down at the thick, curved cock which flexed convulsively against the midshipman's tensed stomach. He wiggled his toes.

A low gasp puffed from an open mouth.

Mick regained his balance. He stood there, feeling a damp spot form in his fine lawn underwear. Unable to pull his eyes from between Orlando's splayed thighs, he dragged his foot back as if in a kick then pressed forward once more.

The man's arse-lips stretched a little further, encompassing the first swell of Mick's instep. The gasp lowered itself to a grunt, then a series of bassy, animal sounds. Mick continued to fuck the prostrate man with his foot, increasing the length and arc of the leg swings as he'd increased the weight of the belt blows, but never completely withdrawing his foot.

Orlando's long, pale cock shuddered with every prod. Well-muscled arms flailed on the floor behind his head. The midshipman arched his back and widened his thighs.

The sight aroused Mick further. His foot slipped once more into the greasy tunnel, but this time he pushed harder. The skin of Orlando's arse-lips had almost disappeared and he could see the pink fleshy lining of the man's rectum tight around the rise of his instep.

Mick's hand found the front of the baggy lawn underwear. He began to stroke himself through the fine fabric, which was now damp with sweat and lust. Goose-grease and arse-slime slicked his foot. His toes curled up in pleasure, extracting another gasp from the man who writhed beneath him.

Orlando was thrashing now, his head flicking from side to side. A fine foam flecked the flaring nostrils as he pushed back on to his attacker's foot, trying to take more and more of the unconventional penetration.

In a frenzy of desire, Mick pulled his own cock free from underbreeches,

Orlando's eyelids, which had been screwed shut, suddenly flew open. 'Give me your water!'

The flesh of his prick pulsed against his sweating palm. Foot buried in the man to the instep, Mick stared into fathomless, irisless eyes.

'Your water! Foul me with your piss, Michael!'

Three tankards of porter churned in his bladder. Mick moved his gaze to the hard length in his fist. Not at this stage of arousal, he couldn't!

Orlando's cries were growing increasingly plaintive. He pushed himself up on to forearms and gazed beseechingly through tear-stained eyes. The purple head of the midshipman's throbbing cock was stiff with slowly drying precome. 'Please –'

Mick looked away from the pleading man and stared at the bare wooden wall just beyond Orlando's head.

Gripping his shaft between thumb and forefinger, he saw beyond the wall.

To his family, back in Ireland.

To the failed crop which had prompted his departure, two years ago.

A frown formed on his rugged features. He had almost forgotten what his family looked like.

Fighting lust and his own need for release, Mick focused his mind on the thin, haggard faces of his brothers and sisters. Tingling in his bladder told him another type of release was now possible.

'Your piss, Michael! Foul me with your water!'

Anguished cries drew him back to the present.

Orlando was now prostrate once more, tugging on the hard flesh of cockmeat which sprouted from a damp pubic bush.

Sinking his foot further in the man's arse, Mick aimed the head of his cock towards the straining, pleasure-creased features and let go.

As the torrent of piss sprang from Mick's slit and cascaded on to the already wet face, Orlando's head and shoulders bucked up from the floor and the man shot a slitful of thick, viscous spunk on to his own heaving chest.

Four

———

How much rum did one tankard hold – half a pint? A pint? How many had he been forced to consume?

On the journey back from London, Christopher glanced from his examination of the passing countryside and stared at his gently snoring father.

More hours ago than he cared to remember, back in the Admiralty Club, he had awoken to the raucous singing of Viscount Fitzgibbons and the gnarled giant of a man.

The other two – the captain's son and the strangely familiar Irishman – were nowhere to be seen.

Christopher flinched at the memory of what had happened next. Everyone insisted on buying ex-Admiral Fitzgibbons's son a drink. It would have been rude to refuse. Most of the tankards he had managed to exchange with either his father's or Captain Rock's ever-empty drinking vessels, but occasionally Christopher had been forced to consume the burning liquid himself.

After that?

His stomach churned then fell into his boots as the carriage swerved to avoid a pothole.

Dancing.

Tables were pushed back. Hats and wigs were discarded, jackets draped over the backs of chairs. The stockily built serving lad had turned out to have a penny-whistle in his quarters at the back of the premises. Several silver pieces persuaded him to provide musical accompaniment as half the assembled naval crew sang lustily and out of tune, while the other half cavorted and jigged around the room.

Christopher's dry lips moved into a moue of distaste. At least no one had noticed his own failure to join in the proceedings: the jaunty hornpipe melody still careered around his brain, an apt air for a bunch of drunken sailors!

Eventually, the merrymaking had ebbed away, due mainly to the advanced age of most of the hornpipers and, amidst fond farewells from a remarkably sober Captain Rock, Christopher had half-carried, half-dragged his father out to their waiting carriage.

On the seat opposite, Viscount Fitzgibbons's nose-hair quivered in a less-gentle snore.

Christopher returned his attention to the window.

Outside, lush pasture gave way to a more wooded landscape. Night was falling. Another day slipped behind a range of tall trees. Another wasted day.

His books and thesis had languished another twenty-four hours in the library.

The carriage lurched, one wheel dipping into a pothole.

Christopher lurched with it, grabbing the side of a richly upholstered seat for balance.

Twenty-four hours' working time had disappeared in the blink of an eye.

The sky darkened further as the carriage moved between a dense avenue of tall trees. Abruptly, from beyond the window, the rhythmic clack of hooves became the ostinato for a high, distinctive call. The sound filled his head, drowning out the clatter of horses' hooves.

Christopher lips curled into a smile. A nightingale. The smile froze.

Last night.

Willicombe's rich country voice identifying the bird's call.

Willicombe's thick black hair falling lazily into one shining eye –

Something solid turned to liquid in Christopher's stomach.

Willicombe's rough fingers tight around Willicombe's thick staff of flesh.

Christopher shuddered. The carriage had suddenly grown rather warm. He tugged at the neck of his high-collared shirt.

One of the few things he'd been grateful for today was the young underfootman's absence from duty. Eight hours in his father's boisterous company was bad enough. Willicombe's presence on the three-hour journey there and back, either up front with the coachman or travelling at the rear, would have been unbearable.

The man popped into his mind and made it reel, even when he was not around. Christopher wiped a single bead of sweat from his forehead and knew he would never be able to look into that handsome, West Country face again without blushing.

Beyond his thoughts, a polka of hooves slowed to a more stately galliard.

Christopher glanced to the window as the carriage slowed further. Then stopped. He watched the tall gates to Fitzgibbons Manor pushed open by a dark outline.

Horses snorted breathlessly.

Then the crack of a whip ground the carriage into motion once more.

Christopher's stomach lurched.

As they swept up the driveway, a boyishly handsome face smiled at him through the half-light, then fell in behind the carriage.

Christopher listened to the pounding of more human feet over those of the horses, and returned his attention to the now-rousing shape of his father.

'An enjoyable day – a very enjoyable day!' Viscount Fitzgibbons rubbed his palms together, grabbed his hat and bounded through the open carriage door.

Christopher reeled as fresh night air hit his face.

The sleep seemed to have rejuvenated his father, who was now striding purposefully up the stone stairs towards the Manor. All signs of his previous inebriation had vanished with the remains of the day.

One foot hovering above the first carriage step, Christopher swayed. He'd felt completely sober and in control on the journey. Now he was reluctant to leave the carriage. A breathless voice at his side made the prospect more unwelcome than ever.

'Did you have a pleasant trip, sir?'

'Er, yes –' Christopher stared straight ahead, scrupulously avoiding the source of the West Country accent. His fingers tightened on the sides of the carriage door. He focused on one of the large stone lions which guarded the grand entrance to Fitzgibbons Manor and prayed for it to solidify.

'Let me give you a hand, sir.'

Before he could protest, strong fingers gripped his elbow, gently but firmly manoeuvring Christopher from his perch on the top step.

'There you go, sir.'

One foot then a second hit gravel with a crunch. Then both knees turned to water, dissolving beneath him. Around him, a circle of stone lions spun. Christopher turned back, searching for the solidity of the carriage. He flailed for purchase.

The grip on his elbow was joined by another around his waist.

'Oops–a–daisy, sir!'

Christopher felt himself steadied by strong arms. His head lolled against a broad shoulder which smelt faintly of horse manure. A low chuckle drifted into his ringing ears.

'You did have a good trip, didn't you?'

The familiarity in Willicombe's low voice made his legs shake more than ever.

'Too much rum, eh?'

Christopher tried to get away, but the more he struggled, the more Willicombe's hold on him increased. And the faster the stone lions pranced before him. Somewhere in the distance, he could hear the coachman's complaints and the snorting of the horses. The carriage moved away and he found himself staggering towards the stone stairs, draped over Willicombe's broad shoulders. Then everything went black.

'Are you sure he's all right?'

'Yes, ma'am. Just a little the worse for wear.'

'Perhaps he'd like some –'

'He'll sleep it off, ma'am – don't you worry yourself.'

'He's not used to travelling – I told his father, but he wouldn't listen. Are you quite sure he's not ill? He has such a delicate constitution.'

Christopher came round to the sound of his mother's solicitous enquiries and a dull pounding in his head. He opened one tentative eye.

His bedroom.

Through the half-dark, he could just make out the shape of the washstand, silhouetted against the closed curtains.

'Yes, I am quite sure, ma'am.'

The second voice identified itself in Christopher's rum-addled brain, just as a hand seized his foot and pulled off his right shoe.

'I'll put him to bed, my lady, if you like.'

Christopher would have flinched, had his body been able to function.

'Well –'

He willed his mother to object.

The hand removed his left shoe.

'– I do have Lady Marlborough in the drawing-room –'

'Leave it to me, ma'am.'

Willicombe's earnest, competent voice erected the hair on the back of Christopher's neck. He moaned. The sound came out more of a snore.

'See, my lady? Mr Christopher's already asleep. Shame to wake him now –'

Hands eased him up from the softness of the bed, manoeuvring his arms from the sleeves of the frockcoat.

'Thank you, Willicombe.'

His mother's grateful voice was further away now. Christopher wanted to call out, but his throat felt like some feathered creature had crawled into it and died there. In the distance, a door opened, then closed softly.

A shiver swept his body.

Alone. With Willicombe.

Wordlessly, the underfootman's fingers moved to the front of Christopher's shirt.

Lying motionless, his body rendered useless by rum and something he didn't want to think about, each touch of the surprisingly deft fingers was another nail in his coffin.

He wanted to leap up. And didn't.

He wanted to race from the room. And didn't.

Christopher wanted away from this man with every fibre of his being –

The underfootman was humming softly to himself.

– and didn't. As he lay there, the slow, West Country melody filling his ears, Christopher remembered Willicombe seemed to believe he was asleep. It would be easier – and less embarrassing – for all concerned if he continued to believe that. Willicombe would leave him his modesty, tuck him in and depart.

Hardly daring to breathe, he allowed himself to be moved sideways as the underfootman eased the shirt from Christopher's chest. Then the cool air was heating up rapidly and a blush tingled over his nipples.

Christopher bit back a groan, half pleasure, half mortification. Beneath the waistband of his best velvet breeches, solidity was returning to his limp, useless body.

Willicombe's fingers moved to the front of those breeches.

What had seemed a good idea, moments earlier, was now the worst decision Christopher had ever made. Panic gave his brain wings. Feigning a snore, he slumped over further, burying his face in the goosedown pillow. He prayed for Willicombe to toss the eiderdown over his body and leave the room. He was half-undressed: surely that would be enough? Christopher sank down further on to the bed.

The motion, however, was double-edged. The fastenings of his breeches were safe from further access, for the moment: but the underfootman's right hand was now trapped against Christopher's stomach.

Behind, a soft sigh of irritation interrupted the humming.

Christopher feigned another wriggle, arching his back and giving the man ample opportunity to withdraw that hand.

Then his face was burning against the cool pillowslip as a second hand joined the first and the underfootman continued to undo the velvet breeches. The humming recommenced.

Christopher's mouth gaped in panic.

Willicombe's fingers were efficient and businesslike.

A dip in the mattress told him the underfootman was now kneeling on the bed beside him, hauling the breeches down over Christopher's arse-cheeks and thighs.

Freed from its velvet cage, the head of his member pushed against the fine lawn underwear as though trying to gouge a furrow into the mattress. Christopher clenched his fists, then remembered he was supposed to be asleep and tried to relax.

His feet were lifted from the bed. Then he was listening to the soft sounds of fabric as the underfootman carefully folded the expensive breeches. Relief washed over his hot skin.

Before he could relax, the hands were back.

Christopher bit the pillow, smothering a cry of horror as Willicombe's practised fingers slipped beneath his body once more and tugged at the drawstrings of the final barrier between his nakedness and the hot, humid air of the dark bedchamber.

He could block out his moans of discomfort, try to ignore the way the man's hands felt against his skin, but the humming was another matter. It filled his head, as tuneful as the nightingale's song but deeper and more masculine. Banished to a hell of the rum's making, Christopher concentrated on the tune, ignoring the feel of Willicombe's rough fingers on the delicate skin of his stomach then thighs.

Now at liberty, the agonizing stiffness between his legs pushed itself harder against the mattress. He tried to halt the movement of his hips but, like everything else which had happened since he'd stumbled drunkenly from that carriage, it was beyond his control.

The hands removed themselves.

Their imprint remained, continuing to arouse Christopher's body as Willicombe moved softly away and began to fold the undergarments.

The humming filled his head. Christopher lay there, naked. He listened to the melody as it wove a spell around his brain. An invisible thread joined Willicombe's voice to the tightness in his groin. With each hummed refrain, his bollocks tightened. With every repetition of the main tune, his hips jutted down then upwards.

Then another sound broke through his delirium – a sound he immediately identified and which drenched his body in a new film of sweat.

The sound of water splashing into porcelain as the underfootman filled the washing-basin.

He froze, mid-thrust. Movement was beyond him now, as was groaning. Suspended in a state of inflamed arousal, he heard the soft slop of a wash-cloth immersed in water. Then wringing. Then the low pad of footsteps as Willicombe made his way back to the bed.

And paused.

Christopher's rigid fists tightened around handfuls of pillow. Beneath him, the mattress dipped, pulling away from his throbbing groin as Willicombe sat down on the bed beside his trembling body.

The humming stopped.

An unreleased scream rose in Christopher's throat, swelling into his head and replacing the soft, West Country air. Just below the smooth, motionless surface of his damp skin, every muscle and sinew was a writhing, thrashing tangle of terror and need.

Seconds passed.

Minutes.

An eternity elapsed.

Then something touched the back of his neck –

Not the wash-cloth.

– something warm and dry.

And fleshy.

Mouth open in a wordless cry, Christopher's fingers dug into the palms of his hands as other lips brushed the nape of his neck. The lips removed themselves. Willicombe's sigh was soft and low.

At the other end of the spectrum, Christopher's member pulsed with a hardness which almost made him feel sick.

The room was swimming.

His lungs expanded, ribs pressed painfully into the organs within.

His stomach lurched and tightened.

Through a gap between his burning face and the goosedown pillow, he managed to suck in tiny breaths of air. The action only made his lungs burn further.

Then the lips were back, moving over his neck and shoulders.

The mattress beneath him was warm and wet. Christopher flinched, disgust at the reactions of his own body and a vague annoyance at the underfootman's forwardness swirling in his mind. He pushed the feelings away, ignoring the tightening in his bollocks and willing his brain to function.

Willicombe kissed his right shoulderblade.

The library. The Miller's Tale. Christopher concentrated on one particularly obscure medieval reference.

Willicombe's mouth moved to his left shoulder.

Christopher frowned. The imagery was oblique. He was vaguely aware his hips were grinding now.

Soft lips hardened, moving to his top vertebra.

Mentally, he brought the specific phrase back into his mind. His body was moving by itself, grinding increasingly large circles into the bed.

Willicombe kissed the nobble of bone then slipped down to the second.

What did Geoffrey Chaucer mean? Somewhere deep inside his body, a muscle tightened, relaxed then retightened. The circles became smaller, more insistent.

The third, fourth and fifth vertebrae were kissed in turn.

Then rough fingers on his waist and a warm mouth at the base of his spine pushed The Miller's Tale back into obscurity. The tightening was travelling up the length of him. Christopher gasped in surprise as wet warmth flooded the mattress beneath his aching groin. Most of the sound was absorbed by the pillow.

His body seemed to be merging with the bed. His mind had drifted off somewhere.

Then other warmth.

In a daze of molten release, Christopher felt the sharp rasp of stubble as Willicombe pressed his face to his buttocks. The mouth delivered a final, almost regretful kiss. Then the rough hands reluctantly left his waist and Christopher was vaguely aware of an eiderdown against his rapidly cooling skin.

Sometime later, he heard the click of a door closing. The last thing Christopher registered as he drifted off into a drunken sleep with a sour taste in his mouth –

– the distant call of a nightingale.

When he awoke, the room was still dark but the nightingale had stopped singing. His tongue had adhered itself to the roof of his mouth. Christopher groaned. Wisps of some terrible nightmare in which he and Willicombe had –

– arms windmilling, Christopher fought his way from under the heavy eiderdown and opened his eyes.

A dream.

Just a dream.

He blinked, rubbing crusty eyes and gazed at the reassuring outlines of the wardrobe, bureau, washstand, ewer and bowl. Grabbing the corner of the eiderdown, he sat up, flicking the covering aside. Christopher staggered out of bed.

Then paused.

The sheet was stuck to his stomach.

He looked down.

Something dry and salty crumbled around the top of his legs. Christopher winced, pulling the sheet away. His nose wrinkled at the smell of his own body. He stared down at the now-dry patches of semen which dotted his stomach and thighs, frosting the still-damp pubic hair.

In panic, he rubbed at it with his hand, then leapt away in disgust as the fine, sea-smelling powder dusted his fingers and clung to his skin.

His head spun.

Christopher sat down heavily, still staring between his pale thighs. The previous day returned.

The Admiralty Club.

Too much rum.

Dozens of rowdy, drunken sailors careering round him like so many base animals.

He coughed, trying to clear his thick throat.

The journey home in the carriage. He'd felt fine until –

– the room was suddenly very claustrophobic. He couldn't breathe.

Memories of his face pressed into a pillow brought back the feelings of suffocation. As quickly as his rubber limbs and throbbing head would allow, Christopher got to his feet and walked slowly to the window. Grabbing the heavy brocade curtains, he wrenched them apart and stared out.

The light hurt his eyes. Blinking in noon sunshine, he shaded his gaze and drew a deep breath into his lungs.

A dream.

Just a dream.

The bright daylight reassured him further. He could remember nothing, after the point when he'd half-fallen from the carriage, in front of the stone lions.

Gripping the sashed ledge, he hauled the window open and felt a cooling breeze on his thighs.

He'd had dreams like this before – wet, uncomfortable nights, when the part of his mind over which he had no control broke loose and wrought its unwanted work on his body.

A dream.

Just a dream.

A smile twitched his lips as he surveyed the lush green fields of his father's estate.

Then a sound. Christopher cocked his head.

A nightingale? At this hour? A cooling breeze continued to caress his thighs as he looked down towards the source of the unexpected bird-call.

Then the cooling breeze became a furnace blast. Christopher stared into the boyishly handsome face.

Outside the stableblock, Willicombe grinned, raised one broad hand in salute then returned to grooming the large black mare before him.

Christopher shrank away from the window, suddenly aware of his nakedness. The underfootman's gesture continued to hover in his mind as he walked to the washing-stand.

A dream?

Yes, just a dream.

Splashing water over his face, he turned his mind towards today, and a long-awaited spell with his beloved books.

Five

———

Midshipman Rock slept long and deeply.

Mick smiled. Rosie the landlady would profit more than she'd anticipated: one hour's rental had stretched into four.

The room above the tavern stank of man-sweat, piss and the cloying smell of animal fat. Pulling his eyes from the limp, unconscious form, Mick wiped the last of the goose-grease from between his toes and dressed. His thick hair was more tangled than usual and lay in an unruly tail over one shoulder. He frowned, noting he had lost two mother-of-pearl buttons from the fine shirt and his breeches were torn. Mick thought about the midshipman's heavy money-pouch, now carefully secreted beneath a loose floorboard. Maybe Rosie could be persuaded to clean and repair the clothes.

As he slipped one foot into a buckle-shoe, a low groan from the bed took his attention.

Mick watched the midshipman ease himself up on to one elbow. He admired the strong muscles of the man's chest.

Orlando's blue eyes were heavy with sleep. Drying piss had stiffened the front of his blond hair, which now stuck up like question marks. A smile of contentment played around full lips. The previously strained face was completely relaxed, if a little embarrassed. 'Michael, I –'

'We'll say no more about it – are we not men of the world, my friend?' Brushing further protestations and thanks aside, Mick sat down on the side of the bed. 'Did you sleep well?'

Orlando sprawled on to his back. 'Better than I have in a very long time, Michael.'

Mick stretched out a hand, smoothing the piss-stiffened hair over the crown of the man's head. A handsome fellow, indeed! Flickers of satisfaction ignited into a wide smile as he remembered three hours earlier.

The toast of naval society!

The pride of Captain Josiah Rock.

Naked, on his knees, before Mick Savage. Writhing in ecstasy, Mick Savage's broad foot rammed deep in his spasming, midshipman's rectum. Bathing in the piss of someone who, only months before, had been scrounging scraps of food from the kitchens of men like himself.

Orlando sighed. 'Will you be in London long?'

The wide smile slipped into a frown. 'Alas, I am expected back in Connemara, the day after tomorrow.'

The blond head turned. 'Must you?' A lock of hair fell over one blue eye.

Mick fixed an expression of regret on his face. Given the disappointment in those eyes, it was almost genuine. Inside the torn breeches, his cock twitched.

Money or not, improving his foot-fucking and lashing technique or not, Mick would have enjoyed a few more encounters with this passionate, unusual man. He pushed the thoughts away. 'I must – my ship is docking in less than a week, and I have estate matters to attend to.'

This was business – not pleasure.

Pleasure was the pixie-faced cut-purse whose eye he had caught on numerous occasions, and whom Mick knew often passed the odd hour downstairs after a hard evening's work of his own. He stood up. 'We should leave, my friend – it is neither fitting nor safe for gentlemen to linger in such –' he managed an expression of distaste '– low establishments as this.' Moving from the bed, he picked up the blue, brass-buttoned midshipman's jacket and draped it over the back of a chair.

'I know.' Another sigh from the bed. Orlando slowly eased long, hair-covered legs on to the floor and grabbed his underwear.

Trying not to smile and fighting a growing heat in his groin, Mick leant against one of the bed's four posts and watched the man dress.

A serving lad was dispatched to secure a carriage. A previous engagement with a naval acquaintance in the other direction allowed Mick to remain behind. Rosie let them exit through her hot, smelly kitchen.

In the doorway, once more hatted and uniformed, Orlando lingered.

The sound of approaching hooves clacked over the sharp crack of ships' rigging and the other night noises of Deptford docks.

Mick shuffled impatiently. The further away from himself Orlando Rock was, when he discovered his lack of money-pouch, the better. Then he felt eyes on him.

The midshipman's handsome face was turned towards him. Full lips parted as if about to speak.

In the background, the kitchen staff clattered about, oblivious.

Mick blinked, stretched out a hand and pressed one finger to the man's mouth. 'Not a word, my friend.'

Orlando seized his wrist. Holding his hand there, the midshipman softly kissed Mick's fingers.

Ships that pass in the night: an apt phrase for an encounter such as theirs. He rested his other hand on the man's broad shoulder, listening to the hooves draw nearer and trying to rein in his own impatience.

The carriage came to a halt opposite the kitchen door. Mick withdrew his hands, smiled. 'May you have a long and happy life, my friend.' He was surprised to find himself almost meaning the words. This sailor had suffered God knew what at the hands of the fierce, twisted brigand El Niño, and had come out of the experience intact – if a little more specific in his desires. He deserved to find contentment and peace.

Orlando bowed his head. 'Will you join my father and me at Rock House, for dinner tomorrow?'

Mick suppressed a grin, imagining the expression on Captain Josiah Rock's gnarled face if he ever found out what had just taken place. He quickly sobered. 'I have business in the East End, my friend. It will not be possible.'

The regret which rose from the man's body was almost palpable. But Orlando quickly gathered himself. 'So be it. I will never forget you, Michael.'

'Nor I you, Orlando.' Mick made a mental note to work on his lashing technique: a man never knew when it would prove useful. Not one for prolonged farewells, he moved towards the carriage, where the horses were pawing the ground impatiently.

Behind, Orlando paused, patting the pockets of his jacket. 'My money-pouch! Where is my – '

'I tried to warn you.' Mick cursed under his breath. Encircling the uniformed shoulders, he urged the man towards the waiting carriage. 'These are dangerous parts.'

Orlando stopped again. The rich voice rose in volume. 'That pouch contained over –'

'Shhh!' Mick lowered his head. 'People are already curious as to what such gentlemen as ourselves were doing in this low alehouse.' He fixed one blue, enraged eye with a persuasive one. 'Do we want them knowing our business?'

Orlando's resolve wavered.

Mick continued. 'And even if, by some slim chance, their curiosity is not aroused further, whatever scurrilous rogue stole your money will be miles away by now.' He watched the logic of his words sink in.

Orlando's anger dissolved, replaced by an appealing helplessness.

Mick sighed, thrust a hand into his own pocket. He held out three silver pieces. 'This should be enough to pay your carriage.'

Orlando stared at the offering. 'No, you have given me enough as it –'

'Take it!' Mick tipped the coins into the midshipman's palm, curling the man's fingers around them. 'One day, you can do the same for me.' Before Orlando could argue further, Mick steered him towards the open carriage door. He raised his head towards the outline of the driver. 'Rock Hall, my good man – and don't spare the horses!'

'Yes, sir!'

Stepping back, Mick watched the midshipman climb into the carriage's interior. His heart hammered in his chest. He moved back further, one hand raised in farewell.

Then Orlando's handsome face appeared at the window, his hand extending into the darkness.

A night breeze swept over Mick's skin. He watched the oil-lamps from the kitchen glint off the object on Orlando Rock's palm.

Go!

Get out of here!

The longer the man lingered, the greater the chance his resolve would return and Rosie's establishment would become the focus of unwanted judicial attention. Mick walked swiftly to the carriage. He stared at the medallion-shaped object.

'For services to His Majesty.' Orlando's deep voice was low with pride and gratitude. 'It was presented to me by Lord Nelson himself. I want you to have it.'

Nervousness tingled on his skin. Mick willed his heart to still. 'Your generosity leaves me speechless.' Deftly, he scooped the silver award from Orlando's hand and slipped it into his pocket, wondering how on earth he had overlooked the treasure in his earlier search of the man's garments. Moving back, Mick slapped the rump of a nearby steed. 'Now home with you!'

Orlando's sombre expression broke into a smile of pleasure. He waved once, before the carriage drove off into the night.

Mick watched the back wheels for a few seconds, then patted his pocket and went back inside.

'How much?'

Rosie stuck the medallion between snaggled teeth and bit. 'Silver.'

Mick laughed, gnawing at a leg of goose. 'Sure, I know that!' He glanced around the busy tavern. Just the usual assortment of rogues, drunken sailors and whores – apart from a group of cassocked figures eating beside the fire, around a heap of luggage. A few feet away, a thin red-headed youth was furiously consuming a bowl of mutton broth.

The landlady removed the medal from her mouth, wiped it on a corner of her apron. She looked at him curiously.

Mick lowered his voice. 'Is there any value in it, over and above the silver content?'

She held the circular object up to an oil-lamp, squinting first at the embossed head of His Majesty George III, then the inscription on the other side. 'Presented to Orlando Rock, on the occasion of His Majesty's investiture, for services over and above the call of duty.' She let out a cackle of mirth. 'Is that what they're calling it now?'

Mick chuckled, grabbed the medal from Rosie's claw-like grip.

She winked. 'I'm not going to ask why you needed a fistful of my best goose-grease, dearie, but I'd say the sooner you got rid of this, the better.' She tapped the side of her hook nose. 'No reminders – nothing to connect you with your ladies and gentlemen friends. Isn't that the way you like to do business?'

Mick stared at the silver circle. He had been more than a little touched by Orlando's parting gesture. But Rosie was right. He set the medallion on the table between them. 'So it's not valuable?'

'A cheap piece of junk.' She lowered her capped head to his conspiratorially. 'Tell you what, my pet: since I like you, I'll take it off your hands – in payment for your extended stay upstairs.' Bony fingers reached out towards the prize.

Mick roared with laughter, snatching the medal away. 'So it is worth something?' He tossed the object into the air.

Rosie clawed for it, but he was too quick for her. He caught the object deftly, slipping it back into his pocket.

She laughed good-naturedly. 'Not much gets past you, does it, dearie?'

'Greed will be your downfall, Rosie.' From his other pocket, he produced the heavy money-pouch. Opening the drawstrings, he counted out four silver pieces and slid them across the table. 'I only take what's owed to me – as should you.'

'Can't blame a girl for trying, can you?' Quick as lightning, she seized the money, cramming it down the front of her tightly corseted blouse. 'You're an honourable man, dearie – I'll give you that.'

'A compliment, from one of the wiliest villians Deptford knows – you honour me further, Rosie!' Mick threw the remains of his goose-leg on to his plate, sucking the juicy fat from his fingers. Fucking – regardless of which of his limbs was involved – always gave him an appetite.

'But you will get rid of it, won't you?' She eyed the pocket in which Orlando's touching keepsake had ended up.

'Fear not.' Mick gripped the tankard of ale, drained it. 'First thing tomorrow.' He leant back in his chair, surveying his drinking companions.

One of the whores had her face in the lap of a burly, laughing sailor.

The red-headed cut-purse had finished the mutton broth and was now chewing on a hunk of bread.

The group of priests were huddled together, talking.

Mick's eye lingered on the large, ornate cross which hung from around one of the cassocked necks. 'Will you do that bit of needlework for me, Rosie?'

She laughed. 'Why not treat yourself to some new clothes, dearie – you make enough money.'

Mick looked away from the priests. He flexed his slowly recovering right arm, then wriggled out of the frockcoat. He showed her the missing buttons and the tear in the fine breeches.

She nodded. 'I'll have them ready for the morning, good as new, pet.'

He stretched out his long, muscular legs.

Rosie cocked her head. 'So, if it's not for the fine things in life, why do you do it?'

Mick's eyes narrowed.

Rosie expanded. 'You're a hard worker, dearie, and you must have quite a nest egg by now. What's it all for?'

Mick narrowed his eyes further but said nothing.

She pressed her suit. 'Is it property you're after? Perhaps an alehouse of your own? I know it took me five long years sucking the cocks of lusty sailors before I had enough to buy this place. But it was worth every drop of spunk I swallowed!'

Mick grinned at the thought.

'Or is it land?' Rosie's curiosity was growing. 'You Irish lads are hard workers – that's obvious to anyone with eyes –' she winked '– or lust to slake. Are you wanting to buy a nice piece of farmland, maybe settle down and raise crops and children?'

Mick laughed out loud. 'To be sure, my plan involves land – and a family.' His eyes moved towards the open door and out into the night. 'But a land far from these shores.'

'You're going back to Ireland?'

Mick shivered at the thought of his bleak, rainy homeland. He stood up, pushed his chair back and moved closer to the fire.

Rosie followed.

Nailed to a wooden ceiling-support, a ragged handbill caught his eye, as it had done two months ago:

That if any young lads, not under fifteen and not exceeding sixteen Years of Age, who can read and write and are virtuously disposed, and can bring sufficient testimonials of the last, will come under Indentures for five years, to serve a gentleman in Jamaica, with the Consent of their nearest Relations, they shall have new Cloathing along with them, their Passage paid, Bed, Board, Washing and Lodging as Customary there, and Ten Pounds Sterling yearly of Wages paid to them, to call at Robert Findlay's in the Newgate of London.

Mick nodded to the handbill and lowered his voice. 'The West Indies, my inquisitive friend.'

Rosie scanned the words, her cracked lips moving slowly. She snorted. 'Virtuously disposed, pet?'

Mick laughed. 'I have no wish to line another man's pocket with the sweat of my brow anyway.' He leant against the flue and felt the welcome heat seep into his chilled bones. 'Land is cheap there – soil is rich and fertile. The weather is clement.' He thought about his mother and his five siblings, huddled round a smoking peat fire, then pushed the image away. He grinned. 'Sugar, rum, fine hardwoods – Have you ever seen a banana, Rosie?'

She goggled. 'A what?'

He laughed. 'A wonderful, yellow fruit which comes in its own protective wrapping! When I have enough money, I intend to take my entire family to the West Indies, where we shall raise bananas and grow old under a warm tropical sun.'

'It's so far away, dearie.'

Mick chuckled. 'That, my friend, is part of its appeal. In the New World, a fellow makes his own destiny. There, I will be a different man: no past to haunt me, no price on my head. No dodging into alleys and stealing the clothes of fine gentlemen.'

She cackled. 'And no fine gentlemen's fine cocks to suck on, remember.'

Mick paused.

'But perhaps, in that foreign land, you'll take a pretty young West Indian boy as your own?'

Mick considered the prospect, staring from the fire to the corner beyond.

The priests were checking their luggage.

The red-haired pickpocket was draining his tankard. Green eyes met brown over the pewter rim. The former twinkled with undisguised interest.

Mick chuckled, cock twitching. 'Yes, Rosie, perhaps I shall have some swarthy companion with whom to enjoy my twilight years.' As he returned his gaze to her hook-nosed face, he caught another twinkle.

From the ornate cross which dangled from a cassocked neck.

Another twitch – in his brain. 'I see someone is after our souls.' Mick casually nodded towards the ecclesiastical group. 'What brought the Brothers in?'

Rosie cackled. 'The weather – and no sense of direction! They are from Cork, I hear. Bound for Manchester, poor fools.'

His mind began to work. 'Cork, you say?'

'Very devout, apparently. In England, two weeks already, raising funds for their –' She broke off, understanding dawning on her pock-marked face. 'Dearie, you're not –'

'Sure, and am I not from Cork myself?' That ornate cross and the large pile of luggage burnt in his mind. Mick grinned. 'And would it not be rude of me if I failed to welcome the good Brothers to our new land?'

Rosie clapped a warty hand over her mouth. 'You'll be the death of me, pet – or yourself, if you're not careful.'

Mick winked. 'It will do a wayward Catholic boy like myself the world of good to have some clerical company.' He lowered his voice, produced another silver coin from his pocket and pushed it towards her. 'But keep that redhead in whatever he's drinking until I return.' He stood up, smoothing down his tangled locks. As he made his way over to the group of priests, her hearty laugh rang in his ears.

'Let me help you with that, Father.'

Half an hour later, he found them a coachman who was prepared to travel to Manchester at such a late hour.

'Thank you, Michael – we are in your debt indeed.'

He smiled at the handsome young priest, then changed his expression to one of more suitable respect. 'God's work requires no debt.' Rain soaked his fine shirt and breeches. Mick staggered through ankle-deep mud, hurling another piece of the Brothers' luggage on to the back of the carriage.

The cassocked figure turned, about to make his way back to the alehouse.

'Let me, Father – this should be the last one.' Mick bounded towards the glow of oil-lamps and what he knew to be two more portmanteaux.

Inside, he thrust the larger piece of luggage under a table, picked up the smaller and raced back into the wet, pouring night.

Four of the priests were already esconced in the carriage. The remaining figure – the handsome-faced man, wearing the large ornate cross – stood waiting, the hood of his cassock drawn up over his fine head. As Mick placed the final piece of luggage on top of the others, the man held out a coin.

'For your trouble, Michael.'

Unheeding of the filth beneath his feet, Mick fell to his knees, kissing the fingers of the robed man as Orlando had kissed his only hours earlier. 'No trouble, Father –' he raised his eyes through the rain, then lowered them in supplication '– it is a privilege to serve God.'

The priest bent in parallel. A broad hand patted Mick's shoulder. 'Blessings on you, my son.'

Mick staggered on to one knee, a hand moving to grip the cross, which he began to kiss as fervently as he'd honoured the man's hand. His mind was working equally feverishly.

Any time now, the crew of the *Invincible* would be returning on board. Drunk as lords, but without the manners of gentlemen, they would be highly amused at the carriage of priests. The diversion was all he needed to –

On cue, the door of the alehouse flew open and at least a dozen semi-undressed sailors were disgorged, shouting and laughing, into the night.

Mick saw the apprehension on the priest's face: Mother Church was not tolerated in these parts.

Hoots of derision behind told him the sailors had spotted the carriage and its occupants.

Mick got to his feet, still holding the cross which was now swathed in the folds of the man's cassock. 'Go, Father –' He pushed the priest towards the carriage.

Behind, amused voices had become darker, angrier.

The cassocked man needed no further bidding. Picking up the skirts of his robe, he fled towards the open carriage door, unaware of the snapping of a finely linked chain.

Mick thrust the cross down the front of his soaking breeches, slammed the door shut then watched the coachman apply the whip to the backs of both horses.

In a whinny of surpise, the steeds bolted forward, hauling their cargo into the distance and away from the angry mob. With a wink to the disappointed sailors who had been denied a bit of sport, Mick strolled back to the alehouse and the luggage which awaited him.

Six

———

Through his pince-nez, Christopher squinted down at the tiny handwriting in front of him and felt a flush of pride.

Four complete stanzas translated and annotated –

He removed and glanced at his pocket-watch.

– in less than four hours. He'd barely been aware of the passing time, so absorbed had he been in his labours.

The library curtains were closed, the way he liked them to be when he worked. His mother hadn't bothered him with any of her usual trivialities, and none of the servants had been in to offer him unwanted meals.

Christopher laid down the quill pen, leant back in his chair and smiled. Perhaps last night's disturbed sleep had worked on his brain in another way. Only another couple of months – three, at most – and his thesis would be finished.

The door burst open.

Christopher jumped.

'So this is where you are!'

His father's booming voice filled the room.

Christopher sighed, closing the ledger and removing his pince-nez.

Viscount Fitzgibbons strode across the library. 'None the worse for yesterday, I see.'

The hand on his shoulder made him flinch further. The previous day came back to him in rolling waves. 'Er, no, Father.'

The hand patted again.

Christopher stared up into his father's beaming face.

'I thought not – a chip off the old block, eh, lad?'

Christopher winced.

'Hold your drink the way you hold your women – tight and soberly, isn't that right?'

Christopher stood up to get away from the iron hand. 'Er, yes, Father.'

A conspiratorial leer flickered around Viscount Fitzgibbons's lips. 'Tell me, man to man, lad: did you give it to her good?'

Christopher recoiled. Heat flushed his pale skin. 'I, er – I don't know what you mean, Father.'

The booming laugh echoed in his head. 'No need to be bashful, my son! Lady Violet is still –' his father winked again '– indisposed.' Viscount Fitzgibbons shook his head. 'Quite the cocksman, aren't you – even if not the seafaring variety.'

The gorge rose in Christopher's throat. He backed away towards the book-lined walls.

His father glanced briefly at the previous four hours' work. 'Perhaps there is more to this studying lark than I thought. What are you labouring away in here at, anyway –'

Christopher hesitated, then felt a tingle of satisfaction. His father had never as much as enquired about the object of his study. Perhaps now, he could share some of the pride and enthusiasm he felt for his thesis with a willing audience. He opened his mouth.

'– when there are maidens to be deflowered and lusts to slake?'

His mouth remained open for a few seconds. When his lips finally closed, it was into the usual tight line of frustration.

Viscount Fitzgibbons strode to the fenestration, drew back the heavy curtains and opened the French windows.

Cool air flooded the room, but only served to increase Christopher's discomfort.

'On a fine evening like this, I'm sure there are several of the parlourmaids –' he turned, winked again '– who would be very grateful for a glimpse of that fine naval rod of yours.'

Christopher managed to gather himself. Replacing the pince-nez, he walked slowly back to his desk. 'I have further work to complete, Father – perhaps, in an hour or two, I will –'

'That's my boy! That's the son of Admiral Fitzgibbons talking now!' The ramrod figure strode past him, slapping his back a second time. 'You get out there and give that rod of yours an airing – after you are married, there will be less opportunity for such dalliances.' With a final wink, his father strode from the room.

Face sweating, Christopher slumped back into his chair.

The marriage.

The marriage.

Bad enough that he had little enthusiasm for what was expected of him. Worse still, his father presumed not only that he was well acquainted with the techniques of the bedroom, but he was already putting those skills into practice.

Christopher stared down at Geoffrey Chaucer's neat hand. Words blurred before his eyes.

He had to do something.

He had to learn.

But how? And from whom?

His father was out of the question. Christopher had no brothers or male cousins on hand, and no friends here.

Who could he consult for a little advice?

Whose discretion could he count on?

A lump of self-consciousness formed in his throat. Could he even form the words of enquiry, even if he did locate a suitable mentor, in these matters?

From outside, the distant call of a nightingale disturbed his musings.

Unexpectedly, the sound caused a tightening in the crotch of his linen pantaloons.

Christopher stared at his manuscripts, picked up the quill pen and tried to re-immerse himself in his work.

The nightingale's high-pitched warble pushed itself further into his thoughts, breaking his fragile concentration and rendering all further study useless.

Last night.

His bedchamber.

A strange dream in which someone was kissing the back of his neck and –

Christopher leapt from his chair and staggered towards the French windows.

A walk.

He'd take a stroll through the grounds. Clear his aching head. Maybe a little night air would refocus his thoughts.

Stumbling from the library, Christopher barely felt the chill as he tried not to remember the rest of the dream.

★

The woods were devoid of all life that night. Christopher found himself wandering aimlessly. Heading for the stables, he changed his mind at the first earthy whiff of horse manure and walked towards the rose gardens instead. Their sweet perfume did little to improve his restless mood, so he set his course on the tall area of trees. Something about the wood's dark density seemed to mirror his frame of mind.

Still no sound. Even the tuneful nightingale had deserted him. The air rang with the sound of his own, heavily beating heart. His head filled with his father's expectations and assumptions. Before he knew where he was going, Christopher found himself following the same path he'd trodden two nights ago. Pushing his way through a thicket, he ploughed on in the direction of the clearing and the fallen tree.

The patch of ground was deserted. The rutting deer had moved on, although he could still see the scores on the bark where the victorious stag had rubbed his antlers. Inadequacy careered through Christopher's veins.

He had always been a failure in his father's eyes, and would be a further disappointment once it became known that, whatever was ailing Violet Marlborough, it had little to do with him.

Christopher Fitzgibbons, heir to the Fitzgibbons fortune and betrothed to the fair Lady Violet, could publish scholarly theses from now until doomsday but he would never gain the approval of Viscount Fitzgibbons –

Christopher slumped against the fallen tree.

– unless he could somehow make true what his father already believed.

Silence pressed in on him. His heart thumped against his chest. Thirst for a different type of knowledge parched his throat and burnt deep into his lungs.

Christopher racked his brain.

Perhaps a woman could help – he could pay a visit to a brothel. The very idea disgusted him. He hardened his resolve. Yes – a brothel. He knew of the existence of an establishment, back in Oxford. Frequented by some of his less cerebral colleagues. Christopher had never felt the need to set foot in such a place. Until now.

But was there a brothel around here?

If so, where? And could he visit, unnoticed?

A sudden rustling broke into his musings.

Christopher's ear strained.

Nothing – then more rustling. And a giggle.

He raised himself from the fallen tree and glanced around, trying to locate the source of the sound.

More rustling. Another giggle. Then a low, masculine voice.

Christopher stared at the bushes.

The sound was distant, emanating from the direction of the lake.

Moving stealthily and surprised at his own forwardness, Christopher crept through the undergrowth towards it.

The moon was up. Its pale luminescence rippled over the smooth surface of the lake.

The giggling had stopped. As had the rustling.

As Christopher emerged from the wood, the first thing he saw was a small rowing boat, beached on the far end of a low jetty. The second thing he saw was a heap of clothes.

Then a shriek of pleasure split the night and two naked figures darted from a bank of reeds and raced into the water.

He recognised Elsa the downstairs parlourmaid by her coarse cry of delight as she threw herself into the water. But Christopher's eyes were now fixed on her companion – in particular, the tightly muscled swell of the man's white arse-cheeks which quivered in the moonlight as he ran deeper into the lake.

With a whoop of abandoned joy, Willicombe's dark, curly head disappeared beneath the surface, only to emerge seconds later in a gasp of shock.

On tiptoe, Christopher moved closer, skirting around behind the rowing boat.

Elsa's laugh tore through the night. Then the sounds of frenzied splashing and more shrieking as the two, waist-deep in the lake's icy waters, hurled handfuls of spray at each other's pale bodies.

Christopher sank to a crouch. In his dark frockcoat, he merged with the half-light. Cowering behind the rowing boat, he watched the childish play and felt his heart leap.

Willicombe was performing a series of tricks, much to the under-parlourmaid's amusement. He bounced through the water, kicking his feet up and laughing.

Christopher's gaze was drawn to the dark, triangular patch of hair between the underfootman's sturdy thighs, and the more slender though equally bouncing length of man-flesh which leapt and wriggled with every antic. Moving forward, he edged closer, creeping around to the far side of the rowing boat.

Willicombe's John Thomas swayed heavily with a momentum of its own, slapping against the underfootman's thighs, then dangling down over the man's stomach as Willicombe skilfully executed an underwater handstand.

A familiar itch gnawed at Christopher's own groin. He ignored it, following the man's every move with narrowed eyes.

Elsa stood in waist-deep water, applauding enthusiastically as the underfootman broke the surface with a back flip.

Willicombe gave a mock bow, pushing wet curls from his eyes.

Christopher bit back a sigh. He could never do that: the very idea of gallivanting naked – even alone – made him shiver. Envy spread over his flushing skin and the itch in his groin grew more urgent.

Willicombe was now chasing Elsa into the shallows. The underfootman looked so at ease, playfully careering through the water, long legs glinting in the moonlight. His thick curly hair was plastered to his skull in a molten cap as he threw himself forward, seizing Elsa around her waist.

Two shrieks filled the air. The pair fell into the reeds.

Part of last night's dream floated into Christopher's mind.

Himself. Willicombe's rough hands undressing him.

Willicombe carefully folding his clothes.

Then soft wet pressure on the back of his neck and a harder, more urgent tension in his groin and –

– Christopher shook his head to clear it. Everything had gone quiet and the naked bathers had disappeared from view. He poked head and shoulders above the edge of the rowing boat, towards where he had last seen them.

The bed of reeds was motionless.

Christopher frowned. Then another sound seeped into his ears and the frown froze.

A moan. Another moan. Then a lower grunt.

Christopher backed away, circling around the beached boat and staring beyond to the forest.

Deer?

On the periphery of his vision, movement. Closer movement. Head swivelling back to the tall bank of reeds which fringed the now-motionless waters, Christopher stared at a section of bulrushes which swayed rhythmically in the still night air.

Another moan.

Silence.

A grunt.

The sounds and movements were unmistakable, even to his green, unworldly ears. Christopher stifled a groan of his own. His father's knowing winks and his own thoughts on brothel visits swam in his head. The Socratic method of learning faded in the face of an older, more basic educational tool.

Imitation.

Christopher staggered to his feet, flinching as the itch in his groin became almost unbearable. Every fall of his buckled shoe seemed to sound like a musket shot on the jetty's wooden slats as he made his way gingerly back on to the lakeside and round towards the reeds. His foot caught in a heap of clothes and he almost stumbled.

Staggering for balance, he righted himself and crept on. There would be no need for any furtive, red-faced visits to brothels if he could watch for himself, here on his father's estate.

The anticipation did strange things to his garments. The soft lawn of his underwear became the scratchiest of hairshirts, brushing against his nipples and making them feel hot and sore. Further down, his breeches seemed to have shrunk in size. Everything was too tight. Fabric rubbed against his suddenly hypersensitive skin and caused little explosions which made him gasp and shiver by turns.

He was closer now, and could see the sway of the reeds.

Heedless of the damage to his clothes, Christopher lowered his stomach to the ground and dragged himself along the wet grass. The movement only served to inflame his anticipation and make his burning face flush further.

He was parallel to the activity, now. The front of his shirt and pantaloons soaked with dew, his underwear drenched by a warmer, thicker moisture, Christopher paused. He raised his head a little. And gasped.

All he could see of Elsa was one white, splayed thigh.

In between that limb and another, hidden leg, Willicombe's strong, thrusting buttocks stood out from the surrounding greenery and the rest of his sunburnt body. Slick with sweat, the underfootman's arms were braced either side of where Elsa's head should be. Willicombe's own head was lowered, the curly hair rapidly drying only to be drenched a second time by sweat.

Christopher couldn't move. He watched the tension in the clenched white buttocks ripple up with each thrust, then ebb away as the man withdrew. Eyes transfixed by the activity, he tried to take mental notes and visualise what was going on below.

His mind permitted no such activity. All he could think about was the pistoning movement of Willicombe's nether regions. He focused on the thick furrow of darkness between the man's arse-cheeks, which narrowed then broadened with each forward motion. Heat condensed in the air around them. He watched a fine sheen of sweat shimmer in the moonlight as it formed on the sunburnt skin above those buttocks. He watched it trickle down and become absorbed by the thick, bristling arse-hair.

Bewitched by the vision, the thought came from nowhere.

Suddenly, Christopher wanted to lick the sweat from that thick band of hair. He wanted to lunge forward, throw himself on top of Willicombe and bury his face between the heaving, hairy buttocks.

Then sounds from beneath the powerful, masculine body broke the spell.

Elsa was panting now. Her laboured breathing found an echo in the object of Christopher's attention.

Willicombe's thrust became strong, faster. The furrow of coarse hair was now a channel of musky perspiration.

Jolted from immobility, Christopher became aware of a parallel increase in the tightness of his underwear.

Elsa's cries were growing higher in pitch. Willicombe's grunts seemed lower than ever.

Christopher thought about the rutting deer, about the clashing of antlers which had preceded the animal coupling.

Then Elsa's legs twisted upwards, wrapping themselves around Willicombe's thrusting arse-cheeks and obscuring Christopher's view.

As quietly as his pounding heart would allow, he moved slowly to the head of the two-backed beast. Christopher's entire body was as damp as that of the man he watched.

Willicombe's shoulders were braced. Mounds of tensed muscle stood out in the half-light, ebbing and flowing as the coupling increased in speed. His handsome boyish face was hidden, dark eyes staring down into the tall rushes.

Christopher's mouth was dry. Something he didn't want to think about pounded in his head as the underfootman pounded into the figure below. If he could have undone his breeches, Christopher would have dragged his own throbbing John Thomas free. But his fingers were as rigid as every other muscle in his slim, pale body: incapable of performing any such delicate operation.

On the bed of reeds, the bestial act continued.

Christopher paused at the head of the entangled bodies. He stared at Willicombe's brow, wanting to see the man's expression, wanting to be part of this lusty embrace.

The dark curls were plastered to the man's skull once more.

A mixture of bravery and abandonment made Christopher sit up. Leaning back on his heels, he perched dog-like, listening to the wet slap of Willicombe's John Thomas and smelling the scent of sweat mix with green night smells.

Abruptly, Willicombe's head shot up.

Christopher flinched. He was in full view here. Unable to drag his eyes from the man's face, he noted with a mixture of disappointment and relief that Willicombe's eyes were tightly shut.

Thick, girlish lashes twitched against slick skin. The boyish face creased, then uncreased, contorted with passion. His full lips were parted, and breath streamed from flaring nostrils.

Transfixed by the man's expression, Christopher watched the full mouth open further. Willicombe dragged air into his lungs, thrusting more urgently into Elsa.

Christopher could no longer hear her cries of encouragement. He could no longer see any part of her. The reeds vanished. The lake melted away. Willicombe's boyishly handsome face filled his mind, his body.

They were alone.

Just he and Willicombe.

Naked.

Erect.

Eyes wide with desire and fixed on the man before him, Christopher's mouth gaped in parallel as Willicombe's jaw fell slack. Something tingled deep inside his body. Before he knew what he was doing, the heel of his hand had found the front of his dew-soaked breeches and Christopher was rubbing himself furiously.

Then a soft grunt drifted into his ears.

Willicombe's eyes shot open.

Christopher stared, watching as the man's body shuddered with pleasure.

For a second, their gazes met – Christopher's intent and horrified, Willicombe's dreamy and unfocused.

Then the underfootman collapsed on to Elsa and Christopher was on his feet, tearing back towards the shelter of the woods.

Seven

'Can't win 'em all, dearie!' Rosie patted his shoulder consolingly, placed two more tankards of ale on the table and sashayed off to attend to other customers.

Mick frowned, staring at the cheap paste cross in his hand. How could he have been so stupid? He'd taken a great risk, and for what? Had the glow from the fire made the cheap adornment seem heavier and more valuable than it was? With a scowl, he cursed his tired eyes and drew back his arm, intending to hurl the worthless object into the flames. Quick as a blink, a strong hand stayed his arm.

'Keep it – you never know when it might prove useful.' The red-haired pickpocket stared down at him. Mick's eyes moved to the grip, and its owner.

The boy's pixie face stared back. 'Keep it, eh?'

Mick nodded, placing the cheap cross back on the table.

The lad's long fingers lingered briefly on his wrist, then moved back to the drinking vessel. 'Typical missionaries, sir.' The cutpurse sighed philosophically and took a deep draught of Rosie's best ale. 'They're after your soul and donations to their cause – they have nothing worth stealing themselves. You should have known better.'

Giving a wry smile at the advice from this slip of a fellow, Mick turned his attention to the contents of the stolen luggage and the rest of the worthless booty: two long woollen cassocks, a variety of coarse underwear and a letter of introduction, addressed to Cardinal Glassford, in Bath.

68

All useless – except perhaps as a source of warmth, should the spring weather turn cold.

Disappointment stiffened his muscles. Mick flexed his shoulders. The ache in his right arm returned with the movement. He winced.

The expression was noted. 'Hard night?' The cutpurse raised a freckled face from the tankard of ale.

Beneath the table, a long-fingered hand settled on Mick's knee. He grinned. 'My nights are always hard, lad – what about yourself? How were the pickings in the Strand, this fine evening?' The long fingers tightened once, then removed themselves.

'Not bad.' The youth patted the side of his loose-fitting jerkin. 'For a Tuesday.'

A light rattle emanated from within the folds of fabric.

The pixie head shook slowly, in mock regret. 'Those wealthy merchants really should be more careful where they hang their purses.'

Mick threw back his head and roared. 'You have spirit, my lad.' He drained his tankard in one gulp.

One green eye winked. 'And I have other skills.' He replaced the tankard on the table, flexed seven long fingers and two curving thumbs.

For the first time since he'd joined the cutpurse half an hour earlier, Mick noticed the pinkie on the lad's left hand was missing. The boy was lucky: cutpurses more often lost a whole hand, if they were unfortunate enough to be caught and appear before the magistrate. Mick reached across the table, slipped his fingers behind a tousled red head and pulled the cutpurse closer. 'What do they call you?'

The cutpurse grinned. 'Cat – because of my nine lives.'

Mick smiled, rubbing the smooth nape of the lad's neck. 'And are these other skills for sale, pray?' He knew, from conversations with Rosie and several of the serving wenches, that Cat's slender fingers could work miracles on tired muscles and stretched sinew. He wondered vaguely what Rosie had told the boy about him.

Cat's green eyes twinkled, an inch from his. 'Let's see.' The hand was back beneath the table, moving up the inside of Mick's thigh. 'I'm yours for –' the eyes narrowed briefly in concentration '– make it a shilling, because I like your face.'

Mick roared again, drew the youth closer and kissed him hard on the lips. Three expert fingers worked their way over his inner thigh. Then a hot ale-bitter tongue snaked into his mouth before the boy broke the kiss.

'Up front, Mr Savage.' Cat tapped the table with three business-like fingers.

Mick wiped the lad's saliva from his lips and grinned at the title: it was nice to be treated with respect, for once. Thrusting a hand into his pocket, he produced Midshipman Rock's money-pouch, loosened the drawstrings and tossed two shillings on to the worn wood. 'Never undervalue yourself, my young friend.'

'I'll remember that, Mr Savage.' The hand on Mick's thigh remained where it was. The other scooped up the coins. Surprising white teeth tested the metal, then he nodded approvingly. The money disappeared into the folds of the loose jerkin. Cat stood up, grabbed the cassocks and staggered slightly. 'For that, I'll carry your belongings back to your lodgings too.'

Mick got to his feet, staring at the slight figure. Eighteen if he was a day. Young in many ways. But Mick knew Cat had probably made his own way in the world since the age of twelve. The loss of a mere finger bore testament to the youth's survival instinct.

Two of a kind. Separated by more than ten years.

United by their chosen profession and – if that kiss was anything to go by – a taste for men's bodies.

'I'll pick this up in the morning.' Catching Rosie's eye, Mick tossed his torn jacket and three coins on to the table then followed the cutpurse out into the night.

The six flights of stairs which led to his attic lodgings were dark and rickety.

Cat padded agiley on ahead, oblivious of their steepness.

Mick focused on his companion's pert buttocks as they disappeared from sight. The growing stiffness in his right shoulder was mirrored by another stiffness, as his engorging cock showed its appreciation of delights to come.

It had been a while. Mick didn't usually permit himself the luxury of as young a body. Tonight – after the exertions of Midshipman Rock – he felt like indulging himself.

Somewhere ahead, the footsteps had stopped. An urgent whisper drifted down.

'Come on, Mr Savage – or do you want me to carry you too?'

Mick stifled a grin at the audacity. He might be past thirty, but he could still give this young buck a run for his money – out of bed, or in.

Dragging keys from his pocket, he put on a sprint, rounding the final bend in the sharp incline in a few seconds.

Green irises glinted in the darkness, feline and shining. Cat's low laugh was lusty and full of promise. 'Watch you don't tire yourself, Mr Savage.' The edge was still there, half-criticism, half-taunt.

Inside his breeches, Mick's rod rose to the challenge. He laughed, thrusting a key into the lock. 'We'll see who tires first, my cocky young friend.' Delivering a sound slap to the cutpurse's firm rear, he pushed him into the room.

Mick was six foot three and strongly built.

Cat's slender frame barely stretched to five-ten, and the urchin couldn't weigh more than one hundred and twenty pounds.

Two candles burned on the window-sill, throwing two very different men's shadows on to the low, sloping ceiling.

From the side of the bed, Mick watched the cutpurse undress. Cat wore several layers of clothing, as was the way of street-dwellers. Beneath the swathing, his body was white and milky, apart from a rash of brown freckles on his smooth chest and the thick thatch of ginger hair between his slender thighs. It was also ripe with the smell of several days' activity. As layer after layer fell away, Mick drank in the rank, musky odour of male sweat and the grime of London's filthy streets.

Eventually, clothes tossed to a heap on the bare floor, Cat stood naked before him, casually scratching one tufted armpit with three fingers.

Mick feasted his eyes on the slim, though well-muscled figure. The trade of a cutpurse required quickness of movement and deftness of touch. Cat carried not one ounce of spare flesh. His body was sinewy and athletic. Those slender legs could break into a sprint at a moment's notice. Those seven elegant fingers could cut a purse from a merchant's belt then merge with the bustling crowd before the theft had even registered. A sharpness of mind was also part of the cutpurse's equipment.

The urchin's brain had been at work, from the moment he checked the coin back in Rosie's alehouse, measuring more than the guinea's value. Mick knew he had been weighed up, surmised, his own mettle tested.

As Cat grinned, then turned to inspect an old flea-bite on his pert arse, Mick knew that razor mind was still at work, showing the pale, freckled body off to its best advantage. He laughed, his hand moving to the front of his corduroy breeches. 'Now come here and make yourself useful!' Mick got up from the bed, planting his feet half a yard apart.

With a sly smile, Cat padded slowly towards him. The movement was nonchalant and unhurried. The green eyes scanned the room, occasionally returning to the source of the request.

Mick stifled a grin, then slipped Midshipman Rock's money-pouch from within his shirt and placed it under his pillow. Standing there, in his gentleman's finery, with his thick black hair tied in a neat loop behind his head, Mick knew he looked good. He had felt practised eyes appraise his body several times already. The two silver shillings were only one of three reasons Cat was here with him, in this dusty room.

The second was the bond they shared – a tie shared with every man trying to make his way in London's grimy underworld. It was good, every now and then, to spend some time with your own.

The third?

Mick's eyes moved to the darker length of flesh which hung between the lad's thighs. He remembered the missionaries and the paste cross. Could his instinct be wrong, twice in a row? Was Cat's only interest in him purely of the business variety?

Then the urchin stood before him.

Mick cupped a hand beneath a pixie chin, tilting the lad's face up to his.

Green eyes twinkled impishly. A professional to the last, neither Cat's body nor face showed any echo of the desire which at present raged against Mick's own stomach.

The possibility was a further challenge. He had coaxed a response from enough men to know he himself had certain skills in that area too. Mick's other hand reached behind the slender waist, pulling the boy closer. Rough fingers stroked the crack of that pert rear, feeling the soft, barely masculine down which separated the cheeks of Cat's arse.

He continued the eye lock, watching for any alteration in the youth's expression. The first sign was a twitch against the left thigh of Mick's breeches. The second was a vague flicker of unease in the emerald eyes.

Both signals sent shivers of anticipation across Mick's bollocks, drawing the heavy sacks up tight against his body.

Cat covered his desire expertly, wriggling away. Arms folded across his chest, he cocked his head and grinned cheekily. 'Well, do you want this massage or not?'

Mick laughed, patting the urchin's rump. 'Sure, is that not why we're here?' He stepped back. 'But I presume these will get in the way.' He plucked at his garments. 'And I intend to get my two shillings' worth.' Mick ran a finger down the lad's downy crack one final time – for now – then moved away. 'Undress me – I am used to a manservant to attend to these matters.' He sat down on the bed and stuck out a silver-buckled shoe. 'And mind you fold my fine clothes carefully, now.'

Cat's cheeky grin wavered slightly, before resuming its previous strength. 'Yes, sir – right away, sir!'

The mocking use of the title only served to inflame Mick's lust further. He enjoyed a game, and this young cutpurse was in for some sport beyond all his world-weary expectations.

Cat hauled off Mick's right shoe and, with exaggerated deference, padded across the room and placed it neatly on the far side. On his return, he straddled the second outstretched leg, giving Mick a full view of his tight white buttocks.

Mick stared at the downy crevice, trying to see past the light covering of hair to the crinkled orifice beneath.

The second shoe was removed, followed by the fine silk socks, which were carefully draped over the back of a chair.

Mick grinned, wiggled his toes and stood up.

In silence, Cat knelt before him, seven fingers deftly undoing fastenings then easing the needlecord breeches down over Mick's thighs.

He stared at the crown of the red head, watching. The tip of Mick's stretching cock was rubbing against his galligaskins, the foreskin retreating to reveal the sensitive glans. Inches below, inside the loose undergarment, his swollen bollocks hung low with need.

With a surprising delicacy, Cat raised each of Mick's bare feet in turn, drawing the breeches free and folding them carefully.

As the youth turned to hang the garment over the chair, Mick caught a sneer of good-natured contempt from the full, rosy lips.

He almost laughed out loud.

You think you're calling the shots, my young friend.

You think you'll have the last laugh here.

Mick stared at the swell of Cat's arse-cheeks, watching the fine play of muscle as the breeches joined the silk socks.

But we'll see who has the energy to laugh longest when my prick is deep in that fine rump!

In a flash, the urchin was back, seven skilful fingers loosening the fastenings of Mick's shirt.

Was it his imagination, or did those experienced fingers shake a little as they brushed the thick hair on Mick's chest? The Irishman's nipples sprang to attention under the cutpurse's cool fingers, tingling deliciously as the fine shirt was removed and placed on top of a nearby bureau.

Mick folded his arms across his well-developed pectorals, eyes fixed on Cat's returning frown.

The length of the lad's cock swayed languidly as he moved, the still-hidden head glancing off the inside of one thigh, then the other. Cat paused, looking down at the bed.

Standing there, in his fine lawn galligaskins, Mick grinned. 'So the masseur is naked, but the massaged must remain covered?' He rubbed the front of the gauzy undergarment.

'My activity will keep me warm.' Cat was bending over the bed, arranging Mick's pillows and smoothing out the rumpled covers. 'You don't want to catch a chill, do you?'

'I don't think coldness will be a problem for either of us.' His eyes drank in the smooth mounds of the lad's arse-cheeks, amazed at the cutpurse's unexpected thoughtfulness.

A low, responding laugh sent a fine shiver of goose-flesh over Cat's skin, erecting the downy air.

The sight caused Mick's rod to flex further, sending arrows of heat through his stomach.

Apparently satisfied, Cat knelt beside the bed and patted the mattress.

Mick adjusted his swollen cock, then moved forward and stretched himself out on the bed's lumpy surface. Despite its unevenness, the mattress felt good against his tired body. The ache returned to his right shoulder, causing him to wince again.

Then firm hands swept up his back and a low voice drifted into his ear.

'Here?'

One of the hands paused at his right shoulderblade.

Mick groaned.

'You're very tense.' The hand began to move in slow clockwise circles.

Mick smiled wryly, feeling the head of his cock jut outwards into the galligaskins' loose crotch-piece.

The circular motions continued, now counter-clockwise. 'What have you been doing to knot the muscles so much?'

Mick debated sharing his encounter with the interesting Midshipman Rock, then thought better of it. In truth, as the soreness slowly ebbed from his body, his ability to speak went with it.

Cat's hands were warm and powerful, pushing his tired muscle inwards with every forward sweep, then dragging it back in retreat. The urchin's lack of a pinkie was no hindrance to the massage, and Mick found himself starting to drift off.

'Tugging on the fine cock of one of your gentleman friends, perhaps?'

Cat's voice was further away now, but Mick was still awake enough to hear the edge of scorn in the words. He grinned into the pillow.

The hands paused.

Mick groaned again, in annoyance at the interruption. A dip in the mattress told him the urchin had risen from the bed. Instantly alert, with ears straining, he listened to the soft pad of the cat-like feet, then the rustle of clothing. He turned his head.

Then Cat was back, his bare knees an inch from Mick's face. He could smell the youth's body, detecting a strange sweetness under the meaty scent of the cutpurse's stale sweat.

And the hands were back too, sweeping down from his shoulders to rub the small of Mick's back.

Different hands.

Moist, fragrant hands.

The scent drifted into Mick's nose. His body began to glow. A moan escaped his lips. 'What's that?'

In one quick movement, Cat was straddling Mick's thighs, pushing up over his ribs and shoulderblades. 'Just an oil.'

Suspicion twitched his brain. 'What sort of oil?'

Cat's laugh was deeper than before. 'Something I obtained from the old Chinaman who taught me my art.' The hands swept back down, pausing at the swell of Mick's hard arse-cheeks. 'A potion of his own recipe, designed to relax muscle, where that is wanted –' the hands swept back up '– and deliver stiffness, when that is lacking.' Three fingers slapped his shoulder lightly. 'Turn over.' Agile as his name, the urchin slipped from Mick's thighs.

The Irishman eased himself on to his back. No sooner had he done so than Cat's deft fingers were undoing the ties of his now-damp galligaskins and sliding the undergarment over Mick's hard, hairy stomach. He yelped as the head of his engorged cock caught in the fine fabric, back arching up from the lumpy mattress.

'Sorry –'

Propped up on his elbows, Mick wached as Cat carefully reached inside the undergarment. Three warm fingers settled around his swollen shaft, skilfully freeing the cock.

The touch inflamed him further. Grasping the lad's slim wrist, Mick stayed the hand.

Cat frowned, tried to pull away. 'It is not –'

'It's my money, my lad! Are you foolish enough to think I paid merely to have my back rubbed?' The words were angrier than he'd intended. Mick's grip tightened on the three fingers, dragging them down to the bristling hair at the root of his cock.

Cat's pretty mouth hardened into a scowl.

Mick arched his back a second time, feeling a fiery sensation seep through his balls and into the very heart of him.

Then Cat tightened his own fingers within Mick's iron grip.

Mick howled, releasing the urchin.

Cat nursed his bruised wrist, still scowling. The red head lowered itself. The lad stared at Mick's full eight inches.

Recovering from the sudden pain, the Irishman grinned proudly. 'A fine length, eh?' He jiggled his cock, holding the length loosely.

His boast was ignored. Cat continued to peer at Mick's cock.

'And thick, with it!' His entire groin was glowing now. Flames of desire licked around his heavy scrotum. The cockskin was tightly stretched beneath a wide, purple head which seemed to pulse as Mick watched it. Eyes moving from self-admiration, he surveyed the slender, milk-white body at present crouching over him with such interest.

A curtain of red hair hid most of the freckled face. Cat seemed almost afraid to touch Mick's member a second time, so engorged and stiff was the mast of flesh.

Mick's gaze moved to between the youth's splayed thighs.

A half-hard length drooped downwards, but at least Cat was slightly more aroused than he had been previously.

Mick rose further to the challenge. Straining up from the bed, he grabbed the youth by his slim, girlish waist, one-handed. The other hand darted downwards, over that pert rear.

Cat gasped as Mick's finger found the object of its search.

Bucking up further, until his shoulders and back were off the bed, Mick's mouth found the full pink lips. As he kissed the lad passionately, his index finger executed another massage. Mick stroked the tight pucker, feeling it tighten then relax under his caresses.

Cat groaned into Mick's mouth, seeming to be trying to say something.

He silenced the mumbles with his tongue, flicking its damp tip around the warm interior of the cutpurse's sweet mouth.

The urchin tried to pull away.

Mick's left hand moved to the small of Cat's back, making escape impossible. He wondered vaguely why the cutpurse's hands were not returning the exploration. Then he gasped himself, easing the first joint of his finger into the urchin's moist body.

Against Mick's stomach, Cat's small balls flinched. The cutpurse gasped into the Irishman's mouth then pulled away.

Damp palms covered Mick's nipples as the cutpurse braced himself against the man's thickly haired chest.

Mick eased more of his finger into the youth's rectum, feeling strong muscle clench and unclench in rippling motions which seemed to almost draw the digit in further. When the lips of Cat's tight arse-hole were clamped around the base of his finger, Mick raised his eyes.

The cutpurse's freckled face was a map of uncharted pleasure. Long ginger lashes lay on pale cheeks. The full mouth was open and Cat was breathing heavily.

Below the lad's left thigh, Mick's cock demanded an increase in pace.

Then words: 'We can't – I have to wash my hands – you must wash your –'

Mick brushed the prudish protestations away with another kiss. He liked the way Cat smelt – the rank, almost fetid stink of the urchin's body was mixing with the sickly smell of the oil and filling his head. A good healthy odour – the smell of men's lust. Curling his finger inside the lad's arse, he drew the now-whimpering form forward, positioning the cutpurse's hole at the head of his aching length.

Cat raised his hips, arms still braced against Mick's chest.

The Irishman felt an anticipatory flinch shiver over the urchin's body. The muscles which embraced his finger were strong, and unused to penetration. Mick thought about the wide, raging head of his throbbing cock and wished he'd brought some of Rosie's goose-grease.

Then he remembered the oil with which Cat had spiced up the massage. Pulling away, he looked at the sweating face. 'Where is it?'

Cat's pupils were dilated with need. Dark circles almost eclipsed the emerald green.

'The oil – where's the oil? I don't want to tear you when I –'

'Put it in me, Mr Savage!' The words flew from the youth's slack mouth, splattering Mick's face with spit. 'Now!' Dragging himself off Mick's finger, he grabbed the solid staff of man-flesh, placing the huge head at the entrance to his body. Then Cat sat down hard.

Mick leapt off the bed as sensation ripped at his cock. Pressure stretched against the sensitive glans. His own grunt almost obliterated the harsh, rasping pants of the fellow above him as Cat gripped his own arse-cheeks, wrenching them apart.

They hovered there, Mick's cock hard against the clenched opening to the cutpurse's body, Cat almost sobbing with need as he bore down on the great mast.

Face wet with sweat and Cat's saliva, Mick bucked up again, twisting against the discomfort. The movement served an unexpected, if welcome purpose.

With a loud, wet sound, Cat's sphincter gave way and Mick drove his cock into the lad's arse. Tight balls impacted with his stomach in a soft slap. Cat's grunt of satisfaction resounded in his ears and joined his own moan of relief.

Then they were moving like a well-oiled crank-shaft, bodies synchronising into the pace of their joint passion.

Mick sprawled back on to the mattress, straining up with semi-focused eyes at the slender body astride him. He gripped handfuls of bed-sheet, thrusting upwards with his hips.

Cat mirrored the movement, using a combination of body-weight and balance to drag himself up Mick's cock, then slam down again.

The cutpurse's rectum was an ever-tightening vice around him. Mick moaned. His cock felt hot, impossibly hard.

Cat took the reins, speeding things up. He rode Mick with wild abandon, lowering his torso to ensure the cock filled every available inch of his man-tunnel and give maximum pleasure for himself and his lover.

The heat had spread to Mick's balls, filling his body with a burning fire he doubted any single orgasm could ever extinguish.

Then Cat was crouching over him, three fingers wrapped around his own, now-burgeoning length. Parallel to the cock pistoning in and out of him, the cutpurse frantically slid his own three-fingered fist up and down his slim length.

Through blurring vision and the motion of the fuck, Mick watched a tiny drop of liquid fly from the pink slit in the head of the lad's cock and land wetly on his cheek. The sight caused a great volcano to erupt somewhere deep in his bollocks. With a low grunt, Mick thrust deeply up into the urchin, just as Cat released a very unfeline sound and shot a volley of thick, milky liquid on to Mick's chin.

The Irishman's hips jutted up again as an intense orgasm made his entire form quiver. Somewhere at the back of his mind, Mick was aware of a lack of wetness in the youth's arse, and a similar lack of waning in his own prick.

Cat fell forward, coaxing the last droplets of spunk from his shuddering length, then staggered off his impaler and ran to the window.

Still dazed, and aware that the burning in his balls had found no unleashing, Mick watched the slender figure lift the cracked washing-ewer from its place in the corner, and turn back towards the bed.

Seconds later, he was spluttering and cursing as a great volume of cold water deluged on to his burning cock and balls.

Eight

___

'I, er –' Christopher shifted uncomfortably further up the loveseat. 'I am glad to see you have recovered from your, er – indisposition, Lady Violet.' He fiddled with the cuff of his jacket.

From the other end of the upholstered couch, a pair of flashing eyes appeared from the top of a flourished fan. 'A spring chill, my love –' the fan flapped dismissively, then lowered itself to allow a view of pouting lips '– but I am a little hurt you neither visited nor sent flowers.'

Christopher looked away and fiddled with his other cuff. 'I, er –' He stared beyond the carefully coiffured head into the garden and tried to form words. A halting half-sentence tumbled forth. 'I was up in London with my father and then I, er –'

'No matter, my pet.' The fan twitched impatiently. Then a slightly less bejewelled than usual hand patted the space between them. 'Come and sit by me, Christopher. I have missed you.' Her high voice took on a less-annoyed edge.

He cringed, edging a fraction of an inch closer.

'I won't bite, you goose!' Lady Violet giggled.

Christopher felt his face begin to redden. He jumped to his feet. 'Is it not a beautiful day!' Every fibre of his being strained towards the French windows and away from the edge in her voice. 'Shall we walk in the garden?'

'I do not think so!' She grabbed his wrist, hauling him down.

Christopher tripped over a small footstool, landing half in the Lady Violet's lap.

She gave a little shriek. 'Why, Christopher – you are so forward!'

Before he had a chance to gather himself, fleshy hands had gripped his arms and were manouevring them around her slim waist. In seconds, the feet slipped from under him and his hot face impacted with her ample bosoms. Now it was Christopher's turn to shriek. Struggling, he tried to get up but she held him fast.

Then two sharp raps on the door sent them both lurching apart.

Christopher turned, and found himself staring at Elsa the under-parlourmaid. Her knowing eyes swept over his face with some amusement, before she slipped past him carrying a tray.

'Tea, sir.' Elsa neatly placed her burden on a small table. Sharp eyes took in his disarray, and the way Lady Violet was hastily re-adjusting her clothing. The underparlourmaid beamed. 'Sorry to disturb you, I'm sure.' With a quick curtsey, she backed out of the room, still beaming.

Last night returned to him in ever-disquieting waves.

Elsa, beneath Willicombe.

Willicombe's white buttcoks.

Willicombe's grunts of animal lust.

Perspiration poured down his face. He was still attempting to collect himself when a low, husky voice drifted into his ear.

'Perhaps we should go into the gardens, after all –'

He shuddered as her breath brushed his ear.

'There are many secluded spots where two yong lovers can be alone to –'

'You must excuse me.' Christopher hauled a handkerchief from his pocket and blew his nose. 'I fear I may have caught that chill of yours.' He wiped his sweating forehead with the back of a shaking hand.

'Oh, my precious!' Lady Violet moved to scan his flushed face. 'You do look rather feverish.'

Her concern made him feel like a scoundrel, but he had to get away.

Lady Violet's tightly corseted figure inched closer. 'My poor baby –'

A supporting hand slipped beneath his elbow.

'– let's get you upstairs and out of those nasty clothes.'

Christopher flinched. The tone was back – the tone which told him Violet Marlborough, like his father, had expectations of him. Suddenly angry, he pulled away. 'I am sorry for the inconvenience, my lady, but I must ask you to leave. I am perfectly capable of undressing myself. I bid you good-day!' With what little dignity he had left, Christopher marched from the drawing-room, leaving a bewildered Lady Violet staring into his wake.

★

He couldn't concentrate on Chaucer today.

He couldn't linger around the house, in case he encountered his father or – worse – Elsa's knowing face.

He couldn't retreat to his room or walk in the gardens: his mother would be bound to pester him with questions about his health.

Half an hour later, Christopher found himself leaving the grounds of Fitzgibbons Manor and wandering aimlessly down the narrow country road which led into town. He wasn't really dressed for walking, and after the first mile his feet began to ache inside his polished shoes. Brushing the dust from his breeches, he carefully wiped the top of a rough stone wall with his handcherchief than sat down, removing his right shoe and stocking.

Inside, his foot was raw and blistering.

Christopher sighed. What a mess – what a disaster!

He needed help – and he needed it now. Tears of frustration formed in the corners of his blue eyes as he rubbed the sole of his sore foot.

Overhead, a bright spring sun mocked his miserable situation.

Christopher sighed again, kicked off his other shoe and rubbed his aching toes. He could run away!

He could hobble on down this road and never return!

From a nearby tree, song-birds laughed at the idea.

Christopher frowned.

He couldn't: he had his work, his family – a wife in the offing. There were appearances to keep up and expectations to fulfil.

Replacing his foot on the ground, Christopher buried his face in his soft, white hands.

If only there was someone from whom he could seek advice – he was a quick learner. He needed only to be shown once – twice, at most – how a man was supposed to behave with a woman and all his problems would be gone.

His father would be happy.

Lady Violet would be happy.

And himself?

Warm tears streamed down Christopher's hot face.

He would always have Geoffrey Chaucer. *The Canterbury Tales* were his source of happiness. Within the pages of that ancient manuscript lay his satisfaction.

Christopher sniffed.

To wish for anything more was unrealistic.

So deep in thought was he, he failed to hear the approaching cart until the two-wheeled vehicle was almost upon him.

Perching there, shoeless and sobbing, his mind recalled a rich, West Country accent, and the soft pressure of a dream kiss on the back of his neck.

'Mr Christopher, sir? Is anything wrong?'

The warm, solicitous enquiry almost caused him to fall off the wall. Flailing for balance, he raised his head and stared into the worried brown eyes of the boyish underfootman. Christopher groaned inside. No – not now, not at this of all times!

Securing the reins around the side of the cart, Willicombe jumped from his seat and ran towards him. 'Are you injured, sir? What has happened? What are you doing, out here on your own?'

The concern in the rich, country voice tugged at his heart. A strong arm draped itself around his shoulder.

'Tell me what happened, sir! Have you been robbed? If vagabonds have molested you, I will –'

'I am fine.' Christopher couldn't move away from the arm. Willicombe's body, hard and warm from driving in the sun, was reassuring and welcome beside his. The feeling cracked the dam in his mind. 'No I'm not!' Suddenly remembering the way the underfootman's eyes had met his, last night by the lake, he slumped against the other man. 'I'm worthless – I'm a disappointment to everyone, I cannot –'

'Steady, sir.' The underfootman perched on the wall beside him and continued to enfold Christopher's shoulders in a strong embrace. 'Now, take it slow, and tell Willicombe all about it.'

Coaxed by the gentle, caring words, Christopher found himself spilling his heart to this virtual stranger – someone to whom, at that precise moment on a sunny, spring afternoon, he felt closer than he'd ever felt to anyone.

An hour later, they were both on the cart and the stone lions of Fitzgibbons Manor were edging back into view.

'That's nothing to be ashamed of, sir.' Willicombe's voice was very comforting.

Christopher sat back against a bale of hay.

'You are a scholarly gentleman – your life, until now, has been filled with scholarly matters. But we've all got to learn sometime. There is no shame in that.'

The mere act of confiding had raised a huge weight from his slender shoulders. Christopher glanced gratefully at the man by his side. 'So what do you advise?'

Just beyond the large gates, Willicombe slowed the horse and turned his curly head. 'I think you are right. A visit to a brothel will sort you out.' An encouraging smile crossed the boyish face. 'And I know just the place – far away enough from here, but still travelable there and back in a day.' Rich brown eyes lowered themselves in deference. 'It would be my pleasure to accompany your good self there, to ensure you are not set upon by robbers or rogues.'

'I would certainly appreciate that.' Christopher drank in the reassurance, bathing in the underfootman's kind offer. The thought of going alone to a house of ill repute had been worrisome.

Willicombe talked on. 'But we need some pretext, in order that this visit remain our secret.'

Christopher found himself smiling idiotically.

Secrets.

He'd never had a secret before.

With a gentle motion of the reins, the underfootman urged the horse back on course. 'Do you, by chance, have any scholarly acquaintances in the good city of Bath, sir?' Willicombe's eyes focused straight ahead.

'Bath?' Christopher frowned. 'I am acquainted with no one in that city. Oxford is where my –'

'Are you quite sure, sir?' Willicombe interrupted, the curly head turning slowly. One dark eye regarded him, then winked.

Christopher took the meaning and laughed. 'Well, as it would happen, there is a certain colleague in that fine city, whose opinion on The Miller's Tale I would be very eager to hear. I will write to him this very afternoon!'

Willicombe's rich chuckle filled his head. His heart swelled with another sensation as the cart carried two laughing young men back into the grounds of Fitzgibbons Manor.

His mother wasn't completely happy about such a long journey, given his delicate health, but relented a little when informed the stalwart underfootman would be travelling with him.

His father snorted about a waste of good courting time, then slapped his back, ruffled his hair and told him he probably needed a rest.

A letter to the fictitious Algernon Parsimmons was 'delivered' by Willicombe.

That evening, meeting behind the barn and giggling like schoolboys, Christopher and the underfootman forged a suitable reply, taking pains to disguise their handwriting.

A welcome by-product of the subterfuge was a return of his concentration. Almost as if he truly were going to consult a colleague on some matter of linguistics, Christopher spent the next two days barricaded in the library. He worked until his eyes hurt and his fingers cramped around the quill pen. He worked long into the night, snatching a few hours' sleep on the library sofa. He accepted his mother's offer of meals happily, and found for once he had a large appetite.

Everything seemed to be coming together in his mind. Coincidentally, Lady Violet and her mother were unexpectedly visiting relatives in Portsmouth, so he had few interruptions from that quarter.

And if he did look up from his furious labours, night or day, he heard the musical call of the nightingale beyond the French windows and knew his future was in safe hands.

The 'reply' arrived, courtesy of a village lad and Willicombe's bribe of two shillings.

Algeron was looking forward to Christopher's visit, and even offered overnight board and lodgings to his fellow scholar and his manservant, should the need arise.

'What should I wear?' His books and papers were packed and waiting downstairs. In his bedchamber, clad only in a nightshirt, Christopher stared balefully into the depths of the wardrobe. Clothes had never been a consideration for him, but now he suddenly felt a great lack of sartorial expertise.

Willicombe's low chuckle drifted over from the wash-stand. 'I doubt you will be in them for long, so I shouldn't think it will matter, sir!'

Christopher smiled.

The nightmare had not returned.

His sleep had been brief and dreamless.

Selecting something his mother had picked out for him months ago, Christopher chose a darkly sober frockcoat, matching breeches and a plain shirt. He turned with a flourish. 'Will these do?' He waved the selection in front of the underfootman, whom his father had permitted to dress in ordinary clothes, since he was to perform the role of Christopher's manservant as well as his coachman.

Willicombe stared, then shook his head. 'Will you allow me to choose for you, sir?'

Christopher shrugged then laughed. 'Please do.'

Wearing tight, hopsack breeches and a white, high-collared shirt, Willicombe grabbed the jacket. 'This will suit you well enough.' He examined the breeches, nodding approvingly. 'As will these.' The underfootman regarded the dark shirt, shook his curly head then grabbed the garment and replaced it in the wardrobe. 'But a brighter hue will set off your colouring to more advantage.'

If what he wore didn't matter – ?

Christopher felt a light flush scurry over his face. Sitting down on the rumpled bed, he drew the nightshirt tightly around his body.

'Let's see –' Willicombe was rummaging now, heaving forth a variety of shirts. He scrutinised each in turn, then tossed them over his shoulder on to the bed.

A mass of dark fabric hit Christopher in the face. He laughed, hauling himself free of the folds of fabric.

'Ah, yes – this one, sir!'

When he could finally see again, Christopher stared at a bright red damask shirt, decorated with darker burgundy butterflies. An aunt had made him a present of the garment several years ago. He had looked at the shirt once, then consigned it to the depths of his wardrobe. Christopher shook his head doubtfully.

Willicombe grinned. Holding the scarlet garment aloft, he walked towards the bed.

Christopher stood up. 'No, really – it is somewhat flamboyant. I cannot –'

'Of course you can, sir!' Pausing an inch away, the underfootman held the shirt against Christopher's chest. 'See? It brings out the colour of your eyes –'

The scurrying flush slowed to a more sedate creep.

'– and the fine texture of your hair.'

In sharp contrast to the soft, low words one rough finger gently stroked a loose strand back from a face which was now dangerously close to matching the garment in intensity of colour.

Beneath the baggy nightshirt, Christopher was aware of a warm tingling between his legs. 'No, er – really –' His hands lose in protestation. 'I would prefer a more restrained –'

'At least try it on, sir.' In one quick movement, the underfootman tucked the garment under one arm then bent down and gripped the edges of Christopher's nightshirt.

Voluminous fabric muffled most of his cry as Willicombe dragged the sleeping-shift up over his raised arms.

'Please?' The underfootman held out the scarlet shirt. 'For me, sir?'

Christopher stood naked, staring into Willicombe's beseeching face. The warm tingle had become a raging fire.

Then the twinkling brown eyes moved away from his, and focused lower. 'Nothing wrong with your equipment, is there, my lord?' The West Country voice was low and playful.

Blushing scarlet, Christopher's hands flew modestly to his genitals. 'I, er – perhaps I will try the shirt on.'

Lightning-like, rough fingers grabbed his wrist, pulling. 'Don't be modest, Mr Christopher – let's have a look at what's in store for those eager whores.' The scarlet shirt was tossed over a broad shoulder and Willicombe's other hand was gripping the remaining wrist.

Something exploded in Christopher's stomach. His head drooped forward.

Willicombe gave a low, admiring whistle.

Staring down at his own blond pubic bush, he moaned in shame at the thick, fleshy rod which poked out towards the man who held his wrists in an iron vice.

'For such a slender fellow, you have a fine weapon, Mr Christopher.'

The nightmare feelings were back. He wanted to close his eyes. Couldn't. He wanted to look away. Couldn't. He longed to touch himself. Couldn't. He wanted the rich country voice to stop. It didn't.

'And you have never – ?'

Christopher heard the disbelief in the voice. And beneath that, something he couldn't quite identify. A trickle of desire made its way from the tiny slit in the head of his swollen member. He raised his scarlet face.

Willicombe was gazing at him with a mixture of surprise and sympathy. And – envy?

'No, I have never –' Neither of them seemed able to say the word. Christopher's eyes moved away from the boyishly handsome face and focused on the raised, hard curve now visible along the left thigh of Willicombe's tight-fitting breeches. The sight made his legs wobble.

'Well, there's a great treat in store for whichever of those low strumpets you choose, Mr Christopher.'

No – not envy? Almost regret. The knowledge turned his thighs to water. Then one sunburnt hand released his right wrist. To his shock, his arm remained where it was. Through blurring vision, Christopher watched in horror.

A rough finger brushed the head of his aching rod, slicking itself with the clear liquid which was now leaking freely from the tiny slit.

His legs gave way. Christopher sat down hard on the bed, unable to pull his eyes away.

Willicombe raised the same finger to his full lips and licked the tip. 'Pity to waste it, eh, sir?' The words were almost a whisper. The underfootman sank to a crouch between Christopher's splayed thighs.

He could smell himself.

Willicombe licked the finger a second time. A strange expression played around the man's large, brown eyes.

Something inside Christopher wanted to seize the underfootman's sunburnt wrist and thrust that finger between his own lips.

Then the man jumped to his feet, thrust the same hand down the front of the tight-fitting breeches. He frowned, readjusting the position of his own swollen length with fingers still damp from the fine, clear liquid.

Christopher wanted to die – he wanted to thrust his own hand down those hopsack trousers and expire with his fingers curled around his friend and confidant's cock. He pushed the thought away and grabbed for the red shirt instead. 'I, er – I think you are right. I will wear the damask.'

Willicombe chuckled softly. 'A good choice, sir. Now, let me help you dress, as a good manservant should.'

His mind was suddenly blank. His body trembled. A tentative knock at the door saved him.

'Should you not be setting off, Christopher dear?'

He had never been as glad to hear his mother's voice. 'Yes, Mamma. We are almost ready!' With a speed that surprised even himself, Christopher hauled on underwear, then the red shirt and the plain, dark pantaloons.

A little away, Willicombe was watching, one hand lingering inside his tight-fitting breeches.

Ten minutes later, they emerged breathless.

Half an hour after that, his best three-cornered hat perched atop his blond head, Christopher sat apprehensively inside the carriage and listened to Willicombe's rich voice urge the horses onwards to Bath.

Nine

Mick leapt from the bed. Icy water soaked his burning cock. His fiery bollocks shivered under the onslaught. 'What – ?'

'Wash it off – quickly!' Cat's voice was hoarse with spent passion and tinged with an edge of urgency. The cutpurse ran to where Mick stood, dripping and open-mouthed.

'Wash what off?' Water dribbled down his thighs.

'The oil!' Dipping a rough cloth into the half-full ewer, the boy knelt and began to scrub vigorously at the throbbing man-staff.

Mick winced, grabbing the slender, freckled shoulders.

Cat was far from delicate. He rubbed abrasively up and down the great rod of stiff flesh, frantically scouring every inch of Mick's over-engorged length. 'I told you: the oil has properties – I tried to warn you. A mixture of exotic cinnamon and a secret, oriental ingredient –'

Grimacing down at the crown of a ginger head, Mick moaned as the almost unbearable heat in his swollen sacks was replaced by another, more familiar but equally intense sensation.

'– as well as a relaxant, this lotion has the opposite effect, when applied to a fellow's nether regions.' Cat rinsed the wash-rag thoroughly. 'I must get rid of every trace, or you will remain hard for a week, Mr Savage.' He gripped the root of Mick's aching length with a three-fingered hand, dragging the already tightly stretched foreskin back further still. More gently this time, he ran the edge of the rough cloth meticulously under and around the huge, purple head.

Mick gasped, fingers tightening on the boy's pale shoulders.

Cat worked diligently, carefully wiping and cleaning.

A more natural stiffening took over. Mick widened his thighs, bending his knees to allow the cutpurse greater access. By the time Cat had laved thoroughly around the rim of the great head and was moving up on to the wide, velvety glans itself, the muscles in Mick's legs were tight and rigid, while the load in his engorged sacks had drawn itself up close to his body. 'Enough!' He tried to pull away.

'I must check, Mr Savage.' A three-fingered grip clasped the root and held him fast.

Mick stared down at the boy who knelt before him.

Moving his hand upwards, the cutpurse increased the circlet of pressure on the glans with his long thumb and forefinger: the digits came nowhere near to meeting around the vast girth.

As Mick watched, his own hands moving upwards to thrust themselves into the boy's red hair, Cat squeezed.

Mick's slit widened, gaping and pink.

With a quick flick of his wrist, the boy snapped a corner of the washcloth inside.

Hips bucking , the Irishman grunted. A clear tear of longing bubbled up from within.

Cat laughed approvingly, raising his freckled face. 'That's you, Mr Savage.' The vast textured head bobbed an inch from the boy's nose. With a smile, he slipped a hand round to the small of Mick's back and planted a kiss on the underside of the quivering length.

His bollocks contracted. Mick inhaled deeply at the touch of the boy's full lips.

Then those lips were parting and Cat was drawing him closer.

A soft tongue flicked out, laving where only moments before the rough surface of the wash-cloth had scoured and inflamed.

Mick's hips pistoned forward. 'Take me in your mouth, lad – before I waste my seed.'

Cat's chuckle was low and teasing.

Mick felt the boy's warm breath on his tightly stretched cockskin. He was well used to postponing his own pleasure for greater gains, but the oil had already delayed his release far longer than any mortal man could bear.

The cutpurse continued the mouth play, licking all around the vast purple head and lapping up the drool which now poured from the still-gaping slit. His left hand caressed the small of Mick's back, before moving lower.

Then a thumb inched into the crevice of the Irishman's arse and a firm mouth slid down over the head of his aching cock.

Mick's spine arched abruptly, his body caught in a cross-current of sensation. Through passion-narrowed eyes, he watched the second and third inches of his rod disappear between the cutpurse's expert lips.

A tongue lapped along the underside of his shaft while sheathed teeth applied more pressure further up the engorged length.

Mick moaned.

A slender thumb was moving up and down his warm, hairy crack, stroking in parallel with the movements of the tongue as Cat continued to take more and more of the Irishman's thick length into his mouth. Then the thumb paused at his spasming hole just as the head of his prick slid over the back of Cat's tongue.

Breath hissed from between Mick's clenched teeth. Hips jutted forward and the sensitive glans impacted with the hard cartilage at the top of the cutpurse's throat.

Cat's choking moan of satisfaction ebbed into Mick's ears. Then he was groaning as the boy's gag overwhelmed him, caressing his shaft in strong, muscular waves.

They paused, Mick entwining his sweating fingers in the damp hair of the boy with a cock in his mouth, Cat breathing heavily through a nose now buried in the Irishman's dense, bristling pubic hair.

Slowly, the waves of muscle ebbed to lower ripples. A crashing shiver shook Mick's broad body as his tight bollocks brushed Cat's downy chin and his glans collided with ridged bone.

The thumb was massaging now, stroking his pucker with practised movements. Then Cat began to ease his firm mouth off Mick's length and his thumb applied more pressure.

Mick gasped at the welcome invasion.

Small whimpering sounds punctuated low groans as the boy continued the mirroring motion. By the time his saliva-slick lips reached just below the head of Mick's thick cock, Cat's thumb was buried inside the man's arse to the hilt.

Mick's ropy thighs shook with the need for release. His bollocks ached and he knew he couldn't postpone much longer. Moving his eyes from his scrutiny of the kneeling boy, he focused on their shadows, thrown high on the sloping ceiling. Gasping breath burned the back of his own throat as he watched the cutpurse lean forward, withdrawing the thumb almost to the lips of Mick's arse just as his mouth began its downward journey once more.

It was too much. Gripping the boy's head tightly, back arching in passion, Mick thrust with his hips and shot into the boy's throat.

Through the force of his orgasm, he was vaguely aware of choking sounds from his groin. But it was too late to stop. His bollocks spasmed a second time, sending a further warm load straight down the cutpurse's gullet.

The strength left his legs. Falling forward, Mick found himself straddling the boy's face as he pumped another slitful of spunk into the warm throat-tunnel. Sweat glistened on his strong, hairy body, which at that moment felt as weak as a lamb's. Falling further, he collapsed on top of Cat, burying the boy completely.

Face pressed against the worn wooden floor, Mick emptied the contents of his aching bollocks into Cat's stomach in a series of racking spasms. The force took his breath away and sent shudders of exhaustion through every limb.

Panting, he registered struggles somewhere beneath him. When he could focus again, and feeling some strength return to his rubber limbs, Mick rolled off the cutpurse.

Cat's face was scarlet. Saliva and a few dregs of milky spunk slicked the full mouth. Which grinned. 'Worth a guinea, Mr Savage?' The voice was hoarse from the face-fucking.

Barely able to speak, Mick could only nod as he scooped the grinning boy up into his arms and carried him towards the bed.

An hour later, as dawn edged through the grime-smeared window, Mick had more than recovered his power of speech. 'Your family disowned you?' Cradled against his vast, hairy chest, he felt the boy's nod.

'I don't blame them, Mr Savage – thirteen mouths are a lot to feed. And I was eleven: well capable of making my own way in the world. Leaving Bristol was easy.'

There was no trace of resentment in the low voice. Mick kissed the crown of the ginger head and wrapped his arms more tightly around the slender boy. 'And what brings you to Deptford?' A sigh brushed his chest hair.

'The great ships. I have attempted to stow away twice, and was discovered both times. Now I want to buy passage.' One arm moved from around Mick's waist.

'Bound where?'

Beneath the covers, three long fingers scratched a freckled arse. Cat chuckled. 'Anywhere! Anywhere warm!' He scratched more vigorously. 'To where the cinnamon tree grows.'

Mick laughed. 'So you wish to follow in Mr Marco Polo's footsteps and lay a parallel Spice Track to his Silk Road?' The slim bundle in his arms pulled away.

Cat's green eyes flashed. 'Do not mock me, my fine gentleman. Why should I not make my fortune? Why should all the riches go to those who are already too wealthy for their own good?' The freckled face contorted itself into a scowl of confrontation. Then an expression of less cerebral discomfort flashed over the boy's face. Struggling up from beneath the covers and out of Mick's embrace, the cutpurse knelt on the bed and raked at the back of his right thigh.

'No reason at all, my young friend – I admire your ambition.' Raising himself on to one elbow, Mick watched the boy's face pain further. 'What's wrong – fleas?'

A snort of indignation escaped the full mouth. 'Fleas be damned – the cinnamon!' Cat raked again. His pale neck craned over one shoulder in an attempt to locate the irritation.

'Let me.' Moving upright, Mick gently seized the skinny biceps, halting the frenzied scratching and easing the boy forward.

Cat's elbows and forearms met the mattress. Still kneeling, his slender thighs stretched outwards and back.

Moving between those splayed lengths of paleness, Mick placed his broad palms on the boy's hard arse-cheeks and pulled gently.

Amidst a channel of soft, downy hair, an angry redness surrounded the moist pucker.

Mick sighed. Being fucked without grease had left the boy's hole dry and sore-looking. Denied even the barrier of the Irishman's spunk, the delicate orifice had been badly irritated by the sweet, inflammatory oil. He glanced briefly around his dim lodgings for some soothing salve. And found none.

Cat's right arm flailed up from the mattress, in an attempt to attack the source of the torment. 'It does not hurt, exactly – it will pass. I just need to scratch and –'

'You will only make it worse.' Mick stayed the motion. Cat's slim wrist was warm in his grip.

Returning his gaze, he noticed trails of a scarlet hue leaking down the back of one thigh, where the lad's nails had done more damage.

Cat wriggled. The movement found an echo in his clenched rosette.

Mick's barely recovered prick twitched. With a grin, he parted the smooth white mounds and lowered his face.

The boy's groan was low and liquid. 'That feels –' Another moan of relief ended the sentence.

Mick lapped over and around the now-spasming rosette. A familiar taste filled his mouth: fiery, and yet diluted by the boy's own musk. It reminded him of the delicately flavoured bonbons he had been fed, two weeks ago, by Lady Snodgrass's own fair fingers, just before her rings had mysteriously disappeared. Grinning more widely, he wrenched Cat's arse-cheeks further apart and lapped more vigorously.

The boy's moans drifted into his ears.

Mick was nuzzling now, thrusting his nose against the quivering pucker. His unshaven chin rasped against Cat's balls.

A yelp.

Mick laughed, moved back slightly and kissed the boy's tight hairy sack.

The yelp became a whimper. 'It tickles.'

Mick's rough fingers fanned themselves out on the boy's hard white mounds.

In front, Cat's red head was lowered. His narrow hips were moving in small, circular motions and he was pushing back into Mick's face. 'More – more –' The words were muffled, the pleasure unmistakable.

His battered and bruised prick was starting to swell again. Mick could feel the tingling which signalled erection as blood flowed into the thickening length. Remembering the cutpurse's solicitous ministrations an hour earlier, he ignored his own pleasure and concentrated on the task in hand – or rather, the task pressed against his eager mouth. Mick opened the boy further, until the dry lips of Cat's arse spread pinkly out to meet his own lips. Then gathering saliva in his mouth, he spat gently on to the spasming ring.

Cat's response was a low grunt and a more fervent push back against Mick's face.

He licked again, coating the rim of the boy's hole with warm saliva, and applying a firmer pressure with his tongue.

Cat was undulating more urgently now. Diluted by his own sweat and Mick's spit, the cinnamon was now soothing where it had previously burnt, healing where it had, moments before, hurt.

Mick closed his eyes. His mouth filled with the taste of the boy – a hot, manly spice. When the lips of Cat's arse were thick and thoroughly wet, swollen with a different, more welcome irritant, Mick pushed with his fingertips.

The boy's hole widened.

Moving back a little, Mick stared at the salmon-pink orifice, then hardened his tongue and flicked the tip inside.

Cat's grunts punctuated each thrust. The inside of the boy's body still tasted of the hot cinnamon oil as Mick tongue-fucked the warm tunnel of muscle. Only hours before, his own overly engorged prick had ploughed this furrow. Now his ministerings were less frenzied, but equally passionate.

Blood continued to pump into his cock. His bollocks grew heavy as he reached further into the cutpurse, curling his strong tongue around the interior of the boy's body until Cat's grunts rose to a high howl and he smashed back on to Mick's sweating face.

Moving his hands to beneath the slender body, Mick grabbed sharp hip bones, lifting Cat's lower body from the bed as the boy's slender cock pumped thick globules of spunk on to the backs of his knuckles.

The cutpurse's thighs flailed around his head. Mick removed his tongue and gnawed at the engorged lips of the boy's arse, sending Cat into a further spasm of ecstasy.

By the time the final shudder of orgasm ebbed from Cat's freckled body, Mick's hand was drenched in the boy's seed. His own need had receded, replaced by a different satisfaction and something akin to affection.

Ten years ago and more, this boy could have been him.

He hoped Cat managed to cut enough purses from the belts of merchants to buy that passage to India.

Slowly, he pulled his face from between the boy's sweating thighs and gently flipped him over.

Cat's face was a mask of exhaustion. A small smile of pleasure hovered around the full, now-slack lips. Green, feline eyes hidden behind sandy-lashed lids, he lowered one shaking hand to his groin, where a frosting of crystallising man-milk iced bristling ginger hairs.

The boy's spunk rapidly cooling on his knuckles, Mick licked the salty-tasting thickness from the back of his hand. 'Better?' He leant over, kissed an eyelid.

The mouth parted in a sigh. Easing them both back beneath the covers, Mick snuggled in behind the near-sleeping boy, resting his half-hard cock in the slick crevice between Cat's arse-cheeks. Arms wrapped around the gently snoring cutpurse, he drifted off into sleep.

★

Mick dreamt of a voyage which had begun two years ago, when he'd left the rainy shores of Ireland, and would end in his crossing the vast ocean on a tall, three-masted ship.

He dreamt of a foreign, faraway land where hands of sweet yellow fruit beckoned to him from strange, exotic-looking trees.

He dreamt of long, satisfying days spent harvesting bananas and warm, balmy nights sitting in front of a house he had built with his own rough hands, in the company of a dark-skinned version of Cat.

Mick smiled in his sleep.

His mind's eye visualised the faces of his victims, back in England. Some waved handkerchiefs and wished him well. Others shook their fists and cursed him.

The smile slipped into a frown and his grimy forehead creased.

The jewellery he obtained from those fine ladies and gentlemen only brought a fraction of its value when he sold it on. But the contents of Midshipman Rock's bulging money-pouch would go a long way to bringing those distant shores a little closer.

His brow relaxed and his arms tightened around Cat's still, warm form.

The boy's body was almost boneless, so at ease was he in the Irishman's embrace.

India. Africa –

The dream moved on. Snatches of overheard conversation changed the setting, and he was back in the Savoy, sipping chocolate beside two expensively dressed gentlemen who had no idea their every word was being stored away by alien ears.

'I heard old man Gloucester hewed it from the mine himself!'

'I heard it is as big as a fellow's fist, and the light from its facets blinds any who look upon it with the naked eye.'

'How much is it worth?'

'Hundreds – perhaps even one thousand pounds.'

Mick sighed, burrowing his face into the back of Cat's soft neck.

The Gloucester Diamond.

Over the past few months, he'd picked up bits and pieces of information about the legendary gemstone, brought back from somewhere in the East by the present Earl of Gloucester's father.

Talk, wild tales – no one knew for sure if the jewel existed or not, but if it did, a jewel of that size, when cut into smaller stones, would more than pay for his family's voyage across the Atlantic, and still leave plenty with which to set themselves up when they reached those shores.

Maybe even enough for another's passage, if a certain cutpurse could be dissuaded from following the Cinnamon Trail. Mick tightened his arms around Cat's waist.

Then a noise stiffened every nerve in his body. He opened one eye and found himself staring into the back of a long, chicken-down bolster.

The room was once again silent.

Mick frowned. He was slightly annoyed Cat had left without saying goodbye, but if that was the way the boy wanted to do things . . .

He turned his head, one arm stretching out stealthily over the side of the bed. Instinctively, with the practised movement of one who guards his hard-earned spoils well, his fingers checked underneath his pillow.

And found nothing.

Opening both eyes, Mick stared at the once-more swathed shape of the cutpurse.

Three fingers were deftly tucking Orlando Rock's bulging wallet into one of those many folds of fabric. The right hand reached for the door handle.

With a roar of disbelief, Mick leapt naked from the bed and threw himself on the boy. 'Oh no you don't!'

Cat screamed and tried to struggle free.

Mick held him fast with one strong hand while the other tugged the money-pouch free and waved it accusingly before green, feline eyes. 'Is this how you repay my trust? Is this how you treat your friends?' He shook the slender form furiously, tossing the money-pouch on to the bed.

'You are no friend of mine!' Cat's teeth rattled. 'A fine gentleman like you? And you can afford it, anyway!'

Mick stared, then found himself laughing. 'A fine gentleman, am I? Exactly how did you form that impression?' He nodded around the shabby room. 'Does this look like the abode of a fine gentleman?' Hauling the boy towards him, he pulled him off his feet and held him dangling there. 'Does this feel like the foppish fist of any lord you've ever encountered?' He brought his face close to Cat's, licking his lips. 'And is this the tongue of anything but a rough, country lad?'

Cat shrieked. 'But your clothes – the way you speak. I –'

Mick's chuckle drowned out the rest of the baffled voice. 'Well, if I can fool an expert such as yourself, I must be getting better.' Gently, he lowered the lad's feet back to the floor.

'I thought this –' eyes glanced around the room '– was where you brought boys to bugger!' Cat's face was a study in confusion.

'This is my home – for now.' Mick slapped the boy on the back. 'We are in the same line of work, my naive young friend. Never go by appearances alone – surely the streets have taught you that much.' Releasing the cutpurse's collar, Mick sat down on the bed. He shook his head of tangled hair. 'The robber robbed – that would have been a fine thing indeed!'

'Forgive me, Mr Savage, I –'

'Save your apologies, boy –' Mick manufactured an offended scowl '– and let me think what your punishment will be.' He looked away to hide the teasing smile which threatened to spoil the moment. His eyes fell on the two cassocks and the visiting card, thrown in a heap by Cat, on the far side of the room. The paste cross sat atop the bundle, its glass stones glinting in the noon sunshine.

'I am truly sorry, Mr Savage.' The cutpurse continued his regrets.

Mick barely heard them. 'You hail from Bristol, you say?'

'Yes, Mr Savage. I –'

'Do you know Bath?' He regarded the cutpurse's contrite expression with renewed enthusiasm.

'Very well, Mr Savage, although it was in that fine town that an evil magistrate relieved me of my little finger, so I cannot –'

'You have a pious face, my lad.' Mick stood up, gripped the boy by the chin and stared into glowing green eyes. 'Are you a religious boy?'

Cat looked confused. 'I know my catechism, but apart from that I –'

'Good – good!' Holding him firmly, Mick led Cat across the grimy room. With his free hand, he seized one of the cassocks, held it aloft in front of the still-apologising figure.

The robe was a little long, but Rosie was adept with a needle. Mick grinned. 'Do you truly want to atone for the insult you have inflicted upon me?'

Cat's red head nodded vigorously.

Mick released the boy's chin, gripped the freckled face between both palms and kissed the lad hard. 'Well, I think I have a way you can help me.'

Ten

The ancient, Roman city of Bath was very different from his scholarly Oxford. As Willicombe urged the carriage up the main street, Christopher stared out of the window, taking in the strangeness of the buildings.

Oxford was full of dreaming spires and dark, redstone structures blackened by centuries of grime.

He gazed at the bright, blond sandstone of what looked like the town hall. In Bath, everything was fresh and new. Noon sun smiled down, reflecting off the fine architecture.

Christopher sat back in his seat.

In Bath, he would learn a different type of knowledge from that which occupied his mind in Oxford.

He lowered his head, regarding the scarlet shirt. Christopher smiled. Willicombe was right – the garment did look good.

Returning his attention to the view outside, he watched the groups of men and women who strolled each side of the broad road, stopping now and then to exchange courteous greetings.

A genteel city. A mannered city.

The nervousness which had plagued his stomach for the past four hours slowly faded.

With Willicombe as his guide, they would find an establishment where the ladies were of a superior, well-born quality. Perhaps a gentlewoman, fallen on hard times, would be his instructress.

She would be educative but patient, coaxing and living up to the title of gentlewoman in every way. Christopher removed his feathered hat, patted his hair then replaced the tricorne. He smiled, almost looking forward to the encounter.

Then the carriage lurched as one wheel dipped into a pothole.

Craning his head, Christopher frowned.

Beyond the window, the scene had changed.

Gone were the bright, sandstone buildings. The sun was now hidden by a towering row of ramshackle wooden structures.

Another pothole caused the carriage to sway alarmingly. A dirty-faced urchin seized the windowsill, hauled himself up and leered in. 'Spare a farthing, good sir?'

Christopher recoiled, just as a shout from Willicombe repelled the unwanted boarder.

Gone were the fine ladies and gentlemen.

Gripping the sides of his seat, Christopher regarded the crowds of ragged citizens who now thronged the streets.

Most had red, pox-marked faces. Many carried bundles of clothing. Others herded a few mangy-looking sheep along the filthy edges of the deeply rutted road. Barrows trundled by, filled with vegetables, crates of squawking chickens and other fowl. On the far side, a pair of cassocked priests picked their way gingerly around a sprawling beggar.

Christopher sighed, not envying the good fathers their task.

In the distance, a cock crowed repeatedly. Somewhere closer, a penny-flute whistled over coarse singing and the clatter of wooden shoes on cobble. The noise of rough chatter was loud and raucous.

Christopher flinched.

And there was a smell.

Thrusting his hand into his pocket, he pressed a lace-edged handkerchief to his twitching nostrils and tried to mask the stench with its lavender fragrance.

The carriage picked up speed. Over the racket he could hear Willicombe exchange greetings with many of the townspeople, pausing to shout warning words to those who refused to get out of their way.

Lurching from side to side as the horses swerved to avoid potholes and crowds of dirty urchins, apprehension swelled once more in Christopher's stomach. He stared down at his polished shoes: perhaps if he ignored it all, it would go away. If he didn't look, the filthy throngs of townspeople weren't there.

Then the din lessened and the carriage turned a corner.

Christopher blinked in the growing gloom. Even the sun had deserted them. Raising his head, he risked a look beyond the window.

The carriage was travelling down a narrow street. A dark narrow street. But at least it was quieter than the previous teeming avenue. Fingers squeezing the lavender-scented handkerchief into a sweaty knot, he became aware of the slowing of hooves.

Minutes later, in front of a tall, rickety-looking building, the carriage came to a halt.

Christopher's stomach was still in motion.

The door opened.

He shrank back against upholstered cushions, bracing himself for an onslaught of chattering beggars.

Willicombe's boyishly handsome face peered through the gloom. 'Here we are, sir!' The underfootman brushed dust from his tight-fitting breeches.

Christopher relaxed a little. He raised himself from his seat and stared past the curly head. 'Where is – here?'

Willicombe was unfurling the set of three steps which led down from the carriage. 'Doxy's!'

Christopher shivered: Doxy didn't sound like the name of some well-bred lady, fallen on hard times.

'The best brothel in Bath!' The underfootman stood back, stretched out a hand. 'Down you come, Mr Christopher – the journey wasn't too uncomfortable, I trust?'

Lurching to his feet, he seized the rough, extended fingers and felt them clamp around his. A flush rose to his face. 'No, no – the journey was fine.' Christopher stepped from the carraige.

'Mind your feet, sir.'

One foot hovered over a puddle of something thick and smelly-looking.

Willicombe's fingers tightened, steering his charge a little to the left. 'That's it, sir.'

The sole of his shoe found dry, solid earth. His heart still floated somewhere outside his chest.

The underfootman closed the carriage door, then inserted two fingers into his mouth.

A piercing whistle filled Christopher's head. He tried to cover his ears but Willicombe still gripped one of his hands.

Out of the half-dark, a gaggle of small, filthy figures scurried into view. One thrust himself forward, pushing the others away. 'Yes, gentlemen? Can I be of service?' The urchin grinned toothlessly.

Willicombe plucked a copper coin from his pocket and flipped it into the air. 'Mind the horses until we return and there will be another half-penny for you!'

Christopher watched the child scramble amidst the filth, then retrieve the coin and beam gummily up at them.

'Certainly, sirs.' Bright against the grime-smeared skin of his face, the urchin's ever-observant eyes regarded their still-clasped hands. A knowing glint flashed. 'Poxy Doxy has some fine boys, at the moment, gentlemen – you will not be disappointed.'

Poxy Doxy? Christopher barely registered the swift disentanglement of Willicombe's fingers from his own. The thought of disease brought a cough to his throat.

'Less of that!'

The urchin's howl, as Willicombe cuffed him soundly behind the ear, rang in his head.

The underfootman turned. 'Doxy runs a clean house, sir – you'll have no fears there.' With a bow, Willicombe moved aside and ushered Christopher over to a flight of steep stairs.

Still coughing, he made his way towards his destiny. Other fears swam once more in his mind.

'Only seventeen but as wise as Aphrodite herself!' The madam tried hard to inject enthusiasm into her voice. 'She'll see you right, sir. Amelia? Say hello to the gentleman, my lovely!'

The whore regarded him with studied disinterest, then resumed darning her stocking.

'She's a beauty, sir.' Half an hour after they'd entered Doxy's establishment, Willicombe's warm, West Country voice was also growing a little desperate. 'Will you not – ?'

'Er, are there any more?' Christopher sighed. None of the nine handsome women he'd half-heartedly inspected so far had done anything for him. He was a lost cause. But he couldn't give up now – not after Willicombe had gone to all this trouble.

Madam Doxy echoed his sigh. 'A few of my older girls –'

'Ah-ha!'

Christopher felt the weight of Willicombe's arm around his shoulders. Breath brushed his face as the underfootman lowered his lips to Christopher's ear.

'Perhaps a more mature strumpet will suit you better, eh, sir?'

Christopher managed a wan smile. 'Yes, perhaps I –' Before he could finish the sentence, the fragment of hope had been seized on by both his friend and Madam Doxy, who was now striding down the shabby corridor to another curtained cubicle. His feet were lead as Willicombe urged him forward. Opposite the row of small rooms, he caught sight of another passageway. 'What's down there?'

Madam Doxy's laugh was dismissive. 'That's the boys' quarters, sir – you'll not be wanting to go there, I think!'

Willicombe's confirmatory chuckle boomed louder than strictly necessary.

A familiar heat filling his groin, Christopher turned back just as the madam whipped a ragged drape aside.

'Charlotte is one of my most knowledgeable girls. You're particularly expert with inexperienced gentlemen, ain't you, my sweet?'

Christopher's mind was back with the other passageway.

Boys?

Willicombe's arm drew him closer. The voice was conspiratorial and too low for the madam to hear. 'You're nervous, eh?'

Christopher could only nod.

'Tell you what –' the arm tightened '– if it will help, I'll come with you, to whichever strumpet takes your fancy. How does that sound?'

An almost forgotten dream exploded in his mind. Tender kisses on the back of his neck. Strong, rough hands freeing his limp body from its prison of clothes.

He pulled away from the embracing arm. 'No, er, no – it's quite all right, thank you.' Inside his breeches, the warmth grew in both temperature and strength. Christopher cleared his throat. 'I, er –'

Willicombe's chuckle obliterated the rest of the words. 'John Thomas has made his choice, eh, sir?'

Christopher stared blankly from the underfootman to Poxy Doxy's now-smiling face. Following the former's twinkling brown eyes, he stared down at the curved outline in the front of his pantaloons. The sight brought a further flush to his cheeks.

The madam gave a rough laugh of obvious relief. 'A fine choice, if I may say so, sir! Charlotte knows all the tricks and you'll leave here a happy man.'

Christopher found himself staring at the side of Willicombe's sun-burnt face. The previous blush drained away from his own cheeks, rushing downwards to inflame his cock further. A grubby palm thrust itself forward.

'Two guineas, gentlemen – full money back guarantee if you are not completely satisfied.'

Moving like a sleepwalker, Christopher handed over a couple of silver coins, which were swiftly pocketed.

'Wash yourself, girl!' Doxy was now addressing the old whore, who sullenly stood up and wandered over to a washstand. Then the stout madam led Christopher down a further series of maze-like corridors, finally flicking aside another curtain. 'You can undress in here.' Her voice was low and understanding. 'When you are ready, Charlotte will be waiting.' With a gentle shove, she pushed him inside.

He'd never undressed so quickly. Easing his lawn underwear over the head of his rapidly expanding member, Christopher gritted his teeth.

He had to do it.

Christopher stared down.

He had the means and, finally, the opportunity. Thinking about his motive, at present visiting relatives in Portsmouth, Christopher became aware of a cooling in his ardour. He pushed thoughts of Lady Violet away and concentrated on a boyishly handsome face.

Willicombe.

His friend.

The only man who had ever listened to him.

The only man he'd ever really talked to.

White buttocks.

White buttocks pounding into Elsa's thrashing form.

White buttocks separated by a dark channel of hair.

Soft kisses on the back of his neck. A wet mouth –

With a cry of abandonment, Christopher seized the moment and lunged towards the curtain. The head of his swollen cock reached the fabric seconds before he did, leading the way. Whipping the drape aside, Christopher strode erect out into the passageway in search of Charlotte.

Left or right?

Had he passed this way before?

In the labyrinth of curtained corridors, Christopher paused, heart pounding.

From within each screened cubicle, grunts and groans greeted his ears.

All occupied.

All filled with men slaking their lust with willing whores.

The thought did strange things to his mind. Christopher clenched his fists and thought about Willicombe.

He couldn't disappoint his friend – the man who had given up his one day off this month to drive Christopher all the way here. The man who had been completely supportive during all his shilly-shallying.

His prick twitched upwards, brushing his right hipbone.

Christopher walked on. The added weight of the erection gave a slight swagger to his gait.

Eventually, he came to another fork.

Right or left?

A frown creased his pale face. Falling to a crouch, he pressed an ear to a space in a nearby curtain.

A grunt, then a curse of release soared out.

Left!

Quickening his pace, Christopher ducked down a narrower aisle and walked more briskly.

Yes, he recognised these curtains. This area was also quieter. No wet, fleshy sounds seeped from behind those cheap drapes. A quiver of expectation shimmered over his slim, hairless body.

He counted five along the row, then paused.

This was it!

This was definitely Charlotte's room.

He vaguely wondered what Willicombe was up to, then smothered a gasp as a further vision of the underfootman's sunburnt shoulders flashed into his mind.

Staring down, Christopher saw that, twelve inches above the purple head of his turgid cock, two tiny buds of pink flesh had swollen in parallel.

His nipples pushed themselves out towards the fabric of the curtain and itched unbearably. Raising a tentative hand from his side, he touched one, and gasped again.

He was ready.

He was willing.

He was able.

It was now or never!

Squeezing his eyes tightly shut, Christopher gripped the curtain and hauled it aside. 'Here I am!' He stepped into the cubicle.

The responding words were low and smoky. 'You are indeed.'

He hadn't expected Charlotte to possess such a rich, husky voice. But, then again, she was older.

'Come closer.'

Nipples itching, Christopher walked blindly towards the sound. A strange elation filled his head. He had expected Charlotte to be some low, common thing, but this was an educated, unaccented voice.

'What is your name, my handsome one?'

'Christopher Fitz – er, Christopher.'

'A fine name for a fine fellow.'

The smoky chuckle seeped into his ears.

'And what's that you have for me, Christopher?'

As if called by name, his cock twitched towards the source of the question.

Then a soft, delicate hand caressed his shaft.

Christopher almost cried out as gentle fingers curled around his aching length and drew him further into the room.

'Good and thick, Christopher – just the way I like it.'

So much blood was pounding into his pulsating length there was none left to work his brain. Far from wanting to buckle, his legs felt invigorated. Christopher strode forward, feeling a soft thumb test the weight of his swollen sack.

'And a fine load you have here for me too.'

He was dizzy with lust. If only Willicombe could see him now. 'I am yours, Charlotte – teach me the ways of men!' Bursting with pride, he opened his eyes –

– and met the amused gaze of a slender, dark-skinned man. 'Call me Charlotte if you wish, good sir.' The fellow was now lounging on a large bed. He wore a white hide waistcoat which hung open, revealing the firm mounds of finely muscled pectorals. Around his neck hung a tiny gold cross. One dark hand still held Christopher's throbbing cock. Apart from the waistcoat, the fellow was naked.

Christopher's jaw dropped.

The man smiled, revealing two rows of even, pearl-white teeth.

Christopher barely noticed. His gaze was fixed on the swollen staff which jutted up and out from the man's bristling groin like the branch of some exotic tree. Where the rest of the fellow's flesh was dark and glossy, the skin which covered his member was darker still – and matt, where the rest of him shone as though polished with oil. Atop the turgid, ebony length, a crown of rosy pink sat like a sprouted bud.

Then a thumb stroked the underside of his length and Christopher gasped.

'My name is Abel –' retaining his grip around the shaft, the fellow eased himself to his feet '– as is my nature.' The glossy black body seemed to glow as the man quickly closed the gap between them.

His eyes remained fixed on the swarthy Abel's thick, black staff, which bounced languidly against his mahogany stomach with every step. Beneath the rosy-pink head, a ruffled collar of matt-black skin was slowly stretching itself further.

'What is your pleasure, Christopher?'

His eyes moved to the hand around his rod.

Abel's palm was paler, but still a shade darker than Christopher's aching shaft. He marvelled at the contrast, unable to draw his gaze from those four black fingers curling loosely around the shaft of his beige-coloured cock.

The fellow continued. 'I am skilled in many of my people's practices, good Christopher –'

The voice was low, the lack of accent even more at odds with the dark, exotic creature himself.

'– during my journey from Ethiopia, I learnt more of the ways of men, as you so delicately put it.'

A gentle thumb stroked just beneath the head of Christopher's swollen cock. His nipples were on fire, ignited by the deep, husky voice which seemed to reverberate up through the fingers around his throbbing staff and resound in his very bowels. He moaned.

Abel's body was a mere fraction of an inch from his now. Christopher could smell the fellow's musky sweat: a mixture of sweet aromatics, with a darker undernote of the sea.

'You like this, I know –' Abel's fingers tightened, then moved slowly down the length of the pale, pulsing meat.

Christopher moaned again. The sound came from deep in his very soul.

'– and this?' Abel's other hand left Christopher's cheek, travelling down the arch of his spine and stopping just above the tight swell of his arse.

Christopher quivered.

Abel's palm was dry and warm.

Every hair on Christopher's body was as stiff as his rigid cock. Staring down between them, he gazed at Abel's member.

Topped by the rosy head, a solid black arc was curving out to meet his own staff. The fellow continued to caress the rise of Christopher's arse.

'You do, my sweet young man. We have all the time in the world to discover what else you like –'

The hand moved downwards, cupping one cheek. Christopher's moans quickened into short, sharp panting sounds.

'– all the time in the world for me to –'

The hand moved up. One finger separated itself from the others and began to circle the moist hole between Christopher's arse-cheeks.

He bit back a cry.

'I will be gentle.' The finger paused. The hand around his length gripped more tightly. A thumb moved lower, stroking the heavy sack of seed. 'We will only do what pleases you, at a speed you yourself will set.'

Staring down between them, Christopher watched two pearls of misty liquid seep from the heads of two very different cocks.

He wanted to burst out of his skin.

He wanted to slough the old Christopher Fitzgibbons aside.

He wanted to throw this dark, exotic creature onto the bed and suck more of that misty liquid from the tiny slit in the great, rosy head.

He wanted –

'Mr Christopher!'

He leapt back, colliding with another body. Whipping round, Christopher stared at the boyishly handsome face.

Willicombe's mouth hung open.

From behind, a low husky laugh. 'Two of you? I hope Doxy has given you a special rate!'

A scarlet shroud of blush draped his body. Christopher blinked in horror.

The underfootman's face was a mask of jumbled emotions. Shock gave way to bewilderment, which in turn was replaced by something akin to disappointment. 'What are you doing in here?' A sunburnt hand grabbed his bare shoulder.

Christopher backed away and bumped into Abel. The curving length of the fellow's black cock pressed into his right arse-cheek. He flinched, caught between two men. 'I, er – I thought this was Charlotte's room. I got lost, er, I –'

Abel chuckled. 'So there really is a Charlotte?'

The cock moved away as Abel sat down on the bed.

Christopher stared at Willicombe, who had apparently recovered his composure.

'Yes, my friend –' the underfootman laughed '– and she is getting somewhat impatient!'

Abel returned the laugh. 'I had no idea.'

'You're new here?'

'Relatively, sir – I arrived two days ago. Your young friend was about to become my first customer.'

Christopher cringed. The two men were talking around him, over his head. It was as if he wasn't there. A sudden anger was swiftly replaced by a deeper, more unsettling sensation.

'Doxy treating you well?'

'Well enough, thank you.'

Wild thoughts of Willicombe's hairy buttocks, of the small dark hole between those mounds, untouched by the sun, circled in his mind. Christopher clenched his fists. 'I –'

'And what part of the world are you from?'

'Africa.'

Images of Abel's thick black cock with its rosy crown tormented his brain. Christopher clenched his fists more tightly. 'I want to –'

'Ah, the Dark Continent?'

Abel laughed. 'They are not all as black as I, my pale friend.'

In his mind's eyes, he watched that great dark cock sliding between those pale, hairy buttocks. Christopher's voice was a desperate whisper. 'I want to go home.' His nails dug into the palms of his sweating hands.

'I hope to see a bit more of the world myself, some day.'

'My country is large and very beautiful, sir – I would be happy to be your guide, should the opportunity arise.'

'I want to go home.' The words were half-whisper, half-sob.

Willicombe and Abel continued to exchange pleasantries. Through rapidly filling eyes, Christopher raised his gaze from scrutiny of his bare feet and glanced right.

Still naked apart from the waistcoat, Abel's curving length had receded somewhat.

He glanced left.

Inside the underfootman's tightly fitted breeches, a far from flaccid length was clearly obvious.

'Well, I suppose I should get Mr Christopher back to Charlotte – if she has not taken another customer.'

'I want to go home!' He roared the words into Willicombe's startled face.

'But, sir, we have come all this way and you have yet to –'

'I want to go home – now! Will you take me?' The raised outline of Willicombe's obvious excitement burnt in his mind. A green, unpleasant emotion coursed through his veins and seemed to turn his already engorged cock to stone.

'Sir –' the underfootman reached out a hand '– Charlotte is –'

'Charlotte be damned!' Christopher stamped his foot in sheer jealous fury. 'If you would rather stay here with this fine fellow, it is no matter – I can return home alone!'

No one said anything.

Tears streaming down his face, Christopher dashed from the room, pounded along endless corridors and out into the afternoon's gloom.

He only realised he was still naked when he collided with a tall, cassocked figure. Strong, unpriestly hands gripped his shoulders.

'Steady there, my son!'

His heart threw itself against his ribcage. Christopher stared up through blurring vision.

A pair of blue, piercing eyes stared back. An iron grip moved him away slightly. Then the gaze shifted from his face to the thick length of unrequited passion which throbbed upwards. A coarse, decidedly unclerical laugh echoed in the dark side street. 'They build 'em big, here in Bath, do they not, Father Caticus?'

With the other priest's giggle of agreement hot in his ears, Christopher twisted away and rushed towards the waiting carriage.

Eleven

A small crowd had gathered, to shriek and point at the naked youth. Mick watched a disappearing view of a white, hairless arse as the lad leapt into the waiting carriage and pulled down the window blinds. That particular part of the young man was new to him. But the ashen face and confused eyes were etched into his memory.

Three days ago: the Admiralty Club.

Two days before that: a ball, announcing Lady Violet Marlborough's betrothal.

Beneath the heavy wool cassock, a shiver of unease coursed over his strong body.

Was he being followed?

Why was this foppish slip of a fellow continually bumping into him?

Mick fingered the paste crucifix around his neck.

The boy's tear-streaked face pressed into his mind. Mick pulled himself together. The fellow seemed too distraught to even register Mick's presence.

He was overreacting, worrying unnecessarily. Moving away from the carriage, he turned and scanned the crowded street for his robed companion.

The space previously occupied by young Cat was now empty.

Mick's quick eyes peered more deeply into the market throng. Eventually, he spotted a slight, cassocked figure standing casually behind a group of haggling farmers.

As the country gentlemen argued over the price of six dozen eggs, a slim, three-fingered hand snaked from within the vast cassocked folds and reached towards one of the farmers' belts.

With a swiftness that belied his priestly garb, Mick ran across the road. In seconds, he had grabbed that slender wrist and hauled the figure away. 'Father Caticus? Come, we must make haste!'

Cat tugged back. His face was a mixture of surprise, disappointment then pain as Mick dug his fingers in between slender bone. 'It would have been so easy, Mr Savage.' The voice was a resentful mutter.

Mick frowned. 'Father Michael – remember?' He hissed the words, half-dragging the cutpurse further from the dangling object of his attention. 'And there are greater prizes at stake here, my stupid friend.'

Tripping over the long hem of his robe, Cat continued to mutter under his breath. 'Such a waste.' He staggered for balance. 'No one gives a second glance to penniless missionaries.' Beneath the voluminous hood, the boy's face was smaller and paler than ever.

Dragging a Bible from one of the vast pockets Rosie had sewn into the underside of their robes, Mick thrust it into the cutpurse's nimble fingers. 'Keep hold of this – and for the Good Lord's sake at least try to look like a priest!'

Cat giggled. 'Yes, Father Michael.' The boy suddenly sobered, bowing his head. 'May our Lord's blessed mother keep us safe.' The sly, audacious voice had taken on a reverential quality.

Mick stared at the transformation.

The former cutpurse walked on, head lowered.

Mick laughed as they turned into a narrower street. With long strides, he retook his place at his curate's side. Then he lowered his voice. 'Let's go over this again. From where do we hail?'

Father Caticus clutched his Bible more tightly. 'Raethlan Island, to the north of Ballycreggan.'

Mick nodded, the contents of the recently steamed open then resealed letter of introduction etched on his sharp brain. 'And why are we here?' It would take the real missionaries at least two more days to make their way to Bath.

'To secure funds for our impoverished parish, Father Michael.'

'Good, good – and what do you do when we get to Cardinal Glassford's abode?' Mick raised his eyes, scrutinising the names of passing streets.

'I let you do all the talking, then I ask if he will hear my sins –' Cat paused. 'But what shall I say?'

Mick smiled. 'Just confess – use your imagination and make something up. It doesn't matter what you tell him, as long as it occupies his attention –' Mick winked, gently lowered the cowl and grinned into the boy's freckled face '– for at least half an hour.'

Cat grinned back. 'A fifty-fifty split, you said?'

Mick tweaked the boy's ear. 'You drive a hard bargain, Father Caticus, but I suppose so.' Dragging the hood back up and pulling it playfully over the boy's eyes, he began walking again. 'Just try to keep that missing pinkie hidden!'

Cardinal Glassford's housekeeper directed them towards St Martha in the Fields, where her employer was conducting Mass.

Slipping into the large, vaulted church, Mick and Cat crossed themselves then took seats at the back of the nave. The congregation was large and wealthy-looking. While Cat bowed his head in prayer, Mick took in the fine gold cross which adorned the altar and a couple of other valuable artifacts. His keen eyes soon located the confessionals, at the far side of the aisle.

A few fine pieces should do it – half an hour would be plenty of time.

Soon, Mass was over and the congregation were leaving. Nudging Cat to his sandalled feet, Mick nodded to where the cardinal, in a wash of altar boys, was exiting. Exchanging small smiles, they followed.

'Your eminence.' Mick knelt, his lips brushing the large purple stone on the man's finger. 'Thank you for seeing us.' He raised his head.

'It is always a pleasure to welcome brothers from overseas, my son.'

Close up, he saw the cardinal was younger than he'd seemed while officiating at Mass.

A mere forty, with a good head of smooth brown hair.

Sitting back on his heels, Mick watched a pretty blond altar boy ease the last of the richly embroidered vestments from the man's remarkably broad shoulders.

'Thank you, Eamonn.' The cardinal's small brown eyes followed the slip of a lad who lovingly carried the heavy robe to a cupboard and placed it inside.

A smile twitched Mick's sombre mouth.

'And how are you finding England, Father Caticus?' The cardinal regarded Cat with discreet interest.

'Sure, it's a fine place, your eminence – full of many fine people.'

In response to an almost imperceptible shoo-ing motion from a strong, ringed hand, the altar boys bowed briefly, then scurried from the room.

'And many fine temptations, my son.'

Mick watched Cat's freckled face assume its pious cast.

'Sure, it's a terrible wicked place, your eminence. Blessed Mary's light grows dimmer with each passing day.'

Mick goggled: the boy had a talent for accents.

The cardinal's interest was pricked further. Slipping his arms into a more modest, dark-coloured garment, he turned to Mick. 'Your young curate has seen some godless sights since he has set foot on these iniquitous shores, I fear.'

Mick stood up, placing a hand on Cat's still-lowered head. 'He has that, your eminence.' They both stared down at the submissive boy, who was still clutching the Bible.

The cardinal's sigh was long and deep. 'One so young should not have to look upon such devilment –'

Mick risked a glance sideways.

The man's small brown eyes grew brighter with every word. 'But it is the way of the world.'

Mick's eyes brushed the front of the cardinal's flowing robe. Was it a flicker of candlelight, or did he detect movement? 'Indeed, your eminence, but Father Caticus is in a better position than most of our brethren to understand those ways.'

The cardinal's bright eyes darted up to meet his. 'This boy has a past?'

He shook his cowled head sadly. 'When I rescued him from the streets of Dublin, only two years ago, he was in with a very rough band of vagabonds.'

'Indeed!' The man sighed again. The sound was breathier, underpinned by more than regret.

'His immortal soul was stained to its very depths.' Beneath his palm, Mick could feel the heat from Cat's lowered head.

'Is this true, my son?'

'Yes, your grace.' The cutpurse's voice was barely audible. 'I pray every night to ask Blessed Mary to intervene for me –'

'You do well, my son.'

'– but she does not listen, your grace! I fear I am damned!' Cat's anguished voice echoed in the small stone vestry.

Mick removed his hand and stepped back as the cardinal moved forward.

Strong hands gently gripped the boy's slim shoulders. 'Control yourself, my son – I will hear your confession, but we must use the –'

'Save me, your eminence!' Cat threw himself forward. Seizing the hem of the man's plain robe, he began to kiss the fabric feverishly. 'Save me from myself!'

The ferocity of the boy's words took Mick by surprise. They also tore the years away. Suddenly self-conscious, Mick made his way towards the door.

Cardinal Glassford's dim vestry faded.

Back in the cathedral, St Martha's vaulted ceilings faded.

Even the glinting gold of the altar cross grew dim and he was once more in Londonderry, eighteen and blushing behind the perforated confessional screen.

'Forgive me, Father, for I have sinned. It has been –' the previous evening shimmered in Mick's teenage mind '– nine hours since my last confession.' From the other side of the door, Father Liam's calm voice drifted into his ear.

'Tell me your sins, my son.'

Mick pressed his face to cool stone and closed his eyes. 'I have harboured evil thoughts, Father.'

'So you told me last time, my son. Have you tried to banish those thoughts from your mind?'

Mick shivered: out of his mind and into action. 'Yes, Father – but it is no use. Last night I –' he could hardly form the words '– lay with a man.' His barely broken voice quivered then cracked.

A sharp intake of breath was audible on the other side of the screen. 'Tell me, my son. The Lord is a merciful god: confess your sins and all will be forgiven.'

Beneath his stolen cassock, Mick's cock was hardening at the memory. That day, almost fifteen years ago, he had been stiff and aching inside his ragged work-trousers. 'I met him on the moors, Father – he was English, over for some sport.'

Disapproval hissed through the screen which separated them. 'Could you not at least find an Irishman, my son?'

Mick barely heard the reprimand. 'He called me over from my plough, asked if I knew the land. He indicated that if I would show him around, there was a silver sixpence in it for me.'

Father Liam sighed. 'They turn the heads and the bodies of our youth with their money, my son. Do not berate yourself – I know your mother has eight of you to raise, now your father is dead.'

Mick stared down at the erect rod of flesh, once more pulsing inside his work-breeches. 'I went willingly, Father. I showed him the best fishing streams, took him deep into the woods where the deer run free.' An unstemmable torrent of words poured forth. 'And when he asked me to unfasten his fine linen breeches and take his John Thomas in my mouth, I fell to my knees and did as he bid me.'

A long exhale brushed his ears. 'Come closer, my son. Tell me it all – tell me everything. Together we will offer supplication to the Blessed Virgin.'

He could still taste the Englishman's hot seed. Mick felt the thick spunk coating the back of his throat. 'I licked him, Father – I licked all around the great crown of his manhood while he buried his fingers in my hair and pulled me closer.' There, in the confessional box, his hand found the firm curve of his own cock. Mick stroked himself through the threadbare fabric.

'Go on, my son.' The priest's urging was a hoarse whisper.

'He tasted of the sea, Father – salty and sour and tangy. His manhood stretched itself in my mouth until I was almost choking. Then I moved to his hairy bollocks, Father – oh, I cannot go on! It is too terrible. My soul will go straight to Hell and devils will prick my arse with their pitchforks and –'

'Continue! Much as it pains me to listen to this filth, you must confess it all!'

Inside his hot woollen robe, Mick's cock was engorged and raging. 'He liked that even more, Father – and I liked it too. Taking each of his big balls into my mouth in turn, I sucked at the puckered flesh and felt it wriggle and tighten under my actions. Then, opening my mouth as wide as I could, I stuffed both of them in there. All the time my Englishman was moaning and panting and trying to force himself into my very throat.'

The head of Mick's cock brushed the rough fabric and left a tiny spot of moisture on the oiled wool.

'I wanted to stay like that for ever, kneeling in front of him, sucking on his vast sack but he pulled out and bid me undo my own breeches.' Mick could still smell the boggy ground beneath his wet knees. 'I did as I was asked, and when he bade me hold the cheeks of my arse open for him I did that too.'

'Oh, my son, my son!'

'I could feel the cool air on my hot hole, Father – the Englishman told me I had a fine arse, one of the finest he'd seen. He knelt behind

116

me and kissed my arse, Father, covered its hairy surface with a multitude of wet kisses.'

'You poor boy – you poor, innocent boy!' A rustling sound seeped from behind the confessional screen.

Mick talked on, hearing the words echo in his head, fifteen years later. 'Then he handed me a small pot of lanolin, and told me to rub it into my hole. It felt good, Father – I have fingered myself before, as I confessed to you last time, but this felt different. To slip my fingers into my own body while another man watched felt strange beyond my wildest fancies.'

'Did it excite you, my son?'

'Oh, very much, Father. At first it was merely two fingers. Then three. If my arm had been longer, I would have forced all my fingers into my own warm hole.' His voice shook at the memory. 'Then my handsome Englishman seized my wrists and his own fingers were pushing into my body, Father. I gripped my knees, trying to stay on my feet. But it felt so good I lost my balance and fell sprawling on to the floor of the forest.'

'Save him, Blessed Mary! Save this boy's soul!'

'He slipped a hand under my belly, hauling me up on to all fours, Father. Holding my arsehole open with one hand and his prick with the other, he guided himself forward. It was huge, Father Liam – I thought he was going to split me in twain. But all the while he was trying to squeeze the vast head of his John Thomas into my tight pucker, my Englishman whispered filthy words to me, and before I knew it he was inside!'

'Oh, this is indeed evil of the worst sort, my son.'

'Will the Blessed Virgin forgive me? Will she ask the Lord Jesus to take pity on my blackened soul?'

'Only if you tell her everything, my son.'

Mick took a deep breath. 'He fucked me for a long time, Father. At first, it hurt a little, but then the head of his great shaft bumped against something deep inside me and my skin began to glow. I thought I would spill my water on to the soft moss beneath me, but that feeling passed. And then I was pushing back on to him, trying to climb on to his thick John Thomas and take everything he had to give me. We scared the birds from the trees with our animal grunts and howls, Father: larks left their roosts in huge flocks, calling above our heads as my Englishman and I spent our passion there in the heart of the forest.'

'Oh, the lustful wickedness of it all – the great, unholy wickedness!'

'I could feel him drawing close to his time, Father Liam. He was fucking me faster, using short sharp jabs to plough my furrow the way I plough the hard-packed fields of our farm. And when he emptied his seed into me, his great English body shook like an earth tremor, knocking me clean to the ground.'

'Oh, Michael – oh, my poor, corrupted boy!'

Mick remembered lying there, the man's sweating body covering his. His lover's panting mouth showered his shoulders with hot kisses as the last tremble of passion sent a further spurt of man-seed deep into his body – and Mick shot his load into a mound of green moss.

'Did he hurt you?'

'No, Father.'

'We must check. Take down your breeches, my son.'

Mick did as he was asked.

From the other side of the partition, more rustling seeped into his ears. Then the low grate of wood on wood as the tiny screen opened. 'Show me your manhood, my son.'

Kneeling on the wooden confessional seat, Mick gripped his swollen rod and pushed it through the small opening.

The priest's side of the booth was dark. Mick couldn't see Father Liam's face. Then a warm mouth enveloped the head of his aching cock and Mick sighed.

He'd barely been able to walk as he'd staggered home, bow-legged, the previous evening with two silver sixpences jangling in his pocket, and the Englishman's slime slowly coursing from his pulsing hole down the back of his thighs.

Reliving each warm caress of Father Liam's specific brand of pastoral attentions as the priest brought his eighteen-year-old self to orgasm a second time, Mick smiled and opened his eyes.

The parish priest had done him two favours, all those years ago: he had confirmed what Mick already suspected, concerning his own lusts and desires. And he had taught Mick the lesson he had put into practice ever since: no man was above the powers of the flesh.

Everyone had their passions. All he did, these days, was tap into those secret desires and take a small token of appreciation, in whatever currency was available.

Recovering himself, Mick gazed around the deserted church. Stealthily, he walked to the altar, lifted the great cross and slipped it into one of Rosie's specially designed pockets. Another smaller gold crucifix came next, followed by a series of gilded portraits of the saints.

As he moved back towards the vestry, his eyes fell on a picture of St Martha, former prostitute. For a second, the worldly face seemed to smile, then wink at him.

Mick suppressed a grin. Before he lost his control and laughed out loud, he remembered where he was, wondering what Cat had ended up confessing. Carefully opening the vestry door, he peered inside. The sight which met his eyes almost took the breath from his lungs.

Cardinal Glassford was seated on a rough wooden bench. Across his spread knees, Cat's bare nether regions poked from within the boy's pulled-up cassock. 'Pray, Father Caticus!' The man's large hand delivered a resounding slap to the lad's bare arse-cheeks.

'Hail Mary, full of grace –' Cat's words were muffled by the cassock which hid his red head.

'Louder, Father Caticus!' The cardinal drew his arm back, then let his broad palm fall a second time.

'– the Lord is with thee –'

Mick stared at the pink handprint which decorated the cutpurse's firm young flesh, then returned his gaze to the cardinal.

The man's face was pink with exertion. His smooth brown hair hung in dark, sweaty tangles around his angular face. The small brown eyes were tightly shut. Four clear drops of perspiration fell from the tip of his patrician nose. Cardinal Glassford continued the spanking. He delivered three more slaps to the cutpurse's rapidly reddening rear while Cat staggered his way through the rest of the Hail Mary.

'Blessed art thou amongst women –' the priest's voice filled the small vestry '– and blessed is the fruit of thy womb, Jesus!' So lost in the spanking was the cleric, he didn't notice Mick creep forward, unfurl the cowled hood and reveal the lad's pink, sweating face.

'Holy Mary, Mother of God –' Cat grinned breathlessly then removed one hand from the depths of the robe and motioned Mick away '– meet you later, back at the Cock and Bollards.' The words were a rushed whisper, almost obliterated by another sound slap and a gasp.

Sinking to his knees, Mick peered between the two men. Previously hidden by the folds of their garments, he now saw the cardinal's left hand was tight beneath Cat, curled around the boy's fine prick, while the cutpurse's three fingers were burrowing back beneath the priest's dark vestments. Nodding his understanding, Mick winked and backed towards the door.

'Your grace, you must punish me further! I have more to tell you – I cannot keep anything from you.'

Readjusting his own swollen length, and Cardinal Glassford's kind donation to the Cause, Cat's eager, supplicatory voice followed Mick out of the church.

Twelve

On the long journey back to Fitzgibbons Manor, he barely noticed the passing hours.

He barely stirred when Willicombe stopped to water the horses and solicitously enquire if Mr Christopher was quite all right.

The carriage travelled through the night. An overturned coach ahead held them up for three hours. Morning came, warming into afternoon then evening.

Christopher couldn't speak. He hadn't uttered a sound since Madam Doxy's establishment.

He hadn't raised his eyes from the floor since Willicombe had silently handed him his clothes and equally wordlessly taken the reins.

It was no use: he was destined to be a failure in matters of the bedroom. Every time he thought about Madam Doxy's selection of whores, the slim, ebony Abel pushed himself into his mind.

If only he'd been quicker.

If only Willicombe hadn't arrived when he did.

If Christopher had only been able to voice the wild desires which careered through his scholarly brain, what could have occurred in that small, curtained room?

In the background, the rhythm of horses' hooves mirrored his galloping thoughts. Misery and regret for lost opportunities soured into resentment, then irritation.

By the time the carriage was making its way up the broad driveway to his home, Christopher was furious.

How dare Willicombe take him to such a place!

How dare his father arrange his betrothal to Violet Marlborough without even consulting him!

How dare everyone presume he wanted anything else but to bury himself with his beloved Chaucer and never re-emerge!

As the hooves slowed, and the coach drew up in a soft, gravelly clatter, Christopher's fury had grown to a fiery rage. He wrenched open the carriage door and leapt from the vehicle before it had stopped. Stalking up the steps past the stone lions, he heard Willicombe's call from behind, but ignored it.

One of the stable lads had evidently been keeping watch at the gates, to gain forewarning of their arrival.

Ahead, at the top of the great sweeping staircase, his father and mother stood waiting. She was weeping. Viscount Fitzgibbons's steely eyes were cold and accusing.

Christopher paused, suddenly confused. His mother made to move forward.

'Oh, Christopher – why? Why?'

The question froze his blood. How did they know? Who had betrayed him?

Viscount Fitzgibbons stayed his wife as she lunged to embrace her son. 'Christopher? Go to the library and wait there for me.'

His father's words were low, all the more ominous for their lack of anger. Christopher's rage faded, diluted by the returning dread which now coursed through his veins. 'Yes, sir.' Automatically, he bowed his weary head and slunk past his sobbing mother, through the tall doors of Fitzgibbons Manor and towards the library.

'What were you thinking of, you idiot?' Hands clasped behind his ramrod back, Viscount Fitzgibbons paced the floor.

Christopher's mouth was dry. He could still smell the sweet, musky aroma of Abel's body.

'Now everything will have to be moved – the banns can be called, this Sunday, with a bit of luck, and I don't suppose anyone will count the months, or wonder why.'

Christopher goggled. He'd waited to be accused of everything from visiting a brothel to harbouring unnatural desires. His father's words made no sense.

Viscount Fitzgibbons continued to pace. 'Idiot – stupid young fool!'

Christopher flinched under the insults and tried to work out what he had done.

'Lord Marlborough was after your head on a plate, you young bounder. But I reminded him of what he'd been like, in his youth.' A harsh laugh filled the library. 'Of course, Lady Marlborough and your good mother have been in tears since they heard the news, but women don't understand that sort of thing, do they, my boy?' The pacing stopped. Viscount Fitzgibbons fixed his son with an expression somewhere between a reprimand and a leer.

Christopher took a step back. 'What sort of thing?'

His father smiled conspiratorially. 'You sly dog – don't pretend you had no idea. Some of those wild oats of yours have taken seed.' The viscount winked.

Christopher stared incomprehendingly. 'Oats?' A strong hand clapped him on the back and almost knocked him from his feet.

'There's no keeping a good Fitzgibbons down, is there my boy? Our seed takes root easily, grows strongly.' The viscount winked again. 'And Lady Violet has a most fertile furrow!'

Christopher blanched. His father talked on.

'Still, she is not the first fair lady to walk down the aisle, having already borne a child, and she will not be the last.'

His heart was pounding. 'I, er –'

'Why did you not use a sheepskin, my boy – or draw out before your moment?'

Christopher took another reverse step. 'It was not me.' The denial was quiet. His father ignored it.

'Youthful passion, eh, my boy? Too caught up in the moment to think about things like children, were you?'

They had never as much as kissed. Christopher's mind reeled back to that moment in the drawing-room, four days ago, when he had tripped and fallen into Lady Violet's plump arms. Was it possible? A hand patted his shoulder in affectionate camaraderie.

'But tell me –' the viscount lowered his thin lips to Christopher's scarlet ear '– was it that night, after the betrothal ball? When you and the Lady Violet disappeared for hours?'

His brain replayed events of almost three weeks previous. The ball. The Irishman with the dark, flashing eyes who had been so attentive to his fiancée and with whom she had danced so often. The duke of somewhere-or-other. Christopher racked his memory for the man's name –

'It was, wasn't it?' His father nudged him lewdly.

– a solid handshake, and another in the Admiralty Club, a week ago.

And from beneath a priestly cowl, the same dark flashing eyes in Bath, only hours before. 'No – never!' Christopher refocused.

His father regarded him curiously. 'What do you mean – never?'

His entire body was shaking. When he eventually found a voice, it was strong and remarkably steady. 'I mean whoever has lain with Lady Violet, it was not me, sir!'

Viscount Fitzgibbons's expression darkened. 'What are you saying, boy?'

Every misapprehension, each mistaken gesture of fatherly pride the man had ever expressed rose up in Christopher's mind. 'I am saying I have not bedded my fiancée – neither on the night of our betrothal ball or any instance since. I am chaste – wedded to my studies, Father. If you cannot accept that, I am sorry, and I suggest Lord Marlborough look to the Emerald Isle for the identity of his daughter's seducer.' His quiet, resolute words hovered in the air between them. Then Christopher turned and walked stiffly from the library.

His resolve lasted until he reached the stables. In warm darkness, with the sound of snuffles and the occasional pawing of a door, Christopher sank limply to a crouch.

He would call off the wedding. There would be a scandal, but he could not live a lie.

Plucking at a handful of hay, he shuffled the stalks in his hand. Though he felt no passion for her, Christopher's sympathy went out to Lady Violet. An unmarried woman with child, her prospects would diminish rapidly despite Lord Marlborough's wealth.

He stared at the chaff in his palm, then threw it into the air.

But she wasn't his problem – nor was the dark-eyed scoundrel who, he had no doubt, had taken Lady Violet's virginity. Christopher cursed the cad whose actions had brought all this to a head. With a heavy heart, he stood up, leaning over one of the half-doors and staring at the glossy rump of one of the mares.

He would leave: go back to Oxford and finish his dissertation in peace. His mother would be upset, but it had to be done. There was nothing for him here but more heartache and further disappointment

Beyond the stables, a nightingale's sweet song quivered through the darkness.

A sad smile played around his lips. Then:

'Christopher? Christopher? Where is that boy, damn him!'

Ducking down behind a bail of hay, his blue eyes darted to the open door.

'Have you seen him, Willicombe?' His father's voice was closer now, and more than a little irritated.

'No, my lord – not since we returned from Bath.'

'Bah! Where the devil is he?'

Christopher held his breath. His father's footsteps clumped towards the open door.

'You might try the lake, my lord – Mr Christopher sometimes walks down there, to rest from his studies.'

'I'll give him studies! That boy has other responsibilities now.'

His lungs were bursting.

The footsteps veered away. 'If you see him, tell him I am looking for him, Willicombe.'

'Yes, my lord – I'll do that, sir.'

As the soles of his father's shoes faded into the distance, air whooshed from Christopher's lungs. A nightingale called through his fuzzy, panicked brain.

Then other footsteps. Softer, less threatening but equally unwelcome.

He was still getting his breath back when tentative words cut through the darkness.

'Are you all right?' A stocky silhouette was framed by the stable's doorway

Christopher could only nod.

Closing the heavy door, Willicombe moved forward.

Christopher was beyond caring about the way the crotch of his pantaloons was suddenly tightening.

The underfootman stopped a little away, leaning on a bale of hay. 'I am truly sorry things did not work out for you at Doxy's, Mr Christopher.'

Christopher waved a hand dismissively. 'It is no matter – I'm sorry I –' he almost laughed '– ran out like that.'

In the half-light of a moon which shone down between the rafters, Willicombe smiled. 'You certainly gave everyone in Bath something to talk about.'

Christopher pushed a lock of errant hair out of his eyes and sat back down. 'I suppose I did.'

The underfootman chuckled, moving closer. 'All is not lost, Mr Christopher – there are other ways we can –'

'Have you not heard?' Christopher would have been surprised if the news wasn't already common knowledge amongst the servants.

Willicombe cleared his throat tactfully.

Christopher was touched by the man's consideration. 'Don't worry – I know what I am. The Lady Violet carries another man's child. I am a cuckold before I'm even wed. That's a fine thing, is it not?' Unexpectedly, tears began to stream down his face.

'Oh, sir – please don't cry.'

A rough hand reached out through the darkness and settled on his knee. The touch was fire. 'I'm not crying.' Christopher wiped his wet cheeks with his sleeve. When he raised his head once more, Willicombe was now kneeling in front of him.

The boyishly handsome face creased with concern. A rough hand moved up on to his thigh. 'I can teach you all you need to know, concerning women and the ways of the bedchamber.'

The scent of the hay and the musky undernote of horse manure mixed with the strong, masculine odour of the man's sweat. Together, with his slowly drying tears and the touch of that rough, sunburnt hand, the smell cleared his head. 'Forget about women – tell me about men!' The words stengthened his resolve. Christopher leant closer until his hot face was a mere inch from Willicombe's snub nose. 'I want to know about men.' He felt the sharp intake of breath. Arms moving by themselves, Christopher found his hands settling on the man's shoulders. He watched the man's skin redden under his tan.

'I too have had such yearnings: for a boyhood friend, back in Bristol.' Willicombe bowed his head. 'It is not right, sir.'

Loins throbbing, and with a bravery his father would have been proud of, the young Fitzgibbons stretched out a hand and stroked a hot cheek. 'It is neither right nor wrong. It merely is.' The words caught in his throat. 'I want –'

His hand was grabbed, knuckles and fingers kissed feverishly. 'Oh, sir –' Rough skin gripped flesh previously accustomed to touching the ancient pages of manuscripts. Red-rimmed eyes flashed up at him from beneath thick, lustrous lashes.

Unable to speak, Christopher watched as Willicombe guided his hand to the front of the rough work-breeches. He gasped, fingers curling around the solid length of desire he found there. He began to stroke through the coarse hopsack.

The underfootman's boyish features ran a gamut of expressions. The full-lipped mouth fell open, the shining eyes closed. Willicombe parted his thighs to allow greater access, slipping his free hand around Christopher's neck.

The man's member was thick beneath a layer of rough fabric. The rod pulsed beneath his increasingly bold fingers. After years of Oxford's dusty libraries, what Christopher held in his hand felt vibrant and more alive than he'd ever dared hope. Somewhere, someone was whimpering. Christopher reached down between Willicombe's tensed thighs, fondling the two heavy sacks he found there while his lust-addled brain searched for some memory of the man's first name.

Then names didn't matter and they were tearing at each other's breeches, fumbling with fastenings and unwieldy knots in their haste to be free of undergarments. Mind reeling with emotions and needs he'd never dreamt of, Christopher pressed himself against the half-naked Willicombe.

An urgent mouth found his.

Christopher gasped. His first kiss! It was messier than he'd imagined it would be: wet and awkward and clumsy and the most wonderful thing he'd ever experienced. The crotch of his trousers grew tighter, chafing his swollen prick as Willicombe's tongue continued to explore his mouth. Christopher's shaking hands slid down the rough work-shirt and gripped the solid flesh of Willicombe's bare buttocks. The warm skin cooled beneath his awkward grip.

Hands seized his waist, pulling him closer.

Linen hose bagging around his ankles, Christopher took a step forward. He could feel the warm hair of the underfootman's groin rasping against his. The itch in his loins was now almost unbearable. Breaking the kiss, Christopher slipped a hand beneath the underfootman's sandpapery chin and tilted the man's face upwards.

Willicombe's eyes were closed.

Christopher stared at the long, thick lashes. The man's skin was warm and damp against his dry palm. Christopher tightened his grip on Willicombe's shoulder and raised him to his feet.

They stood there, in the stables, while the horses snuffled and whinnied around them.

'I want to lie with you, Willicombe.' The words were out before he could stop them. 'I want to lie naked with you, as you lay with Elsa. I want to rut with you as the deer in the forest rut. I want to taste you in my mouth and push my John Thomas into your strong body. I want to feel your release when I am inside you. I want to –'

'Oh, Mr Christopher!'

Before he knew what was happening, Willicombe's hot lips were on his and Christopher was falling backwards. In a tangle of arms and legs they writhed on the straw. With one hand, Christopher hauled at the underfootman's white cotton shirt while rougher hands roamed all over his body.

Then pressure against his lips was forcing them open and Willicombe's tongue pushed its way into his mouth.

He was suffocating. Rough stubble ground against his downy chin. Christopher's tongue was in Willicombe's mouth. Lips twined as two very different chests pressed against each other. Slowly, they sank to their knees.

Nipples met nipples. Christopher's buds sprang to attention. The hair on Willicombe's chest was thick and soft, brushing Christopher's smooth pectorals in a delicious grinding movement.

The underfootman moaned.

Christopher felt the sound within his mouth, on his tongue and deep in his stomach.

Willicombe was gnawing now.

Christopher returned the ferocity of the kiss. He gouged with his lips, feeling their passion increase each time the underfootman's teeth glanced off his.

Thigh to thigh, belly to belly, their chests pressed together.

Cupping a hand behind the man's neck, Christopher tilted Willicombe's head left. He wanted to thrust his tongue down the man's throat. He wanted to choke him with his need – and he wanted to feel the same.

'Let me hold it.' The words were mumbled into his mouth. Then Willicombe's panting mouth nuzzled his neck. 'Let me hold your John Thomas, sir – oh, let me hold it and caress it and feel its great weight in my hand.'

Christopher's rod responded to the request. He stared into lust-engorged pupils.

Willicombe's breath rose in great steaming clouds. He lowered his face.

A rough hand curled around his length. Gasping, Christopher stared at the crown of a curly head, then almost cried out as a warm tongue flicked over the wet tip of his manhood.

Before he could respond, they were kissing again. His mouth burnt with the tang of the clear milky liquid which was now seeping from his slit.

Willicombe was on top of him, one fist wrapped around Christopher's throbbing prick. The other hand was massaging the small of Christopher's back, which arched up from the bed of straw.

Eventually, he managed to drag the underfootman's breeches and underwear down as far as the man's hairy thighs. Then Willicombe pulled away and Christopher sprawled back on the hay, the underfootman's lips settling around one pink, aching nipple.

He flailed for purchase. His fingers buried themselves in the thick curly hair on the man's head.

Willicombe licked and sucked by turns until the nipple throbbed with an unbearable mixture of pain and pleasure.

Christopher's back arched a second time. His full bollocks clenched against the side of the underfootman's hand. 'Let me take you! Let me mount you as the stag mounts his mate!' His lusty voice soared up through the rafters, scattering nesting birds and making the horses whinny in response. 'Oh, please let me –'

'Shhh! Remember your father.' A rough palm clamped itself over his mouth and Willicombe's frantic lips moved to his left nipple.

Christopher moaned and kissed every crease of that rough palm as the underfootman's mouth continued to arouse him beyond his wildest dreams. Straw dug into his thighs and shoulders.

Willicombe's teeth nipped once, then the frenzied mouth released his aching bud and began to track a wet trail down Christopher's stomach.

Silenced by the man's hand, he could only moan as Willicombe's other hand spread his pale thighs. Then the palm left his mouth. Sunburnt thighs were clasped each side of his thrashing head. Christopher's face was pressed into the underfootman's bristling pubic hair.

He grabbed the man's legs, hauling them apart. With a wild cry of abandon, Christopher opened his mouth and tried to take the slim length of the man's erection.

Between his own thighs, more skilful lips were nuzzling and mouthing the head of Christopher's manhood. The sensation made him try harder than ever to take everything the underfootman had to offer.

But it was too distracting – he wanted to enjoy the feelings which were coursing through his veins like some powerful, out-of-control engine. So he moved to Willicombe's heavy, musky sack, flicking and licking with his tongue.

Abruptly, Willicombe pulled away.

Christopher moaned with disappointment. The boyishly handsome face was very close to his.

Willicombe's skin was flushed. His full lips quivered, slick and swollen from the kiss. 'Take me, sir – take me now.' Turning, Willicombe knelt on his hands and knees, his firm white buttocks undulating in the moonlight.

His heart was about to leap out of his chest. His John Thomas throbbed with an urgency he could barely control. Christopher seized his aching length. His cock flexed against his sweating palm as he moved towards the waiting man.

'I want you, sir – I've wanted you since that day I carried your books from the carriage. As far back as that first day I saw you, I hoped you would be my lover.'

Willicombe's hoarse words made Christopher's balls clench and unclench. He wanted to reply, but doubted he'd ever utter another coherent sentence. One shaking hand reached out. Christopher ran a tentative finger down the furry crack between the man's arse-cheeks.

The responding moan from the underfootman filled his ears. In his fist, his pulsing cock reached out towards the object of its passion.

'In the forest, I wanted you,' Christopher gasped. 'When we watched the deer rut, I wanted you –'

The skin on his cock strained unbearably. He moved his finger back down the thick furrow of hair, pausing at the tiny, spasming hole.

Willicombe groaned. 'I knew you were watching me and Elsa, down by the lake. I saw you, hiding behind the rowing boat. I wanted you with us – wanted to feel your great cock ploughing into me as I bore down into her soft quim –'

Hardly able to breathe, Christopher positioned the pink crown of his manhood against the strong pucker of flesh. It flinched as he did so, sending arrows of need shooting into his bollocks.

'– and I wanted you in Doxy's. I would take you with another man – I would have you take me anyway you wish, oh Mr Christopher!'

Christopher's stomach churned. The tight ball-sack contracted abruptly. Sweat plastered his blond hair to his face. Bracing one arm against the underfootman's right buttock, he gripped his shaft more tightly. And pushed.

Willicombe howled.

The door to the stable burst open and the light from at least four candle-lamps illuminated their bed of straw. 'Perhaps he's in – what in God's name – ?'

The pressure was too much. Barely the first inch of his pulsing rod inside Willicombe's hot body, Christopher roared in response and fell backwards. Through dazzled eyes, he watched a thick wad of creamy liquid land with a splatter just above Willicombe's right buttock. He felt dizzy. Elation shuddered through his body.

'You animals!'

Just as a second load propelled itself from his spasming bollocks, a strong hand grabbed his shoulder and Christopher fired a further ecstatic volley on to the front of his father's well-cut knee-breeches.

Willicombe was dismissed on the spot.

Two hours later, Christopher sat in the library, head in hands. His books and papers lay on the desk. He couldn't look at them – or himself. After the appalled expression on his father's face, Christopher doubted he'd ever look anyone in the eye again.

A door opened.

Christopher raised his head.

Wordlessly, Viscount Fitzgibbons closed the library door and walked stiffly towards him, hands clasped behind a ram-rod straight back.

Steel eyes pinned him.

Christopher stared, unsure what to say. It didn't seem to matter.

'Lord Marlborough has been appraised of Lady Violet's indiscretion. He is at present making enquiries as to the whereabouts of this Duke of Connemara, in order to exact suitable retribution. However, the wedding will go ahead –'

Christopher sighed.

'– in fourteen months' time. Lady Violet departs tomorrow for Scotland. She will stay there until her time.'

Willicombe's strong, sunburnt body blazed in Christopher's mind.

'That, however, is the least of my concerns.'

Steel eyes peered into his very soul. Christopher tried to look away. Couldn't.

'In just over a year you will have a wife, and sometime in the not too distant future you will take over the running of Fitzgibbons Manor – do you understand what that means?'

Before he could open his mouth, his father's voice rose in volume.

'Responsibilities – adult responsibilities. And expectations.'

'I know.' Christopher looked away from his father's angry eyes and stared at the blurring letters on the desk in front of him. 'I just want to finished my research before I –'

'This isn't natural!' Barely restrained frustration burst from Viscount Fitzgibbons's thin lips as he swept books and papers from the desk.

Christopher scrambled to retrieve weeks of painstaking work. He knew he was a disappointment to his father, and his studies were the least of that disappointment. The voice railed above him.

'You spend all your time either in here poring over these –' scorn now tinged the rage '– books, or out in the stables getting up to Lord knows what with the servants.'

Christopher flinched, gathering papers into his arms. Words rained down on him.

'I thought Lady Violet could make a difference – I hoped the prospect of marriage would pull you from all this –' his father's foot kicked a heap of books '– namby-pamby studying and make you worthy of the Fitzgibbons name. But I was wrong.'

Christopher scrambled to his feet, arms laden, legs shaking.

Viscount Fitzgibbons eyed him with barely concealed loathing. 'Only one thing can make a man of you now.' A fist hit the desk.

Christopher's blood turned to ice water.

His father's eyes were glacial. 'I have received a letter from my old friend Josiah Rock. In ten days' time HMS *Impregnable* sails for the West Indies with a cargo of indentured labour. I have secured the post of midshipman on board for you.'

Papers fluttered from his arms. Christopher stared at his father.

A hint of disgust creased the edges of Viscount Fitzgibbon's thin lips. 'If anything can bring you to your senses and make you fit for marriage, it will be a spell under the influence of one of the greatest captains I have ever known!'

Thirteen

Mick spent the next day waiting. He left a message with Rosie, when he slipped out for an hour to sell the cross and other artifacts. The price he received was less than he'd hoped. As he sat in the Cock and Bollards, impatiently awaiting the young cutpurse's return, his mind wandered once more on to the mythical Gloucester gem.

Two hours later, he left Cat's half of the Bath spoils with the smiling landlady and headed north.

'More port?'

In the lavish drawing-room, Mick smiled and nudged his empty glass forward. 'I may have had too much already!' He wiped his mouth and burped noisily.

'Nonsense!' Nathaniel, Lord Emley, son of the Earl of Gloucester and Master of the Sandhurst Hunt, tipped a crystal decanter upright. 'Riding to hounds gives one a thirst.'

Mick grinned, watching the ruby liquid fill his glass. 'Well, thank you – for this and all your hospitality, sir.' No trace of an accent tainted his words.

'Think nothing of it – you've earned it.' Lord Emley ripped open the buttons of his hunting pink and stretched back on the couch, thighs splayed. 'Where did you say your estate was, Lord Marchbank?'

'Let us dispense with the formalities: when a fellow picks another out of a ditch, titles do not matter – please call me Michael.'

Lord Emley roared. 'Can happen to anyone, Michael! But it is a pity we missed the kill.'

Mick recalled a damp half hour lying in wait for the horseman and tried to look similarly disappointed. 'Since you ask, I have a small place in Devonshire – just a few hundred acres – but the bulk of my estate is in County Antrim.' He studied the solid, aristocratic face. 'Do you know Ireland?'

'Thankfully, no.' The man planted a pair of booted feet more widely apart and slapped Mick on the back. 'The place is cold, damp and full of truculent Irishmen, from what I hear.' Thin, cruel lips curled in distaste. 'Or what pass for men over there – if you take my meaning, sir.' The man rubbed his hands together.

Mick bit back a retort and pushed his own glass away.

'If you ask me, the Irish should be flushed from their earths and chased with hounds like the vermin they are. That would put a stop to their whining.'

Mick scowled. Well-built and handsome though he was, Lord Emley was a bore and a bigot of the worst variety. He'd already had to listen to hours of bragging and boasting about this sport and that, along with several less veiled slights on the Emerald Isle and its inhabitants.

Time to speed things up a little: the potted aspidistra had already received enough ruby red liquid to ensure alcoholic poisoning and this boorish fellow seemed to possess hollow legs. Mick moved along the richly brocaded sofa towards Lord Emley. 'I'm finding myself yearning for some of that cool Irish air at the moment.' He deftly unfastened the silver buttons of his own hunting-jacket, stolen from the cloakroom of the Huntsman's Inn, and hurled it over the back of the sofa.

'That's it, Michael – make yourself at home. The old boy's away on one of his preposterous expeditions, so we won't stand on ceremony!' The man roared again, slapping a jodhpured thigh for emphasis. 'And call me Nathaniel, if you will.'

Mick stifled a yawn, wishing the fifty-year-old earl was here instead of this lout, who was apparently immune to all Mick's wiles.

'Pray tell what you find to hold your attention in Ireland?' Nathaniel poured himself another glass of port and slurped loudly. 'You're not one of those unnatural buggers, are you?' The man lowered his voice. 'There's a lot of it about, you know. I had to thrash two of my kennel boys, just last week.'

Mick casually stretched his arms over his head, flexing strong musculature and regretting he'd not come disguised as a whore of the female variety. 'Shooting and fishing, mainly. I have a river stocked with salmon.' Eyes swept the room, alighting on silver candle-sticks and a collection of ornate snuff boxes which sat on top of a beautiful satinwood bureau. He lowered his arms, mind straying to the contents of the other rooms and further delights in store, if only he could somehow distract this boor. 'You must join me sometime and allow Irish hospitality to change your opinion of the Emerald Isle: summer days in Ireland are very pleasant.'

Nathaniel nudged Mick in the ribs with his elbow. 'And what about the nights, eh?'

'The nights?'

Nathaniel nudged again. 'Plenty of willing Irish country girls to keep you warm, a fine manly fellow like you!'

Mick's eyes brushed bejewelled fingers. 'Blazing log fires and good brandy, my friend.' He risked a fraternal hand on the man's hosed thigh. 'But they are no substitute for human companionship.' The sadness came easily to his eyes. 'Lady Marchbank has been dead these four months, and my bed is a very empty place.' His other arm stretching casually behind the man's lolling neck, Mick dug his nails into his palm and felt tears spring to his eyes. 'To be honest, the desire no long visits my loins.'

Nathaniel looked uncomfortable.

Mick withdrew his hand, regretting the gesture. This strategy wasn't working either. Then a broad palm patted his knee.

'I know what you need, friend.' Nathaniel's fingers tightened, then patted again.

Mick returned his gaze to the once-more grinning face.

'I have quite a collection of –' he chuckled '– artistic material. Several new pieces arrived from France, just yesterday, and I have not had the chance to inspect them.' Nathaniel stood up. 'Will you join me?'

Mick brightened: progress of a sort. 'I will try anything, sir.' He patted the front of his riding breeches. 'Four months, and not a stirring.'

Nathaniel brushed the information aside. 'No man is immune to my etchings. Get your engine up and running in minutes, or –' the cruel eyes twinkled '– your name isn't Michael Marchbank. Are you a betting man?'

Mick cocked his head. 'I have been known to indulge.'

Nathaniel winked. 'Well, I'll wager anything you like that your stout staff is throbbing with life by the time I've finished with you – agreed?'

Mick almost laughed. Despite the man's boorishness, if Mick wasn't hard the minute he entered Nathaniel's bedroom, something was indeed wrong with his equipment. 'Agreed.' He nodded sadly. 'But do not wager anything of value. I do not hold out much hope.' Turning away, Mick tugged at the neck of his taffeta shirt, undoing the drawstring and pulling the fabric free from the waistband of his riding breeches. 'I must be more drunk than I thought.' Cool air brushed the thick coating of hair on his chest. His nipples rose.

Nathaniel's guffaw was loud and uproarious. 'Good idea! Let us get out of these tight clothes.' In one brisk movement, he had pulled off his own shirt and tie. He threw them on to the floor, slung his hunting-jacket over one broad shoulder and strode towards the door. 'Come on then! I don't know about you, but I am hardening at the very thought of those comely French fillies.'

Watching the firm cheeks of the man's arse, Mick smiled and followed his host through the great double doors and towards a candle-lit staircase.

'Look at the tits on her! Does that not get your rod up and around, Michael?'

Stomach pressed into a pile of rumpled sheets and with his face very close to the handsome, aristocratic one, Mick shook his head at the crude etching. 'She is beautiful, certainly, but –' he sighed '– it is going to take something very special to arouse me, I fear. Let us annul our wager, for you will surely lose.'

Nathaniel grumbled. 'Not at all – in fact, we can up the stakes. Fifty guineas is a mere trifle.'

They lay there, side by side, like two lusty schoolboys: Nathaniel was down to his underwear, while Mick still wore his shirt.

'No, I will not take your money, friend.' Mick turned away, rolling over on the great four-poster bed and eyeing several large paintings which adorned the walls: rather bad paintings, at that, and of little value. 'I am a lost cause.'

'Nonsense!' Nathaniel whipped the etching away and fumbled under the bed.

Mick's gaze fell on a small jewellery box but his mind was on the real reason he had spent a tiring afternoon galloping around Gloucestershire in search of the man. He looked around for some heavy, blunt object with which he could stun this bore into insensibility.

'Have a look at this – is it not most special?'

136

The back of Mick's neck was gripped and he found himself staring at a sketch of a serving-wench, under service of a different type.

One lusty, well-muscled Frenchman was easing his cock into her pert rear, while another shoved himself between rosebud lips. Her wrists were bound, her neat ankles tied wide apart.

Mick could feel the warmth from the man's palm on the back of his neck. He was also aware of another warmth, much lower. He sighed again. 'Sorry – nothing.'

Nathaniel was angry now. 'If this last one does not have you beating your meat, I will –'

Mick turned slowly, dragging his swollen length along the rumpled sheets and trying not to gasp. His interest was more than pricked by the tone of desperation in the man's voice.

'– retire from the Sandhurst Hunt!'

Mick's brow creased with disappointment. This was taking far too long. There were servants in the house – and Nathaniel's wife, somewhere around.

Nathaniel lay on his back, his strong arms clasped behind his head. The handsome face was furrowed in frustrated concentration.

Mick sneaked a glance at the front of the man's underwear and saw that the last half-hour's perusal of sub-standard French erotica had at least had the desired effect on one of them.

The man's cock was a solid, curving arc, stretching up from his groin and twitching against the man's left hipbone.

The sight made Mick's nipples tingle. He racked his brain. Then smiled. 'Do you and Lady Emley ever play games, sir?'

'Games? What do you mean – games?'

Mick crawled slowly to the foot of the great bed and fumbled for his riding breeches. With a flourish, he whipped six fine, silken scarves from the pocket and dangled them in front of curious eyes.

A flicker of panic crossed Nathaniel's noble features.

Mick smiled. 'An old Irish custom, Nathaniel. The late Lady Marchbank and I used to amuse ourselves with it. Perhaps –'

'Sounds pretty queer to me, fellow.' Nathaniel's eyes glinted sceptically.

Mick separated one of the scarves from the bundle and brushed its silken length along the man's chest. 'Not at all. It's merely a game –' his eyes moved to where Nathaniel's curving prick, despite the man's scorn, was flexing with interest '– and always got me harder than the stoutest staff, when my late wife and I played.' His own length was now pushing at the waistband of his purloined underwear. 'Still want to up the stakes of our wager?'

'I am a man of my word, Michael. One hundred guineas it is!'

Mick grinned. 'Done – but you must be naked when it happens.'

The cruel lips twisted into a sneer. 'This has the air of buggers about it.'

'Does it, indeed?' Mick leant back as Nathaniel stretched out his arms. Then he darted forward, deftly securing wrists then ankles to the four posts of the huge bed. 'I would not stick my prick into your arsehole if it was the last orifice on earth, you ill-bred English fool!'

Nathaniel roared. 'How dare you! How dare –'

The shout of outrage was cut short as Mick expertly pushed the fifth scarf into the man's open mouth and tied it behind his head. 'Sorry. I know you want me hard, so you can suck the seed from my slit, but I have other matters to attend to.' Straddling the man's thighs, Mick stroked his own, now fully erect shaft. 'Console yourself with the knowledge that you won the wager, sir.'

Scarlet-faced, Nathaniel heaved at his bonds.

A smile crossed Mick's face: the upper classes favoured silk because it was expensive and fashionable. Few of them had any idea of its strength. He moved back a little. Gripping the waistband of Nathaniel's fine lawn underwear, Mick hauled the fabric down over the man's hips.

And stared.

Lord Emley was a fine figure of a fellow, with a fine, upstanding cock. Mick quickly looped the sixth scarf around the base of a pair of lust-engorged bollocks and tightened it, ensuring the man's cock would remain upstanding for as long as it suited his purposes.

With one last smile, he gazed at the trussed, naked figure then playfully flicked the head of the man's swollen cock before jumping from the bed.

Nathaniel's narrowed eyes followed him as he moved around the four-postered structure. A muffled grunt escaped from behind the silken gag.

Shirt flapping open, chest hair damp with sweat, Mick grinned and walked his fingers down the man's right arm to the wrist and beyond.

A curled fist flexed in fury.

In seconds, Mick had slipped three rings past sweat-slicked knuckles and into his pocket.

As Lord Emley writhed and heaved, Mick laughed and sauntered to the left hand. He plucked the heavy signet band from the man's pinkie and raised it to his mouth. Expert teeth bit into soft, unadulterated gold. 'You have excellent taste, my lord.' He dropped the ring into his pocket. 'In trinkets, at least.' He let the brogue drift back into his voice.

A snort of indignation puffed from furious nostrils.

'To be sure, your choice of drinking partner is a little more ill-advised.' Mick perched on the edge of the bed and surveyed the rest of the room. His eyes came to rest on Nathaniel's hunting-jacket. Seconds later, a thorough search of its pockets had secured a wallet containing twenty pounds and a silver fob-watch. He turned back to the bed, wafting the notes under an outraged nose. 'You didn't even have the money to cover our wager, my lord!' With his other hand, he stroked the front of his own riding-breeches and feigned a frown. 'That alters things, I think. You forfeit the bet. Wonder how I should take my winnings?'

The aristocratic face was scarlet with fury.

Mick could almost feel the man's sphincter clench. He chuckled, pocketing the money and the watch, then covered Nathaniel's still-hard cock with a broad palm. 'Don't worry, my beauty –'

Snorts of indignation coursed from Nathaniel's flared nostrils.

Mick curled his fingers around the damp skin of the man's prick. 'I'll think of something.' With a wink, he released the throbbing length and bounded over to the small jewellery box he'd noticed earlier. Pulling on his jodhpurs, Mick raised the calico pouch from where it had snuggled all evening against his own prick and quickly tipped the contents inside. He lifted a candle from the bureau and turned.

Lord Emley was about to explode. Mick smiled. 'Don't go anywhere – I'll be back.' In stocking soles, holding riding-boots and the candle, he tiptoed to the door and unlocked it.

A vague muffle of fury followed him out into the silent hallway in search of richer pickings.

An hour later, in the library, he found them.

Mick's eyes widened as he eased the Gloucester diamond from its hiding place behind a portrait of His Majesty King George.

The sparkling rock almost filled his palm, reflecting the light from the candle in a thousand shimmering prisms.

Mick stifled a whoop of joy. Fingers closing around the huge gemstone, he replaced the portrait on the wall and smiled.

No more hanging around the streets of the East End in stolen clothing.

No more accidental meetings with lords and ladies.

No more lies and fabrications to get into their beds.

No more thrusting his face into countless cocks and cunts.

With this, he would be lord of his own plantation, far from these wet shores.

Slipping the diamond into the pocket of his hunting-jacket, he left the room and made his way noiselessly across the grand hallway to the front door. Inches away, he paused, eyes glancing up the great staircase.

On the floor above, that rude, unmannerly bigot was probably still thrashing in his bonds. Mick smiled, aware of a throbbing beside the breech-pouch as he remembered the feel of the man's cock against his palm and the insulting slights the fellow had delivered on Mick's native land.

Hunted like foxes indeed!

The smile spread into a grin: maybe there was time for another type of sport, before he left.

Placing his boots on the bottom step, he rubbed his crotch and silently reclimbed the stairs.

Lord Emley's prick was an aching rod of unreleased arousal which bucked and flexed as the man struggled against the silken restraints.

Mick couldn't take his eyes off the engorged length. 'Told you I'd be back.' Tugging at his riding-breeches and underwear, he hauled the garments over his thighs and crouched above the swollen staff.

The fifth scarf was still in place.

Seizing the loose ends of the length, Mick quickly crisscrossed them up and across the man's bollocks, securing a tight knot around the root of the swollen rod. Hardness was still ensured, but the second binding would prevent any orgasm. Mick gripped Nathaniel's prick, pulling it away from the man's tensed stomach. Gathering a mouthful of saliva, he spat onto the engorged, purple head. To the accompaniment of muffled roars he coated the first inch with spit, then moistened the fingers of his other hand and raised himself on to his knees.

As Mick thrust one then two fingers into his own body and lubricated his spasming hole, a shiver of pleasure trembled deep in his balls. Mick inhaled sharply.

A muffled snort from further up the bed took his attention.

Mick removed the digits from his arse and stared at the flushed, furious face. He grinned and gripped a nipple. 'Now, what shall I do with you?'

140

A trussed prick jutted against Mick's tight balls as Lord Emley's hips shot up from the bed in pain.

He grabbed the stiff length and positioned the engorged head against the opening to his body. 'Although you could not cover your bet, you did make me hard.'

Nathaniel tried to pull away.

'Oh yes! This is all your own doing, my beauty. How could I resist someone who invited me up to his bedchamber to look at his –' he winked '– etchings.' Mick pinched the man's nipple a second time, then gasped as an involuntary thrust from his captive pushed the velvet glans into his greased hole.

A low moan of fury filled his ears. The lips of his arse stretched wide to accommodate the great bulb. A groan of pleasure seeped from between his teeth. Knees spread each side of the narrow hips, Mick paused and tried to relax. He needed to get used to the massive helmet of flesh inside him, but the dangers and risks of the rest of the evening had filled his veins with adrenalin.

He stared into Lord Emley's angry eyes and felt his prick twitch. With a laugh, Mick bore down, allowing the rest of the thick shaft into his body.

The head on the bed twisted from left to right.

Mick gripped the aristocratic chin, holding it steady.

Nathaniel closed furious eyes in an attempt to get away from this final indignity.

As the cheeks of his arse met the full hairiness of the man's bollocks, Mick seized both nipples and pinched.

Aristocratic eyelids shot open. The pale body flexed on the bed. Buried in his arse, Lord Emley's hostage prick burrowed deeper.

Mick bit back a howl, arching his back as the iron length impaled him. Then he slackened his hold on the man's swollen buds and began to move.

The muscles in his thighs quivered and shook. Mick hauled himself back up the length of his prisoner, savouring the invasion as rings of sinew clenched around the pulsating rod. Just below the fat head he paused.

Sweat drenched his body, soaking the thick mat of hair on his chest. Mick swivelled his hips, feeling his arse-lips widen once more. Beneath him, the man was struggling more urgently. A grin played around his open mouth as he hovered there, enjoying something his boorish lover was giving by mere dint of his bonds. 'The hunter has been hunted down and trapped, Nathaniel!' Then he nipped already tender buds and slammed back on to the welcome sword of flesh.

A whoosh of affront flew from Lord Emley's nostrils, followed quickly by a moan of discomfort.

Lost in his own passion, Mick continued to fuck himself on the Master of the Hunt, using the man's wriggles and writhes to ensure maximum pleasure. Every time he bore back on to the bound prick, damp silk tickled the hair on his arse and his fingers tightened on Nathaniel's nipples.

The great bed was shaking. Somewhere in the distance, Mick heard the sound of wood on wood as he pounded down on to the infuriated figure below.

Pressure built in his balls, a sensation made all the sweeter by the great Gloucester Diamond snuggling in his pocket and the taking of another prize from another Gloucester. Mick removed his right hand from a tender nipple and gripped his own cock. Altering the angle of penetration, Mick leant lower on the furious man. The feel of his own fingers around his shaft broke waves of pleasure in his spasming balls. As he stroked his prick and drove himself closer to the edge, Mick aimed the drooling head at Lord Emley's gagged mouth and hauled the Gloucester Diamond from his pocket. 'I have taken something else of yours –' the words were rasping grunts, as he jabbed himself more furiously with the man's trussed length '– so it is only fair you take something of –'

The final word was carried away by a deep sigh of release. Sweat plastered his hair to his face as a shower of milky spunk exploded from his slit and splattered Lord Emley's scarlet, aristocratic cheeks.

Then the door burst open and the barrel of a musket pressed a cold circle into the skin on the back of his neck.

Fourteen

'Silence in court!'

Four short raps of the gavel cut through the crowd's chattering voices and into Mick's brain. He cursed all manservants for their sharp ears – Why had he gone back?

If he'd left with the Gloucester Diamond, he would not be standing here, manacled and filthy after three days in the depths of Newgate Prison.

Mick scowled, cursing himself and the thick, tethered aristocratic prick which had been his downfall. He caught Rosie's eye, raised his chained wrists to the gallery in salute.

A cheer. Four more gavel raps.

Eventually, the courtroom settled down.

Behind his rostrum, the sheriff flicked through papers then removed his pince-nez and glared. 'Lord Marchbank?'

Mick bowed respectfully. 'Your Honour.'

The sheriff nodded, then glanced around. 'And where are the Duke of Connemara, the Marquess of Antrim and Michael Savage?'

Mick scanned the room, past the still-outraged eye of the young Lord Emley. 'Sure, I have no idea, Your Honour.'

'Liar!' The accusation rose through mounting whispers.

Tracking down the source of the voice, Mick stared at a man he didn't recognise. The carefully coiffured hair and pouting lips of the wench at the fellow's side were all too familiar, however.

'You have a further charge to bring against this man, Lord Marlborough?' The sheriff replaced his pince-nez and peered.

The face of Lady Violet's father was a portrait in fury. 'He seduced and robbed my daughter, Your Honour –'

'He accosted me, three weeks ago, in an alley!'

'And me – stripped me of my garments also!'

'Deceived my wife and me, then made off with most of our jewellery!'

'Molested me in my own home!'

With a sigh, Mick tried to cover his ears with his manacled hands.

The cries of allegation increased. The sheriff was scribbling on a piece of paper, eyes moving from the clerk of the court to Mick.

He held the gaze and tried to look ignorant, then decided a penitent expression might be more useful.

The sheriff's steely gaze was convinced by neither.

Mick lowered his head. At least neither Cardinal Glassford nor young Orlando Rock were present, though he knew two lesser charges would hardly matter, when the rest of his crimes were taken into consideration: a man could only be hanged once. Rubbing the angry red scores caused by the heavy manacles around his wrists, Mick braced himself and prepared for the worst.

'Michael Savage – or whatever your name is – you have been found guilty of deception, fraud and theft. Before I pass sentence, have you anything to say in your defence?'

Mick looked up, locked eyes with the sheriff then glanced around the courtroom.

The faces of those whose bodies he knew intimately, in whose beds he had lain and from whom he had taken merely small mementos, glared back.

The jewels had been replaced by other jewels, the fine clothes barely missed. Even the money he had taken would make those lords and ladies only infinitesimally the poorer.

Then he looked down at his own ragged garments. Raising one manacled hand, Mick rubbed the thick beard which now covered most of his handsome face. Puzzled eyes returned to the waiting sheriff. 'To be sure, I never hurt anyone, Your Honour –'

'My daughter is with child, you scoundrel!' Lord Marlborough leapt to his feet.

Mick smiled sadly at the blushing Lady Violet. 'It may be mine, sir – or its father may be any of the dandified fops for whom the lady raised her skirts before I came along.'

Lord Marlborough's face creased with fury. 'How dare you! I'll have your head for this!'

The gavel banged so many times Mick lost count. Then the sheriff's voice soared over the crowd's increasing discontent. 'Michael Savage, you are a wicked, evil man who shows no remorse for his crimes against the good people of this country. However, you have a strong body and, from all evidence, a quick mind. Accordingly, you will be taken to His Majesty's Colonies in the West Indies, to serve fifteen years as indentured labour –'

Mick barely heard the rest of the sheriff's words.

The West Indies.

For nearly twelve months he had connived to obtain funds to do this himself. Mick smiled at the irony.

The expression did not go unnoticed. '– and another five for your insolence!'

The crowd booed and hissed its discontent.

Two strong bailiffs gripped his biceps and made to lead him from the court. The smile became a mocking grin. Mick wrestled free and tugged an unruly forelock. 'A thousand thanks, Your Honour!' He wouldn't let them see the fear and apprehension which was growing inside him.

The crowded laughed raucously.

Mick executed a leg-pulling bow. 'Please feel free to visit my banana plantation, if your good self is ever in that part of the world.'

The crowd were cheering now.

'Take this ruffian back to the cells!' The sheriff rapped four times with his gavel.

Mick waved two-handed as he was dragged shuffling from the courtroom. The grin was fixed, and remained so as to mask the trepidation which drenched his skin in a clammy sweat.

Seeping in from the nearby Thames, the trickle of water oozed from between moss-covered brick behind him and joined the pool around his feet. He watched it spread past his boots and over the bare toes of the man on his right. Mick raised his gaze from the sludgy floor and stared at the tiny barred window high up in the cell wall.

In the distance, the gentle slap of waves told him the tide was rising.

Mick ran a manacled hand through his long matted hair and tried to stem the rising tide of defeat in his chest.

Someone coughed.

Someone else moved.

In the cramped cell beneath Newgate Prison, Mick listened to the slow, laboured steps as the man dragged chained feet through an inch of filthy water.

A shard of moon slipped into view, bisected by iron bars.

Over whispered threats and low pleading, Mick focused on it and tried not to think about others who would be seeing that moon from even more lugubrious surroundings.

His mother, his sister Lizzy, eleven-year-old Peter and three others.

He might be going to the West Indies, but his family remained in Ireland. He had let them down – only the knowledge that Rosie would forward the most recent of his acquired money to the usual address eased his sorrow. He tore his eyes from the moon.

From the secret pocket, sewn carefully into his underwear, Mick withdrew a silver-coloured object. Orlando Rock's keepsake glinted in the moonlight. He'd considered trying to bribe one of the guards into allowing his escape, then decided the medal would have other uses as soon as they docked in the West Indies. Slipping the object back into its hiding-place, Mick sighed. The moon ducked behind a bank of cloud and plunged the cell back into darkness.

The door burst open. 'Feeding time!' A gaoler hurled the contents of a basket on to the muddy floor.

He watched the outlines of starving men throw themselves on to scraps of rotting meat and stale bread.

The cell door slammed shut.

His hard, muscular stomach was beyond hunger. As the cramped space filled with the sound of frenzied eating, his mind was back with his hungry family, in their one-room, run-down farm back in Ballymena.

In the background, angry voices argued over the last few scraps of food.

Mick's rugged face creased with pain.

'Here!' The word was a whisper in the dark, over-crowded cell.

Long fingers pressed something stale into his manacled hand and broke the train of thought. Mick glanced from the piece of stale bread to a munching, mud-streaked face.

'Eat it quickly!' The words were whispered.

Mick stuffed the morsel into his mouth, taking in his unexpected provider as he chewed.

Less than five foot eight inches tall and slimly built, shrewd eyes darted around the tiny cell from beneath an unruly tangle of ginger hair. A smile hovered near the edges of pixie lips.

'By God, Cat!' The scrap of bread hit Mick's stomach and brought back the hunger. 'I hoped you had got away, my young friend.'

The cutpurse frowned. 'I did.' He swallowed noisily. 'The temptation of further purses in Bath was too much.'

Mick stared at the boy's roughly bandaged left hand.

'Then they sent me back here.' Cat laughed wryly. 'Two fingers and a thumb will still see me right, for most purposes.' He winked. 'As will my mouth, eh, Mr Savage?'

Mick smiled. The boy's forbearance lifted his spirits.

Around them, men were settling down into sleep. Cat's feline eyes lived up to their name. He lowered his voice. 'I have an idea – Are you game?'

Mick stared, then nodded.

'Then follow my lead.'

Before Mick could enquire further, Cat plunged through huddles of sleeping men towards the door.

'The pox! The pox!' Two slim fists pounded on the door. 'They have the pox! Get them out of here!' Turning, he winked one green eye in the darkness.

Roused from their uncomfortable doze, men shrank away from each other. Mick made his way towards the door and joined the pounding. Other panicked shouts augmented theirs, until no one was sure who had raised the alarm.

'What's going on in there?' The gaoler's voice was tight with irritation.

At his side, Cat had stopped pounding and was now pinching sections of his freckled skin.

Mick did likewise. Soon both their faces were a mass of angry, raised areas. Together, they turned.

Horrified expressions met theirs and backed away further. 'There's pox in here! We will all die!'

Mick suppressed a smile: dead indentured labour was no good to anyone. Seconds later, heavy keys were again scraping at the lock.

'All right, all right – although who should care about a couple more scurvy pox victims, I –'

As the door opened, Mick threw his weight against it. In a flash, Cat was sprinting from the cell. Pushing the startled gaoler to the ground, Mick followed. They tore through a rabbit-warren of dank corridors –

– and straight into the broad chests of three pistol-wielding men.

In the head gaoler's small office, the red patches faded.

Sandwiched between two burly turnkeys, Mick glanced from the stout, balding man who was eating the remains of a chicken to where Cat stood, nursing his hand. Mick's mouth watered.

'You know the punishment for absconding from His Majesty's pleasure?' The stout man sucked the last of the grease from a wing, then got up from his chair, large hands spread across a larger belly.

Mick knew only too well. He stepped forward. 'It was my idea. Let the boy go –'

'Your idea, was it?' Cat frowned. 'I do not think so!'

The gaoler's laugh was deep and genuine. Wiping greasy fingers on already stained thighs, he nodded to the turnkeys. 'I'll deal with them – get back to your duties.'

The men left the room.

Mick watched them go, thinking about Orlando Rock's silver medal and wondering about its value to this large, hairy gaoler.

'Now then, my boys –'

Something in the man's voice pricked Mick's interest. He turned back, and saw Cat had moved closer to the desk.

'– I presume you are both pox-free?'

The cutpurse grinned. 'Clean as a whistle, sir.' He moved his good hand to the front of ragged breeches. 'Do you wish to make certain?'

'I might.' The gaoler's small brown eyes darted over the boy's slender body. 'Or I might prefer you to carry out another type of inspection.'

The face was ruddy, roughly shaven. Greying stubble coated a short neck, which led down to a vast, barrel chest. Beneath a tight waistcoat, the gaoler's large belly was barely held in check. And, below that, baggy breeches could not hide the man's excitement.

The outline of a thick prick was clearly visible inside the stained fabric.

'What about you?'

Mick felt himself under scrutiny. He smiled. 'The boy is good, sir – I can vouch for his skills.' Out of the corner of one eye, he saw Cat was fondling himself.

The gaoler's ruddy face took on a leering cast. 'Can you indeed!' He patted his large belly, then began to unfasten straining buttons. 'And who can vouch for you?' The gaoler eased his vast body from the waistcoat and tugged his loose shirt over his balding head. 'I've already hanged three today, who were not as obliging.'

Mick's eyes widened. He stared at the gaoler's enormous chest.

Thick silver hair covered the vast expanse of flesh, sweeping down to the waistband of his breeches. Great folds of white belly hung over his belt, like the fleshy ruffles of a formal shirt, and swayed temptingly with every movement.

He liked a bit of meat on a man. Mick grinned. 'Michael Obliging Savage, at your service, sir!'

The gaoler chuckled and the great belly rippled. 'I have a cleaning job which has defeated the strongest stomachs, Michael Savage.'

Mick's eyes flicked to a pair of mops and buckets which stood in a corner. His gorge rose. A good few of the prisoners in Newgate's fetid cells were true pox victims, and swabbing out their quarters was not a task he would have taken willingly. But it was better than the gallows. He risked a glance at Cat.

The red head was cocked, uncertainly.

Catching one green eye, Mick winked. 'Sure, we're your boys, sir.' He rubbed his palms together in a parody of anticipation.

'Really clean, mind you – every scrap?' Two large thumbs eased themselves into the waistband of the breeches.

'May God strike us blind if we flinch an inch!'

The gaoler's responding guffaw was loud and enthusiastic.

Then the huge hands were hauling down the baggy breeches and Mick found himself staring at the lowest-hanging bollocks he'd ever seen.

The man's sack was a vast, pendulous mass which swung between his thick thighs almost to his knees. A short, stubby cock seemed tiny in comparison, but Mick knew the shaft would fill his or Cat's mouth as much as any man's.

Eyes returning to the huge dangling bag, Mick rubbed the crotch of his threadbare breeches and felt the beginnings of arousal. He could imagine those bollocks swinging over his face as he lay prostrate on the floor. He could visualise the stout gaoler squatting over his mouth as Mick reared up, sucking one then the other and finally both giant testicles between his lips and feasting on them.

The gaoler kicked off his shoes, bending to drag breeches and badly stained underwear free of his feet.

A strong, male odour filled the small office, increasing to an overwhelming stench as the man turned, exposing his huge backside.

Cat gasped. 'Holy Mother of God!'

Mick smiled across the gaoler's lowered back. 'No, my young friend – just a man's arse in need of cleaning.'

In response to his words, the gaoler moved to a small couch and leant over it. Gripping each of those huge mounds of flesh, he wrenched his cheeks apart. 'Do a good job, and I'll throw in extra rations.'

Mick looked at Cat, who was rolling up his ragged sleeves.

Apprehension had given way to eagerness: after all, there were two of them, and extra food could make life a lot more bearable.

The cutpurse grinned and moved forward.

Falling to a crouch, Mick joined the boy between the gaoler's splayed thighs. At closer quarters, the stench was more powerful. He inhaled great lungfuls of the man's body, staring at the smears of grime, urine and worse which decorated the deep crack.

The gaoler's hole was almost obscured by a mass of thick, matted hair.

Mick's crotch tightened. The head of his desire pushed its way towards the wasitband of his shabby breeches.

Cat whispered, 'You take the behind, I'll take the bollocks.' In one fluid movement, Cat was on his back, full lips positioned just beneath the heavy sack.

Mick was glad the decision had been made for him – it was quite a choice. Delivering a light tap to the man's right buttock, he replaced the gaoler's hands with his own and plunged into the fetid crack.

The stench was eye-watering: the man hadn't washed for weeks, maybe months. The hair in his furrow was stiff with sweat and muck, rasping and scratching the unbearded areas of Mick's face. Gathering a throat full of saliva, he spat into the crack, then began to swirl and soften with his tongue.

A bassy groan resounded in the gaoler's body. Over the slurps of his own ministrations, Mick could hear Cat lapping and sucking the filthy skin of the man's balls.

The crack-hair was losing some of its former stiffness. Rigidity had taken possession of Mick's cock and he knew from the moans that another two pricks were thoroughly engorged. He teased the hair with his teeth, combing muck from matted tufts. The taste filled his mouth as he swallowed – sickened to the pit of his stomach and highly aroused at the same time. As he worked, he tried to identify each odour, in an attempt to keep his mind off the clenching in his balls.

Piss – old piss. The alkaline urine took on a dull, musty perfume when allowed to remain on the skin and clothing.

Sweat – layers of sweat. The rank, meaty fragrance of the man's body was a testament to the foods he ate. Mick grinned, running his nose down the slick furrow and back up again.

Chicken?

Brisket?

He pushed great handfuls of flesh further apart and buried himself in the very depths of the gaoler. The man's arsehole was more accessible now. A fragrant bouquet filled Mick's head as he pushed with his thumbs.

The orifice popped open. The blast of the ensuing fart knocked him off his feet.

Mick sprawled backwards, landing on Cat who was now writhing and bucking as he caressed the man's spit-drenched sack.

'Sorry, my friend!' The gaoler's chuckle was anything but regretful. Mick laughed, Cat heaving beneath him. He wasn't about to be defeated by mere hot air. Turning, he attacked the man's bottom with renewed vigour.

Having divested itself of the internal pressure, the pucker gaped wide to admit his tongue.

Mick threw himself into the task, licking and gnawing until in a frenzy of passion his hands slipped and the cheeks of the gaoler's vast behind closed around him. The vibrations of the man's orgasm trembled in his ears. Wondering if Cat's full lips had been in a position to catch any of the spunk, Mick gasped as his own need took over. Pulling himself reluctantly from the prison of arse-flesh, he moved back on to his knees, straddling Cat's groaning form. He wrenched down his breeches, gripped his prick and delivered the few quick strokes necessary for relief.

Inches beneath him, his pixie face still obliterated by the man's contracting sack, Cat was also hauling on his slim member. The sight tightened Mick's own bollocks. As the shivers of climax shimmered up from deep inside and into his shaft, Mick aimed the head of his prick at the gleaming hole.

Through swimming vision, he watched one, two then three wads of spunk deposited dead on target.

The gaoler's orgasm was retreating as Mick lurched forward, rubbing his fluids into the man's hairy furrow. Panting, he pressed his face to the spasming hole one last time, and breathlessly licked the gaoler's crack clean.

'I would let you boys go, if I could.' The man pulled up his smelly underwear, refastened the belt around his vast belly and beamed at them both. The expression was tinged with genuine regret.

Cat wiped a smear of semen from his cheek. His boyish face was pink with effort.

'It is no matter, sir.' Mick had barely recovered his breath. The man's odiferous musk drenched his beard and filled his lungs. Tucking his softening prick back inside his breeches, he threw an arm around the cutpurse's slim shoulders. 'But you did promise –' He nodded towards the remnants of the man's supper.

The gaoler chuckled. 'Be my guests, please.'

Mick and Cat threw themselves on the food, filling their bellies as they had sated other appetites only minutes before.

Fifteen

Seagulls swooped and wheeled overhead, screaming their derision.

His mother fussed around him, smoothing the heavy felt of his midshipman's jacket. 'You will be all right, won't you, my precious?' She'd sobbed all the way from Fitzgibbons Manor to the docks, and those plaintive words heralded the arrival of another downpour.

Christopher cringed. 'I will be fine, Mamma – really!' He pulled away, before her tears started his own.

'Of course he will – fresh air and hard work are just what he needs!' His father's broad hand slapped his back.

'You coddle the boy too much, Martha – you've always coddled him! I wouldn't be surprised if that is at the root of all his problems.'

Christopher winced, trying to move out from under his father's palm. The hand tightened around his shoulders.

'Smell it, my boy? Smell the sea?' Viscount Fitzgibbons took a deep breath, puffing out his chest.

Christopher inhaled and coughed.

A heavy palm slapped his back, inducing a further spluttering fit. 'Straighten up there, lad – you're a Fitzgibbons! Never forget that!'

Almost bent double, a sharp pain racked Christopher's slim chest. Managing to stagger to a nearby bollard, he took his ease until the coughs subsided.

He didn't feel like a Fitzgibbons – he felt like an impostor. When he'd examined himself in the mirror, four hours ago, the pale fellow in the smart midshipman's uniform was a stranger. Rows of shiny brass buttons mocked him. The gold braid on his cuffs glinted, ridiculing him and making his long, slender fingers look more useless than usual.

Despite the severe, masculine cut of garments which signalled he was serving on board one of His Majesty's merchant ships, from beneath the fine hat, the face of a frightened boy had looked back at him.

Christopher coughed one last time, patting breast pockets for a handkerchief.

Inches from the toe of his highly polished boot, a splatter of seagull dropping hit the ground.

He frowned. Not a good omen – not a good omen at all. Christopher raised his eyes to where Viscount Fitzgibbons was berating his mother. Behind sat his meagre luggage. He'd wanted to bring his copy of *The Canterbury Tales*, and perhaps a few notebooks, but his father wouldn't hear of it.

His small knapsack only contained a change of underwear, and the bright silk scarf he'd found hidden amongst his underclothing when packing, earlier that morning.

Christopher sighed. He'd thought about Willicombe for the past two weeks. It was his fault the underfootman had been dismissed, banished from the Fitzgibbons estate that fateful night. All attempts to discover Willicombe's home had been ineffectual: he dared not broach the subject with his father, and every time he tried to question the servants, they turned away.

His heart sank further. What would be the point anyway? What could he do? He had no money of his own – not until he turned twenty-one, in three months' time. There was no way he could compensate the handsome underfootman for the sour fruits of their one brief moment of forbidden pleasure.

Christopher stood up, glancing over the side of the dock into the murky water of the Thames. He had been unable to eat any breakfast that morning, but his empty stomach nevertheless gurgled at the motion of the waves.

You are a Fitzgibbons – never forget that!

He stared into the dark depths.

The first Fitzgibbons to feel sea-sick before he'd even boarded a ship.

The first Fitzgibbons on whom the fine naval uniform hung like stolen garments.

The first Fitzgibbons to disgrace the family name and have a deflowered fiancée.

An image of his noble ancestors pranced around him. Christopher swayed slightly. Maybe it would be better for everyone concerned if he just threw himself into the Thames, here and now, rather than –

A light hand touched his shoulder.

He staggered back, nearly carrying out his threat.

Elsa's grip steadied him. 'Be careful, sir.'

Christopher stared at the pretty underparlourmaid, who had accompanied his mother in the carriage. Her flashing eyes and thick hair reminded him of Willicombe. He bit back a sob.

She steered him purposefully away from the edge and over to a cart loaded with supplies for the voyage. 'I have a message for you, sir.' Her voice was low with urgency. Elsa flattened herself against a pile of sacks, pulling him beside her.

Christopher's eyes widened.

The underparlourmaid lowered her mouth to his ear. 'Tommy says not to blame yourself – he is thinking of you, and will see you again soon.'

Christopher stared blankly.

Elsa frowned. 'Has it been so long you have forgotten his name, sir? Before he left, he gave me his kerchief to slip in with your undergarments, as a keepsake.'

'Willicombe? Willicombe is thinking of me? Oh, where is he, Elsa – tell me, and I will go to him this very instant!' Christopher leapt back, grabbing her wrist.

'Shhh!' She raised a finger to his lips and moved closer. 'Your parents are close by. Listen carefully, sir –'

He removed his hat, lowered his ear to her mouth and tried to stay his beating heart.

'Tommy has gone home, to his family in Bristol. But he will be with you –'

'Saying your farewells, young Fitzgibbons?'

Christopher jumped. Elsa curtsied hurriedly, then scurried away, leaving him to stare into the vaguely familiar craggy face which topped the towering mountain of a man. One vast hand held a stout stick. While he fumbled for words, his father appeared.

'So this is where you are, lad – not up to any mischief, is he, Josiah?'

The craggy face cracked a knowing grin. 'Saying goodbye to one of your pretty servants, if my eyes do not deceive me!' Captain Rock glanced in the direction of Elsa.

Viscount Fitzgibbons snorted. 'A bit too free with the ladies in general, I fear, Josiah – that's when he can tear himself away from stable-lads and books!'

Christopher blanched, stooping to retrieve his midshipman's hat: his father still believed he was lying about the Lady Violet.

Josiah Rock chuckled. 'Chip off the old block, eh?'

'He needs experience and responsibility – something to make a man of him. I trust I can rely on you in this department?'

'Completely, you old sea-dog, you! After all, does he not have the Fitzgibbons blood in his veins? That's almost pure salt-water, these days –' the captain laughed '– laced liberally with rum, of course.'

Christopher wanted to crawl under the cart. Then, unexpectedly, the vehicle moved, and the tall masts of a great, black ship filled his vision.

'What do you think of your home for the next six months, young master Fitzgibbons?'

Christopher could only stare. As his father and the captain began to walk down the quayside, he found himself trailing in their wake.

'HMS *Impregnable* – know what that means, Midshipman Fitzgibbons?'

The title made him falter. 'Er, unassailable?' Christopher paused, watching as an army of sailors and merchants carried supplies up several narrow gangplanks.

'That which cannot be taken by force!' The stout stick slapped against a sea-roughened palm.

Captain Josiah Rock's voice vibrated in his ears: 'Neither the sea, the elements or the French – not even that knavish dog El Niño can defeat the *Impregnable*, young Fitzgibbons.' The stick slapped again.

They paused. Christopher took in the boastful words, still focusing on the tarred hull of the great, two-masted vessel.

'How is your own son faring, Josiah?' Viscount Fitzgibbons' voice was low and concerned.

'Not good, I fear – after he seemed to be recovering from his encounter with that foul Spanish brigand, Orlando suffered a nervous set-back, and is now unfit to sail.' The captain's words were quiet, grief-stricken. 'On top of everything else, he was robbed – the cads even stole his medal, awarded to him for services to Lord Nelson himself!'

'I am sorry, my old friend. It grieves me to –'

'No matter!' Captain Rock's tone hardened. 'I'm sure Master Fitzgibbons here will prove an admirable replacement – eh, lad?'

The stout stick tapped Christopher's slim shoulder.

'Together we will deliver our cargo of prisoners to the other side of the stormy Atlantic, and bring back a ship loaded with tobacco and sugar.' Josiah's voice rose up through the dockside noise and the cries of the gulls. 'And if we should happen to meet that dirty Spanish dog, I know I can count on your boy here to fight by my side!'

Christopher shivered.

The Atlantic!

Prisoners!

Storms!

Pirates!

Battles!

Was there no end to the trials which awaited him?

'Indeed you can, Josiah – a Rock and a Fitzgibbons, battling side by side. Just like the good old days!'

As Christopher paled further, a sound drifted into his ears: crying – and beyond that, the drag of chains and the slow tramp of many footsteps. He spun round, eyes narrowing at the gathering crowd of women and children, in front of the long procession of manacled men which was making its way from Newgate Gaol.

Two weeks of constant near-darkness had given his skin a white, unhealthy pallor. A fortnight of fighting for every scrap of food had slimmed him down to a lean, muscular shadow of himself. Not an inch of surplus fat remained on his rangy body.

Mick narrowed his eyes against the sunshine. His beard itched. The hair on his head was tangled and filthy, stretching down to brush his broad shoulders. Remnants of tattered shirt and breeches clung on by threads as, with nearly two hundred others, he staggered from the stinking cell and hobbled towards the waiting ship.

At his side, a two-fingered hand manacled to Mick's, Cat was as alert as ever. Vibrant green eyes searched the passing streets. 'Keep a look-out for my mam – she said she'd come.'

The optimistic words brought a smile to Mick's dry lips. Many of his fellow prisoners were also peering hopefully into the waiting crowd of mothers, sisters, wives and children.

Who was here to see him off?

Who cared, one way or the other, what happened to Mick Savage?

Pulling his mind from such self-pitying thoughts, he glanced at the red-haired boy and trudged on towards the docks.

Slightly built to begin with, the cutpurse had eaten surprisingly well

– in every sense. He had made a favourable impression on the fat gaoler that first night and, every evening, the boy had been summoned to the man's office for cleaning service, in return for his leavings. The offer had extended to Mick also, but he had declined: the stout gaoler cleaned most of his plate, and Cat's need was greater than Mick's.

'Mam! Mam! There she is, Mr Savage!' The pixie face beamed. Cat began to wave furiously.

Mick glanced briefly to where a ginger-haired woman stood with three young children, then returned his attention to the quayside. He could see the ship now: a huge hulk, two-masted and high in the water. It looked like a brigantine, or a snow – two hundred tons burden, at least, and over sixty feet long. Great carts of supplies were being unloaded into her hold, supervised by a harassed-looking boatswain. In front of one of the gangways, a huddle of naval uniforms were further overseeing the process.

Blinking, Mick registered a tall figure, wielding a heavy stick, and a smaller, slighter fellow in midshipman's garb. His eyes moved away, flicking to the steerage section, where he and his companions would spend the next twenty-four weeks. A sudden yank on his wrist tore his gaze away.

Cat lunged towards where his mother was desperately trying to manoeuvre herself and a basket of bread through the swelling crowd of wives and loved ones. Three squealing children snatched at her skirts, slowing her progress.

Mick smiled wryly, breaking ranks to aid the cutpurse. The action had repercussions for the men both in front and behind, who lurched and stumbled.

'Catch, my dear!' As Cat's mother gave up and began to lob hunks of bread in the direction of her son, the snake of chained prisoners veered left. Following her example, several other wives and mothers rained stale missiles and the odd piece of meat into the line of prisoners.

His arms filled with food, Cat passed several to Mick. 'Told you she'd come, didn't I? I'm the first of my family to venture overseas!'

Mick laughed. Others heard the remark, and low chuckles broke out along the chained length of men.

'What's going on down there? Get back in line, you rogues!'

Something in the voice was familiar. Mick turned, watching as the tall man with the stick bore down on their merriment. The young midshipman tagged along behind.

Cat's mother was sobbing now. 'Take care, my dear – write to me!'

'That I will, mam.' One arm cradling the bread, the cutpurse raised his damaged hand in salute.

The movement dragged Mick left, and before he knew what was happening he was face down in the mud, and Cat was on top of him. Around them, six others descended into the mire.

'Fighting already, you scoundrels?'

An iron hand seized his shoulder, hauling him to his knees.

'Only over food, sir.' Mick wiped smears of filth from his face and grinned up. 'The kitchens of the Savoy let us down this morning, I fear.'

Behind, someone stifled a snigger.

Mick's eyes moved from a craggy, angry face to a paler, less confident visage beneath a midshipman's hat.

Memory returned with a vengeance.

The streets of Bath. Lady Violet's betrothal ball. The Admiralty Club.

'Less of your insolence, fellow!'

Recognition made Mick lower his face as he considered the countenance of the older man.

Orlando Rock.

Orlando Rock's father.

Instinctively, his hand dipped into the secret pocket inside his underwear. Around him, prisoners were staggering to their feet. Someone bumped against him. Mick fingered the keepsake.

'On your feet, wretch!'

Amidst the jumble of bodies, the iron grip on his shoulder tugged his hand free.

Orlando Rock's silver medallion rolled gently across the cobbled stone, stopping in front of the toe of a well-polished boot.

'What the – ?'

Lurching backwards, Mick found his feet, hauling Cat upwards.

Countless pairs of eyes followed the progress of a gnarled hand as it picked up the medal and held it aloft. Shards of sun glinted off the silver surface.

'To whom does this belong?' The voice was barely audible and stiff with rage.

An ominous silence greeted the question. Even the gulls declined to answer.

'To whom?'

Mick stared at the ground. Of all the ships in all the world –

159

'Answer me, you pox-ridden blaggards, or by God I'll throw every last loaf of bread into the Thames before we –'

'It is mine, sir.' Mick raised his head and moved forward. The eyes which fixed his burnt with hatred.

'Where did you get this?'

Mick considered lying, then decided against it. 'A friend presented it to me, sir.'

The burning eyes flared. 'A friend? Some other thieving ruffian, more like! What is this friend's name?'

Mick said nothing.

Josiah Rock raised the stout length of wood high above one vast shoulder. 'Tell me, or by God you will feel the weight of this staff across your back!'

'Orlando – Orlando Rock, sir. Your son, I believe.' Mick's words were clear and unmistakable.

The heavy silence on the quayside was almost palpable.

The captain lowered his arm and brought his clean-shaven face closer to the bearded one. He peered. 'I know you!' Outraged recognition dawned. 'My son would never part willingly with this medallion – you robbed him, you knave! You inveigled your way into his and my company, accepted our hospitality, then you took advantage of his ill-health and –' the craggy face was scarlet with fury '– ravished him!'

Mick knew the words fell on his ears only. He raised one hand in protest. 'Sir, I stole his money, I will not deny that, but his body and the keepsake he gave willingly. Please, I –'

'How dare you!'

Before Mick could finish the sentence, Josiah Rock's arm drew back a second time, and the stout stick was descending towards Mick's face. He heard Cat's cry and he raised his arms to protect them both.

Then a voice: 'Captain Rock! No!'

Mick cowered there for what seemed like hours, awaiting a blow which never came.

The voice talked on. 'It was an accident – I saw it all. He slipped when the other prisoner tried to catch the bread. Do not punish him for something which was not his doing.'

Tentatively, Mick uncovered his head.

A slim fist was clamped around Josiah Rock's broad wrist. The stick hovered mere inches from his skull, trembling with barely restrained frustration.

A pale, horrified face stared into a furious, craggy countenance.

'Don't you agree, Captain?' The young midshipman continued to plead Mick's case.

Then another, basser voice boomed in. 'Come on, old friend – Christopher's right. No real harm done anyway, is there?'

On his knees, Mick couldn't tear his eyes from the earnest, beseeching features. On the periphery of his vision, the stout stick lowered itself to the ground near his bare feet. Cold grey eyes bored into his skull. The voice which eventually replied was icily calm: 'You are partly right, Mr Fitzgibbons. But insolence must be stamped out as soon as it raises its ugly head. These ruffians are animals – they need to be kept in line. However, this is neither the time nor the place. Any punishment due will take place on board the *Impregnable*, under naval discipline.'

Mick flinched as an iron hand hauled him to his feet.

'What's your name, animal?'

Mick rebelled against the scorn, holding his shaggy head high and defiant. 'Michael Savage.'

Rock laughed. 'Savage by name and savage by nature, I'll be bound. Let's see if twenty lashes can tame you, Savage! Mr Fitzgibbons? This can be your first lesson as a midshipman – how's your right arm?'

The pale boy didn't reply.

Then emotionless words seeped into Mick's ear: 'I will break you, for what you did to my son. You will never see the shores of the West Indies, you scurvy rogue.'

Pushed onward amidst the farewells and cries of wives and mothers, Mick stumbled on board HMS *Impregnable*. The pale midshipman's face shone like a beacon in his mind.

Sixteen

A further half hour saw all prisoners and crew on board. Propitiously, the turn of the tide brought a wind from the east. The anchor was raised, the first sail dropped free of tethers. From the poop-deck, at the stern of the *Impregnable*, Christopher watched his sobbing mother and stone-faced father fade into the distance. A flock of seagulls squawked, replacing the cries of farewell.

Above his head, the second great sail was unfurling, let loose by dozens of ant-like seamen aloft in the vast, intricate rigging which creaked in rhythm with the ship's progress.

He continued to stare into the vessel's wake. The bustle of Deptford gave way to a series of dockside villages then green pasture land as the *Impregnable* glided on towards Tilbury.

Around him, the boatswain shouted orders. Men scurried to obey, singing as they did so.

Christopher's stomach sang a less jaunty song as he swallowed back another rising tide of queasy anticipation. The motion of the ship was surprisingly smooth, but his grasp of geography told him the journey out into the English Channel would be calm, and unrepresentative of the Atlantic's open waters. Wiping a tear from his eye, he took a deep breath and inhaled the sharp tang of sea air.

A pain shot across his slender chest, only partly due to the cool, salty breeze.

Christopher winced, eyes focused landwards.

Somewhere, back there, was the Lady Violet's seducer – the cause of Christopher's presence here.

162

Somewhere, back there, was Willicombe.

As the ship eased away from the riverbank and into the deeper channel in the Thames, he repeated Elsa's message over and over in his mind. The underfootman was obviously unaware of Christopher's fate. Despite the man's relayed words to the contrary, Christopher knew he would never look upon that handsomely boyish face again.

The knowledge sent another stab of misery into his chest.

Only God knew if he would ever return to England at all. Even if the *Impregnable* reached the West Indies safely – and that was doubtful enough – there was the journey back to consider.

The West Indies.

Christopher sighed. A sail whooshed above his head.

The strange, distant land seemed impossibly far away. Six months away.

Unexpectedly, his mind turned to his beloved Chaucer, and another journey – to Canterbury. He recalled the setbacks and encounters which had dogged that fictional trip – and that was on land!

Willicombe – strong sunburnt arms. Tight white buttocks.

The feel of Willicombe's mouth on his.

The feel of Willicombe's fingers around his John Thomas.

The thick furrow of sweaty hair between Willicombe's –

No!

The word blasted itself into his mind as Christopher became aware of a swelling at the front of his midshipman's breeches.

For all his misunderstandings, Viscount Fitzgibbons had been right about one thing: Christopher must forget Willicombe – forget Chaucer. Forget everything he had ever known.

Only the stupid held out hope where there was none.

Resolve hardened, mirroring the stiffening in his groin. Christopher took another deep breath. Over the smell of the sea and the tarry odour of the taut rigging, another scent drifted into his nostrils.

The greasy fragrance of cooking meat.

His stomach rebelled against the stench. Stifling a dry heave, he tore his eyes from the riverbank and spun round.

Below, on the main deck.

Rows of men – dozens. Hundreds!

Christopher blinked, recalling Captain Rock's words that the *Impregnable* was carrying two hundred and fifty prisoners, as well as a full complement of crew.

The reality of their numbers was a staggering sight.

He stared at the mass of men, who stood still chained together. At the far end, towards the bow, a barechested figure sat beside a glowing brazier. The boatswain stood beside him. Over the sound of the waves and the creaks of the rigging, names were called.

Manacles clanked. Men moved forward, obscuring his view of the figure beside the brazier. Something yellow and blazing glinted, then disappeared.

A sizzling, then a gasp filled his ears. Followed by: 'Found your sea legs yet, Mr Fitzgibbons?'

Christopher jumped, eyes focusing on the giant form of Captain Josiah Rock, who had appeared at his side. 'Almost, sir!'

The captain grinned, lowering a spyglass. 'Good – I knew you would.' He nodded towards the ranks of men. 'That's us past the five-mile line – naval law takes over. Come!' Josiah Rock tucked the telescope under one arm and began to move towards the stairs. 'Now that these animals officially belong to me, you can have the pleasure of carrying out your first order under my command.'

Another gasp. Muffled, this time.

Christopher blanched: he'd forgotten about the quayside incident. As he followed, listening to the sharp click of his boots on weathered wood, he took in the long rows of men, who were now shuffling along the deck.

To one side, separated from the rest and flanked by two burly seamen, a rangy tangle-haired figure stood waiting. The fellow's head was lowered as if in penitence, but even at this distance Christopher could feel the animosity.

Josiah Rock talked on: 'Ever seen a branding, Mr Fitzgibbons?'

The smell of roasting meat placed itself. 'Er, no –' As they walked along the front row of waiting prisoners, Christopher's stomach turned over and he paled further. He raised a lace-edged handkerchief to his nose.

Someone sniggered.

Quick as a flash, the captain's fist impacted with the side of the offender's head. 'Mouth shut, animal!'

The man staggered.

Josiah Rock lowered his voice. 'Never show weakness, Mr Fitzgibbons. These beasts will cut your throat at the slightest sign of humanity. Remember that.'

Christopher's heart pounded. A greasy film of sweat drenched his face. Desperate to avoid the spectacle taking place around the brazier, he scanned the deck for something to focus on –

– and found himself staring into the dark, sullen eyes of the man who had tripped on the quayside. Hurriedly, he looked away – and bumped into the captain, who had paused. Christopher's hat fell off. He grabbed it, cramming the headgear back on top of his fine blond hair.

A low chuckle swept the rows of waiting men.

'Silence!'

The chuckle ebbed away.

'Move along!'

Christopher watched with horror as the line of prisoners shuffled left, and another man lowered his breeches, baring his arse to the shirtless sailor who held the branding iron.

'You are nothing!'

The sizzle of hot metal on delicate skin fizzled in Christopher's ears.

'You are cattle – no, lower than cattle.'

He wanted to look away. Couldn't. His eyes were drawn back to the branding.

Another man lowered his breeches. The fellow gripped his knees for balance. One of his hands bore only two fingers.

Christopher stared over the top of a red head, transfixed. He watched the glowing, R-shaped brand as it drew nearer to the white, quivering flesh.

'And you will be marked as cattle are marked. If you attempt escape – either during the journey, or after we reach our destination – it will be an easy matter to identify and retrieve you. From this day forth, your scurvy flesh will bear my brand.'

A member of the crew stepped forward, placing a broad hand on the redhead's slim neck as the R-shaped iron contacted with delicate skin. Tissue sizzled.

'Mother of God!'

Christopher's heart leapt as the man cried out.

Stumbling, the prisoner fell forward, before being yanked to his feet.

The ginger head raised itself, and Christopher saw the face of a boy, barely out of his teens.

Tears of pain streaked freckled cheeks.

A spasm of sympathy racked Christopher's chest. He moved forward.

Captain Rock raised a restraining hand as the boy was pushed, still trying to cover himself, towards an open deck-hatch. 'Save your pity for the good people these animals robbed and murdered, Mr Fitzgibbons.'

The boy staggered, bow-legged, into the dark hole beneath the deck. In seconds, another man had taken his place. Another arse was about to be marked. Christopher turned away, sickened to his very stomach.

The movement was misinterpreted. Josiah Rock laid a paternal arm around his shoulder. 'Good – I see you are a quick learner, Midshipman Fitzgibbons. Now let's find out if those scholarly ways of yours have weakened your muscles completely.'

Before he knew what was happening, Christopher found himself steered from the branding and over to where the rangy, bearded figure was awaiting punishment.

'Mr Barber?' the captain roared.

'Sir!' A young man, in a uniform identical to Christopher's, sprang forward, holding a length of rolled calico. He held it out.

'Thank you!' Josiah Rock seized the fabric and turned to a pile of coiled ropes. He set the tube down and began to unroll it. 'Only two things are worth their salt at sea, Mr Fitzgibbons: a loyal crew –' the captain unfurled the last inches of the length with a flourish '– and a strong right arm.'

Christopher stared at the array of objects which appeared from within the folds of calico.

'The cat-o'-nine-tails, the lash, the rope's end, the cane –'

Christopher's palms began to sweat. He wiped his hands on the thighs of his breeches.

'– a fine selection, eh, Mr Fitzgibbons?'

Christopher watched, appalled.

The captain picked up a long, flexible-looking length of wood. Around the thicker end, a ring of metal was tightly clasped. 'I see the ferule takes your fancy, sir.'

Christopher tried to back away. His feet wouldn't move.

The weapon was at least three feet long. Josiah Rock raised the length over one broad shoulder, then brought it down through the air.

A sharp crack made Christopher's knees turn to water.

'Excellent choice, Mr Fitzgibbons. Good for a beginner, but still capable of making the necessary impression.' Gripping both ends of the slender rod, the captain flexed the ferule.

Christopher watched the weapon bend almost in two without breaking. He risked a glance at the tall, bearded prisoner.

Dark eyes stared out from within a sullen countenance. Then the head turned away.

Josiah Rock strode forward, seizing a handful of shoulder-length hair.

The man's head jerked up. White teeth clenched against the movement. But he went with the tug as Josiah Rock pulled harder.

The captain's laugh was low and menacing. 'Not so brave now are you, Savage? Your insolent tongue is strangely still.'

The rigging fell quiet, sails ballooning then deflating. The sizzle of branding iron on flesh died. Even the gulls were silent.

A strong, Irish accent soared up into the salty air. 'There is nothing more to be said.'

The words seemed to inflame the captain further. Christopher watched as Josiah Rock unflexed the ferule, sliding its tip beneath the man's bearded chin. 'Is there not, you ruffian?'

The man made no reply.

The captain's voice shook with fury. 'You will be a little more vocal, I'll be bound – after thirty strokes of this.' He pushed more of the rod beneath the man's chin, forcing his tangled head back until the prisoner's eyes regarded the blue sky above.

Thirty? On the quayside, the punishment had been twenty! Christopher opened his mouth to correct the captain. Before the words could come, Josiah Rock had thrust the instrument of punishment into Christopher's hand and was tearing the ragged shirt from the man's strong shoulders.

'Tie him to the mizzen mast!'

As the two burly seamen released their grip to carry out the order, the prisoner broke free.

Christopher would not have blamed the man if he had dived overboard and taken his chances with the current. Instead, he watched in amazement as the tall fellow turned, stretching out his arms against the perpendicular spar, which cut across the short mast, of his own free will.

The gesture only served to enrage the already furious captain. 'Tie him I say!'

Christopher's fingers tightened sweatily around the ferule, which was almost weightless.

The two guards obeyed, securing the Irishman's wrists roughly to the spar.

'And his feet!' The captain's order echoed up into the sails.

Christopher watched strong legs wrenched apart. His eyes took in the swell of the Irishman's clenched buttocks. The threadbare shirt hung in tatters from his waist. Long muscle played across the man's back, up over his biceps and raised forearms.

A tail of thick tangled hair brushed twitching shoulders.

The rod in Christopher's hand was slippy with dread.

'Now, Mr Fitzgibbons – thirty clean strokes!'

The captain's lips moved closer to his ear: 'Every eye is on you, boy – flinch and your naval career will be over before it has even begun.'

Christopher gritted his teeth. His head told him Josiah Rock was right: this had to be done. His heart rebelled against the instruction. His body was drenched in a sudden heat as he stared at the Irishman's leanly muscled body. This fellow's only crime was to stumble on the quayside: Christopher couldn't –

'Sending a boy to do a man's job, sir?'

The words were low, emanating from a lowered, thickly haired head.

Boy?

Boy?

The mocking tone touched a nerve deep inside Christopher's body, bringing back every taunt his father had ever uttered. And prompting the desired response. Never having struck another creature in his life – the very idea of violence usually sending him screaming in the opposite direction – Christopher stepped away from the captain, drew the ferule high above his shoulder and brought it down in the direction of the fellow's broad back.

It took less force than he'd thought. The crack of wood on flesh filled his ears. Along with the captain, crew and assorted prisoners, Christopher waited for the corresponding flinch.

It never came.

Maybe it didn't hurt as much as it looked. Drawing back his right arm again, Christopher let the ferule impact with the sinew a second time.

Then a third.

And a fourth.

By the fifth stroke, sweat was running into his eyes. Wrenching off his hat and jacket, Christopher threw them to the other midshipman, who caught the garments and grinned.

'I envy you the task, my friend.'

Christopher barely heard the words. Still smarting from the Irishman's taunt, he rolled up his sleeves.

The next five strokes fell easily. His arm ached, the muscles in his shoulder stretching with each blow. Six strokes later, Christopher was transported to another world, deep in the rhythm of the punishment.

He no longer saw the Irishman.

He no longer heard the captain's exhorting words.

Barely aware of his surroundings, Christopher's total attention was focused on the arc and fall of the ferule.

After another five, he found all that was needed was a flick of the wrist to deliver sufficient impact.

Still the Irishman made no sound.

Christopher was breathing heavily. The whack of the ferule and each inflation of his lungs were completely synchronised. His blond hair came loose, falling around his pale face. Moving with a grace which belied his scholarly bearing, he threw his weight into the punishment. For extra leverage, his fingers slipped down around the metal circlet, which encompassed the thicker end of the rod.

Something strange and unfamiliar galloped through his veins. His head spun. His breath quickened. The crotch of his midshipman's breeches was tighter than ever. He felt invigorated – elated. Charged with a newly discovered energy, he felt he could go on for ever.

Five strokes later his strength let him down. He paused. His eyes refocused. Then widened.

Although he had neither flinched nor uttered a sound, the Irishman's strong shoulders were now a mass of angry red scores.

Christopher gasped. The knowledge of what he had done descended on him like a heavy stone. He stared, open-mouthed, then tossed the ferule away as if it were as white-hot as the branding iron.

The rod landed on the deck, with a soft clatter.

'There are still ten to go, Mr Fitzgibbons.' The captain's words were quiet. 'Pick it up.'

Christopher shook his spinning head. His groin throbbed. The marks on the Irishman's back and shoulders reddened further under his gaze, rising up to taunt him.

'Pick up the ferule.'

Christopher stepped back, unable to tear his eyes from the damage he had done.

'Pick it up, damn you!'

'Twenty was your first order, Captain – twenty I have delivered.' Christopher's reply was equally low, and breathier as he gulped air into his lungs.

'Are you disobeying an order, Mr Fitzgibbons?'

169

'I am obeying the instruction you gave me, sir.' Exhaustion gave way to a new strength. Christopher focused on Josiah Rock's craggy face, pushing a lock of sweaty hair from his brow.

The captain's small grey eyes held his gaze for what seemed like an eternity, then looked away. Reaching down to the deck, he grabbed the ferule. 'If you will not finish the punishment, then I shall. Sir – this is for Orlando, you dog!'

As Christopher tried to make sense of the man's impassioned cry, he was elbowed aside.

Josiah Rock now stood where he had stood. The ferule whipped through the air, delivering another ten resounding strokes to the Irishman's back.

Christopher closed his eyes.

The beating continued.

He heard the flick of wood on skin, listened to the jerky, arhythmic rasp of the captain's laboured breathing as he threw himself into the task and beyond. Beneath Christopher's feet, the *Impregnable* lurched. The vessel herself was rebelling against the injustice.

'Enough, Captain!' The boatswain's gruff voice scythed through the lashes.

When Christopher opened his eyes, the stocky man was gently removing the ferule from within Josiah Rock's iron fist.

. The captain remained where he was: one arm raised to the heavens, fingers curled around a weapon no longer there. His craggy face was contorted by an expression of sheer hatred.

'Take him below – his branding can wait!'

The two seamen were staring at the captain. No one moved – every eye was focused on the broad, ossified shape of Josiah Rock.

Then the boatswain took charge, loosening the bonds at the man's wrists and ankles.

A click from the overhead rigging broke whatever spell Josiah Rock's frenzy of rage had cast over the ship. Christopher darted forward to assist as the Irishman's bleeding shoulders and arms were lowered. His hand gripped a sweating bicep. 'I'll get the ship's doctor, you'll –'

'I will be fine, sir.' The man pulled away and turned stiffly.

Christopher stared into a pink face. 'But you are hurt. Let me –'

'I think you have done enough.' The thick beard was drenched with sweat. Behind a cocky grin, barely disguised pain shimmered over the strong features.

'Jump to it, lads! Get him below!'

Spurred into action by the boatswain's command, the two burly seamen grabbed the Irishman, dragging him towards the hold.

Christopher watched the rangy fellow break free a second time and walk slowly, if unsteadily, towards the dark hole.

At the edge of the hold, the Irishman stumbled and fell.

Christopher's mouth was dry. His body pulsed with a thousand sensations, most of which were completely alien.

Shards of sunlight dappled the wealed skin on the Irishman's back and shoulders as he dragged himself to his feet.

Then he was gone, and Christopher's body was drenched in a hot prickle of uneasy disappointment.

Seventeen

Thirty tongues of fire licked at his skin.

Mick frowned. At least he hadn't been branded – they could mark him with their whips, but he would never suffer another man's imprint of property. He stared to where the young cutpurse was peering over a slender shoulder at the bright red R on his left buttock.

'How am I supposed to sit down?'

The question brought a smile to his cracked lips. 'Cats always land on their feet, I presume – or their knees.'

The cutpurse giggled. 'You have a point, Mr Savage.' The impish face took on a more serious cast. 'Let me see your back.' Cat moved towards him.

Instinctively, Mick edged away. He wanted to retreat to a corner and lick his wounds, like the animal they said he was, but the cramped hold and his manacles made this impossible.

Cat folded thin arms across his chest and regarded him through narrowed eyes. 'I won't bite –' the boy grinned '– at least, not unless you want me to.'

Mick laughed. 'Thank you, no.' The cutpurse's easy, off-hand joke penetrated his anger and humiliation. He turned, exposing his tender shoulders. 'At the moment I have enough bites to contend with.'

'Call these bites? I've had fleas deliver more damage!'

Staring to where a group of chained men were nursing their own wounds, Mick smiled wryly. Cat kept up a barrage of flip comments as he examined his friend's injuries.

For his part, Mick tried not to wince when skilful fingers contacted with a particularly sensitive area.

'A little salve will do the trick – by God, I wish I had my oils and herbs with me.' The hands moved away.

Mick pushed his mind from the discomfort and back to its source.

The punishment had started bearably enough. Bracing himself for the onslaught, he'd been surprised at the skill of the young midshipman. From his appearance, Mick had presumed the boy to have little experience of anything, let alone the nous to deliver a lashing.

He searched his memory for the lad's name. Fitzgibbons – Mr Fitzgibbons.

Obviously, it was the lad's first voyage. Anyone could see that.

But when the first stroke of the ferule contacted with his shoulders, Mick sensed he was in the hands of an expert.

The young midshipman instinctively knew the exact degree of weight and force necessary to make his stinging point, but do no permanent damage.

Staring at the floor of the filthy hold, he closed his eyes and saw the deck once more.

After the first decade of lashes, something had happened. His shoulders almost numb, a strange heat had suddenly injected itself into his veins. His body became light, almost weightless. His breathing steadied and, just for a second, a peculiar relaxation pervaded his entire being.

He found himself trying to relive the next ten lashes – or, rather, bring back to his mind the rhythm and cadence of the ferule. He'd barely felt the fall of the instrument on his shoulders, but when it stopped he'd been tempted to cry out for the first time.

Through the pounding blood in his ears, he'd heard the near-argument between Orlando Rock's father and the young midshipman. Then he'd been transported from somewhere just outside Heaven into the depths of Hell.

Josiah Rock possessed none of the finesse of Mick's previous pun-isher. The strokes his arm had delivered were designed to maim. Mick had felt resentment grow hot in his veins as a battery of blows rained on to his back and shoulders, biting into already tenderised flesh and sending arrows of fury through his body.

He had been beaten thus, many times before.

The hunting-shooting gentry visited his homeland each autumn, to bag themselves grouse and pheasant. In his youth, Mick and his brothers earned a few pennies, carrying the guns of the well-dressed lords and helping to scare the birds from their hides amongst the scrub-grass.

Sometimes it was a good season, and game abounded.

Other years, breeding was late and the few birds available for the gentlemen's sport proved cunning prey. On those occasions, Mick and his brothers became the object of another type of sport.

He'd been beaten in frustration.

He'd been beaten in disappointment.

He'd been beaten unfairly – was it his fault the gentry couldn't shoot straight?

A cold rage flooded his veins. Mick knew what he'd experienced at the hands of Josiah Rock was only a taste of things to come.

You will never see the shores of the West Indies.

The man bore him a grudge, and misplaced though that grudge might be, Mick was in no doubt the captain had every intention of carrying out his threat.

There would be ample opportunities: if the Rock did not break Mick's back with more beatings on equally flimsy pretexts, he could be starved or worked to death. It would not be difficult: the six months' voyage was hard enough to survive for those who did not bear the full weight of Josiah Rock's vengeance.

Accidents could happen. He could find himself thrown overboard, dead or alive, at any point.

Escape: the idea thrust itself into his brain.

He didn't know how, or when, or even to where, but Mick knew his only chance of survival was to get off the *Impregnable* as soon as possible.

Out of nowhere, a strange glow spread over his skin. The feel of Josiah Rock's fury-motivated blows receded.

Mick gasped.

Never before had he experienced a beating like the first twenty strokes at the hand of the young midshipman. And it was all the more painful when one of those same hands had touched his arm and requested a doctor.

When Cat's practised fingers resettled on Mick's shoulders, he barely felt them. Something cool and slightly abrasive slicked the boy's palms.

'Spiders' webs and dried salt-water.' The cutpurse's explanatory words were quiet as he gently moved his hands across Mick's back. 'Amazing what is available, even in a stinking hole such as this.'

Mick slumped forward on to his knees. 'You are very resourceful, my young friend.' Tangled hair fell over his face. He leant the crown of his head against the curved wall of the hold.

Cat's laugh was soft. 'Thank that old Chinaman, Mr Savage – not me.'

Gentle lips kissed the side of Mick's neck.

'This should help –' the mouth moved away '– although your wounds seem to be healing on their own.'

Mick felt the imprint of a kiss, aware of a vague stirring in his groin. For the briefest of moments he fancied those lips belonged to another young man – a slight midshipman with a master's way with the ferule.

'A fine bunch we are to travel with, eh, Mr Savage?'

The question pulled his mind from its musings. Turning slowly, Mick regarded his fellow prisoners, each of whom was either studying his own or the scorched arse of his neighbour, and complaining.

As his eyes acclimatised to the darkness, he saw the hold was huge. It stretched from behind him to as far as he could see. The bulk of the area was below the waterline, and waves slopped softly against the vessel's tarred sides. Mick raised his eyes.

Overhead, tiny untarred areas and knot-holes let in pinpricks of light which broadened into bright beams and criss-crossed the space above them.

'A fine bunch indeed.' Mick's gaze lowered itself to the nearest group, who were talking in low voices.

From within their midst, a heavy-set fellow returned his gaze. Then stood up.

Mick got up from his crouch.

The man was over six feet tall, in his thirties, with a girth to match his height. The fellow had the sullen, antagonistic bearing of one who had been forced to fight for everything –

Mick's eyes took in the bulging muscles.

– perhaps even fight for his living, literally, in the boxing dens of London's East End. He glanced at the fellow's knuckles, noting the callused, cracked skin.

Dressed only in a ragged shirt, the man's strong, thickly haired legs ended in a pair of very large, bare feet. Great clumps of bristly hirsuteness sprouted from each toe. He took a step forward.

So did Mick.

Through the threadbare weave of the man's shirt, vast shaggy patches were visible. A dense stubble coated his jutting chin and upper lip. His dome-like head was completely bald. Thin lips frowned.

So did Mick. He had little idea what his travelling companions had made of the beating, but of one thing he could be sure: word would have quickly got round the prisoners that someone of specific interest to the captain was on board. And that could spell trouble for them all.

Unblinkingly, he held the man's gaze. A dull hum of discontented conversation drifted into his ears from further down the hold.

'Aye, married only three hours – tore me from her arms, they did.'

'She was on the quayside, waving. I could almost smell her!'

'Six months, they say – six months without a woman. I fear I shall go mad!'

A smile twitched the corners of Mick's mouth. He watched a similar movement on the surly face opposite his. The complaints continued, taking on a lustier tone.

'I have a cob on me that would shame a stallion!'

'The ache in my bollocks is worse than the pain of the branding!'

'I would fuck one of those high knot-holes, if my legs would carry me aloft!'

Mick's lips stretched further. Another stretching was also taking place, inside his shabby breeches. The pain in his shoulders had vanished – whether due to Cat's spiders' webs, he wasn't sure – and he knew the minds of the men around him were moving from contemplation of their sore arses to thoughts of their raging libidos. Instinctively, his eyes dropped to the low-hanging front of the bald man's shirt. Then he laughed.

The fabric was slowly raising, pushed outwards by a great mast.

'Do you find me amusing?'

'Not at all, my smooth-pated fellow!' Mick took a step forward, closing the gap between them. 'My mirth is at our shared situation.'

The response was less than convinced. 'I would have thought those thirty lashes on your back would have taken your sense of humour as thoroughly as they removed a layer of skin.'

Mick watched a sail of fabric continue to rise until it stuck out at a forty-five degree angle. The man's staff was as strong and thick as the rest of his body. Mick longed to whip the shirt-flap aside and feast on the cock's great, bulbous head. But someone beat him to it.

In a flash, the cutpurse nipped in between them. 'Jeremiah Roscoth at your service, sir – call me Cat.' The cutpurse executed a neat bow, his red head lowering itself to the man's crotch. 'It is less of a mouthful –'

The bald man took a step back.

As he did so, Cat raised his head, nudging the mast of flesh. The shirt-flaps parted. 'And talking of mouthfuls –'

Mick moved to the side, watching.

The cutpurse's green, feline eyes gazed into the man's densely haired groin. Inches from his full, watering lips, the cock's purple head was a swollen invitation.

Mick felt the boy's lust, which mirrored a throbbing in his own groin. Conversation ebbed away, and the hold was now filled with the sound of dragging chains as a circle of prisoners gathered around them.

'And of whom will I have the pleasure?' Sitting back on his knees, Cat stared appealingly upwards.

The balding fellow's face creased with confusion.

Cat smiled. 'Your name, sir?'

The huge man with the jutting cock cleared his throat. 'Thomas – Jonathon Thomas.'

Mick grinned. How apt! The length and girth of the man's member bore testament to the title.

Cat's pixie face showed no amusement. 'It is good to make your acquaintance, Mr Thomas.' The words were sober and respectful. Then a two-fingered hand snaked up and seized the man's staff in greeting. 'I am sure our friendship will be long and mutually satisfying.' He pumped his slender arm up and down.

Mick's eyes moved to the heavily stubbled face.

The man's expression was a mixture of bemusement and annoyance. But when Cat's deft fingers tightened, all other emotions fled the stony countenance and his shaft lengthened another inch. 'Cat, eh?'

'That's what they call me, sir.'

'And what makes you purr, Cat?' The voice was hoarse with need.

The growing crowd of onlookers chuckled.

Cat's response was wordless but unambiguous. Maintaining his unconventional handshake and sheathing his fine white teeth behind his lips, Cat held Jonathon's gaze and slipped his mouth over the velvet glans.

Mick uttered a moan, feeling his own aching length flex inside his breeches.

Jonathon threw back his head in undisguised pleasure.

Cat closed his lips just below the rim. And exerted a little pressure. Then a low, animal sound rumbled deep in the boy's throat, escaping his nostrils.

Purring.

Around them, chuckles died and were replaced by sighs of envy and frustration.

Mick drank in the arousal of dozens of men. He ripped the shreds of his torn shirt aside and stroked the front of his threadbare breeches.

Cat took his time, lapping and sucking on the vast purple head until Jonathon's huge hands gripped the boy's slender shoulders and pushed his ginger skull lower.

He could smell them – Cat and Jonathon and the bodies of the men who pressed their bodies behind his.

He could hear them – the rustle of fabric thrust aside and the rough glide of fist on cock.

Mick leant back, tearing at breech fastenings in his haste. His fingers tightened around seven inches of engorged meat.

And he could feel them – on either side of him. Shoulder to shoulder, thigh to thigh, at least a dozen men had formed a close circle around Cat and Jonathon. Some were gazing fixedly on the slim redhead's lips as they slid slowly down the bald giant's thick length. Some stared up towards the hold's dark ceiling, their minds elsewhere. Some gazed straight ahead, through lust-blurred vision.

Mick caught one, two then three sets of eyes.

Others sneaked glances at the men at their sides or the fellows opposite, hauling on their cocks more vigorously as the atmosphere in the hold grew hotter and more tense.

Cat's ginger head was now flush with Jonathon's groin. One mana-cled hand gripped the man's waist for balance. The other exerted a two-fingered barrier around the root of the stout cock to prevent himself choking.

The bald giant's knees buckled as he thrust down then up in scooping movements, hauling his thick shaft from between the boy's o-shaped lips then ramming himself back in.

Mick slumped to a crouch. Cat's grunts and smothered groans filled his head. Side on to the spectacle, he watched Jonathon's large ball-sac collide with the boy's hairless chin each time he drove himself forward. Odours filled his head: the stench of unwashed flesh, the meaty smell of singed skin and the salty sweetness of arousal. His cock pulsed in his fist. Mick slid his hand up the shaft, gasping as a tiny drop of pre-come formed on his slit – a pearl in a pigsty.

Then something warm and muscular pushed against his back and Mick almost howled.

Behind, one of his fellow prisoners was bucking his hips and thrusting his tensed thighs against Mick's damaged shoulders.

Pain shot through his body. His fist tightened around the base of his length. In a parallel movement a quiver of approaching climax clenched his balls. He bit his tongue, fighting discomfort as the man's legs thrust against him again.

Again his bollocks twisted against each other. Then his hand was moving by itself.

Inches away, Cat had toppled on to his back.

Mick heard the gasp as the boy's branded buttocks came in contact with the floor of the hold. Mick moaned – in sympathy and longing.

Before the writhing cutpurse could shift position, Jonathon was straddling the lad's slender, heaving chest, forcing Cat's head up and back.

Mick's unseen assailant seized a shoulder, digging broad fingers into his flesh with barely restrained passion.

Mick clenched his teeth and jerked his aching shaft.

As Cat's throat opened up by the change in position, Jonathon threw himself into the final straights of the face-fuck. Sweat glistened on every inch of the man's vast body. It glistened on his bald pate, gathered on his stubbly upper lip and dropped down on to the floor behind the cutpurse's head in streaming rivulets.

Mick's back was on fire. His shoulders throbbed, each laceration inflamed further with each thrust of the man behind. Mick pushed himself onward, hauling on his cock like a man possessed as the entire hold quivered on the verge of release. He couldn't see Cat's face at all, now. The cutpurse's red head was completely obscured by Jonathon's great thighs. Mick focused on the thick covering of sweat-soaked hair, watching the man piston in and out of the boy's open throat.

He barely registered the first orgasm. The sudden cry of release was quickly followed by others. Mick pumped himself more vigorously.

Bare feet planted on the hold's sludgy floor, Cat's groin bucked heavenward. One two-fingered fist jerked up and down his slender cock.

Something wet and warm landed on Mick's burning shoulders. The splatter coincided with another three climaxes. Through the roaring in his ears, he heard Jonathon's great grunt of release, seconds behind his own. Somewhere beyond that, as spunk rushed up the length of his cock and exploded from his slit in a thick wad, Cat's choking gurgle rose to a smothered gasp.

Mick fell forward, coaxing another slitful of milky come from the head of his trembling prick.

Jonathon's vast musculature slowly relaxed.

More groans of satisfaction indicated the climax of another four prisoners. Men fell panting to their knees, shooting in all directions. Another volley caught Mick in the face. He grinned through receding waves of pleasure, catching a salty gobbet with his dry tongue.

Then voices. 'Pass the boy over here!'

'I want some of that!'

'Is his arse as good as his mouth?'

Mick chuckled. Climbing to his knees, he crawled over to where Jonathon was pulling his softening length from between the cutpurse's lips.

Cat's green eyes were glazed, hazy with spent passion. He gazed dopily up at Mick with huge pupils.

'I see you ended up on your back after all, my young friend.' Mick flicked the head of the boy's come-coated cock.

Slowly, realisation dawn. The pixie face creased with pain. Leaping to his feet, Cat howled and stared over his shoulder.

The shouts continued. 'Give him some water then it's my turn!'

'No, mine!'

'Mine, I say!'

Chuckling, Mick slipped one manacled hand behind Cat's knees and draped the other around the boy's shoulders. In one easy movement, he lifted the surprised boy off his feet and carried him through the disappointed crowd of aroused men.

'Tomorrow, my good fellows – you shall have your pleasure tomorrow!' Cat swivelled his head and grinned at a sea of frustrated faces. 'Meanwhile, I could do with some of that water.'

An hour later, Cat lay naked across Mick's lap, his freckled face aimed at the floor.

Mixing the water Jonathon had brought with a little of his own spunk and some cobwebs, the cutpurse had created a soothing salve.

Gently, Mick applied more of the balm to the raised red letter on the boy's arse-cheek.

Cat moaned, gripping Mick's calves, then relaxed. 'We'll make a physician of you yet, Mr Savage.'

Mick smiled, feeling the boy's soft cock twitch against his thigh. 'You've made several friends there, my lad.'

Cat giggled. 'And gone some way to filling my belly. Now I know why whores are always well-padded. Whatever else happens, I will not go hungry these next six months!'

Mick laughed. Below his feet, the ship lurched.

The movement sobered his mood and reminded him where he was. And for how long.

Six months.

Six long months.

Ample time for Orlando Rock's vengeful father to extract whatever punishments he chose. On his lap, Cat wriggled round to face him.

The freckled skin was pink with exertion. The cutpurse raised two manacled hands and draped them around Mick's neck. 'What ails you, Mr Savage? Is it your wounds? Let me help.'

Circling the boy's waist, Mick shook his head. 'I am merely tired.' Josiah Rock was his problem, and his alone.

Raising his damaged arse-cheek, Cat altered his position and rested his red head in the crook of Mick's neck. 'Well, let us sleep.' The boy snuggled in, pressing his slim chest against broader, hairier pectorals.

In minutes, soft snoring sounds drifted up.

Mick kissed the top of Cat's sweat-drenched head and tightened his arms around the sleeping figure. Staring into darkness, he wondered if he dared risk the luxury of Morpheus' embrace.

Eighteen

A n hour after Captain Rock had stalked off to his cabin, leaving Christopher bewildered and trembling on deck, the young man was still shaking.

He'd stared at the sea: that only increased his discomfort.

He'd returned to the poop deck: the boatswain and the First Officer were both engrossed in a study of charts, and barely acknowledged his presence.

He walked from stern to bow, trying to acquaint himself with naval activity and longing to feel part of the crew.

Stalwart seamen with tarred pigtails and wind-hardened skins scurried to obey orders: checking sails, tightening ropes and cleaning the two small cannons which sat on the port and starboard sides of the *Impregnable*.

Christopher merely got in the way.

Everyone seemed to have a function.

Everyone seemed to regard the lashing of the tangle-haired Irishman as par for the course.

Everyone was industriously engaged in some task or other and acted as if nothing had happened.

Every bone in Christopher's body shivered. His right arm throbbed, and he was sure it now hung an inch longer than his left. But it was the pain in his mind which bothered him most – and the odd exhilaration that prevented him from just curling up in a corner somewhere and pretending it was all a bad dream.

In the tiny three-bunk cabin to which he had finally been directed, he tried again to unpack his meagre possessions from the small knapsack. Palsy shook his fingers when they contacted with Willicombe's brightly coloured kerchief, forcing him to give up. He leant back on the bunk, pulled in contrary directions: he'd wanted to please his captain, and he'd wanted to spare the prisoner, but had done neither. His mind swam with self-hatred. Christopher clenched his fists and tried to relax.

Four deep breaths later, he had almost managed it. His blood no longer pounded to the same extent. His pulse had lessened to a more sedate pace.

Staring at the opposite wall he saw the contorted features of Captain Rock as he delivered more than twenty extra strokes to the broad Irishman's back. Christopher gasped and closed his eyes.

The vision changed. Strobing on his pale lids, he saw an image of a lowered head. Long black hair obscured the roguish face. But the words were clearly audible: *Send a boy to do a man's job –*

He squeezed his eyes more tightly shut, biting back resentment as his heart began to race once more. He could still feel the ferule in his hand, still hear the crack as the rod whipped through the air and landed squarely on the Irishman's shoulders.

Christopher flinched – then leapt to his feet as a frisson shimmered along the length of his cock. His brain was still reeling from the unexpected reaction when the cabin door opened and two figures were grinning at him.

'Blotted your copybook there, Mr Fitzgibbons!'

Christopher grabbed his knapsack and held it in front of his swelling crotch. He stared blankly at the stocky, wigged man who also wore the blue jacket of a midshipman. While he was still searching for an appropriate reply, the other, taller fellow chimed in: 'Pay Samuel no heed, Mr Fitzgibbons – I am sure the captain will not hold first-day nerves against you.'

Grateful for the friendly tone in the man's voice, Christopher found a smile and moved back to allow the two other officers into the cramped space.

The taller of his two cabin mates talked on. 'Please permit me to introduce myself. Laurence Mims, Mr Fitzgibbons. And this joker –'

The stocky midshipman vaulted up on to the top of three bunks.

'– is Mr Samuel Barber.'

He stared at the offered hand, then took it in his. 'Christopher Fitzgibbons, sir.'

The grip was easy. 'Glad to meet you.'

As he withdrew his fingers and turned to the upper bunk, the stocky man grinned down.

'I wonder how long you will remain the Rock's favourite after that little display on deck, Mr Christopher Fitzgibbons.'

His handshake was returned briefly. A myriad questions circled in his head. As Laurence removed his hat and began to unfasten the brass buttons of his blue-and-gold jacket, Christopher broached the first with his cabin mates. 'Why do you call him the Rock, Mr Mims?'

The answer came from Midshipman Barber's thin, sneering lips. 'Because he's built like a mountain, sir – solid and unmoveable. Because he is cold, hard and unemotional –'

Christopher recalled the unrestrained passion which had been evident during the lashing of the Irish rogue.

'– and because, if he ever does crack, God help any mere mortals in the vicinity!' The speech ended in a harsh, braying laugh.

Christopher flinched. Then an arm encircled his shoulder.

'Ignore Sam, Mr Fitzgibbons – he is only jealous.'

'I am not!'

'Indeed you are!' Laurence laughed, tightening his arm and lowering his voice. 'Mr Barber is from a fine seafaring family – he expects preferential treatment. But whatever else the Rock is, he is not one who shows favouritism –'

'Unless your ancestors sailed with Drake to the New World! Unless your father served with Nelson!'

Christopher could hear the bile in the man's voice.

'Then, of course, you are taken under the Rock's wing and given the benefit of his own special brand of naval discipline. I –'

'You are worse than a gossiping fishwife, Sam! Now be quiet!'

Christopher edged away from the fraternal arm, unsettled by the stocky man's outburst. There was so much he didn't know, so much he needed to know. He wanted to hear more, and he didn't. Moving over to his bunk – the lowest of the three – he sat down. The memory of his failure to carry out an order circled in his confused brain. 'I have not made a very good first impression, have I?' He looked beseechingly up at Laurence Mims' aristocratic face.

The midshipman sighed. 'It would have been better had you been able to complete the punishment, I will admit, but –'

'I could have done it! I could have whipped that Irish dog to within an inch of his worthless life. I would not have disgraced myself in front of my captain, had I –'

'Yes, I'm sure you would have, Sam –' Laurence's tone was weary '– then gone on to keelhaul the entire crew if any of them as much as looked at you the wrong way.'

Sam snorted. 'Nothing wrong with a bit of discipline, before God!'

'I like to think God would have shown the same mercy Mr Fitzgibbons did, my fierce friend.' Laurence turned back to Christopher. 'But that doesn't help you much, does it?'

Christopher sighed. 'It does not – and I do so want to get off on the right foot.' The ship lurched. He grabbed the side of the bunk to steady himself. His stomach gave a queasy flip and he was again glad he had refused breakfast.

'Well, there is a way.'

He looked up.

A plump, bewigged face dangled down from the top bunk. 'The Rock is, amongst other things, a stickler for tradition.'

Christopher brightened. 'He is?'

The upside-down face beamed. 'Indeed he is. So many old naval customs are dying out and falling by the wayside.'

Christopher's expression sobered as he recalled the raucous dancing and drinking, back at the Admiralty Club. 'You mean, er – hornpipes and the like?'

The wigged head shook and Mr Barber's eyes took on a regretful cast. 'More ancient customs, Mr Fitzgibbons, dating back to your great-great-grandfather's time and beyond.'

Christopher frowned, again disheartened by his inadequacy. 'I am a scholar of literature. I know little of nautical traditions.'

The inverted face winked. 'But I do.'

'Are you sure this will impress Captain Rock?'

His blue-and-gold jacket was draped over the back of a chair. His tight breeches and underwear sat in a neat heap. Dressed only in his black midshipman's hat and knee-boots, his long-fingered hands shielding his curled member, Christopher glanced uncertainly from Laurence to Sam and back again.

'Positive, Mr Fitzgibbons!' Mr Barber's confirmation was loud and cheerful. All signs of his previous sneering tone had vanished.

Laurence Mims' aristocratic face creased. 'Sam, this is not right. We cannot –'

'No, you and I cannot, because we have sailed before.' Jumping down from his perch on the top bunk, Midshipman Samuel Barber regarded Christopher's exposed chest and stomach with a critical eye. 'But it is his maiden voyage – and all maidens were once required to appear thus at the captain's table, their first night on board.' Meticulously, he altered the position of the large hat to a more rakish angle, then strolled to one side.

A frisson of expectation swept over Christopher's skin, erecting the downy hair on his arms and legs. He stared straight ahead, focusing on a portrait of the king which hung on the wall opposite.

On the periphery of his vision, Sam circled slowly. 'Yes, yes –'

Christopher felt a twitch against his right palm. He cupped his long fingers more tightly between his legs, curling the digits down until he was cradling his own bollocks. Something about the way Sam was scrutinising his body was having an effect on Christopher's member.

'– you'll do nicely. Just one thing more –'

The cupping only served to increase the movement against his palm. Christopher froze, eyes still directed at the painting of poor mad King George. He had never been looked at quite like this before. Shivers of unease trembled up from deep inside. Behind his cupped palms, something warm and insistent was making its presence felt. 'One more thing?' He tried to keep the quaver out of his voice.

'Salute your king, Midshipman Fitzgibbons!'

Instinctively, Christopher's left hand shot up to his eyebrow, shading his eyes from the majesty of the monarch, as his father had taught him. His other hand hung limply by his side.

To his left, Sam chuckled, then nodded approvingly. 'A fine sight, eh, Laurence? The captain will be most surprised –'

Midshipman Mims was silent.

'– and pleased, of course.'

Christopher's body flushed up. Droplets of sweat ran from between his collarbones and trickled down his chest. A cool breeze wafted against his groin, but only served to increase the throbbing there. He could feel himself under scrutiny from other quarters. Maintaining the salute and desperate to please, he turned slowly and met an intense, narrowed gaze. 'Er, do you think so?'

Another, more unconventional salute did not go unnoticed. Christopher's fine cock stuck out, flexing towards the man in its search for approval.

Laurence's eyes shot from the level of Christopher's crotch. 'I am taking no part in this.' The man lowered his head, briskly refastened the brass buttons of his jacket and walked swiftly towards the door. 'You should be ashamed of yourself!'

Christopher's hands fled back to his groin. A blush rose to his pale cheeks.

'Where's the harm, eh? Fitzgibbons wants to make an impression –' the stocky man chuckled '– and an impression he will make!'

Quivering with a mixture of anticipation and self-disgust, Christopher watched the way Midshipman Mims' angular shoulders moved beneath his tight blue jacket, then found himself wondering what the man looked like naked. A tingle rippled across his slim, hairless chest, resounding in each of his suddenly hard nipples and finding an echo in his erect member. He pushed the thought away, along with his doubts.

Everything that had happened since he'd set foot on board this dreadful ship had been alien and strange. He'd already made a pig's ear of his first order but, however odd this piece of naval lore might seem, he would not miss the opportunity to recover some of the lost ground.

In the distance, four bells rang.

Christopher took a deep breath. 'Shall we go to dinner, then?' His belly growled.

Midshipman Barber laughed raucously. 'So you do know something of seagoing protocol?'

Christopher beamed at the compliment, although the rumbling in his stomach had more to do with the remark than any knowledge of marine time and bells which had been ringing off and on for hours. He took a step towards the door.

Sam placed a restraining hand on his chest.

Christopher inhaled sharply at the touch.

Midshipman Barber lowered his voice. 'Let us go on ahead to the mess, eh? You must make your –' he sniggered '– entrance when all the officers are already seated.' He winked. 'Wait fifteen minutes, then follow.'

Christopher nodded like an eager puppy. 'Thank you for all your help. I am very grateful.' He smiled enthusiastically

Midshipman Mims was already out of the door and disappearing down the narrow corridor.

'Think nothing of it, Mr Fitzgibbons: what are friends for? Remember, fifteen minutes.' Sam grinned one last time, then hid his mouth behind his hand and left the cabin.

★

The smell of food led him, sometime later, along a maze of narrow aisles. Christopher passed no one, but could hear the boatswain's gruff voice on the deck above his head.

The motion of the *Impregnable* was so slight that he could almost believe he was back on land. He walked slowly, stomach rumbling, listening to the soft clack of his boot-heels on the polished timber floors.

He was a sailor now.

Christopher Fitzgibbons – scholar and man of letters – had been left behind in Deptford.

Aboard one of His Majesty's great ships, under the captaincy of Josiah Rock, he would learn the ways of sailors.

He would beat a man, when ordered.

He would study the charts and navigational aids.

He would take his turn on deck, watching as the ship made her way through the night.

If there were storms, he would weather them.

If there were pirates, he would fight them.

He would not flinch nor swerve from his duty to king and captain!

The smell of food was getting stronger, now accompanied by loud voices. Christopher paused, cocking his head.

At the end of this corridor.

A double door.

Removing his hands from his crotch, Christopher threw back his slender shoulders and clenched his fists.

He would climb the mizzen mast, if he had to.

He would spend time in the crow's nest, scanning for Spanish vessels and pirate ships.

He would do whatever had to be done.

With a manly stride, he stepped forward, walking more quickly. He held his head high, and proudly.

He was a man.

He was a sailor – a sailor who knew the most ancient of naval traditions.

The voices were louder now. Christopher recognised the ingratiating tones of Midshipman Barber, and the low, bassy response of the captain.

Adjusting the angle of his hat, he wiped his palms on his bare thighs then grabbed two handles. Hauling the double doors open, he walked jauntily into the room. 'Good evening, gentlemen!' His voice was louder than he'd intended.

It echoed in the messroom, bouncing off the wood-panels and rising up to the ceiling.

Five heads looked up from their meal.

Ten pairs of eyes stared at him.

Christopher deftly closed the doors behind himself and bowed to the head of the table. 'Captain Rock, I present myself for inspection, on my first night at sea.'

Silence.

Then a snigger.

The first flickers of uncertainty shot through his semi-naked body. Christopher tentatively examined the seated men. Five pairs of hands held five sets of cutlery.

On the right side of the table, Midshipman Barber was grinning broadly. At his side, Mr Mims averted his face.

Opposite, a hunched figure with a sparse head of hair regarded him with faint amusement through pince-nez. To his right, a stern-looking man Christopher recognised as the First Officer raised a bushy eyebrow.

'Mr Fitzgibbons!'

His eyes darted to the head of the table.

Cloaked and hatted, Captain Rock was on his feet, bearing down on Christopher with iron-grey eyes.

Sam Barber's voice was filled with barely disguised mirth. 'Cover yourself, sir! Don't you know such behaviour is an insult to the captain's table?'

The strength left Christopher's body. He felt himself shrink in stature. Unable to move a muscle, he could not even force his hands to his exposed genitals.

Midshipman Barber talked on. 'Fine impression to make! I would not be surprised if you never sail again, and –'

'Hold your tongue, sir!' The captain's voice was low and controlled. 'Approach, Mr Fitzgibbons.'

He could not disobey. Christopher slunk around the table, pausing a yard from where Josiah Rock loomed, huge and dominating. He couldn't look at the man's face, so stared at the toes of his own highly polished boots.

'Here –'

Christopher glanced up, scarlet-faced. He regarded the long, navy-coloured cape which the captain held out.

'Now sit down and eat, before you catch your death of cold, lad!' Josiah Rock chuckled good-heartedly.

A different, stunned silence filled the mess, emanating most noticeably from a disappointed Midshipman Barber.

Christopher responded to the kind words. 'Thank you, sir.' Taking the serge cloak, he draped it around his shaking shoulders and took a seat beside the captain. 'I am deeply sorry for any offence I may have –'

'Save your apologies, young Fitzgibbons.' Josiah Rock moved his iron gaze to where Midshipman Barber was now gnawing discontentedly on a hunk of salted beef. 'My own first night at sea – more years ago than you've been on this good earth – was spent polishing the breasts of the ship's figurehead, a task someone took on himself to inform me was every midshipman's duty. Fell into the Channel twice, trying to do so, before your own father rescued me.'

Christopher found himself laughing. 'He did not mention that, Captain.' A hand patted his shoulder.

'He wouldn't, lad: your father is a modest man.' The Rock chuckled teasingly. 'Unlike his son, to whom mere modesty seems an alien concept.'

A shiver shook his body. Christopher blushed, but continued to laugh.

'Let's chase that chill from your seafaring bones, lad.' The captain thumped the table. 'Rum for the midshipman here!'

'Right away, sir!' From a stool in the far corner, a slight, ebony-skinned youth bounded forward, holding a flagon. He tipped it upwards, filling Christopher's tankard and gifting him with a broad, admiring smile.

A memory of Poxy Doxy, and Abel's dark, exotic face, pushed its way through Christopher's relief. Around the base of the tankard, his hand shook.

Then Josiah Rock was pounding the table again. 'Rum for everyone! I have a very good feeling about this voyage. To the *Impregnable*, the finest crew she's ever seen, and death to the pirate knave El Niño!'

'The *Impregnable*!' Raising his tankard, Christopher jumped to his feet and joined in the toast. His five dining companions drank deeply and, as a warm glow of acceptance seeped into his groin, Christopher did likewise.

Nineteen

Time passed. Night and day merged into one.

The atmosphere in the hold was sticky and oppressive, the ideal breeding ground for disease. Although the wounds on his back were healing, the damp fetid conditions and the increasingly lurching motion of the ship brought another malady. In the grip of a fierce fever, Mick slept fitfully. He tossed and turned, mumbling and lashing out at imaginary assailants who held ferules and regarded him with gentle, confused faces.

Occasionally, he was aware of someone bathing his forehead and slicking his dry lips with water while a soothing voice told him they must wait for the fever to break.

His skin burned unbearably. Icy shivers made his teeth chatter. In contrast to their first night on board, Mick found himself held in Cat's slender arms, his sweat-drenched hair and forehead stroked by two delicate fingers.

Eventually, his temperature began to drop.

Slowly, Mick's body returned to normal, although he still felt a little removed from reality.

Grunts and sighs drifted into his ears. And words:

'Later, my friend – I need to rest.' Cat's voice was breathy.

'Later be damned! I have waited two days!'

'So another hour or so will not hurt you.' The breathy tones took on an edge of irritation.

'Hurt me? I have been hard for nearly forty-eight hours! My groin throbs when I go to sleep, and aches when I wake up.'

Cat's response was weary. 'Use your hand, my good fellow, and let me take my ease for a few moments. Then –'

'No! I have waited long enough.'

Rustling and the thump of something hitting the floor shimmered up into Mick's curled body.

'No red-blooded man can spend two days watching you couple with dozens of others and not desire you himself! I want my cock inside you, young fellow, and I want it now!' More thumps. Then silence, and a long exhale of breath.

Wrapped in a bundle of rags and lying against the hold's curved side, Mick opened one bleary eye.

A face. A freckled face. Parallel with his.

Through sweat-blurred eyes, he stared at the cutpurse's straining features a mere yard from his own.

Six fingers and two thumbs were spread out on the floor of the hold. A length of heavy rusty chain covered the distance between slim wrists. On his hands and knees, the boy's slender body shuddered while a burly fellow pushed his hard cock into Cat's reluctant rectum.

Mick propped himself up on one elbow. He watched the boy's lips part in parallel to other, grossly stretched lips as his brutish lover pumped more of his thick length into the cutpurse's groaning body.

He listened to the wet intrusion of flesh into flesh.

He inhaled the smell of male lust.

Moving his still-sleepy eyes to the naked boy's groin, Mick smiled at the growing rod of sticky arousal which was slowly sprouting from within a bristling ginger bush.

A grunt from behind the pale form found an echo in the cutpurse. Mick could almost feel the firm hairiness of the prisoner's bollocks as they impacted heavily against the cheeks of Cat's arse. Dragging himself out from the wall, Mick crawled forward for a better view.

The man's cock was buried to its hilt in the boy's hole. Ten grubby fingers gripped Cat's slender haunches, pulling the cutpurse back still more as if he intended to thrust further and split him in two.

Unwrapping himself from his bundle of rags, Mick rubbed his itching beard and peered more closely at the man who was using Cat.

The fellow was bulky – more broadly built than even Jonathon – and the darkness on his fingers was not dirt. His sweating arms were draped in a mass of black hair, which spread down from muscular shoulders over his thick wrists to the backs of his huge hands and on as far as his knuckles. Crouching motionless behind the panting cutpurse, in order to allow the boy to become accustomed to his girth, the hairy bear of a man looked like some vast, ominous predator biding his time before an attack. Then one hairy hand released the cutpurse's waist and slapped the side of the boy's right buttock soundly. 'Tighten up there, lad – I want to feel what I'm fucking! You are looser than an old whore's cunt.'

His well-used rectum crammed with unwanted man-meat, Cat's mouth sloped into a sneer of resentment. 'You want it tight, you make it so.'

Mick grinned through cracked lips. This was going to be interesting. From his brief acquaintance with the young cutpurse, Mick knew Cat to be an enthusiastic lover. He also knew the boy could be slippery and dangerous, when pushed too far.

'Is that a challenge, lad?'

'You tell me: you're the one who needs release.' Cat managed to inject a note of complete disinterest into his voice, although Mick could see the boy's own rod lengthening with every word. 'I've already spent my seed countless times: it is no matter to me whether I am tight or not.'

'You've a stiff neck, boy, and by God your prick will match it by the time I've finished with you!'

Cat simulated a yawn. 'Well, I can sleep in most positions. Wake me up when you've finished, my good fellow.' The cutpurse slumped forward, resting his freckled face on the back of a two-fingered hand and thrusting his arse up towards the Bear.

Mick almost laughed out loud.

The massive prisoner's upper lip curled back in a snarl of resentful lust. Every muscle in the Bear's vast body rippled. 'Let's make this interesting, you cheeky young devil. Whoever spills his seed first gets the other's rations for the next three days. Agreed?'

Bored tones drifted up from below. 'Are you still there? Please lower your voice, sir, I am trying to sleep.'

With a grunt of annoyance, the Bear gripped Cat's haunches more firmly. 'Agreed?'

Cat sighed. 'I look forward to feasting, my friend. Now, goodnight.'

'You are very confident.' The hairy man's face creased with pleasure as he slowly withdrew.

Cat's imitation of a snore was low and almost convincing.

The man turned to Mick, irritation now replacing desire. 'You shall judge this contest. Are you a fair man?'

Still a little dazed, Mick smiled then nodded. 'Fairer than most. It will be my pleasure, sir.'

The Cat and The Bear: one known for his languid agility, sharp claws and mind, the other for sheer brutish strength. But the young cutpurse had already used up most of his nine lives, and the man at present with his thick cock sunk deep into the boy's arse was no fool.

The wager was double-edged: to ensure victory, each had to concentrate on the other's pleasure: something in which neither was particularly interested.

Easing back on to his haunches, Mick settled down to watch the battle.

The Bear continued to withdraw, pulling his prick out of the boy's body until the swollen head was the only thing holding them together. The engorged glans stretched the cutpurse's arse-lips once more, widening the circle of muscle to a paper-thin seven inches' circumference. A moan of frustrated desire escaped the man's mouth.

The rhythm of Cat's snores tripped a little, then got back on course.

Mick couldn't see the cutpurse's freckled face, but the burgeoning girth of the boy's prick was clearly visible between his raised thighs. He shifted his gaze to the Bear's straining face.

Then Mick flinched as the man pistoned roughly forward. The Bear put the weight of his whole body behind the movement, shunting Cat's relaxed form a good four inches along the floor of the deck.

A grunt accompanied the thrust – and a gasp.

No longer snoring, Cat yelped as the head of the mighty cock careered up into him.

The Bear grinned with satisfaction. Withdrawing, he pushed again.

Cat's six fingers scrabbled on rough wood as he tried to get away.

Huge hands slid under the boy's slim waist, settling on his hip bones and hauling him off his hands and down on to the throbbing sword of flesh. 'Not so cocky now, are you, lad?' The deep voice was hoarse with need.

Cat squirmed on the vast prick, wriggling in indignation.

The Bear's laugh was cut short by a moan of pleasure as the boy lunged forward, twisting away from the assault.

Between his pale thighs, Cat's prick was a full seven inches of twitching need. It quivered in mid air, then flexed upwards as the Bear lurched back. The cutpurse's bare feet left the floor and he found himself squatting in the gasping man's lap.

'Struggle all you like, my young friend.' The words were punctuated by rasping breaths. 'The more your writhe and wriggle, the tighter your arse becomes around my cock.'

Cat's scarlet face bore testament to the truth of the words – and a further veracity: the more he tried to escape, the more pleasurable the fucking became for himself.

Free of his fever, another heat now had Mick in its grasp. His member pulsed against the ragged fabric of his breeches. But he was still weak: too weak to even free his length.

One of the Bear's monumental arms easily encircled Cat's skinny chest. The other moved downwards. Four thick fingers and a thumb grasped the boy's flexing shaft. As he raised the flailing cutpurse up the length of his engorged prick, the Bear slowly stroked Cat's member.

The sound from the boy's lips was somewhere between a yowl of aggression and a groan of defeat.

But the battle was far from over.

In the ensuing combat, the boy tried a number of tricks. He collapsed limply in his user's arms, forcing his thin body to go with the motion of the lusty attack.

The strategy merely allowed the Bear greater access to the cutpurse's cock and bollocks. After a few surprisingly skilled caresses, Cat was arching his back and fucking the air in front of him.

He tried to make his body rigid, clenching every muscle over which he still had control and turning himself into a stiff, unwieldy lover.

The grunts of passion from behind his soaking red head were accompanied by a more enthusiastic thrusting, and as the velvety glans impacted again and again with his overstimulated prostate, Cat felt all resistance leave his body.

Mick watched, enthralled. The front of his ragged breeches wet with arousal, he knew what would be going through the wily cutpurse's mind.

Three days' worth of rations.

Three days' worth of warm, dirty water and stale bread.

A prize worth fighting for – to the bitter-sweet end.

Through the wet slap of lusty combat, the Bear's voice was low and controlled. 'As you said, my boy, I have waited two days already. It was good practice, and another short while will not hurt me.'

In sweaty desperation, Cat turned to his more feline skills. Slipping his long arms beneath his thrusting assailant's bulky thighs, deft fingers located the delicate skin of the Bear's spunk-bloated balls. As the man's thick prick impaled him again and again, Cat took a deep breath – and dug in his nails.

The Bear growled, increasing the speed of the fuck.

Rendered almost senseless by the force of the man's thrusts, Cat clenched his teeth – and dug in again. Harder.

The Bear roared.

With a gasp of satisfaction, Cat found himself thrown forward on to the floor.

Releasing the cutpurse's chest and prick, the Bear grabbed the boy's lightly muscled legs instead, pushing them up towards the thin chest and pounding into Cat.

A frown of worry creased Mick's features. The ferocity of the fucking would have forced any ordinary man to shoot his seed long ago. Maybe Cat had passed out.

Maybe the boy was unconscious.

Concern for his young friend made him move closer. He watched Cat's tight ball-sac clench and unclench. The head of the boy's prick was slick with a scum of greasy arousal.

Then, through a veil of damp red hair, one twinkling green eye caught his.

Face pink with exertion, Cat chewed his lip in concentration –

Mick focused, watching as the cutpurse used another of his manifold skills to treat a different ailment.

– then raked sharp nails over his furious lover's bollocks.

With a bellow that shook the bones of every prisoner in the hold and reverberated through the ship's sea-weathered timbers, the Bear shot his load into Cat's quivering arsehole.

Seconds later, the scummy crust of pre-come broke to release the cutpurse's own orgasm.

Mick grinned with relief, watching a shower of milky fluid splatter the floor near his face.

The Bear was still mid-release when Cat dragged himself off the spasming rod and curled into a ball, massaging the rest of his own seed from seven flexing inches.

Mick leapt forward, grabbed the cutpurse and hauled the boy to his feet. 'The winner!'

Cat raised one exhausted fist into the air and leant back against Mick's broad chest. 'Aye, the winner!'

On his knees now, the Bear shot a final load on to the floor, then raised a surly head. 'A draw, I think. The wager is null and void.'

'I think not, fellow.' Mick frowned, holding Cat's shaking form tightly. 'Admit defeat like a man, sir: the boy bested you by at least four seconds. I was appointed judge, and my word is final.'

The Bear staggered upright, one hand massaging his pinched sack. Upright, the man was much taller and, even post-orgasm, looked highly displeased. 'A draw! I would have forced the spunk from his body first, had he not cheated and grabbed my balls.'

'No rules were set, sir, and only one objective. You appointed me yourself.' Mick squared up to the sore loser. Cat twisted free.

'Three days' worth of rations –' he turned, his freckled body slick with sweat '– you all heard him. I won, and I claim my prize.' The cutpurse regarded the gathered crowd of men, seeking support.

Some mumbled in agreement.

A few shouted their support.

Others sided with the Bear, moving around the giant, discontented figure who still nursed his injured balls.

'It's a fix! They're in it together – he cannot judge fairly!'

The accusation made Mick bristle. 'Are you impugning my honesty?'

'I only want what is due to me, sir, what I won fair and square.' The Bear pointed to where Cat stood, scratching at the wet trail of spunk which trickled down the back of one pale thigh. 'His rations for the next four days.'

'Three! By God, it was three: you are a liar as well as a rogue!' Naked and scowling, Cat threw himself on to his lover of minutes ago, seizing the man's thick neck in an armlock.

Then someone grabbed Mick, and before he knew what was happening, the entire hold was a heaving, grunting mass of brawling men.

Still weakened by his fever, he only just managed to throw his attacker.

Another replaced him.

Mick lashed out with feet and fist. He kicked and punched his way through the jostling thong towards where the two naked men were wrestling.

In terms of sheer physical strength, Cat was no match for the burly Bear. The heavier man had the cutpurse on his back, and was delivering blow after vicious blow to the boy's freckled face.

Eyes never leaving his friend, Mick fought onward through the melée, surprised at his own returning energy.

Then he paused, watching in amazement as Cat's slender legs

appeared at the Bear's huge shoulders. Slim, freckled ankles twisted themselves around the man's neck and tightened.

'You want to fight dirty, you dog?' Arching his back, Cat flipped forward.

A crack filled the hold as the top of a red-headed skull impacted with a broad forehead.

The Bear's mouth fell open. His eyes rolled in his head. He gasped silently, toppling backwards as Cat dug his heels into the man's windpipe.

The cutpurse seized the advantage, straddling the man's chest then moving forward until he was sitting on the fellow's shocked face. 'I won the contest – admit it!'

Mick marvelled at the boy's agility. Cat's ankles were still around the Bear's throat. The cutpurse had his opponent in the strangest leg-lock he had ever seen.

'Admit it! The prize is mine!' Tightening his ankles, Cat pushed forward.

The Bear's skull slammed off the floor.

'Admit it, damn you!' The exhortation was accompanied by another thump of bone on wood.

Mick elbowed a tangle of scrapping prisoners out of the way. A frown of worry shimmered down his spine as he stared at the twosome.

Cat's face was wild with fury. He continued to bang the Bear's head against the floor, crushing the man's windpipe with his legs and smothering his captive with his arse and balls.

'Enough!' Mick lunged forward, seizing the boy's skinny shoulders.

Cat ignored him. 'We are not liars! We play fair –'

Another crack.

'– it is ruffians like this fellow who get us all a bad name. Whatever happened to honesty amongst thieves?'

Mick pulled harder.

Impervious to everything around him, Cat continued the assault. 'Let's see how much good your rations will do you, dead! We will share them amongst all of us. That will teach you! That will –'

With a supreme effort, Mick dragged the howling boy from the Bear's face. The legs loosened their grip. In seconds, the man had recovered and was back on his feet, punching furiously at both Mick and Cat.

'What's going on down there?'

Through the rising tide of violence, the boatswain's gruff voice barely registered.

One restraining arm around Cat's waist, Mick struck the Bear with his free fist.

The returning punch knocked him off his feet and loosened several teeth.

Mick grunted his annoyance, and found himself sitting on the vast man's legs while Cat grabbed the Bear's pink ears.

'Hit Mr Savage, would you?'

'Break it up!'

Mick's head reeled. Then he felt the butt of a musket impact with his stomach. Knocked sprawling, he was seized and hauled upright by a stalwart seaman.

Another held a writhing, spitting Cat while a third was dragging a bleeding and bruised Bear to his feet.

'Have you not got enough problems without fighting amongst yourselves?' The boatswain's voice was sharp with annoyance. 'Who started this?'

'He did!' Scores of fingers pointed in a dozen directions.

The Bear's dazed tones resounded through the hold. 'He did!' A vast, hairy forefinger indicated Mick.

'He reneged on a wager!' Cat's indignant voice contradicted the accusation.

The boatswain's narrowed eyes took in all three of them. His gaze flicked between the Bear's battered face, Cat's bleeding mouth and Mick's winded countenance. 'Is someone man enough to tell the truth here?'

Mick sighed and stepped forward: Cat's thin shoulders could never endure the ferocity of a punishment beating. 'It was my fault. I –'

'I threw the first punch, sir –' the cutpurse's voice scythed across Mick's words '– but only under extreme provocation! I despise violence, as a general rule.'

The boatswain regarded Cat's still-curled fists and shook his head. 'All three of you – on deck! The captain can settle this.'

Mick rubbed his belly where the butt of the musket had impacted. This was the last thing he needed. As Cat's wriggling form was pushed towards the stairs leading into daylight, Mick's steps were heavier than any blows he'd received.

Twenty

'Steady as she goes, Mister – hold her tight!'

The sun glinted off the brass buttons of Christopher's uniform. Smiling broadly, he gripped the wheel more firmly and urged the wooden spars back a fraction of an inch. An approving palm patted his shoulder.

'That's it, Midshipman –' Mr Mims removed his hand and stood back '– we'll making a seaman of you yet!'

Christopher beamed. The last three days had passed in a blur of orders and instructions. After that dreadful night in the mess – and perhaps the quantity of rum he had consumed in the ensuing meal – matters had taken an unexpected turn.

The sea remained calm.

He did not feel ill.

On the contrary, three days of shipboard activity brought a rosy tingle to muscle and sinew he didn't know he had. Each night he collapsed, exhausted, into his bunk. But it was not the exhaustion of a mind strained and frustrated by study. The satisfying tiredness which brought sleep as soon as his blond head hit the pillow was borne out of hard, physical labour.

He hadn't coughed in days.

He felt better than he had in years.

Each morning, when he washed and dressed, his uniform was slightly tighter, and Christopher knew he was going to be forced to give it to the captain's cabin boy, to let out.

Expanding his broadening chest, he inhaled deeply. The air was fresh and clean.

Under his increasingly skilled guidance, the *Impregnable*'s sharp bow dipped down and rose upwards, ploughing ever forward through the waters of the Atlantic. Overhead, the great sails billowed. The wind had been good to them, so far.

Christopher chuckled, surprised to find himself even thinking in such naval terms. Land was many miles away. His previous life even more distant.

'Glad to see you do not bear a grudge, Mister!'

Christopher glanced left.

Midshipman Mims had been joined by Samuel Barber, who had been behaving somewhat sheepishly for the last three days.

Christopher laughed. 'The incident is already forgotten, sir!' Here, on the poop deck, guiding this majestic two-master on her course to the West Indies, he was in charge of his own destiny and, indeed, the fate of the entire crew. He could afford to be magnanimous.

Midshipman Barber flicked the brim of Christopher's hat playfully. 'You are a good sport, sir. Perhaps on the return voyage we will take on other midshipmen, and it can be your turn to enjoy a little fun at their green expense.'

Christopher nodded abstractedly. His attention had been taken by some sort of rumpus around the hatch which led down to the hold. As he strained his eyes to see more, the conversation behind him took a different path.

'Where's the Rock?'

'In his cabin, poring over those charts again.'

'When did he order this change of route? Is it not easier to follow the currents?'

'Easier – and safer.' Midshipman Mims' voice took on a cautionary tone. 'This way is rife with pirates. Did that barque not signal yesterday that she had sighted at least two Spanish vessels?'

Still watching the hatch, Christopher's ears pricked up.

Early yesterday the *Binning* had identified herself, off the starboard bow. The First Officer had returned signal, and had received a report of bad weather and unfriendly ships ahead.

He moved his gaze from the hatch and stared up at the bright blue sky. White, fluffy clouds scudded across the face of the smiling sun, blown by the east wind. His eyes lowered, focusing on the froth-topped waves which rippled in all directions as far as he could see.

No indications of storms.

No sign of any other ships.

Midshipman Mims continued. 'He gave me the new route himself, late last night.'

'But why?'

'The Rock is a seasoned sailor, Sam, as well as captain. You know it is not our place to question any of his instructions.'

Midshipman Barber's reply was almost a whisper. 'I hear he has scores to settle with that knave El Niño, and he doesn't care how many lives he endangers to –'

A sudden scuffle around the hold-hatch both cut the man's sentence short and refocused Christopher's attention.

Emerging from the dark pit and shading their eyes from the sunlight, three half-naked figures staggered on deck. Flanked by a barrage of musketed seamen and protesting loudly, the trio were pushed forward by the boatswain.

Christopher goggled, his hands suddenly slippery on the wheel's polished surface.

At their head, he recognised the tall, rangy figure with the matted beard.

Alerted, the deck crew paused in their duties and watched as the guarded men were marched in front of the main mast. Some laughed at the prisoners' naked state. Others grinned and nudged each other.

'Fetch the captain, Midshipman Barber! There is a dispute to be settled here.'

Christopher's palms were sweating freely now. His grip slackened. As Sam darted off, Mr Mims voice was low in his ear: 'Unless you want to witness another act of cruelty, I'd make myself scarce, if I were you.' More skilful hands eased the wheel from his.

Christopher couldn't take his eyes off the three shackled men who now stood below him.

Two were completely naked: the young, red-headed boy who had been involved in the ructions, back on the quayside, and a huge bear of a man with a bruised face who was cradling his groin. Each was hurling insults at the other across the man who stood between them.

Christopher barely registered their nakedness.

Like a moth to a flame, his gaze remained on the rangy Irishman: Savage.

Still dressed in the ragged breeches, but now shirtless, the man stood silently.

Christopher took in the flush of fever on the fellow's cheeks.

Focused straight ahead but seeing nothing, the Irishman's blue eyes burnt unnaturally brightly, where his two unclothed companions squinted in the sunlight. His leanly muscled chest shone with fresh sweat, where the strong breeze had already dried the perspiring bodies of the naked twosome. He held his fettered hands at his sides, the link of chain dropping across his hard, underfed stomach.

Christopher moved away from the wheel and gripped the smooth wooden railing. The memory of their last encounter, when he'd beaten this man's back and shoulders, gave way to another familiarity. Had he seen this tall, handsome Savage somewhere other than in his dreams?

A tightening in the groin of his already too small breeches signalled something Christopher didn't want to think about.

Then the Irishman's eyes met his and he knew what he had to do. Tearing his gaze from fiery irises, Christopher turned, stumbling down the steps –

– and straight into the captain's barrel chest.

Josiah Rock smiled. 'You are keen, lad, but there are some duties which remain mine.' He draped a paternal arm around Christopher's broadening shoulders. 'However, I admire your willingness. Come!' The Rock turned back to the still-grumbling twosome and their silent third party, who was now staring at his feet. 'Together we will sort this out.'

Heart pounding, Christopher edged forward.

'You again!'

Mick raised his eyes from the deck. The cool air made his mind reel. Clenching his fists to keep himself upright, he regarded the cold, grey eyes of Orlando Rock's father but said nothing.

'Found the prisoners brawling down below, Captain. I couldn't bring them all on deck, so –'

'These are the ringleaders, eh?' The Rock took a step towards them.

At his sides, Cat and the Bear stopped arguing. Both shrank back in the face of the captain's menacing words. Mick held his ground.

The boatswain's gruff voice continued. 'So I brought you a sample. No one will admit who caused the fight.'

'I threw the first punch, but he started it.' Cat's voice was low and sullenly accusatory. Two fingers indicated the Bear.

'They were trying to steal my rations, sir.' The huge, naked man's words dripped with mock respect. 'I was only trying to defend myself and –'

'Liar!'

'Cheat!'

Mick turned his head.

Cat's face was a spitting mask of freckled fury, directed towards the Bear. 'You are a poor loser – and, moreover, an unsatisfying fuck! I could have gone hours and not spilt my seed!'

The Bear roared his response. Hair-covered hands reached for the cutpurse's slim throat.

Amidst chuckles and shouts from the assembled crew, armed guards pulled the scrapping pair apart.

'What is your name, you young ruffian?' The captain seized the cutpurse by one pink ear.

'Cat, sir.' The boy swung another punch in the direction of the Bear, who had to be held back by five burly seamen.

'Cat, eh? I will not have brawling in the hold! Mr Barber? Bring me my tools.'

The fresh air was making Mick dizzy. He struggled to stop himself swaying. The conversation swam around him, ebbing into his ears then flowing out on rippling waves.

A stocky midshipman unrolled a familiar length of canvas and spread it out on the deck.

'Have you nine lives, you pugilistic rogue, as my cat has nine tails?' The captain dangled a fearsome-looking whip in front of the boy's freckled face.

The deck fell silent.

The mocking question thrust itself through Mick's swimming mind. He watched Cat's expression sober. He moved his eyes to the means of punishment, noting the tiny knots of leather which tipped the end of each leather thong.

The cat-o'-nine-tails was vicious and maiming. The cutpurse's slender shoulders could never survive a beating with that particular lash.

'Cat got your tongue, boy?' The captain roared with laughter.

The crew remained silent.

Sweat leaked from every pore of Mick's body. He felt as if it were lit from within by some blazing fire. Mick took an uncertain step forward. 'I take responsibility.' His voice was hoarse. He stared at the captain. 'Do not punish the boy. It was my fault.'

Grey eyes darkened to the colour of lead. 'I should have known!'

A hand gripped his bearded chin. Mick frowned, but did not pull away. Despite the personal grudge, Josiah Rock was a businessman and as such was concerned with profit: a hold full of corpses was no good to anyone. Mick said, 'If my fellow prisoners fight over food, it is because the meagre rations we are given are rotten and inedible. Feed us good salt beef and clean water, and I promise you there will be no more trouble.'

The attempt to reason backfired. Josiah Rock's eyes darkened further. Black caverns glowered at Mick. 'Are you trying to tell me how to run my ship?'

The grip on his chin tightened. 'No, sir –' Mick could feel the man's fingers digging into his skin '– I am merely offering a suggestion as to –'

'Save your suggestions for those who need them.' Josiah Rock's voice was all the more terrifying for its quietness. 'I see it is going to take more than a few lashes of the ferule to break you, you scurvy dog. Mr Fitzgibbons?'

The name sent a shiver of dread down Mick's spine.

'Captain?'

The gentle voice hurt Mick more than any lashing ever could. He looked at the midshipman's pale face.

The captain flicked nine thongs of brine-hardened leather against a rough palm. 'Tie the blaggard over the cannon!'

'The fellow is ill, Captain. Do you not see the way his skin is flushed with ague?'

'With insolence, more like, Mr Fitzgibbons! Do as you are ordered!'

'His back has only just healed, Captain. Any further beating could result in ulceration.'

The midshipman's soft words pierced the fog of fever which had descended over Mick's mind like a winding-sheet.

'Then his arse can take it this time! Boatswain? Aid Mr Fitzgibbons.'

The hand released Mick's chin and other equally rough grips tightened around his bare forearms. Dragged to the port side of the ship then pushed forward, a delicious coldness rose up beneath his burning chest.

The cannon was curved and smooth as ice. As his manacled hands were slipped over its firing aperture and tied in place, Mick pressed his face to the cool, iron surface. Then other hands were tearing at the tattered waistband of his breeches, and in seconds his quivering, hairy arse was bared to the assembly.

Mick flinched. The remains of his breeches and undergarments were hauled free. His cock shivered against the cannon's barrel, still half-hard from watching Cat and the Bear race towards climax only fifteen minutes earlier. Heavy with undischarged lust, his swollen bollocks drew themselves tightly against his body, trying to escape the sudden chill and the approaching onslaught. Instinctively, his back arched.

'Hold him, Mr Fitzgibbons! He is a coward as well as a rogue and will try to move away from my cat!'

The captain's words bored into Mick's brain. He felt open, naked and vulnerable. Every eye was on him. He couldn't see the assembled crew, but knew they could see him. A frisson of fear shimmered through his groin. His balls clenched again. He thought about the eyes of the midshipman who had pleaded for him. His half-hard prick twitched. Then firm, smooth hands gripped his upper arms and a whisper drifted into his right ear.

'Try to relax – it might hurt less.'

Mick's prick twitched again, edging its way along the cannon's less-cool barrel. He could feel the young midshipman's breath on his ear, feel the surprising strength with which his arms were held. A great shiver of anticipation shook his body.

Then a sharp, scorching heat flashed across his arse-cheeks. Mick winced, his chest and belly arching up off the cannon.

'I know who you are.'

The cat's tangled thongs fell a second time. Mick flinched away from the lash.

'I know what you've done.'

Mick's strong shoulders shivered under another blow. Raising his head, he caught the eyes of the handsome midshipman. The stinging heat increased, as did the burning ache between his spread legs.

'And, by God, I will make your life the hell you have made mine.'

The fists around his upper arms gripped more tightly. A different voice ebbed into his ears. 'Easy, my friend. It will be over soon.'

Iron manacles dug painfully into his wrists as the cat descended a third time.

And a fourth.

Sweat gathered between his shoulderblades, trickling down past the base of his spine and slicking his buttocks.

The lubricant only served to intensify the heat from the cat's nine vicious knots. The beating continued.

'Relax, relax – do not fight it, my friend.'

The low words were an uncomfortable accompaniment to the biting tongues of leather. Mick tried to clear his mind and do as the young midshipman urged. He tried to anticipate each lash of the thongs.

But Josiah Rock's strokes varied in pace. There was no rhythm to go with. Each time he relaxed, his prick rubbed achingly against the cannon's slick barrel, and every time he braced himself, the cat fell again.

Unexpectedly, one of the hands left his biceps and Mick groaned as something soft and absorbent caressed his shoulders and back.

'What are you doing, Mister?'

'His fever is worse, sir. The more he sweats, the deeper your lashes bite. Do not give him unnecessary suffering, Captain Rock. I – ow!'

'Keep your hands clear, Fitzgibbons! I do not wish to accidentally hit you again.'

Mick moaned. He felt the other man's pain, saw the midshipman's shock in his addled mind's eye. Then the strokes of the cat were coming harder, more furious, and Mick sank below the surface of a sea of pain.

With each flick of the vicious, knotted tails the fingers on his biceps clutched more tightly. Then began to massage.

Mick's arse was a numb expanse of angry weals. Wet with tears or sweat, his vision blurred. His arms and legs hung limply across the cannon. His head lolled, both cheeks burning. Slowly, the agony faded and he was only aware of two things: the firm fingers which caressed his biceps and the throbbing ache between his thighs.

The punishment continued somewhere in the distance. Mick's prick was as hard as the cannon along which it stretched and flexed. His shaft pulsed with need – a need that increased with every breath on his ear.

'Soon, my friend – soon it will be over. I will get the ship's doctor. He will ease your suffering.'

The voice filled his head, pushing each fall of the cat outwards and away. Mick was only aware of his prick and the young man's grip. He inhaled each warm breath the man exhaled, drew it into his own scorching lungs and tasted its sweetness. The lean muscles in his arms filled with blood and pulsed against the midshipman's palms as his swollen shaft pressed against the cannon's slick surface.

Then he was moving – not away from the blows, but into them. With each arc of his back he ploughed his aching prick along the barrel of the cannon, and with each retreat his shaft was dragged back. The thunder of his heart pounded in his ears, deafening him to everything except the midshipman's reassuring words.

'That's it, my friend. Almost over. You are a brave man.'

Mick's balls swelled at the praise, then tightened unexpectedly. As the final, angry blow fell across his arse-cheeks, his heavy sack knitted together and a force greater than anything a weapon could deliver sent a lightning-bolt of release from deep in his body.

He jerked up from the cannon, shackles cutting into his wrists and ropes rasping against his ankles. A gasp escaped his cracked lips and the iron between his thighs spurted molten metal over the cannon's lifeless surface.

'That'll teach you, you savage!'

The hands had left his shoulders and were fumbling somewhere beneath him. Seconds later, Mick shot another volley of milky release. Then the hands were back, slipping under his chest and he was cradled against the stiff fabric of a midshipman's uniform. Mick groaned, panting and shaken by the sheer force of his orgasm.

'Now tie him to the mizzen and let the gulls peck at his wounds!' Josiah Rock's rage-filled words seeped through the glow of post-climax.

'No!'

Then silence. Then: '*What* did you say?'

'Captain, the fellow is sick with fever.'

'Are you questioning another order, Midshipman Fitzgibbons?'

Mick's legs turned to water. He slumped into his saviour's arms, feeling the cool brass buttons against his hot skin.

The response was diplomatic. 'I am asking you to reconsider, Captain. The fellow is not at his strongest. Maybe it would be better to –'

'Tie him to the mizzen, boatswain. And you, Fitzgibbons: in my cabin. Now!'

Spunk drying rapidly on his receding foreskin, Mick moaned as he was torn from Christopher Fitzgibbons's embrace and dragged across the deck. He opened tear-sticky eyes and stared bitterly at the departing outline of a blue midshipman's uniform.

Then ropes were tight around his wrists and ankles and unconsciousness claimed him.

Twenty-One

'That was uncalled for!'

'Who are you to say what is and is not called for, on board my vessel?'

Christopher's fists balled with anger. 'It was unfair and overly cruel, Captain! The fellow is ill – could you not see that? And if you ask me, those other two with him looked more capable of any brawling than he.'

'No one is asking you, Midshipman. I urge you to remember where you are and to whom you are talking.'

'These poor wretches have been dragged from their families and homes, and are already paying dearly for their crimes. Why punish them further?'

'Because they are all beasts. And he is the most bestial of them all.'

Christopher stared at the captain's face, which was still scarlet with exertion. 'What is your quarrel with the Irishman, Captain?'

The Rock fell silent. A flicker of something Christopher couldn't identify twitched a muscle in the man's right cheek.

'Whatever it is, I am sure it cannot merit the treatment I have seen meted out to him at every opportunity.'

'Your remarks have the air of mutiny about them, sir.' The Rock's words were low and almost inaudible.

Christopher ignored them. 'I have visited the hold – conditions are appalling! There is no fresh water. As the Irishman Savage tried to tell you, Captain, most of the fighting is over food.'

'Food be damned, sir!' Josiah Rock's huge fist slammed down on the desk of charts and papers. 'Would you have them hale and hearty, well equipped to take possession of the *Impregnable* and force her to sail wherever they see fit?' The captain turned away.

Christopher flinched as if he, not the desk, had been struck. The gesture reminded him of his father. A glib retort was on his lips before he could prevent it. 'The ship cannot be taken by force, Captain Rock – you said so yourself.'

The giant of a man spun back round. Josiah's craggy face was etched with lines of fury. A frozen hatred frosted his eyes.

His blood up, Christopher met and held the cold stare. He thought of the immovable qualities which gave rise to the captain's nickname. At that precise moment, Josiah Rock seemed more iceberg than mountain: a massive, icy edifice, with the bulk of itself hidden.

There was more to this matter than he – or anyone – knew.

Then the rugged face cracked into a grin, and hearty laughter filled the cabin. 'A fine feat of logic, young Fitzgibbons! You have spirit indeed, to turn my own words around and hang me with them!' Josiah Rock strode around the table and threw an arm over Christopher's startled shoulders. 'You are every inch the scholar your father says.' Rough fingers sorted through the scattered array of charts and navigational aids on the surface of the desk. 'Perhaps you will be so good as to give me your opinion on another matter.'

'I am no cartographer, sir.' Confused by the abrupt change of subject, Christopher gazed down.

'But you know how to use your mind. Look: here is the *Impregnable*.' One stubby finger indicated a small dot on the map. 'And here are the last reported sightings of the *Caliente*.'

Christopher narrowed his eyes, following the projected line which led out from the *Impregnable*'s present position. 'But we are heading straight towards where El Niño's pirate vessel was last reported!'

'Exactly, Midshipman! The best form of defence is attack, eh, sir? That arrogant knave will be counting on us to weave a circuitous course in order to avoid him. The last thing he will expect is for us to seek out him!'

Naval strategy was far from Christopher's strong point, but even he knew a complement of four cannons was far below the usual armoury of a vessel intending battle. 'Are we equipped for such an attack, sir?'

'We will have the element of surprise, lad! El Niño is a coward at heart – all pirates are. They prey on the weak and defenceless. As soon as the *Impregnable* appears on the horizon, he will run. And we will give chase.'

The arm around Christopher's shoulders increased its bone-crushing pressure.

'Unencumbered by weighty cannons, and with the prevailing wind in our larger sails, we will catch and board the *Caliente*.'

Christopher gasped. The captain was squeezing the very breath from his body.

'Then they will pay – they will both pay for what they did to my Orlando.'

With supreme effort, Christopher pulled away. 'What did El Niño –'

A sharp rap on wood interrupted his question.

The door to the cabin opened.

Christopher stared at the wizen, round-shouldered form.

The ship's doctor bowed. 'My apologies, Captain, but I have examined the prisoner you have ordered be tied the yardarm. He is ill – it could be contagious. Unless I treat him, the entire crew may fall ill with disease.'

'Stuff and nonsense, Sawbones! You are as bad as young Fitzgibbons here.' The captain snorted in disgusted, then pounded his great fists against his own barrel chest. 'Fresh sea air: that's the best cure for any fever.'

The doctor shook his sparsely greying head. 'Suspended above the deck, in his weakened state, I doubt he will last the night – especially with the approaching storm.'

As if to emphasise the wizened surgeon's warning, a sudden lurch threw them all to portside.

Christopher's stomach heaved its contents upwards. He fought the retch, scrambling for his sealegs as the ship pitched starboard.

'Haul in the sails! Make fast the rigging! All hands on deck – now!' The captain made his way towards the door, bellowing orders out into the corridor.

Staggering after him, Christopher thanked God the storm had come when it did, saving the rangy Irishman from further pain.

His thanks were premature.

As he stumbled on deck, Christopher's eyes rose heavenward, to the boom seventy feet above his head.

'Get up there, you dogs! Furl those sails before the wind tears them to shreds!'

Armies of seamen were already clambering up ropes and shinning along yardarms.

Christopher barely registered the frenzy of aerial activity. Silhouetted against the now-black sky and suspended from the top jib, a pale body shone like a beacon.

A motionless beacon.

His heart sank. He felt no seasickness. A far greater nausea twisted in his chest.

If only he'd pleaded harder.

If only he'd remained on deck.

If only he had interrupted the beating, a man would not be swinging lifelessly from the *Impregnable*'s great mast.

A sudden urge to howl like an animal flooded his body. Tears sprang to his eyes. The wind blasted his face, sucking the breath from his lungs. Then, as he stared through blurring vision, Christopher gasped.

High above his head, the Irishman's feet moved. And moved again, in an attempt to locate a spar on which to ease his not-yet-dead weight. A glimmer of hope sparkled in Christopher's mind.

'Jump to it, Midshipman! Help lower that anchor!' Josiah Rock's words were carried away by a particularly strong gust.

Another urge sent adrenalin shooting through Christopher's veins. Tearing at his jacket and hurling his hat to the deck, Christopher scanned the busy deck. He spotted what he was looking for, close to the ship's wheel. With one hand, he grabbed the water bottle and tucked it into the waistband of his pantaloons. The other fist curled into a tight ball of determination.

Oblivious to the churn of the sea and the violent motion of the waves, Christopher sprinted to the foot of the tall mast and began to climb.

Shouts of warning accompanied him up the first fifteen feet.

Overhead, a crack of thunder roared in his ears.

The leather boots made ascent more difficult, so he paused, kicking them free and feeling the soles of his bare feet contact with rough wood.

Seamen called to him, motioning caution with their hands as they scrabbled to lower the sails.

Another rumble of thunder was followed by an eye-searing flash.

Christopher barely saw the lightning. He stared straight ahead and climbed on. By the time he passed the lowest jib, the first drops of rain pattered on to his blond head. Canvas flapped to his left, buffeting his progress.

By the time he reached the second boom great sheets of rain soaked his body, plastering his hair to his head. Every muscle in his body throbbed with a desperate energy. The mast to which he clung swayed alarmingly, and he nearly lost his footing. Raising his wet head, he stared up –

– and met the dark eyes of one staring down from twenty feet above.

'Hold on!' he yelled over the sound of the howling gale. 'I'm coming!'

His foot slipped a second time.

Christopher cursed under his breath, dragging his eyes from the face of the dangling man. Then a surprisingly strong voice cut through the wind.

'Don't look down – whatever you do, don't look down!'

Curling a drenched arm around the mast, Christopher glanced instinctively in the direction of his flailing feet.

It was his first mistake.

His eyes widened. What seemed like miles below, the deck swarmed with tiny ant-like people. He gasped in horror: heights terrified him. His father had joked that Christopher got vertigo in the upper storey of a house.

Ploughing on into the very heart of the storm, the *Impregnable* lurched sickly from side to side. Both Christopher's feet slipped. Howling in terror, he clung on desperately and cursed himself for a fool.

Why was he here?

What was this man to him?

If he'd stayed on deck, obeyed the orders he had been given, he could be snug and safe in his cabin by now.

The ship dipped further, then swayed right.

Spray from the waves soaked his bare toes. The muscles in his arms stretched to breaking point. Every shred of strength left his body. Then the voice called again, weaker and barely audible over the storm.

'Go left – grab that rope and go left.'

Christopher clung on tighter than ever and closed his eyes. He couldn't move: neither up nor down was an option. He would stay here until his wrists snapped and a wave swept him away.

As the wind whipped cruelly around him and the ship pitched and heaved, an image of another cruelty thrust itself into his mind.

Steeling himself against the motion of the mast, Christopher swung his body like a pendulum. Gripping the length of thick sisal between

his thighs, he grabbed the rope and hauled himself ever upwards –
because someone needed him.

– because the man suspended above his head was in pain.

– because the prisoner tied to the highest yardarm was ill.

– because someone else suddenly mattered, apart from Christopher
Fitzgibbons and Christopher Fitzgibbons's problems.

As he dragged himself up the last few feet, his mind was filled with
dark, flashing eyes and a lilting, Irish voice. The crotch of his breeches
rubbed against the rough surface of the rope.

Emblazoned on his eyelids he saw the man's whipped buttocks and
felt the pain on his own flesh. He remembered holding the fellow in his
arms, and the strange mixture of emotions which had torn through his
own body.

Groin pressed to course hemp, Christopher shinned up the last foot.

Then a hand grabbed his.

Eyelids shot open. Staring right, he blinked through the rain at a
soaking, half-smiling face.

'Now that you've arrived, we must ensure you stay.' Shouting
hoarsely over the din of the storm, the tangled head nodded upwards to
where ropes writhed like snakes. 'Secure one of those loose lengths
around your waist.'

Panting, and hardly able to believe he was still here at all, Christopher
did as he was bid. Quickly, he untied the Irishman's wrists and hauled
him up on to the great wooden beam. Only when they were both
sitting, tightly looped to each other and the main mast, did he remember
the purpose of his climb.

Christopher's hand shook as he eased his fingers into the waistband
of his pantaloons. 'I thought you might need –' As he pulled the water
bottle free, a sudden lurch wrenched it from his grip. A low laugh
drifted into his ears. Christopher sighed, watching the bottle plummet
deckwards.

'Thank you, anyway –'

Rain continued to pelt their shivering bodies.

'– but I have all the water I can handle, Mr Fitzgibbons.'

Wet fingers ruffled his hair, increasing his surprise that the man knew
his name.

'It may still do some good, however. We can always hope it lands on
Josiah Rock's head.'

Christopher frowned to where a bearded face was directed towards
the deck. Then a strong arm encircled his waist and the hairy counten-

ance grinned. Suddenly, laughing, Christopher slid an arm behind the rangy Irishman's back and pulled the man closer. A tangled head rested against his.

'So what do we do now, Midshipman?'

Christopher's trembling body swelled with pride. No one had ever asked for his opinion before. He knew they should probably begin to climb down, before the storm reached its height, but the man's arms must be tired, and his own body ached in a way which had less to do with the climb up and more to do with the presence of this fellow and the closeness of his naked body. Fingers stroking the man's hard, wet skin, he shouted through increasingly violent thunder rumbles: 'We wait until the rain stops, of course!'

A rich laugh greeted his reply. 'Aye, aye, sir! But do you mind if we change position?'

Christopher met suddenly uncertain eyes.

'My arse feels like it is being eaten alive by vipers!'

'Oh –' Suddenly concerned, Christopher slackened his grip. 'What is more comfortable for you?'

'I would stand, but my legs are not up it it.' The Irishman smiled ruefully. 'In truth, my belly is the only part of me which does not hurt.'

Christopher frowned. The logistics seemed beyond him at first. Then he moved a little away and patted his wet knees. 'Lie across me: I will hold you, you will not roll off.'

The smile wavered. 'Rolling off is the least of my concerns, sir.'

'Christopher, please.' He thought about extending a hand, but needed both to stay on the jib. He also knew that whatever was between himself and this rangy bearded fellow had passed the stage of formal introductions days ago.

'Michael – Michael Savage. Mick, to my friends.'

Christopher gently took the man's shoulders, easing him down and across his lap. 'I hope you will count me amongst your friends, Mick Savage.'

'More than you will ever know.' Mick went with the motion. His words caught and held captive by the wind, he felt the twitch of arousal as he flattened his naked body across his rescuer's thighs.

They sat there, one staring out into the black depths of the storm with a new sense of purpose, the other filled with a longing he'd never before experienced.

★

Eventually, the storm blew itself out. Anchored, the *Impregnable* swayed rhythmically, her sails still lowered. In the rigging, rope whacked wetly against wood. Dawn's first rays warmed the skin on Mick's back. With a soft groan, he awoke to find a touch other than that of the sun on his naked, aching body. He raised his head from a damp thigh.

'Sorry, did I hurt you?' The hands stopped.

'No – please continue. It is very soothing.' Mick smiled dreamily, turning his head to watch the great globe of orange rise above the eastern horizon.

For as long as Mick could remember, the dawn merely heralded another day of his struggle to survive; of dodging bailiffs and conning rich ladies and gentlemen. Even now, each rise of the sun brought new trials and onslaughts –

Soft fingers recommenced stroking his shoulders, moving up into his matted locks.

– but for once, Mick was glad to be alive. The fingers paused in his hair.

'Can I ask you a question?'

Mick moaned softly. 'Anything.'

'Why does the captain hate you so?'

Mick sighed, feeling the old tension return to his body. 'He blames me for something I did not do.'

The fingers massaged his scalp, untangling his rat's tails. 'You had his son's medal in your possession, I know that.'

Shifting position, Mick turned over on to his back. 'Orlando and I were –' he searched for an appropriate term '– friends. He gave me the medal of his own free will, as a keepsake.' Staring up into the normally pale face, Mick noticed the sallow cheeks were flushed. He examined Christopher's eyes for any sign of disbelief – and found none. Sparkling blue irises bored into his.

'The captain's son was meant to sail with us, this voyage: I know he loves his son very much, but that love sours into hate at what has become of Orlando, so I hear.'

Mick groaned as gentle fingers brushed a lock of hair from his face.

'I met him once, I think.' Christopher was staring out to sea again.

Sprawled in the man's lap, Mick was just as glad. The attentions were having a very obvious effect on his rangy body.

'At the Admiralty Club – my father took me there, months ago.'

216

The words stirred something other than Mick's cock, which was pushing its sturdy way up the inside of his thigh. He tried to change the subject. 'Can I ask what a refined gentleman such as yourself is doing on board a hulk like the *Impregnable*?'

Christopher chuckled, returning his gaze to Mick's face. 'Blame – or thank – my father.' The chuckle died. Mick watched the handsome face sour with something approaching resentment. 'Or rather, blame the man who seduced my fiancée! If I ever get my hands on him, I will not be responsible for my actions!'

Unwanted memory returned with a vengeance.

A ball: to celebrate someone's betrothal.

A fine house: Lady Something-or-other's batting eyelids and soft thighs.

And the wan, self-conscious smile of a slip of a boy, whose hand he had almost crushed.

Christopher Fitzgibbons, heir to Fitzgibbons Manor and cuckolded husband-to-be, lowered his face and softly kissed Mick's creased forehead. 'But none of that matters now.'

Mick flinched. With a mind of its own, his throbbing cock continued to inch up over his left hipbone.

Christopher sighed happily. 'I have found everything for which I have been searching, in the most unexpected of places.'

Mick felt himself blush at the double-edged compliment.

'Tell me you feel the same, Mick.' The tone was suddenly uncertain.

His prick answered for him, thrusting upwards on to his hairy stomach and jutting out in the direction of Christopher's voice while every other muscle in Mick's body told him to throw himself into the Atlantic. He laughed self-consciously, then flinched again as Christopher lowered his blond head and planted another kiss on the velvety glans.

'I want you –' the words hoarsened '– I desire you in a way I have never desired another man.'

Mick's heart pounded. He reciprocated everything his beautiful saviour felt. Somewhere at the back of his mind, a tiny voice urged him to come clean and identify himself. Another, louder voice reminded him he would lose the only man who had ever shown him any humanity if he did so. He stared up into the drying fabric of Christopher's shirt as his lover's lips worked their way over the head of his prick and down the shaft.

He needed to ask for, and be granted, forgiveness.

Mick's cock throbbed unbearably. The words would not form: he had never asked anything of any man before.

He had taken, because taking meant you were never refused. Silently, in his mind, Mick's heart spoke for him: *Fuck me, sir – fuck me here and now.*

The lips paused. 'We should go below.'

Mick felt the reluctance vibrate deep into his bollocks. He knew it was true – and he knew his own thoughts were madness: they would both fall to their depths. But if he had to die, he wanted to die here and now, with Christopher's rod rammed up his arse. *I am yours – I have been yours from the second you brought the ferule down on my back.*

A soft hand cupped his balls, hefting their weight and need. Gasping, Mick followed the line of Christopher's chest to the ample bulge in the front of the younger man's still-damp breeches.

'Fear not, my beloved. I will plead your case all the more fervently to the captain. You have not been branded so – if the worst comes to the worst – I will buy you from him.'

The idea sent a further shiver of bitter-sweet longing through Mick's sack. His arsehole spasmed unexpectedly, his body pleading to be taken – to be filled and used in whatever way this young man pleased.

Lady Violet-whatever had been a worthless, faithless flibbertigibbet.

The idea of this fine gentleman married to such a fickle chit made Mick almost glad he had dipped his wick in her quim and left his seed there.

Through the haze of arousal, his own thoughts resounded back on him.

He was the worthless chit.

He was lower than the rags with which Christopher wiped his arse.

'Then we will be together for ever, perhaps even with the captain's blessing.'

Hot lips kissed his burgeoning ball-sac. Then his mouth. Panic shot through his body. But before he could protest, a tiny droplet of desire seeped from his slit and he found himself eased to his feet.

As he stood there, naked and trembling, his brine-encrusted skin glowed with shame. Held tightly in strong arms, Mick could not share his young friend's optimism.

Even if Christopher was at present unaware of the facts, Mick knew any further pleading of his case, with Josiah Rock, would merely serve to prompt the midshipman's memory.

Then a shout from below pulled him from his musings.

'Stowaway! Stowaway!'

Staring down at the deck, Mick shaded his eyes and peered at the growing crowd of seamen.

Then he was gripping the mast, climbing down behind Christopher towards the deck and hoping whatever was going on would distract the captain from the fact that the object of his revenge was not dead.

Twenty-Two

As Christopher's feet neared the deck, the fresh tang smell of salt water which was drying on his clothes and skin gave way to a heavier, more familiar odour.

'Strip him! Tar his bollocks and throw him into the sea!' The shouts grew in volume, accompanied by lurching cries and whoops of revelry.

Christopher slid down the last few yards of the mast to the smell of rum and the noise of drunken laughter. He scanned the deck, noting three open and empty kegs.

Beyond, the boatswain was dancing an inebriated, half-naked hornpipe around the mizzen mast with midshipmen Mims and Barber. Many of the crew were already slumped in rum-soaked slumber. Some had unfastened their breeches and were holding their members, measuring them against the pricks of other laughing seamen. The rest had formed a jeering circle around something – or someone – Christopher couldn't see.

Captain Josiah Rock was nowhere in sight.

Jumping up on the poop deck, Christopher stared at the compass. The storm had blown the *Impregnable* far off course, despite the anchor having been dropped.

Matters were out of control: someone had to take charge.

Christopher frowned. He ran back to where the Irishman still stood, looking bemused and apprehensive. Wrenching his arms free of his shirt, Christopher draped it around Mick's naked shoulders and nodded towards the unguarded hatch. 'Go below: it is the safest place for you, at the moment.'

The thickly bearded face creased with further confusion.

Behind them, the jeering circle became more antagonistic. Christopher gripped an arm and gave the fellow a shove. 'Go now! I will come for you later.' Turning away before his resolve collapsed and he kissed the fellow again, Christopher strode forward, pushing drunken men out of his path. 'What's going on here? Who ordered the mainbrace to be spliced? Where's this stowaway?'

'There are few rations left, Mr Midshipman!'

'And now another mouth to feed.'

'Enough of this rabble!' Christopher reached the middle of the circle –

– and could not believe what he saw.

Cowering in front of a heap of jute, a pair of anguished eyes met his. Then Willicombe lowered his boyishly handsome face and threw himself at Christopher's feet.

'Oh, sir – you are safe! Thank God!'

Christopher goggled. 'How – ?'

'I could not let you endure this alone. After your father dismissed me from Fitzgibbons Manor, I asked around at Deptford and found out which ship you were on.' The words brushed Christopher's bare toes. 'I have been hiding under that tarpaulin for two weeks, waiting for the chance to see you.'

Around them, the jeering and bustle fell silent.

Christopher fell to a crouch, slipping his hands under Willicombe's hunger-thin arms and easing the underfootman upright.

The man's cheeks were hollow, but he smiled. 'Everything will be all right now, sir – I can look after you. I can –'

'What's going on here? Why is the poop deck unmanned?' Josiah Rock's craggy form pushed its way into the spectacle.

Christopher jumped to attention and saluted. 'Stowaway, sir! But I know the fellow: he means no harm. I suggest we give him a good meal and –'

'Meal be damned! Throw the blaggard into the hold! There is a vessel off the starboard bow. Haul anchor immediately!'

Christopher lowered his hand. 'But there is no wind, sir.'

The Rock's face was stone. 'Then we will row for a wind, Mister! Boatswain? Lower the boats and get the men into them. If that vessel is the *Caliente*, we must give chase.'

Midshipman Mims' voice protested feebly. 'Sir, the crew are too drunk to be of any use.'

'Then keelhaul every last man of them, Mister, and get into boats and row yourself if you have to!'

Christopher stared at Josiah Rock.

The man's eyes glittered with an unnatural light. Every muscle in his rugged body was rigid with anticipation. His great, iron-grey head turned slowly. 'You'll do it, won't you, Fitzgibbons? You'll lead the rowing crew.'

Christopher blinked.

The captain's eyes glowed like icy coals. 'I know I can count on you, sir. A fellow who spent all night up a mast is my kind of sailor – you are a credit to your father.'

A vast hand clamped itself on to Christopher's bare shoulder. Suddenly, the reality of what he'd actually done the previous evening roared into his body. Every shred of strength left his legs and he collapsed on top of Willicombe.

He swam naked through a great darkness towards a pair of darker eyes. Between his aching thighs, his cock pulsed with need. Then the Irishman's face was replaced by Willicombe's sunburnt arms and the smell of hay and horses was strong in his nostrils.

Christopher moaned, tossing and turning. Sweat poured from his body. He could feel the soft bushiness of Mick's beard as the Irishman's mouth roved over his chest, pausing to suck at his swollen nipples. He reached out, snatching at air and wanting to feel the man's hard, rangy form twist beneath his.

The heat in his groin was unbearable. His bollocks tightened. He thrust with his hips, pushing his groin against solid mounds of flesh. Moaning, Christopher's fingers fumbled for the opening to the man's body. He wanted to feel the clench of man-muscle around his knuckles. He wanted to hear his lover gasp with pleasure as he stroked the spasming pucker. His mouth opened in a wordless plea, longing to suck Mick's tongue between his lips and taste the man as he guided his own swollen and flexing cock into another orifice. He could almost feel the pressure around his glans, savour the man's tightness and hear Mick groan into his mouth.

His body twisted with frustration.

Hands snatched the air again –

– and made contact. Fingers curling into fists, the vision changed and Mick was tied to the mast, his naked, weal-striped arse pushing out towards the strokes of the ferule.

Gasping, Christopher raised the rod and lunged forward. His eyelids sprang open.

A worried gaze met his. Then a pair of small, surprisingly strong hands seized his naked shoulders and eased him back down on to the bed. 'You are dreaming, sir. It is the fever.'

Christopher blinked as the swarthy-faced boy wiped sweat from his eyes with a rag. He tore the cloth away. 'Where am I? What – ?'

'Rest, sir: you have been ill.'

Straining up off the bed, Christopher recognised the interior of his quarters. He sank back down, exhausted, on to the bunk.

'That's it, sir – try to rest.' The cabin boy dipped the rag into a bucket of brine, squeezed out the excess and continued to bathe him.

Christopher closed his eyes, searching for the dream in which Willicombe, somehow on board the *Impregnable*, was rolling naked with him and Mick. As he lay there, distant sounds of singing drifted into his ears through the porthole. 'What's happening?'

Gentle hands moved the cool cloth on to his neck. 'They are singing for a wind, sir: three days and nights they have been at it, but still no wind comes.'

Memory returned through the dregs of dreams. 'The *Caliente*?'

'Captain Rock thinks so, sir, although there is no way of telling for sure.' The cabin boy eased the damp sheet from Christopher's chest and began to wash lower. 'I don't think he cares, to be truthful. He is like a man possessed.'

Christopher sighed.

'If it is the *Caliente*, El Niño will be waiting for him – playing with him, no doubt. That pirate likes a game.'

Christopher opened his eyes as the cool cloth brushed his stomach. 'How do you know so much?'

The cabin boy smiled. 'I listen, sir.'

Curiosity roused him further. 'Who is this El Niño?'

'They call him the Boy, sir, because of his slight stature and hairless face. But a man's blood pounds through his twisted veins – a nobleman's blood, at that. They wrongly name him Spanish, but he is half-Moorish, born on the teeming streets of Cadiz. His mother was Gipsy, his father the great warrior and chieftain Ben Amin from the coast of the Dark Continent.'

Christopher stared at the crown of the cabin boy's head. Skilful hands eased the sheet down over his thighs, then rinsed the washing cloth once more.

223

'King Philip beheaded Ben Amin in front of El Niño's very eyes. English sailors ravished then killed his mother. That pirate has scores of his own to settle with both Spain and England, I think.'

The cabin boy eased Christopher's burning thighs apart and began to bathe the insides.

A shiver shook his hot body. 'What is your name?'

'James, sir.' The cabin boy slipped one hand beneath Christopher's heavy bollocks and raised the sack from the bed.

Christopher groaned. 'Tell me more, James.' He closed his eyes and let sensation fill his body.

'It is said El Niño could sail before he could walk. From the age of two, his only companions were nomadic fishermen and hawks.' The wash cloth gently rubbed at the puckered, hairy skin.

Christopher felt a spasming deep in his body. 'Hawks?'

'Yes, sir. El Niño has a strange affinity with the kestrels and other hunting birds which nest in the tall cypress trees of his birthland. They watch their prey from a distance, carefully planning their attack. And when they swoop, it is quick and merciless.'

Another shiver – half-fear, half-longing – flexed Christopher's prick up from his smooth belly.

'Skilled in the art of falconry, he never travels without at least one hawk. It is said a sailor will never starve, as long as he has a bird on his wrist, to fish for him.' The gentle hand hefted his aching balls again and the cooling rag moved to the root of his engorged prick.

'More – oh, please, more!' Christopher's back arched up off the bunk.

'People say he plunders ships only to throw their rich cargoes into the sea, and make his captives watch as he does so. He is a strange, wild fellow: legend tells that he has not set foot on land for over two decades. His home is the rough surface of the Atlantic, his purpose patrolling its stormy waters year after year. Spanish vessels, French or English, he cares not what flag his conquests sail under.' James' voice took on a darker tone. 'And what he does with his human booty does not bear thinking about.'

The cloth was now wrapped around his straining shaft. Christopher could feel the cabin boy's slim fingers. Biting back a vision of Mick's rugged face, he recalled Orlando Rock's pale, haggard countenance, when they had met briefly, back at the Admiralty Club. 'But he spares their lives, does he not?'

James' fist tightened, then moved upwards.

Christopher gasped.

'What worth a man's life, when his very soul has been taken?' The cabin boy's voice trembled with dread.

'Soul?' Christopher bucked his hips, ramming his aching length between rag-covered fingers.

'Not a mark on them – physically. El Niño has his fun, then sets his captives adrift in boats. But those who return to tell of his hospitality are broken seamen: scarred inside, where no man can see – or should wish to see!' The hand paused.

Whether due to the boy's words, his soothing ministrations or the pressure of his fist, the fever had left Christopher. In its place was a fiery, urgent need for action. Energy pulsed through his body, gathered from every corner of his being and focused in the burgeoning weightiness at the root of his swollen cock. Lunging up off the bed, he covered James' fingers with his, just as they made to move away. There was one piece of information he had to have. 'I know why the captain hates El Niño, but why does he hate the Irishman Savage? Such intensity of passion does not come from the mere theft of a medallion.'

The boy's eyes were wide with fear.

Christopher's grip tightened around James' hand and, by proxy, his own flexing shaft. 'Tell me – you seem to know everything!' His request was hoarse with two needs.

The cabin boy flinched. 'The captain mumbles in his sleep. He rants about how the Irishman robbed his son, then exacted further retribution.'

Christopher guided the boy's hand down his prick, to where his bollocks clenched with tension. 'What did he do – what did the Irishman do?'

'He –' James gasped as Christopher dragged the washrag and the fingers back up to the vast purple glans. 'He – please do not, sir! I was sent to care for you, not to be the object of your lusts.'

'Lusts be damned!' The words flew from his mouth. Half-appalled at his own actions, Christopher was beyond the point of no return. 'Tell me before I spurt my seed over your eavesdropping, swarthy face!' He fucked the cabin boy's fist furiously, feeling heat build deep inside his body.

'He ravished the captain's son with his foot! Then the Irishman pissed his water on to Orlando Rock's noble head! Leave me alone, sir: please do not –'

As the cabin boy tried to pull away, Christopher's hips pistoned forward and he shot into a grip of fingers and washrag. At the exact moment of his release, his mind was filled with contradictory images.

Mick sprawling, erect and moaning across his lap.

The sound of the man's gasps of pain as the ferule cut deeply into his shoulders.

The feel of his own rod, hot and pulsing, as he had delivered the beating.

Then a crystal clarity replaced the jumble of thoughts. Still spurting, he pushed a startled James aside and leapt from the bed.

Whatever Mick had done in the past, he was a different man now – they both were. And despite his vow of vengeance against his son's humiliator, Josiah Rock was at present dealing with another matter.

An opportunity presented itself.

Grabbing his clothes, and with spunk still dripping from his slowly softening cock, Christopher hauled on his uniform then sprinted from the cabin.

Twenty-Three

He barely registered his now shackle-free wrists as Cat vigorously massaged his arms and shoulders.

'We thought you to be dead, for sure.'

Mick smiled wryly. 'I would have been, if it was not for that midshipman.' He lowered his eyes to the floor of the hold where Christopher's shirt, and the bailing-hook which still snuggled within its folds, lay unnoticed. It had taken all his resolve not to use the sharp marlinspike then and there, when the crew was too drunk to protest.

But this had to be planned – and it had to be planned properly.

Cat's six fingers paused. 'What took place, on that yardarm?'

The voice was low in Mick's ears.

'You have been a different man, since you returned. Tell me what happened.'

Mick turned. 'I'm not sure, my friend.' He stared into curious, feline eyes, noticing the strain on the urchin's freckled face. The young cutpurse had evidently spent last night the way he passed most – sucking on some fellow's manhood – and, despite his offer to soothe Mick's aching muscles, Cat's duties were obviously taking their toll. Briefly, he outlined the gist of his time with Christopher.

'You have a strange look about you, Mr Savage.' Cat grinned. 'If I didn't know better, I'd say you were in love.'

Mick chuckled. The fresh air of deck and the words of the young midshipman were swept away by the dank, stuffy air of the hold. 'Love is for fools: only gentlemen and dreamers have time for love!' His chuckle rang a little hollow. 'Anyway, do not forget this same

227

midshipman beat the living Jesus out of my shoulders and looked like he enjoyed it. What kind of love is that?'

Cat raised a sceptical eyebrow to Mick's scorn. 'Love has many faces, my friend.'

Mick rubbed his thick beard. His skin itched beneath the soft hair.

The cutpurse talked on. 'And any of those faces can smile upon the best – and the worst – of us, when we least expect it.'

The philosophical note in Cat's voice was tinged with regret. Mick cocked his head in surprise. 'There is someone in your life?' He'd had the youth pegged as a free spirit and loner, like himself.

Cat's feline eyes glinted in the darkness. 'Was: I have not seen him for years.' The cutpurse leant against the hold's curved wall. 'We were boys together, back in Bristol. It was a naïve, childish love.' The freckled face looked up into the darkness. 'But I still think of him from time to time.'

Hearing the longing in his friend's voice, Mick felt a pang of sympathy for this wild rascal, alone on the streets since the age of twelve. Although far from passionate, his own feelings for Cat were a mixture of admiration, lust and friendship: they had been through a lot together, and he genuinely liked the wily cutpurse. Gently, he slipped a hand beneath Cat's downy chin and turned the impish face to his. 'To have loved and lost is better than to have never known love at all.'

Cat smiled ruefully. 'Talking like a poet?' He playfully ruffled Mick's tangled hair. 'You are truly smitten, Mr Savage. And an officer, too!' The cutpurse rested his red head against Mick's shoulder. 'Take a chance: love is too rare a jewel to let slip through your fingers, as I did.'

Mick draped an arm around the sleepy urchin.

There were other times.

And other places.

His manacled hands now free, and with the bailing-hook in his possession, vague plans took on a more solid purpose and shape.

But they needed opportunity; and, in his weakened state, help. He smoothed Cat's red hair back from his freckled forehead. 'If your love were here, what would you do?'

The cutpurse's reply was solid, despite the exhaustion in his voice. 'Tommy never knew how I felt about him – even when I discovered he was moving away to begin service at a London ostler's, I never told him. Were he here, now, I would remedy that.'

Mick smiled. Even here, in the bowels of this stinking, devilish vessel, there was hope. Cat's snores drifting into his ears, he eased the cutpurse

228

on to the floor, and grabbed Christopher's shirt. Mick pressed his face into the fabric, inhaling the smell of the man's body. The outline of the bailing-hook shattered the moment. He lowered the sweat-soaked garment.

At the far end of the hold, prisoners were talking in low, angry voices. Since the boats had been lowered, no rations had been thrown through the hatch. Soon, they would be tempted to drink the brine which leaked from between the tarred planks of the ship's hull.

That way lay certain madness and death.

But how much could a hold full of manacled men do against guns and muskets, even with the marlinspike?

Girding himself with Cat's salutary words, Mick made his way through semi-conscious prisoners to the group who still had the strength for discontent. As he neared, exchanges were audible:

'I heard the crew talking, before they lowered the boats: that evil bastard Rock has some vendetta on his mind that will be the ruin of us all.'

'But what can we do?' Chains rattled. 'The hatch is soundly battened down: four of us heaved against it, and it did not give!'

'We will all perish. If we do not starve, a watery grave awaits us. Hey, you! What do you know of the Rock's intentions?'

As Mick pushed his way through the group of men, his gaze fell on the curly-haired stowaway who had been thrown into the hold after him.

The lad cowered in a corner, petrified with fear. 'Nothing! I can tell you nothing!'

One of the heavier men got to his feet. 'Then we will find another use for that mouth, eh, lads? If I am to join Davy Jones in his locker, I want a pair of firm lips around my prick when I do so!'

Lust raised their spirits and gave them strength. Other men joined the heavy fellow, slowly making their manacled way towards the cringing stowaway.

Mick sighed. There would be no reasoning with them until that lust had been slaked. He too moved forward, trying to catch the lad's eye. 'What's your name, fellow?'

'Willicombe, sir.' The reply trembled.

A West Country accent greeted Mick's ears. 'Don't try to fight it, Willicombe. Ever had a man's prick up your arse?'

The curly head shook slowly. 'Almost, but his father came in.' The sunburnt face blanched.

One of the prisoners grabbed the stowaway's legs and began to tear at his breeches.

Mick smiled reassuringly. 'This time, there will be no interruptions.' He joined in the frantic stripping process, leaving the fellow his shirt and jacket.

Seconds later, the stowaway stood there, naked from the waist down.

Mick eyed the lad's sturdy cock which, despite Willicombe's apprehension, was steadily swelling. Inexperienced and scared, this lad was no Cat. But if he was to take each of the six fellows who had already formed an impatient queue, he would need to learn fast. Gripping Willicombe's broad shoulders, Mick sank to a crouch and flipped him into a supine position.

The lad shrieked as his spine hit the floor.

Mick seized hairy thighs, wrenching them apart. He lowered his mouth to Willicombe's ear. 'Do as I tell you and you will be fine.' His own arse hit the floor, and he slipped his unfettered hands under those hairy thighs, widening them further. Mick leant forward, catching one of Willicombe's legs with each shoulder and raising them over the lad's chest and head. He stared down through the V of flesh into terrified eyes. 'Relax, my friend. Your body will take over if you only let it.'

Semi-inverted, Willicombe's prick was stretching downwards over his well-muscled stomach in the direction of parted, gasping lips.

'Hold him open, fellow!' The demand came from the head of the queue. 'He is a tight one.'

Mick's gaze darted from Willicombe's panicky face and focused on the man's thick, throbbing length gripped tightly in his fist. Mick's heart fell.

This was too much for a virgin to bear. But the slow leak of fluid from the man's slim slit told him there would be no time for gentle introductions.

Moving his hands from their grip around the stowaway's ankles, Mick thrust his palms under two fuzzy mounds of muscle and hauled Willicombe's arse-cheeks apart.

The lad's hole gaped.

A whoop of anticipation from the queue was followed by bawdy laughter and the firm strokes of fist on waiting shaft.

Then the fellow spat into his rough palm, gave his prick a cursory coating of saliva and fell to his knees.

'Easy – easy, my friend.' Head lowered, Mick watched Willicombe's face crease with pain. He heard the grunts of the stowaway's unbidden lover turn to moans of pleasure, then curses of frustration as the lad's sphincter quivered under the onslaught but refused to give.

'Wider, Savage! Open him wider – he's tighter than a drum!'

Willicombe's curly hair was damp against Mick's stomach. Still murmuring low words of reassurance, he dug in his fingers more firmly and pressed.

Involuntarily, the rigid pucker spasmed. Muscle parted and Mick felt the thrust as the prisoner rammed himself deep into the stowaway's body.

Willicombe arched like a bow. A deep cry of discomfort filled Mick's ears. The lad's legs tensed on his shoulders.

The prisoner moaned, withdrew then thrust again.

Willicombe's cry was lower, this time.

Mick stared at an red, agony-creased face. 'Keep your mind occupied. Let your body respond and the pain will turn to pleasure.' He tried to smile, though he knew the energy and force with which the thick-set man was now fucking the lad's hole was rough and brutal. 'Imagine he is that fellow, whose father interrupted your love-making.'

Willicombe's mouth opened in parallel to his arsehole.

Mick braced himself, pushed back against the wall of the hold by the force of the attack. He moved his hands to the inside of the stowaway's thighs and began to stroke. 'He was a fine fellow, I am sure.'

Willicombe's eyes rolled in his head. Sunburnt arms flailed for grip, then found purchase under Mick's.

The heavy prisoner was thrusting in short jabs now. Mick could smell him, almost taste the man's lust for the curly-haired stowaway. He could feel Willicombe's hands slipping up and over his shoulders, clinging on for dear life.

This was taking too long – and there was a multitude still to take their turn.

Mick moved one of his own hands from the youth's arse-cheek, under his right thigh, and stroked the prisoner's burgeoning ball-sac.

The fellow's body became rigid. With a silent, open-mouthed howl he shot into the stowaway, shuddering and shaking.

Before he could unload his seed a second time, the man between Willicombe's legs was hauled away and another, leaner fellow had taken his place.

Willicombe's rectum was slick with spunk. Now greased, the second penetration was less painful. As the first man staggered to get his breath back, the wiry fellow began to pleasure himself.

Mick watched the stowaway's cock flex against his sunburnt belly. His own shaft was dragging itself along the nobbles of the lad's spine.

This lover had a different style. He fucked slowly, almost teasing himself. Each time his bollocks impacted with the white cheeks of Willicombe's arse, the wiry fellow twisted his hips.

The stowaway roared. A dribble of need oozed from his slit, slicking the velvety head of his now fully hard cock.

The corkscrew attack continued. Around them, men were once more stroking themselves, watching and waiting with mounting impatience. The crowd was noisy in its arousal, and soon other prisoners were awakened from sleep and had joined the throng.

Mick held the stowaway tightly, for the lad was now writhing with pleasure. Each time the lean man twisted his hips and jabbed deep inside the stowaway's arse, Willicombe gave a low grunt of lust.

Somewhere to his right, a prisoner brought himself to orgasm and a shower of warm spunk hit Mick's face.

Minutes later, Corkscrew came quickly and efficiently, leaving a trail of man-slime which seeped slowly from Willicombe's rectum and dripped on to Mick's sweating groin.

He barely registered the next three men.

The stowaway had now released Mick's shoulders and was lunging up to meet his new lovers, embracing one after another with growing passion.

Realising he was no longer required, Mick disentangled himself from Willicombe and moved back, amazed at the lad's powers of postponement. Already over-aroused from watching, the stowaway's succession of six partners came quickly and soon the patch of floor where he lay was thick with congealing man-seed. Mick grinned, stroking his own prick: this lad and Cat would make a good pair.

'What's happening?'

Mick rolled his eyes. Talk of the devil! The cutpurse had evidently come over to investigate the competition. Then the sleepy voice at his shoulder took on a startled tone: 'Tommy?'

Before he could turn round, a sharp elbow had nudged Mick out of the way and Cat was holding the half-naked, spunk-slicked Willicombe.

'Jeremiah?'

While lover Number Eleven continued to pound between the

stowaway's thighs, a pair of green eyes and a set of darker irises gazed into one another.

Just as Willicombe's final partner grunted his release, Cat lowered his head, veiling the other youth's face in a mass of red hair.

The touch of the cutpurse's lips pushed Willicombe over the edge. Roaring, he spurted into mid air, showering his own shirt and most of Cat's freckled cheeks with milky warmth.

Mick chuckled. His young, red-haired friend had been right: love could grow in the most unexpected of places – and boyhood friends could be united in the same way. Then he remembered the bailing-hook and his own plans. Lifting Christopher's shirt from the floor, he unsheathed the sharp spike and draped the garment around the embracing boys then made his way towards a now far more amenable group of prisoners.

'It is not merely for my own sake: you know the Rock will take us all to our doom in his quest for El Niño.' Mick beckoned the next manacled man over, deftly picking the lock on the fetters with the bailing-hook. 'We must take control of the ship.'

The man gratefully massaged his sore wrists. 'But how?'

Mick passed the marlinspike to another, unshackled prisoner who took over the task of releasing his fellow travellers. 'If we have to, we will tear the very planks from the hatch with our bare hands.' Followed by two hundred eyes, Mick's gaze strayed towards the small, reinforced square which stood between them and freedom.

'And what then, if you are so clever?' The Bear's sceptical tones cut through the general assent. 'What is one bailing-hook against the power of muskets?' He scraped at his own fetters, eventually freeing himself.

Mick sighed. He had no answer. Brute force was no match for firearms.

A slice of daylight suddenly dazzled his eyes. Mick shaded his vision, peering as the shard broadened to a narrow rectangle then a full square.

The hatch was opening!

He edged forward.

A whisper joined the unexpected illumination. 'Mick?'

Before he could respond, a palm clamped itself over his mouth.

A booted foot appeared on the first step. 'Mick?' The whisper was more insistent. Another foot appeared. 'Are you there?'

Mick bit the Bear's hand and lunged forward to warn Christopher.

But the huge, hairy man was quicker. Still holding the bailing-hook, the Bear seized two booted feet.

A shriek of shock echoed in the silent hold.

Then Mick was staring into a pair of horrified blue eyes and the marlinspike's vicious point was pressed against Christopher's pale throat.

Twenty-Four

H e didn't struggle. Held in a grip of iron, Christopher hardly dared breathe. His Adam's apple bobbed convulsively against the tip of the bailing-hook.

'Well, well! Look what the Good Lord has sent us!'

The huge, half-naked man's snide, bassy tones rumbled into Christopher's spine as he was dragged further into the dark, stinking hold.

'A pretty midshipman. Our prayers have been answered.'

Christopher found a voice. 'I mean you no harm. Take me to Mick and I –' Gruff laughter rumbled through the body behind his.

'He means us no harm, men! Oh well, we can relax now, eh?'

The laughter grew in volume. Christopher gasped. The point of the blade stroked the hollow of his throat.

'I was shaking in my boots, for a moment there –'

The grip around his arms increased. Pain jolted into his shoulders.

'– but since you're not going to harm us –'

Another twist sent jagged spikes of agony through his very bones.

'– I feel much better!'

The vast man who held him was now shaking with laughter. Christopher's face flushed up. Scanning the darkness, he could make out only vague, man-shaped forms. 'Please release me! I come in friendship.'

'I'm afraid I cannot do that, my pretty midshipman. Now that we have you, I am sure the captain will be more easily persuaded to listen to our demands –'

A bristling chin brushed his ear. Christopher's pink face blanched.

'– in a little while.' The man made coarse kissing sounds.

Then the great arm released his wrists and thrust itself between his legs. Five thick fingers fondled his crotch. Christopher gasped. The deep voice in his ear was hoarse with lust.

'I will fuck you until you black out, little midshipman. And then I will pass you around this hold until every man has had his way with you.' The huge fellow chuckled evilly.

The hand squeezed Christopher's sensitive bollocks. His eyes widened and watered. He blinked desperately. Then a voice boomed out of the darkness, 'Let him go, sir. While he is our hostage, he will not be harmed.' A familiar, bearded face moved forward.

Christopher sighed with relief. He tried to smile into Mick's eyes, but instead grimaced in pain as the hand between his legs lifted him clean off his feet.

'Our hostage? He is my hostage, fellow! I captured him.'

The sharp point of the bailing-hook ripped swiftly down the front of the midshipman's jacket.

'And I will do as I please with him.'

His shirt and midshipman's jacket gaped open. Christopher's heart pounded against his ribs. Then the tip of the hook was back, tracking none too delicate circles around his right nipple.

'Come, come, sir; this benefits none of us. The captain will not bargain for a dead officer.'

Mick's studiedly calm words brought home the reality of his situation. Christopher shrank back, but only succeeded in pressing himself more firmly against his captor's barrel chest.

'See? He likes me – don't you, pretty boy?'

In a flash, the torn garments were wrenched from his shoulders and the tip of the blade was circling his left nipple. Christopher bit through his lower lip.

'Look how his buds respond to the marlinspike.'

Appalled, Christopher focused on Mick's face. His nipples were straining outwards, while every other part of him tried to get away. On the periphery of his vision, he was vaguely aware of two smaller shapes moving apart from the crowd of prisoners.

'Give him to me, sir,' said Mick. 'Let me take him on deck to show the Rock. Then you can do what you will with him.'

The response was a cruel snigger. 'Think I am stupid, Savage?'

Christopher's feet hit the floor. His legs crumpled and the heels of his boots dragged on bare wood as his captor began slowly to retreat.

'Quite the contrary, sir. I know you to be a reasonable fellow.' The calm voice talked on. The Irishman inched forward. 'Give me the spike, at least – we do not want any bloodshed.'

The sharp tip paused on Christopher's chest, then scored roughly over his left nipple. Unable to bear it any longer, he howled.

'Unhand Mr Christopher, you ruffian!'

Something launched itself on them from behind, just as Mick darted forward, seizing the hairy man's wrist. Arms and legs thrashed. Willicombe's cry ringing in his ears, Christopher wrenched himself free of a now-weaker embrace and fell to the floor.

As he lay there, dazed and bleeding, he became aware of movement beneath him.

Solid, swaying movement.

After three days of rowing, a wind had appeared.

Some distant, nautical part of Christopher was glad. The rowers could rest and the *Impregnable* would be once more back on course. Then strong hands hauled him to his feet and pressed a rag to his bloody chest. Oblivious to his wound, Christopher stared at Mick. 'You saved my life!'

Blue, glinting eyes stared back, then looked away. 'I merely returned the favour.'

Christopher was still trying to work out why his rangy Irishman had now assumed such a cool tone when sunburnt arms threw themselves around his neck.

'Mr Christopher! Oh, Mr Christopher!'

Willicombe's embrace was almost painful. Gently disentangling himself, Christopher held the underfootman's wrists and smiled.

The boyishly handsome face was streaked with tears. 'Oh, sir – you are hurt. We must get you out of here. This is no place for a fine gentleman such as yourself.'

Christopher rubbed his nipple. The sight of the man's curly hair and worried face made his skin tingle further. 'I am fine, Willicombe. No harm done.'

A little way away, the great bear of a man was being restrained by six other prisoners.

His eyes had become accustomed to the gloom. Christopher could now see the hatch, and the swelling number of men standing beneath it. Then Mick was at his side once more, holding the bailing-hook.

'I would not do this, if there were any other way.'

The words were low, for Christopher's ears only.

'You will not be harmed, but you are a valuable commodity. Do you understand?'

Christopher looked from the sombre, bearded face to Willicombe's sunburnt countenance and back again. 'Not only do I understand but I am on your side.' Stooping, he picked up what remained of his naval jacket and struggled into it. 'There is no time like the present. Come.' Flanked by Mick, Willicombe and a thin, red-headed boy, Christopher strode towards the hatch. 'Mr Mims? Mr Barber? Bosun?' he yelled up through the half-open trapdoor.

The only response was the thundering of feet overhead.

He raised his voice. 'Get the captain! I have been taken hostage!'

The pounding increased in volume.

Sweat broke out on Christopher's brow. Cupping his hands around his mouth, Christopher roared, 'They have me captive! Please – someone! Anyone!'

The footsteps lessened. Then the hatch yawned ajar.

Christopher squinted in the sunlight, peering at Midshipman Mims' aristocratic face. 'Summon the captain. The prisoners have demands. They will surely kill me if Captain Rock does not –'

'Does not what, Mister?'

Midshipman Mims' worried face was pushed away and Josiah Rock's craggy visage glowered down. One hand held a telescope. The other fist was gripping a pistol.

Christopher cleared his throat. 'Sir, please listen. I –'

'We have a wind, Mr Fitzgibbons: a strong wind, blowing from the east. Do you not feel it?' The captain's gaze was glassy. 'Our prayers have been answered. The sails are filling. The *Caliente* is in our sights and we have the advantage of the sun.'

'Captain, the prisoners are starving and dehydrated. Please give them water. They –'

'I believe I saw El Niño through my spyglass, Mr Fitzgibbons. Standing on the bridge of his hulk of a vessel, laughing at me!'

Christopher stared at the twisted features. 'Sir, listen to me.'

A great crack appeared in the Rock's craggy countenance. 'Let him laugh! Let him blast us with his Spanish cannons! Let him blow our masts to smithereens. We'll see if he is still laughing when the *Impregnable*'s bow rams the *Caliente*'s port side!'

From out of the fissure which had replaced the captain's mouth, a hellish parody of laughter filled Christopher's ears.

'Then we will board her and I will personally wipe the smile from El Niño's scurvy face.'

Christopher stiffened. 'What about the prisoners, sir? The hold is below the waterline. When the *Impregnable* rams El Niño's vessel they will –'

'Join me, Mr Fitzgibbons! Join me in my finest hour!' Tucking the telescope under one arm, and with the pistol still pointed into the dark hold, Josiah Rock stuck out a hand towards Christopher. His eyes were as hard as ice.

'Will you release the prisoners, sir? Against El Niño, they will stand by your side and fight the Spanish brigand, I am sure.'

The captain's glacial gaze hardened further. 'Only one of those animals is of interest to me, Mr Fitzgibbons.' Josiah Rock's eyes moved to Christopher's side. He lowered the pistol towards Mick.

Instinctively, Christopher moved into the line of fire. 'I cannot allow this!' Behind, Mick's naked body trembled against his. Hands gripped his shoulders, trying to push him aside. Christopher dug the heels of his boots into the damp floor. 'Permit me to talk with you, sir. Whatever Michael Savage did, he has more than paid for his crimes.'

'Your words have the air of mutiny about them, sir! I will ask you only once.' The barrel of the pistol continued to point at his chest. 'Get out of the way.'

Christopher remained as a shield between the captain and Mick. He groped for words, but knew the captain was beyond reasoning.

His actions spoke for him. 'Then rot in Hell, Fitzgibbons. You are a disgrace to your father and your naval forebears.' The hatch slammed down, the hold plunged back into darkness.

Stunned, Christopher listened to the pounding of his heart – and the sound of something large and heavy being moved overhead, on top of their only means of escape. He had failed. Slowly, he turned.

Mick's face was difficult to read.

Christopher stretched out a hand and stroked the sallow cheek. 'I am sorry – I tried my best.'

Around them, the prisoners were silent. An air of defeat had descended over two hundred men. The end seemed inevitable.

Mick's reply was low and unemotional. 'It was foolhardy to even try. Now we are all doomed.' Lowering his eyes, he walked past a startled Christopher over to the far end of the hold.

★

He sat with his head in his hands.

Think!

Think!

Beneath him, the *Impregnable* was gathering speed. A great heaviness filled Mick's heart. He had no idea how far away the Spanish vessel was, but knew there was little time to do whatever had to be done.

Think!

Think!

The pale midshipman had come over four times, in the last two hours, to enquire if he was quite all right.

Mick had feigned a sulk. In truth, and despite the desperation of the situation, his body yearned for the man with an almost unbearable fire. And that was the last thing he needed, right now.

Raising his weary eyes, he looked to where blond Christopher was sitting with Cat and the curly-haired stowaway, fiddling with the buttons of his jacket. The trio looked so young, and Mick suddenly felt very old.

The thought blasted itself into his mind.

Thirty-five years: it had been a good life, all things considered. He'd had his fill of cock and quim. He'd lived fast and furiously – if a little ignobly – and if death had to come, it might as well be now.

As he rose to his feet, something tugged at his brain. Maybe it was his distant, Catholic upbringing, or the irrational urge to test a love which had already been measured on numerous occasions. Whatever the reason, Mick knew there was one last thing he must do before he gave himself to the Rock.

Hauling on someone's discarded breeches, he made his way across to the young trio. 'Mr Fitzgibbons?'

Cat and the stowaway were snuggled up together, thick as thieves. Christopher raised his blond head.

Mick nodded to a corner. 'A word, if you please.' He walked away.

Brow furrowing, Christopher followed.

In the semi-privacy of the quiet spot, Mick stared into the younger man's puzzled face. 'You do not recognise me, do you?'

The pale forehead creased further. Then the midshipman smiled. 'I recognise that you haunt my dreams, and I know I will do anything for you. But, now that you mention it, I do seem to know your face from somewhere else.'

Mick steeled himself. 'Bath, perhaps? You ran naked from a brothel, into the arms of a startled priest?'

The pale face reddened slightly at the memory. Christopher gasped. 'That was you?'

Mick nodded. 'And two weeks before, at the Admiralty Club?'

The blue eyes narrowed in concentration. Then a blond eyebrow shot up. 'With Orlando Rock and the captain?' The voice was amazed.

Mick nodded more slowly. 'A conman and a thief. I make no apology for what I am, sir.' After years of pretence, the truth was an awkward bullet to bite. He waited apprehensively for a response, then flinched as Christopher laid a cool palm on his shoulder.

'That was then – this is now. You had your reasons, no doubt, and I believed you when you told me the captain's son was a willing partner in whatever went on between the two of you.' The midshipman's face took on a sadder cast. His blue eyes sloped up to the deck above. 'Although it is not me you have to convince.'

Mick swallowed a hard lump in his throat – a lump which was mirrored two feet below, in the resolute thickening of his cock. He silently cursed his body.

Christopher talked on. 'I thank you for telling me this, my friend, but none of it matters to me.'

Mick opened his mouth. 'Fitzgibbons Manor. Early May. A ball. I –'

'You were there? At my betrothal? Why didn't I meet you?' Christopher goggled. 'Oh, of course: I remember now. I was so fed up that evening. All the dancing, and Violet's crowds of admirers made me retire early.'

Then his blond head rested itself on Mick's shoulder. 'If I had known you were there, I would have waited longer.'

Mick felt the low laugh vibrate through his bones.

'May I be so bold as to ask whom you robbed, that evening? There was so much finery around, I dare say you were spoiled for choice.'

Nothing the Rock could do to him could be more painful than this. Mick clenched his teeth. 'I –' A finger pressed itself against his lips.

'So do not talk any more, Mick. Let me kiss you. Whatever happens next, we are all in God's hands. But I will not go to my doom without having felt your mouth on mine.'

Before he could pull away, strong hands were gripping his waist and warm breath caressed his beard. Chest met chest. Thighs touched. Mick groaned, feeling the hard outline of his love's prick thick beside his. Their hips ground together.

Christopher's mouth moved closer. 'You have taught me what it is to truly desire another man. You have shown me another side of myself:

a strong, masculine side which is the perfect counterpart to my more bookish nature.'

Mick's arms draped themselves around the uniformed shoulders. He tilted his head. He was a coward. The words were beguiling him. Just as his lips parted to suck Christopher's sweet tongue into his mouth, an odour twitched his nostrils.

A burning odour

Christopher smelt it too, and pulled away. They both turned.

All eyes were focused on where Cat and Willicombe, eyes alight, were holding the latter's slowly smouldering shirt aloft. The crafty pair had managed to create sparks in more ways than one.

'Fire! Fire in the hold!' Cat darted forward, wafting the burning garment under the hatch.

Mick watched the smoke thicken, its tendrils snaking up between tarred planks.

Other men were tearing at their garments, igniting them from the now brightly burning fabric.

It would take more than a few flaming shirts to set fire to this damp hulk of a ship, but could Josiah Rock take that risk?

Seconds later, Mick's silent question was answered.

The hatch flew open. Armed with muskets, several pigtailed seamen leapt down, lowering buckets of brine from the deck.

Cat and the stowaway shrieked as they were doused with icy water.

Mick scowled: little had been achieved, but an opportunity now presented itself. Striding forward, he stopped, naked and collared, in front of the bosun. 'Release the prisoners: they have done nothing. If the Rock wants me dead, here I am!'

The response boomed down from above. 'Dead? You'll beg for death by the time I have finished. Bring him to me, Bosun. We'll see how cocky he is after a keelhauling!'

Over Christopher's cries of protest, and with four muskets aimed at his head, Mick allowed himself to be manhandled through the hatch and up on to the deck.

Twenty-Five

A fter the darkness of the hold, the daylight hurt his eyes. Scrambling through the hatch, hot on Mick's heels, Christopher was grabbed and hauled to his feet.

'I should hang you from the yardarm, sir, for mutiny.' The Rock's strangely calm face was very close to his. 'But I am a fair man. A court-martial back in England will decide your fate. Clap him in irons and bring him to the bow!' The captain stalked away.

Barely aware of the manacles as they encircled his wrists and ankles, Christopher stared to where a pale, rangy figure stood, at the portside. Thick ropes were already attached to Mick's arms and legs. A shiver of dread shook Christopher's aching body.

Keelhauling.

Dragged under water from port to starboard, beneath the ship's keel.

If the sharp barnacles did not rip Mick to shreds, if the ropes did not loosen his arms and legs from the rest of his body, up to fifteen minutes underwater would surely drown him.

Christopher's heart hammered in time with the rhythmic tattoo from a band of side drums.

The anchor had been dropped, and the *Impregnable* sat motionless in the water. The crew stood in sombre ranks behind the drummers. Even the crow's nest was empty. Every eye was on Mick, who stood stiffly, his long, tangled hair falling over his broad naked shoulders. Raised up by a pulley, his arms were secured high above his body.

Staring somewhere into middle distance, the Irishman held his head high and proudly. He did not fight the ropes. Nor did he flinch from the volley of insults and blows which the captain rained down on to his defenceless face.

Desperation and a sudden anger made him brave. Lifted almost off his feet by his guard of sturdy seamen, Christopher clenched his fists and wrenched himself from their grip. 'A fair man? You are a bully and a coward!' Chains rattled and clanked as he strode towards the captain and Mick. 'This is a mockery of naval justice!'

Slowly, the Rock turned.

Christopher glowered past the craggy features to Mick's bruised face. One lip was cut and bleeding.

The thick hair of his beard was matted with blood and sweat.

Christopher's heart melted. Stepping forward, he gently dabbed at the injury with the ragged sleeve of his shirt. 'You should be ashamed of yourself, Josiah Rock!'

'Shame?' The word was almost a whisper. 'Do not talk to me of shame. My Orlando is filled with unnatural urges, because of this devil! Why do you plead for a blaggard, who shows neither regret nor contrition for his crimes?'

Christopher stared into Mick's bottomless eyes. A background drum roll almost obliterated his low voice. 'Apologise: save your life and beg his forgiveness.'

Mick blinked a droplet of sweat from one thickly lashed eye. Lips set in a determined scowl, he averted his gaze but remained silent.

The captain's words were tight with warning. 'The fellow is evil incarnate, Fitzgibbons. He has beguiled you as he beguiled my boy Orlando. Save your soul before he steals that too.'

Christopher felt himself wrenched away, his shirtsleeve wet with his love's blood.

'No last requests, Savage? What, no final brave words before I send you to Hell?'

Christopher struggled in the seamen's grip, but they held him firmly.

Then Mick spoke. Dark eyes levelled with Christopher's darting pupils, his voice soared over the drum tattoo. 'I would like to meet my maker clean-shaven.'

The Rock's laugh chilled Christopher's skin. 'Lucifer will not care one way or another what you look like, but I cannot refuse a last request. Bosun? Fetch a razor!'

What was Mick up to? Christopher strained at his bonds. Would he try to grab the blade and free himself? Christopher's chest tightened. He gazed at the man in confusion.

The deck, the assembled crew – even the captain's muttered curses – faded away.

Mick's calm, unreadable eyes filled his vision and annulled all Christopher's questions. All the unspoken words – all the dreams and hopes for the future – were held captive by those eyes. His skin flushed pink. Sweat trickled from his left armpit. Beneath the waistband of the filthy breeches, his cock stirred as he pondered opportunities lost and a love fated never to be.

Then he thought about Mick's fate: an agonising death alone, beneath the waves. He could not allow that. Holding the gaze, Christopher directed a final, selfless plea to the captain. 'Let me shave him, sir.'

The Rock snorted. 'You are a disgrace to the uniform, Fitzgibbons, but I suppose there is no harm in your request. Bosun?'

Released, Christopher gripped the bone handle of the open, cut-throat razor and staggered forward. One fettered hand cupped Mick's chin. In the quivering fingers of his other fist, the blade trembled.

The soft hair on Mick chest was ruffled by the breeze.

Christopher lowered one shaking hand to the man's cheek. He scraped gently but firmly, talking in a low voice. 'You and I, my Mick –'

One denuded cheek appeared from beneath its hirsute cover.

'– we are too special for this world.'

A second expanse of pale skin became visible.

Christopher wiped the blade on the thigh of his breeches then scraped it carefully over Mick's upper lip. If his beloved had to die, he would slit his own throat after he had dragged the razor across Mick's hairy neck and they would go to Hell together.

The face now showing itself was younger, and more handsome.

He moved the blade to the left of Mick's chin, where the growth was heavier.

The blade stuck.

Christopher wrenched the razor free, wiped it again then pressed harder. Sweat ran down his back. His bollocks tightened inside his breeches, whether through trepidation or arousal he wasn't sure. But the straining of his prick against his stomach was unmistakable.

'Get on with it, Fitzgibbons! We haven't got all day!'

Christopher flinched. His face was very close to Mick's as he continued to shave. The transformation amazed him. Smooth-skinned, Mick had an almost noble cast to his features. Then the Irishman's body went limp and his eyes back rolled in his head. Christopher cried out.

'Slacken his arms, please: he is losing consciousness!' He wanted Mick to be with him when he did it.

Josiah Rock sighed. 'Anything to speed this up. Lower the pulley a foot or so, Bosun.'

As the Irishman slumped forward, Christopher released Mick's chin and slid one manacled hand around the man's slick waist. 'Soon, my love –' He scraped more roughly at the last few patches of hair on Mick's face. A strange, unexpected familiarity fizzled in his brain. Christopher blinked. Then stared. And continued to stare.

The ball. Talking with Lady Violet. Violet's buzzing swarm of admiring fops.

The razor paused, and Christopher moved back a little to take in the almost aristocratic face of the tall Irishman in his arms.

One admirer in particular. Not a fop. Tall. Dark, ponytailed hair. Twinkling eyes.

No!

It couldn't be!

Then strong fingers seized his wrist in a crushing grip and a low voice confirmed his worst nightmares. 'You remember me now, Mr Fitzgibbons?'

Christopher's blood ran cold, then boiled in anger.

'Lady Violet – your betrothed, and the reason you are here at all – lay with me, the night of your betrothal ball. It was I who left seed in her. I made you a cuckold, Christopher, and for that I deserve to die.' Mick lowered his head. His stubbly throat pressed against the razor's sharp blade. 'You have the right, sir, more so than Josiah Rock.'

Rage filled his head, but was soon replaced by a strange, gnawing hurt. Grabbing the long tangle of Mick's hair, Christopher wrenched the Irishman's face upwards. 'Why? Why?'

Before Mick had the chance to answer, a heavy thud impacted on the deck. Then another.

The razor fell. Knocked off his feet, Christopher grabbed the rigging. The captain was roaring orders over the racket, but no one heard them. Around him, the crew scrambled for cover, but it was too late.

Dazed, his head full of thunder, Christopher stared over the portside.

Another huge cannonball soared over his head and smashed into the *Impregnable*'s mizzen mast.

Christopher gasped, raising his eyes to the skull and crossed-bones flag which fluttered jauntily against a blue sky.

Less than fifty feet away, the billowing sails of a huge Spanish galleon bore down on them. On the bridge, some great bird clamped to his wrist, the swarthy, grinning face of El Niño watched gleefully as his pirate crew swung across the frothy waves on to the *Impregnable*'s deck.

Muskets exploded loudly around him. Clashing steel filled his head.

Terror froze his muscles. Christopher couldn't move. He looked around for his fellow officers, but Midshipmen Mims and Barber were nowhere to be seen. His eyes fell upon a rangy figure, who had hauled open the door to the hold and was now helping the prisoners up on to the deck.

Then a whooshing of wings overhead made him flinch. Tearing his eyes from Mick's firm backside, Christopher shrieked. He ducked, trying to get away from the circling hawk as it swooped down on him with its sharp claws. Before he could recover, low laughter drifted into his ear and the blade of a cutlass was sharp against his throat.

'And what is this? Trying to steal Ramon, eh?'

His head wrenched back further, his blond hair skimming his shoulders, Christopher stared into the coffee-coloured face.

El Niño laughed, spinning Christopher around. 'What's your name, pretty one?'

Christopher scowled at the slight figure. The swarthy fellow was no taller than he, and slimmer. 'Midshipman Fitzgibbons.'

The handsome pirate grinned more broadly, showing gleaming white teeth. Releasing Christopher's throat, he executed a mock bow. 'Will you accept my hospitality and join me on the *Caliente*, Midshipman Fitzgibbons?'

Christopher hesitated. His attention had been taken by El Niño's right hand – or rather, his lack of hand. Where wrist and fingers should have been, a thick, eight-inch wooden spar protruded from the cuff of the pirate's tightly laced shirt.

El Niño cocked his head and folded his arms across his slim chest. 'Your friends are coming. Will you not join us?' The pirate winked. 'Or you can stay here, if you fancy a swim.'

Christopher looked beyond the mocking face to where what was left of the crew were throwing themselves from the *Impregnable*'s burning deck into the sea. Then he saw a huddle of uniforms, at cutlass-point, picking their way across the narrow plank which now joined the two ships. In the middle, the Rock's craggy countenance was stony. Mick was nowhere in sight. Christopher felt his heart sink along with his vessel.

How could he have been so stupid! The captain was right: the

Irishman Savage was an animal. If it was not for him, and what he had done, Christopher would be back in England, finishing his thesis on Geoffrey Chaucer.

His stomach churned. The dusty libraries of Oxford suddenly seemed very far away, and as his mind turned to Mick's strong arms, the crotch of his breeches tightened. Then other, sinewy arms swept the feet from under him.

'I will not take no for an answer, my pretty Englishman.'

Struggling, and scarlet with shame, Christopher had no choice but to let himself be carried by the surprisingly strong El Niño over to the *Caliente*.

He glanced one last time at the burning hulk of the *Impregnable*, as the vessel sank beneath the waves in a frothing mass of foam. Then Mick slung an arm around the shoulders of Cat and the stowaway, ushering them to a place of safety behind three tall barrels of rum. Around him, the rest of the prisoners eyed El Niño's crew with guarded suspicion. Striding forward, Mick pushed his way to where the officers and captain had been lined up on the *Caliente*'s deck.

Josiah Rock had other matters on his mind now.

One fate had been averted.

Looking to where the slight, dark-skinned figure with the peg hand was dumping a writhing Christopher unceremoniously on to a heap of ropes, Mick wondered what the pirate had in store for them all.

He frowned, biting back an overwhelming sadness that he had lost his handsome, blond midshipman for ever. The future held little for Mick, whatever El Niño's intentions –

His head swivelled to where the young cutpurse and the curly-haired Willicombe held each other, cowering behind the kegs of rum. Their faces were pale with fear.

– but others deserved a chance of happiness.

Over the sound of Josiah Rock's blustering outrage and El Niño's sneering jibes, Mick raised his voice. 'We have no quarrel with you, sir. Nor you with us.' He strode forward.

The line of naval uniforms parted wordlessly to let him through.

Mick stopped a foot from where the pirate stood. Extending his right arm, he indicated his fellow criminals. 'Do not harm the prisoners: they have suffered enough at the hands of that brute already.' He pointed to Josiah Rock. 'Even his own crew have grown to despise him, I think.'

El Niño cocked his pigtailed head. The high cheekboned face creased with curiosity. 'You are English, nonetheless. I despise all Englishmen.'

'English? Sure, am I not Irish through and through? I have as much hatred for the English as you, my Moorish fellow, and by God they hate us back!'

El Niño's full lips hardened in consideration of the words. 'Mine enemy's enemy is my friend?'

Mick smiled. 'Indeed! And if you need any help to dispose of this crowd of blaggards, you will not lack for volunteers!' Behind him, the prisoners murmured in agreement.

El Niño remained suspicious. 'Why should I trust you, fellow?'

Mick curled his outstretched arm in a gesture of respect and bowed his neck to the colourfully dressed pirate. 'I give you my word.'

Abruptly, the air was filled with the flapping of great wings. Mick gasped as sharp claws gripped the flesh of his forearm. His head shot up and he stared at the huge bird now casually preening itself on his wrist.

A hearty laugh broke from the pirate's lips. 'Well, Ramon has taken a liking to you – and my hawk cannot stomach a liar. Your name, fellow?'

The hunting bird's claws digging painfully into his skin, Mick grabbed the tresses which hung from its talons and walked slowly forward. 'Michael Savage, sir.' Carefully, he held his arm parallel to El Niño's arm and the hawk hopped neatly back on to its master's wrist.

El Niño grinned. '*Mi casa, su casa*, Miguel! You and your friends will not be harmed.'

'Thank you.' Mick fell to one knee and bowed his head again. As he did so, he caught a glimpse of Christopher's pale face.

Their eyes met for a second, then the midshipman looked away.

El Niño chuckled, sweeping away Mick's wistful thoughts. 'Get up, get up! I can see you are a fellow of spirit. No man bows to another on board my vessel. We will talk later, Michael –'

Mick raised his head.

El Niño grabbed Christopher's waist and pulled the young man towards him. '– after this pretty thing and I have had time to get better acquainted.'

A pang of jealousy twisted Mick's guts. In his mind's eye, he saw the pale English gentleman and the dark-skinned pirate entwined naked together. He saw El Niño's darker, curving cock gripped in white, smooth fingers and two very different mouths wet and hungry upon each other. Then his own prick was uncurling from its nest of bristling pubic hair, betraying the pain in his heart that he would never feel Christopher's hand on his prick or taste his lord's sweet lips. 'As you wish, sir.'

El Niño released the hawk's jesses and the bird flew high into the rigging. He grabbed Christopher's hand. 'My name is Renato, Miguel.'

The midshipman growled.

Mick felt the blood pumping into his cock. Every fibre of his being longed for any touch – even the pain of the lash – if it was delivered by Christopher's hand.

Then El Niño was hefting the flailing midshipman off the deck and throwing him over one shoulder. Eyes as bright as embers met Mick's. 'Ramon will keep watch.' The pirate winked. 'I am sure you will find plenty to amuse you, until I return.' And with that, the man carried a protesting Christopher off below deck.

Twenty-Six

Hurled through the open doorway, Christopher's face impacted with a great, soft bed.

'Let's see if the rest of you is as inviting as those sweet lips, pretty boy.' El Niño slammed and locked the cabin door behind himself.

Thrown amongst luxurious satins and silks which swayed gently with the motion of the ship, Christopher spluttered with indignation. He scrambled to get away, but a firm hand grabbed his ankle, hauling him back.

'Not shy, are we?'

The mocking tone in the pirate's voice made his blood boil. It was also having a profound effect on the crotch of his already tightening breeches. Christopher shrieked as a sharp twist on his ankle flipped him over on to his back.

Straddling the midshipman's legs, El Niño grinned down at him. His long, plaited pigtail lay heavily on his shoulder like a thick, sleeping snake. 'Come, come, my pretty –'

Nimble fingers tore at Christopher's shirt and jacket, ripping the fabric. He gasped, and the serpentine uncurling of his own man-snake made him flinch.

'– I've seen it all before. What have you got that is so special?' The pirate tutted impatiently, then leant back and grabbed the waistband of Christopher's breeches. 'You English are so repressed.' El Niño tugged resolutely. 'Let's have a look at you!'

Christopher's boots hit the floor with a thud. His breeches and

251

undergarments were thrown through the air. Christopher's hands flew to his exposed crotch.

His wrists were flicked away. 'Oh-ho. What have we here?'

Before he could fight back, both arms were pinned above his head in a single, vice-like grip. Christopher's head thrashed from side to side. His back arched, his eyes focused on an ornate chandelier which hung from the centre of the ceiling. Then something warm and solid edged under his swollen shaft.

'Muhammad has favoured you indeed, pretty boy. Who would have thought such a slender fellow would possess such a beast of a cock?'

Scarlet with horror, Christopher stopped thrashing. He lifted his head from the heap of soft pillows and looked down to where El Niño's peg hand was edging along the underside of his member.

'You are popular with the ladies, I'll wager.' The thick wooden spar flicked.

His inability to give Lady Violet what she wanted – and the memory of who, in fact, had – flashed into his mind. Christopher scowled resentfully.

El Niño flicked his peg hand again.

Christopher groaned. His cock leapt into the air then landed back on the wooden spar with a solid slap.

El Niño raised an eyebrow. 'Or are you *maricon*, my pretty one?' He released Christopher's wrists and ran one finger down the delicate skin of his inner arm. 'Eh?'

Christopher shivered. A moan of pleasure escaped his scowling lips.

'I should have guessed!' El Niño chuckled, flicking his peg hand and causing Christopher's engorged shaft to bounce once more. 'This monster would ravage all but the most robust of orifices. So you like the boys, pretty one?'

Unexpectedly, Christopher found himself rolling and the next thing he knew his head left the bed and he was straddling the pirate's slender waist.

With his good hand, El Niño gripped Christopher's neck and brought the midshipman's face very close to his. 'Shall I tell you a secret, Englishman?'

His swollen bollocks rubbed against the worsted fabric of the pirate's waistcoat then swung heavily between his legs as he was pulled off his knees, and closer.

'So do I.' El Niño chuckled, then winked.

Christopher's bare arse thrust itself ceilingwards. The hand on the back of his neck gripped more tightly. Then laughing lips delivered a resounding kiss to his open mouth. Dazed by the lip attack, Christopher's confused mind wondered where the pirate's other hand was.

Before he could ponder its whereabouts further, something hard and warm moved down the crack of his arse.

Christopher's body moved by itself. Groaning, he closed his eyes and undulated back against the solid length. Then he realised what he was doing. With a howl, he pulled away from the exquisite caress.

El Niño sighed. 'Ah, you want to be wooed, do you, my pretty?' He rolled his dark, flashing eyes. 'You want the black kisses before I take you, eh?'

Christopher had no idea what he wanted. His blond hair hung into his eyes in a sweaty mass. The grip on his neck slackened but he didn't move away. 'What are – black kisses?'

Executing a limber flip, El Niño arched up off the bed and Christopher found himself once more flat on his back, with his legs over the lusty pirate's slim shoulders.

'Ah, I forget you English do not have the custom.' El Niño moved down slightly, slyly licking the inside of Christopher's thighs. 'Even the Spanish frown upon such practices, but we Moors know the way to a man's heart – and it is not through his stomach!'

The breath left his body in a great whoosh as his legs met his chest and were held there by the eight-inch wooden spar which protruded from the frilled cuff of the pirate's colourful shirt. Christopher's arms flailed uselessly behind his head. His arse-cheeks quivered, lifted off the bed. Then he howled again as something warm and wet tracked the length of his sweating crack.

'Black kisses –'

The tongue circled his spasming pucker and the two words vibrated on his skin.

'– the dark, sweet kisses no man can resist.'

The tongue broadened out, laving just behind Christopher's balls then lapping back up to where his hole clenched. The blood left his face, pounding lower until a tiny droplet of arousal slicked the head of his aching prick.

'I taste your very essence, my pretty Englishman: the rich, aromatic flavour which is yours and only yours.'

Christopher writhed in pleasure. He wanted to grab his shaft and stroke himself to orgasm – and he wanted to lose himself in the movements of the pirate's tongue until the seed shot from his slit of its own accord.

El Niño's voice was husky with need. 'You want me – don't you, pretty boy?' Narrowing his tongue, the pirate eased the tip beyond Christopher's spasming sphincter.

Christopher closed his eyes. 'Oh yes –'

The pirate filled his lusty mouth with saliva, then gnawed wetly at the tender lips of Christopher's arse. 'You want me inside you.'

Christopher arched, until only his shoulders remained on the bed. Almost upside down, his head thrashed from side to side. His engorged prick twitched mere inches from his own gasping mouth. 'Oh please –'

'You'll take anything I choose to shove into you.'

'Yes! Anything!'

The pirate's delighted chuckle erected every hair on Christopher's balls. 'I lost my hand in battle, fighting for my people and my father's memory. The English captain who sliced it from my wrist laughed on the other side of his face when I cut his throat and sank his scurvy vessel! But the dog did me a favour: my ship's carpenter fashioned this spar from a piece of strong cypress wood. And it never lets me down.'

Apprehension tinged Christopher's lust. El Niño's nibbling and gnawing paused. Then the tongue snaked deliciously over Christopher's bollocks.

'A fine pair of *cojones* you have, pretty one. But do you have the balls where it counts?'

Christopher shivered. He opened his eyes. 'What do you mean?' El Niño's pigtail slapped off his thigh as the pirate's grinning face appeared between his splayed legs.

The pirate tapped the side of his swarthy head with his peg hand. 'Up here!' He winked. 'Any fool has a sack between his legs, but *cojones* are more than mere flesh. It is a – how do you say? A state of mind, no?'

The state of Christopher's mind prevented any rational thought or answer. The aching throb in his arse was all he knew. He stared at the eight inches of polished, curving wood, mesmerised by the idea. 'Have you, er, had a lot of men with –?' He managed a nod in the direction of the pirate's peg hand.

El Niño held the length of wood in front of his own, sweating face then sensuously licked the spar. 'Many times. They were very special men: men with *mucho cojones*. I can still taste their arses along its absorbent surface. Spanish, French, English, Moorish. Each has left its own special fragrance on my carved hand. Now it will have yours, my beautiful one.' The head ducked back down.

The teeth nibbled on, nipping and tenderising until Christopher could bear it no longer. 'Put it in me! Put it in me now!' Then a firmer, smoother warmth replaced El Niño's wet tongue against the opening to his body and Christopher began to pant.

'Easy, my handsome sailor –'

El Niño was kissing the inside of his thighs, covering the sweaty skin with his musky saliva.

Christopher thrust his own hands underneath himself, lifting his body up and parting the cheeks of his arse. The rounded knob at the end of the wooden spar pressed more firmly. He tried to relax.

El Niño moved from between his legs and crouched beside him on the bed. 'Take it, pretty boy. Take it all.'

Christopher watched, open-mouthed. He bore down on the spar, feeling its polished surface against the slick lips of his arse. Through his own moans and El Niño's breathy exhortations, a sharp, twisting sound echoed in his ears. Then the pirate's lips were forcing two sets of lips apart and a hot, Moorish tongue probed the inside of his mouth as the first five inches of the pirate's peg hand slipped effortlessly into Christopher's body.

He howled as the object stretched and filled his arse, ploughing on up inside him. He grabbed for the swarthy fellow, and felt sinewy arms grip his shoulders, lowering him back down on to the bed.

Two sinewy arms.

Through the barrage of sensations, Christopher's mind tried to deal with the contradiction as the pirate embraced and kissed him passionately. His eyes slowly focused, and when they did so, El Niño had leapt from the bed and was unfastening his flamboyant pantaloons. 'Your hand? Where's –?' Craning his neck, Christopher stared down to where two inches of wood protruded from between his arse-cheeks.

Then he fell back on the bed and the pirate was gripping Christopher's swollen rod and chuckling. 'They say I am more than a mere man, my pretty one – what do you think?'

Christopher's brain ceased to function as the pirate's brown left hand tightened around his aching prick and guided it up into his own, wiry body.

The cuff of his right sleeve hung loose and empty.

Then, as El Niño bore down on to him, Christopher's balls spasmed under two lusty attacks. Pushed flat on to the bed, the last two inches of El Niño's peg hand slid inside him, and his own prick was gripped in a tight, warm wetness.

The pirate rode him roughly, like he rode the waves of the stormy Atlantic. Impaled on Christopher's vast cock, El Niño roared with passion, using his sinewy thighs to pleasure himself and clasp his lover's length in a tight embrace.

Christopher's head swam. He thrust upwards, gasping as his cock ploughed into the pirate's body, then howled when the down-stroke drove the polished spar deeper and deeper into his arse.

Locked in a double-fuck, Christopher gripped his ravisher's waist, watching in awe.

El Niño's great pigtail thrashed from side to side. Sweat poured from his scalp, trickling down his handsome, lust-creased face and dangling from the arc of his single gold earring.

The peg hand pounded up into Christopher's rectum, driving him on to fuck El Niño harder and faster. Flat on the bed, with his arse full and a vice-like grip around his cock, he arched and shivered with desires he'd never dreamt of.

The pirate's mouth was slack with passion. His noble head drooped down and he lowered his body on to Christopher's.

The change of angle tingled up Christopher's prick. Muscles in his arse tightened around the spar, trying to suck more of the intrusion up into himself. Releasing his lover's waist, Christopher clawed at the pirate's tightly laced doublet.

El Niño laughed hoarsely and twisted away, pushing back on to Christopher's throbbing length.

Then a hot tingle was rushing through his veins. Christopher roared, thrusting up one final time. As his balls clenched and he shot deep into the pirate's body, El Niño's husky whoop of release wasn't far behind. The midshipman's fingers tightened on his lover's jerkin as he shot a second time.

El Niño's hole flexed around Christopher's spurting prick and he fell forward on to his lover, breathless and moaning.

Christopher felt each of the spasms as they coaxed more spunk from his jerking length. The pirate bucked with his hips again and again, sending shivers of sensation along Christopher's trembling shaft. Fucked almost raw, his arse-muscles gripped one last, vigorous time and pushed the invading peg hand from his body.

El Niño buried his face in his captive's neck, sweating and exhausted.

Slinging one arm over the pirate's waist, Christopher stared at the ceiling, watching as the swinging chandelier slowly refocused.

Every muscle in his body had been stretched to breaking point and beyond, then relaxed more deeply than ever before. He felt renewed – reborn! Slowly, his softening prick slipped wetly from El Niño's body. Christopher barely noticed.

His mind was miles away, filled with regret for the wasted years and lost opportunities. Why had no one told him what his body could do for him, given the right partner?

A frown formed on his lips, marring his smile of satisfaction and spoiling the moment. Suddenly angry, he wriggled out from beneath El Niño and stood up.

The pirate's laugh was breathy and full of admiration. 'You are stronger than you look, my lusty midshipman!' Sprawling, one hand reached down to haul up the extravagant pantaloons. 'Even I need a few minutes to recover myself.'

Christopher looked down, then goggled. El Niño's tightly laced doublet had been ripped during their passion, and as the pirate gripped the frayed edges, he caught a glimpse of two small, brown-nippled breasts.

His gaze was registered. El Niño laughed, stretched up and tapped a tousled, blond head with a peg hand still slick from Christopher's arse. '*Cojones*, remember? Where it counts.'

Christopher continued to frown, his head suddenly full of the tall, rangy Irishman.

El Niño jumped to his feet and draped an arm around Christopher's naked, sweating shoulders. 'Something tells me there is more than my little secret on your mind, my friend.' Guiding him to a nearby decanter of wine, the pirate filled two pewter tankards. 'Is there anything I can do?'

Christopher took the tankard and emptied it in one gulp. The ruby liquid warmed his stomach and loosened his lips.

A few minutes later they were sitting on the bed, and Christopher was spilling his heart.

'So you still want him?' El Niño had exchanged his torn garments for a white silk shirt and a jewelled waistcoat. He cocked his head.

Christopher sighed. 'Mick stirs something strange inside me, Renato – something I cannot ignore. But he caused me much dishonour, back in England.'

The pigtailed head nodded understandingly. 'Next to his *cojones*, a man's honour is his most prized possession.' He drained his glass. 'Because of the great dishonour done to me – by Dona Nature, the Spanish and the English – I sail the Atlantic for ever, exacting retribution at my whim.'

From the deck above, the sounds of bawdy laughter and dancing drifted down, accompanied by the rhythmic strumming of a guitar.

Christopher looked at the smooth, boyish chin, then into the pirate's large, soulful eyes. He felt a pang of empathy for the beguiling El Niño.

The pirate scowled, then laughed. 'Do not pity me, pretty one. It is a fine life – I have a loyal crew, all the men I could ever want, and my revenge on the world is sweet. As Muhammad says, paradise is under the shadow of a sword.' He sobered. 'But, to return to your problem –' El Niño sighed '– it would be a shame if such a love as you bear your Irish savage were to be lost.'

Christopher mirrored the sigh. Above their heads on deck, the rowdy celebrations were increasing in volume and intensity.

El Niño talked on. 'I think I got the – how do you say? – measure of Miguel, when he asked for the lives of his friends. We share much, your Irishman and I. He is a proud, angry man, from a proud and angry race. Centuries of subjugation by others have made him bitter and suspicious. I saw him looking at you, my lusty Cristóbal, and there was both desire and anger in that look. Perhaps you represent those centuries of subjugation: he has feelings for you, but cannot bring himself to trust you, or even himself. And – as, I think, your captain found out – he cannot be taken by force.'

'Impregnable.' Christopher muttered the adjective under his breath.

'*Qué?*' El Niño cocked a pigtailed head.

Christopher explained.

A smile crept on to the smooth, boyish face. 'If he will give himself to you freely, he loves you indeed, my friend. But how will you – ?'

An anguished cry of rage from above cut the sentence short: 'Break me, you dog? Oh no – you will never do that! But I will break you!'

Recognising Mick's voice, Christopher leapt from the bed and grabbed his clothes.

El Niño frowned. 'What is going on up there? I told them to enjoy themselves, not rip each other to shreds.'

Barely hearing the words, Christopher hauled on what was left of his midshipman's breeches and dashed towards the door.

Twenty-Seven

M ick aimed a kick at the empty barrel of rum and inched towards
   the terrified captain, who was now tied to the *Caliente*'s mast.

He knew he was drunk.

He knew this was madness.

Stripped to the waist, his hairy body slick with sweat and his mind a
seething mass of long-suppressed anger, Mick lurched forward. He
pressed the edge of the cutlass against the Rock's scrawny throat and
grabbed a handful of the man's greasy grey hair. 'Not so brave now, are
you, sir?' From behind, six fingers hauled at the waistband of his
breeches.

'Leave him, Mr Savage. He is not worth it.'

'Oh, he is worth it all right –' Mick released Josiah Rock's hair and
flailed backwards with his arm, sending the young cutpurse sprawling
on to the deck. '– piece of English shit that he is! Like his son was.'

Cat scrambled to his feet and tried again to reason with Mick. 'He is
the pirates' prisoner, not yours, Mr Savage. Let El Niño exact
punishment.'

Mick pushed the boy away a second time, bringing his face very
close to the Rock's craggy countenance. 'Orlando begged me to do it,
sir – begged me to piss on him.'

The captain tried to turn his head.

Mick gripped the strong chin and forced the man to look into his
eyes. 'And do you know something, sir? He liked it – nay, he loved it!
Your son shot his seed the minute my piss struck his handsome face.'

Around them, the strumming guitars died away. The good-hearted cheering faded from Mick's ears, replaced by the throb of angry blood. Moving back, but keeping the tip of the cutlass against his tormentor's bobbing Adam's apple, Mick walked slowly around the mast. 'You blame me for causing a change in Orlando? I made him happy – and I was happy to do it!'

The cutlass point pressed into Josiah Rock's stubbly throat. 'You are an evil devil, Savage.'

Mick laughed, blood roaring in his ears. 'You are the evil one, sir! You endangered the life of your crew to settle some stupid score with a pirate who has now captured us all.' He strolled on, staggering slightly and propping himself up on the mast, just behind the captain's ear. 'And, worse still, you do not understand your own son. I wager Orlando tried to confide his tastes, man to man, but you poured scorn on his desires. In fact, you threw him into my arms, sir. It is neither I nor El Niño who is responsible for the way Orlando now is: you are!'

The Rock strained against his bonds. Then, defeated, the angry head sank on to the man's grizzled chest.

Mick grinned drunkenly. The truth of the words had punished the captain more than any beating ever could. But years of bitter resentment drove the Irishman onward.

His own father, dead from overwork and hunger at the age of twenty-seven.

His family, back in Ireland, starving and abandoned.

Every proud lord and lady who had looked down on him.

The English mockery of a court which had sent him here.

And finally, the one Englishman who had been kind to him – a man he had wronged, and who now lay below deck with the handsome brigand El Niño.

Someone had to pay. Mick didn't care what happened to himself, but someone had to pay for the loss of what might have been. Every muscle in his rangy, half-starved body pulsed with rage. 'An animal, am I?' His features distorted by a scowl, his reason soaked with rum, Mick seized the captain's head and hauled it back. 'I will slaughter you like a pig, Rock: I will watch the blood drain from your veins then dance on your lifeless body.' Drawing back the cutlass, he pressed the blade to the man's throat.

'Drop your weapon!'

Mick stiffened, but remained where he was.

'Drop it, I say, or by Muhammad I will kill every prisoner with my bare hands!'

Mick swayed. The cutlass slipped from suddenly slack fingers and clattered to the deck. Then he found himself hauled away from Josiah Rock's terror-streaked face and staring into furious, opalesque eyes.

'You forget where you are, Irishman! This is my ship – my hostage! You do me a great insult.'

His head spinning, Mick was shoved roughly to his knees. Through a drunken haze, a different voice seeped into his ears.

'Do not hurt him, Renato. He is angry and does not know what he is doing.'

Mick scowled, raising his head.

Christopher's face was flushed. Naked to the waist, the skin on his slim chest glowed with exertion.

The source of that exertion twisted a blade deeper into Mick's heart. 'Do not plead for me, boy: I do not want your sympathy. Your betrothed was more of a man than you are.'

Christopher blanched.

Behind, El Niño growled. 'You attack my hostage and abuse my friend. For this you will pay, Irish dog! Get up!'

On his knees, Mick stared up into Christopher's blue eyes. He saw the double hurt there, then remembered the pain on his back and shoulders when the young midshipman had lashed him. Something hot and unwanted tingled in his groin.

'Stop cowering there like some spineless creature. Get up, I say!'

The strength left Mick's body. He could only gaze into Christopher's face. The man's eyes stripped everything away. Oh, to meet his maker, naked and writhing, as Christopher brought the exquisite ferule down on his arching body.

'Get him to his feet: if he cannot act like a man, he does not deserve to die like one!'

Mick was roughly manhandled upright, held tightly by a pair of scowling pirates.

El Niño turned to his crew. 'We have not had any real, Moorish entertainment since that last Spanish vessel, have we, lads?'

The assembly of scarfed and brightly dressed men cheered their assent. From overhead, the great hawk swooped down, landing gracefully on its master's wrist.

The pirate leader swung his other arm around Christopher's bare shoulder. 'How is your head-lock, my friend?'

Christopher blinked quizzically.

El Niño kicked the cutlass into the guttering and clenched his good hand into a fist. 'Wrestling, Cristóbal – winner takes the loser in the way of my ancestors, while my crew watches. Agreed?'

Blood was rushing from his brain straight to his swelling prick. Mick couldn't think straight. He shook his stupefied head to clear it.

The pirate laughed. 'He does not want this – and he does. See, Cristóbal?'

Mick growled as El Niño's peg hand tapped the burgeoning length inside his tattered breeches. The last shreds of drunkenness left him.

'Strip him, lads! We'll do this properly. I will hold your clothes, Cristóbal, while you exact your revenge on this dog.' El Niño moved back, nodding to his hawk. 'My faithful Ramon enjoys a bit of sport.'

As the breeches were ripped unceremoniously from his thighs, Mick thought he saw El Niño wink. Then all thoughts of exactly what this Moorish custom consisted of fled from his brain and he was staring in awe at Christopher's slim, naked body.

The crowd of onlookers moved back, giving the wrestlers room and forming a wide circle around them.

A sudden gust of wind struck his face as Christopher tossed his underwear towards El Niño. Turning back to his opponent, Christopher felt the breeze erect the soft hair on the inside of his thighs.

Mick was more impressive than ever. Without the beard, and with his long mane of tangled hair hanging over his strong shoulders, he looked like some pale, Celtic god. The thick mat over his firm pectorals was frosted with salt crystals. Hardened by the wind, his nipples thrust outward through the forest of hair which narrowed into a broad channel on to well-defined abdominals. Even after weeks of near-starvation, his rangy body rippled with lean muscle. And between his bristling thighs, his heavy, half-hard cock swung as he slowly circled left.

Christopher mirrored the motion. He had never wrestled in his life. He had no idea what to do, but when Mick bent his knees and continued left, he approximated the stance and did likewise.

Overhead, the gentle creak of the rigging was the only sound other than the fall of their bare feet on the deck.

Christopher chewed his bottom lip. This wasn't fair: Mick was drunk and, despite the Irishman's greater strength and size, Christopher knew he had the man at a disadvantage.

Then the object of his desire belied his inebriated state and darted forward, gripping Christopher's right arm and twisting it up behind his back.

With a howl, the slender midshipman managed to wrench himself free, only to be grabbed again, this time around the waist. As Mick's arms tightened, Christopher felt his feet leave the deck.

The prisoners cheered.

The pirates booed.

El Niño stepped forward. 'This is not going to be much of a fight.' The husky laugh was tinged with disappointment. 'Cook? Bring that pot of fish oil!'

Wriggling in mid air, Christopher felt the crisp hair on Mick's chest rasp against the skin on his back. Then a lukewarm, greasy mass hit him in the face and the arms slipped away. As his feet returned to the deck, Christopher lunged forward.

And slid.

The crew laughed uproariously.

Tentatively, Christopher climbed to his feet. He stared down at his body. A slick, stinking film drenched his chest, arms and legs, even coating his cock which was now a greasy, shining curve.

El Niño was applauding. 'This will even up the odds, I think. Ten doubloons on the Englishman!'

'I'll give you five on the Irish fellow!'

'Six!'

'Eight!'

Wiping a smear of oil from his eyes, Christopher felt the sliminess of the palms of his hands. He blinked at Mick, then gasped.

The fish oil had transformed the Irishman into a sleek, otter-like creature. His hair was greased back over his head. His chest shone like the pelt of some aquatic mammal and his strong legs gleamed in the hot, noon sunshine. Mick turned, trying to wipe the oil from his back and shoulders.

The greasy mounds of the Irishman's arse filled Christopher's eyes.

Separating two rock-hard buttocks, a furrow of glossy hair caught the light and spangled blue-black. Awkwardly, Mick lifted one foot, then another, clumping around the deck in obvious disorientation.

Despite his revulsion at the smell and the seriousness of their situation, Christopher chuckled.

With a howl, Mick spun round. 'Laugh at me, would you?' Hair plastered to his skull, the Irishman launched himself forward.

Their bodies collided in a wet, oily slap.

The impact knocked the breath from Christopher's body.

Mick's hands scrabbled for purchase and failed.

Recovering himself, Christopher seized his opponent in a treacly embrace, only to find his arms sliding down Mick's slippery waist and settling around the man's arse-cheeks. His face was buried in a sea of greasy chest-hair.

Then Mick arched his back and the two wrestlers slid over each other.

The Irishman's slick legs twisted up over Christopher's shoulders. Thighs tightened around his neck. The man's cock slapped off one cheek and Christopher's head was thrust into an oily groin. He gasped. Mick's weighty ball-sac ground against his nose, cutting the breath from his lungs.

The Irishman was crushing Christopher's bones, thrusting down with his vice-like hips.

Christopher's mouth gaped as he struggled to breathe, while Mick's fingers scrabbled uselessly around his ankles. Then heavy hairiness filled his mouth and he found himself sucking on the Irishman's bollocks. He groaned, rolling his tongue over the puckered, sweaty skin and feeling the flesh shiver beneath his touch.

The grip around his ankles slackened. The body on top of his went limp then stiffened.

Seizing the opportunity, Christopher roared and arched up with all his strength. He thrust his fists into Mick's stomach and threw the man off. By the time he'd scrambled to his feet, Mick was staggering to his.

The assembly of pirates and prisoners whooped their approval: a good fight was more welcome than any particular outcome.

Trying to keep his footing firm, Christopher took a step towards his opponent.

This time, Mick followed the sweating midshipman's lead, cautiously advancing.

Cries of encouragement accompanied their movements: 'Look, they are both stiff! Each wants to best the other – each wants the prize!'

Breathing heavily, Christopher glanced down. His eyes widened as he gazed at his throbbing, full nine inches of aching manhood. The mere proximity of Mick, the grappling and wrestling, had aroused him more than ever – and so soon, after his time with Renato.

Amazement was almost his downfall. Mesmerised by the curve and tilt of his own prick, Christopher failed to either see or hear Mick's approach as the man darted behind him. He groaned as he was pulled backwards. The breath hissed through his teeth as a greasy arm reached between his legs and a strong fist clasped around his aching length.

The crowd went wild. 'The Irishman has him now! He has him in the palm of his hand!'

The combination of pain and desire blanked Christopher's mind. Reaching around, he slid his hands down over the small of Mick's back and grabbed the man's arse-cheeks. His fingers burrowed deep into the thickly furred crevice. 'Let me go!'

The response was low and breathy. 'Never, sir – never!'

Christopher leant forward, bending his knees and trying to lessen the pressure against his bollocks. Mick's fist slid up then down, bringing flush after flush to Christopher's already scarlet face and swelling his gripped shaft further. With a low howl, he released the Irishman's arse, slipped his hands between himself and his attacker and thrust his own head between his knees. 'Never?'

The crowd roared as one, watching Mick sail cleanly over Christopher's hunched shoulders and land with a thud.

Before the Irishman could recover, Christopher threw himself on top of him, nudging Mick's thickly haired legs apart and holding the fellow's wrists flat against the deck.

Tangled locks fanned out behind Mick's thrashing head. His blue irises were fiery with anger, hate, humiliation –

Heart pounding, Christopher brought his face very close to the furious one. His curving, oily prick flexed against another.

– and desire. Mick stared into Christopher's eyes.

Christopher stared back. His lips parted, and he lowered his mouth on to the Irishman's.

Somewhere behind, the assembled pirates and prisoners cheered their approval.

Mick didn't hear them.

Neither did Christopher.

Eye-lock paralleled lip-lock. Gazing into dark, lust-filled pupils, Christopher slipped his tongue into Mick's mouth and felt the responding groan through every straining muscle.

Mick's kiss was rough and hard. He gouged at Christopher's lips, thrusting back with his tongue and filling his subduer's mouth with saliva.

Christopher returned the passion, feeling two pricks flex as one against his stomach as he ground his lips on to Mick's teeth.

Then the Irishman pulled away.

The crown hissed its disappointment.

'Take me, Christopher — I am yours, for ever.' The words were barely audible. 'Your kiss has finished what your ferule began. I want your prick inside me — here and now, for everyone to see.'

Christopher's breath caught in his throat. His grip slackened around Mick's wrists. His bollocks throbbing, Christopher moved back, ducking down to raise strong, quivering legs on to his own, slender shoulders.

Mick arched his back, feeling his conqueror's fingers moving over the cheeks of his arse. A great tremble shook his very bones as the vast helmet of flesh positioned itself against the entrance to his body.

Christopher thrust forward, cradling Mick's shoulders, while with his other hand he guided his prick home.

Mick whimpered. Slick with fish oil and sex-sweat, the thick head entered him in one strong thrust, stretching the lips of his arse to a thin, tingling membrane of muscle. The vast rod throbbed on, blazing a trail of fire as it pushed on up inside him. He was vaguely aware of a wet splatter against his oil-slicked chest as his own cock shot its release.

Mick could feel the man's breath on his face, taste the sweat which dripped from Christopher's forehead, smell the rich masculine stench of their passion.

His body was no longer his own.

The wads of spunk which pumped from his gaping slit were mere tributes to his blond, lusty lover.

The spangling on the periphery of his vision was nothing compared to the flashing pull of his midshipman's eyes — and the flexing length of flesh which pushed on up into him like the prow of a great ship.

Everything he had was Christopher's.

His only thought — nay, purpose — was to feel that rod of flesh shoot its seed into his tight, unworthy hole.

Filling his rectum, Christopher paused, panting. Then the thickness in Mick's arse was receding.

Tears rolled down Mick's face as he shot another volley on to his right nipple.

He was nothing — without his lover's prick in his arse he was less than nothing.

As the swollen length of Christopher's cock moved slowly out of him, Mick writhed and thrashed, clenching walls of muscle and trying to keep it there. Then the great, turgid head was widening the lips of his arse again. Mick roared.

He was being torn apart, ripped and rent asunder by the burgeoning glans. The pain of being so stretched and the emptiness inside him was nothing compared to the naked need in his mind.

Just as he thought he might tear, Christopher's mouth covered his and his lover's rod rammed back into him.

Mick arched up into the kiss, clinging on. Despite the fish oil, and the number of cocks he'd had inside him over the years, this felt like the first time – and like nothing else he'd ever experienced.

He didn't matter.

The agony didn't matter.

Nothing mattered, except Mick's need to feel Christopher's hot spunk in his arse.

His lover fucked him furiously. Long, thorough strokes became shorter, jabbing movements and the prow in his arse became the ferule on his back.

The burning in his rectum altered to a faint throbbing which built to a bone-shattering vibration. Mick gasped into Christopher's mouth, sucking his lover's tongue between his lips as the prick in his arse twisted and changed angle. The urge to piss was overwhelming.

Then he was howling, choking on saliva as the obligation to empty his bladder was replaced by a new sensation. His sturdy, half-hard cock was swelling again. Desire pumped through the thick veins which curled around the shaft until they stood out, blue and pulsing.

Christopher's strokes increased in speed and force. Mick's shoulders stung, his vertebrae scraped almost raw as his back was dragged along the rough surface of the deck.

The midshipman's body went rigid. His lover's mouth left his. A deep roar of anguish tore itself free from inside Mick. Before he could take another breath, the prick inside him flexed one final time. Screaming his fucker's name, Mick came again just as Christopher's spunk filled his spasming rectum.

He shot again and again, feeling Christopher's seed hot and fiery against quivering walls of muscle.

Then rough hands were wrenching them both to their feet.

Dazed by the release, and with his prick still spurting against his stomach, Mick's right arm was raised to the skies.

'The winners!'

On one side of a grinning El Niño, Mick blinked at Christopher's glowing eyes.

The midshipman's bruised lips formed three short words, then Mick's legs gave way and he crumpled into a heap.

His last sight, as Christopher's cooling seed tracked a slimy trail down the back of his thighs, was of his beloved's concerned face.

Twenty-Eight

He came round to the gentle swaying of a much smaller vessel and loud cries of farewell. Raising himself from Christopher's lap, Mick blinked at the *Caliente*'s departing hulk and the waving figures which lined her portside. Arms tightened around his still-oily waist. A soft kiss brushed the top of his head.

'You are mine, Mick: I am yours, you are mine and we are free.'

He smiled at a small, red-headed figure who was leaping about on deck, six-fingered hands cupped around his full-lipped mouth. 'Be happy, Mr Savage!'

Mick grinned, eyes moving to the curly-haired boy at Cat's side. 'I will never forget you, Mr Christopher!'

Mick turned his head, and looked into his lover's soulful eyes.

Christopher sighed. 'I have a lot to thank Willicombe for. He accidentally taught me my true nature and, I think, discovered his own along the way.'

Both their eyes refocused back to the *Caliente*. Between Cat and Willicombe, the Bear's large hairy form was now visible, one great arm around each of the boys' shoulders. 'You are a man of honour, Savage. I salute you, and wish you well.'

Mick smiled happily, leaning back against Christopher's chest. As their small rowing boat drifted further away, he caught sight of two very different shapes standing on the bow of the Spanish galleon. The larger of the two leant over the side.

'Michael Savage, you broke me when I tried mistakenly to break you. If this rascally pirate ever releases me, my first action will be to embrace my son, Orlando, and I thank you, sir!'

Christopher kissed Mick's ear. 'He understands, my love. At last Josiah Rock realises all men are impregnable, unless they wish to be taken.'

Then they both ducked in surprise as large wings swooped low over the rowing boat and dropped a wriggling fish at Mick's bare feet.

'*Hola*, my friends! Ramon gives you my parting gift. Although you are both now rich beyond any worldly treasure, even lovers must eat!' El Niño had climbed up the rigging, and was now stretching out his peg hand to receive his hawk. 'There is also fresh water and salt beef in those kegs, to sustain you on your voyage.'

Christopher grabbed the fish and waved it aloft. 'Thank you, Renato – thank you for everything! May you also find what you are searching for!'

Mick arched a brow. 'What is it for which El Niño searches, anyway?' The response was a rumbling laugh from his beloved.

'That which we all crave. Someone with whom we can be ourselves. But as long as he has his lusty crew, Renato will be a happy man.' Christopher moved around, slipping between Mick's hairy thighs and taking the Irishman's half-hard cock between his lips.

Mick groaned. 'What about your studies? Lady Violet? You are still betrothed, and you have a thesis to finish.'

'Damn them both! Lady Violet's father will buy her another husband, and the last thing Geoffrey Chaucer needs is another pretentious interpretation of his work!' Christopher chuckled then fell silent, allowing Mick's stretching cock to lie in his mouth and slowly fill it.

Mick moaned, tangling his fingers in his lover's blond hair and parting his thighs further.

As the *Caliente*'s great sails billowed and the wind drove her west towards the distant Indies, Mick felt his foreskin eased back by the pressure of his growing arousal and the ministrations of Christopher's tongue and teeth.

Christopher nibbled playfully at the heavy folds of skin.

Mick arched his back off the side of the rowing boat. His bollocks tightened, knitting together in a sudden clench as the blond man gripped his shaft and poked the tip of his tongue under the collar of skin. Mick's voice was hoarse. 'I have fucked the arses of many lords, sucked their pricks and tasted their hot desire but nothing has ever felt like this!'

Christopher's laugh came via his nostrils, pouring a stream of warm air on to Mick's tensed stomach. Sliding his mouth back along Mick's prick to the swelling head, he looked up from between the Irishman's thighs.

Their eyes met, and spoke volumes.

Mick stared down at his Englishman's handsome, lust-creased face. As he watched, Christopher's lips tightened into an O-shape just below the head of Mick's now-aching cock then slid over the curving shaft to the very root.

Mick growled. Sensation shimmered over his glans as it impacted with the roof of his Englishman's mouth. His entire torso left the small rowing boat and he quivered, supported only by his shoulders and heels.

Then Christopher's hands were gripping the cheeks of his arse, two strong pinkies caressing his crack and the man was moving more slickly up and down Mick's length.

Mick ran his fingers over Christopher's head, feeling the softness of his man's blond hair. Each descent of the mouth brought him closer to heaven, each retreat of the firm O urging him beyond.

Sweating palms cradled the cheeks of his arse as they tensed and flexed. Mick clenched his fists in Christopher's hair, rising upwards then thudding back down. The edge of the boat slammed into his shoulders, heavier than the ferule but equally arousing.

His nipples pushed up towards a cloudless sky, swollen and tingling. Every muscle on his belly tightened, mirrored by a longing deep in his very bowels.

Christopher sucked Mick's prick with less force than he'd ploughed his beloved's arse on the *Caliente* in front of a cheering crowd of drunken sailors, and with a different intensity than when he'd brought the vicious ferule down on Mick's back and shoulders. But his mouth was as determined as his cock and arm had been, and he showed no mercy.

Thighs splayed, eyes rolling, Mick surrendered himself, body, mind and soul to his lover. Christopher's lips paused at the root of him, then retreated slowly and deliciously. Surrounded by warm, tight wetness, Mick's shaft receded towards his man's lip-sheathed teeth. As his shoulders impacted with the rim of the boat again, he jerked forward and looked down.

Christopher was gazing up, face sweating. Their eyes met a second time, before the midshipman tilted his head back. His strong chin rough with days of growth, the bristling stubble against Mick's shaft was the final straw.

When Christopher skilfully flicked the tip of his tongue over the velvet glans and into the tiny slit, it was as sharp and inflaming as the touch of the cruel ferule. Thighs tightening, bollocks twisting, Mick's fingers curled into fists amidst Christopher's sweat-soaked blond hair and he shot into his beloved's mouth. He barely heard the half-smothered gasps of pleasure from the man between his legs as his balls clenched again and again.

Then his prick was a quivering curl against his own and Christopher's stomach. A salty mouth pressed itself to his. Tasting himself on his lover's breath, Mick moaned into the kiss and slumped into Christopher's arms.

On the third day, they spotted land.

Passing the last of the fresh water to Christopher, Mick shaded his eyes and peered. 'They are small, but definitely islands of some sort.'

'Uninhabited, do you think?'

Christopher nodded. 'There will be much work to do, building a shelter and such.' He flicked the tip of his makeshift fishing rod against Mick's shoulders and heard the gasp of response. 'It is a good thing I have a man with me who is not afraid of honest labour and enjoys the lash.'

Mick blushed scarlet. 'I am yours until I am old and grey, my lord, for whatever use you see fit to put me.'

Christopher kissed Mick's ear then whooped. 'We will probably be the first men to set foot on these islands! We must name them!'

A gentle breeze pushed their tiny boat onward.

'New England?' Mick smiled.

'No, something special – something from us.'

Mick grinned. 'Christopherland?'

The sun-tanned blond by his side laughed. 'No.' He delivered a mock punch to Mick's stubbly face, then stared up. 'The sky is so blue: like your eyes, Mick. What about the Azures?'

The Irishman repeated the words, caressing them in his mouth as he had savoured and caressed every inch of his saviour's strong body over the past three idyllic days.

Christopher seized his lover's hand. 'Your accent makes it sound better – the Azores it is!' He twined his fingers with Mick's and together they watched their new home shimmer against a cloudless sky.

IDOL NEW BOOKS

Also published:

THE KING'S MEN
Christian Fall

Ned Medcombe, spoilt son of an Oxfordshire landowner, has always remembered his first love: the beautiful, golden-haired Lewis. But seventeenth-century England forbids such a love and Ned is content to indulge his domineering passions with the willing members of the local community, including the submissive parish cleric. Until the Civil War changes his world, and he is forced to pursue his desires as a soldier in Cromwell's army – while his long-lost lover fights as one of the King's men.

ISBN 0 352 33207 7

THE VELVET WEB
Christopher Summerisle

The year is 1889. Daniel McGaw arrives at Calverdale, a centre of academic excellence buried deep in the English countryside. But this is like no other college. As Daniel explores, he discovers secret passages in the grounds and forbidden texts in the library. The young male students, isolated from the outside world, share a darkly bizarre brotherhood based on the most extreme forms of erotic expression. It isn't long before Daniel is initiated into the rites that bind together the youths of Calverdale in a web of desire.

ISBN 0 352 33208 5

CHAINS OF DECEIT
Paul C. Alexander

Journalist Nathan Dexter's life is turned around when he meets a young student called Scott – someone who offers him the relationship for which he's been searching. Then Nathan's best friend goes missing, and Nathan uncovers evidence that he has become the victim of a slavery ring which is rumoured to be operating out of London's leather scene. To rescue their friend and expose the perverted slave trade, Nathan and Scott must go undercover, risking detection and betrayal at every turn.

ISBN 0 352 33206 9

HALL OF MIRRORS
Robert Black

Tom Jarrett operates the Big Wheel at Gamlin's Fair. When young runaway Jason Bradley tries to rob him, events are set in motion which draw the two together in a tangled web of mutual mistrust and growing fascination. Each carries a burden of old guilt and tragic unspoken history; each is running from something. But the fair is a place of magic and mystery where normal rules don't apply, and Jason is soon on a journey of self-discovery, unbridled sexuality and growing love.

ISBN 0 352 33209 3

THE SLAVE TRADE
James Masters

Barely eighteen and innocent of the desires of men, Marc is the sole survivor of a noble British family. When his home village falls to the invading Romans, he is forced to flee for his life. He first finds sanctuary with Karl, a barbarian from far-off Germanica, whose words seem kind but whose eyes conceal a dark and brooding menace. And then they are captured by Gaius, a general in Caesar's all-conquering army, in whose camp they learn the true meaning – and pleasures – of slavery.

ISBN 0 352 33228 X

DARK RIDER
Jack Gordon

While the rulers of a remote Scottish island play bizarre games of sexual dominance with the Argentinian Angelo, his friend Robert – consumed with jealous longing for his coffee-skinned companion – assuages his desires with the willing locals.

ISBN 0 352 33243 3

CONQUISTADOR
Jeff Hunter

It is the dying days of the Aztec empire. Axaten and Quetzel are members of the Stable, servants of the Sun Prince chosen for their bravery and beauty. But it is not just an honour and a duty to join this society, it is also the ultimate sexual achievement. Until the arrival of Juan, a young Spanish conquistador, sets the men of the Stable on an adventure of bondage, lust and deception.

ISBN 0 352 33244 1

TO SERVE TWO MASTERS
Gordon Neale

In the isolated land of Ilyria men are bought and sold as slaves. Rock, brought up to expect to be treated as mere 'livestock', yearns to be sold to the beautiful youth Dorian. But Dorian's brother is as cruel as he is handsome, and if Rock is bought by one brother he will be owned by both.

ISBN 0 352 33245 X

CUSTOMS OF THE COUNTRY
Rupert Thomas

James Cardell has left school and is looking forward to going to Oxford. That summer of 1924, however, he will spend with his cousins in a tiny village in rural Kent. There he finds he can pursue his love of painting – and begin to explore his obsession with the male physique.

ISBN 0 352 33246 8

DOCTOR REYNARD'S EXPERIMENT
Robert Black

A dark world of secret brothels, dungeons and sexual cabarets exists behind the respectable facade of Victorian London. The degenerate Lord Spearman introduces Dr Richard Reynard, dashing bachelor, to this hidden world. And Walter Starling, the doctor's new footman, finds himself torn between affection for his master and the attractions of London's underworld.

ISBN 0 352 33252 2

CODE OF SUBMISSION
Paul C. Alexander

Having uncovered and defeated a slave ring operating in London's leather scene, journalist Nathan Dexter had hoped to enjoy a peaceful life with his boyfriend Scott. But when it becomes clear that the perverted slave trade has started again, Nathan has no choice but to travel across Europe and America in his bid to stop it.

ISBN 0 352 33272 7

SLAVES OF TARNE
Gordon Neale

Pascal willingly follows the mysterious and alluring Casper to Tarne, a community of men enslaved to men. Tarne is everything that Pascal has ever fantasised about, but he he begins to sense a sinister aspect to Casper's magnetism. Pascal has to choose between the pleasures of submission and acting to save the people he loves.

ISBN 0 352 33273 5

ROUGH WITH THE SMOOTH
Dominic Arrow

Amid the crime, violence and unemployment of North London, the young men who attend Jonathan Carey's drop-in centre have few choices. One of the young men, Stewart, finds himself torn between the increasingly intimate horseplay of his fellows and the perverse allure of the criminal underworld. Can Jonathan save Stewart from the bullies on the streets and behind bars?

ISBN 0 352 33292 1

CONVICT CHAINS
Philip Markham

Peter Warren, printer's apprentice in the London of the 1830s, discovers his sexuality and taste for submission at the hands of Richard Barkworth. Thus begins a downward spiral of degradation, of which transportation to the Australian colonies is only the beginning.

ISBN 0 352 33300 6

SHAME
Raydon Pelham

On holiday in West Hollywood, Briton Martyn Townsend meets and falls in love with the daredevil Scott. When Scott is murdered, Martyn's hunt for the truth and for the mysterious Peter, Scott's ex-lover, leads him to the clubs of London and Ibiza.

ISBN 0 352 33302 2

WE NEED YOUR HELP . . .

to plan the future of Idol books —

Yours are the only opinions that matter. Idol is a new and exciting venture: the first British series of books devoted to homoerotic fiction for men.

We're going to do our best to provide the sexiest, best-written books you can buy. And we'd like you to help in these early stages. Tell us what you want to read. There's a freepost address for your filled-in questionnaires, so you won't even need to buy a stamp.

THE IDOL QUESTIONNAIRE

SECTION ONE: ABOUT YOU

1.1 Sex *(we presume you are male, but just in case)*
      Are you?
      Male   ☐
      Female   ☐

1.2 Age
      under 21   ☐   21–30   ☐
      31–40   ☐   41–50   ☐
      51–60   ☐   over 60   ☐

1.3 At what age did you leave full-time education?
      still in education   ☐   16 or younger   ☐
      17–19   ☐   20 or older   ☐

1.4 Occupation _____

1.5 Annual household income _____

1.6 We are perfectly happy for you to remain anonymous; but if you would like us to send you a free booklist of Idol books, please insert your name and address

_____

_____

_____

_____

SECTION TWO: ABOUT BUYING IDOL BOOKS

2.1 Where did you get this copy of *HMS Submission*?
    Bought at chain book shop ☐
    Bought at independent book shop ☐
    Bought at supermarket ☐
    Bought at book exchange or used book shop ☐
    I borrowed it/found it ☐
    My partner bought it ☐

2.2 How did you find out about Idol books?
    I saw them in a shop ☐
    I saw them advertised in a magazine ☐
    I read about them in _____
    Other _____

2.3 Please tick the following statements you agree with:
    I would be less embarrassed about buying Idol
    books if the cover pictures were less explicit ☐
    I think that in general the pictures on Idol
    books are about right ☐
    I think Idol cover pictures should be as
    explicit as possible ☐

2.4 Would you read an Idol book in a public place – on a train for instance?
    Yes ☐   No ☐

SECTION THREE: ABOUT THIS IDOL BOOK

3.1 Do you think the sex content in this book is:
    Too much ☐   About right ☐
    Not enough ☐

3.2 Do you think the writing style in this book is:

Too unreal/escapist	☐	About right	☐
Too down to earth	☐		

3.3 Do you think the story in this book is:

Too complicated	☐	About right	☐
Too boring/simple	☐		

3.4 Do you think the cover of this book is:

Too explicit	☐	About right	☐
Not explicit enough	☐		

Here's a space for any other comments:

SECTION FOUR: ABOUT OTHER IDOL BOOKS

4.1 How many Idol books have you read?

4.2 If more than one, which one did you prefer?

_____

4.3 Why?

SECTION FIVE: ABOUT YOUR IDEAL EROTIC NOVEL

We want to publish the books you want to read – so this is your chance to tell us exactly what your ideal erotic novel would be like.

5.1 Using a scale of 1 to 5 (1 = no interest at all, 5 = your ideal), please rate the following possible settings for an erotic novel:

Roman / Ancient World	☐
Medieval / barbarian / sword 'n' sorcery	☐
Renaissance / Elizabethan / Restoration	☐
Victorian / Edwardian	☐
1920s & 1930s	☐
Present day	☐
Future / Science Fiction	☐

5.2 Using the same scale of 1 to 5, please rate the following themes you may find in an erotic novel:

Bondage / fetishism ☐
Romantic love ☐
SM / corporal punishment ☐
Bisexuality ☐
Group sex ☐
Watersports ☐
Rent / sex for money ☐

5.3 Using the same scale of 1 to 5, please rate the following styles in which an erotic novel could be written:

Gritty realism, down to earth ☐
Set in real life but ignoring its more unpleasant aspects ☐
Escapist fantasy, but just about believable ☐
Complete escapism, totally unrealistic ☐

5.4 In a book that features power differentials or sexual initiation, would you prefer the writing to be from the viewpoint of the dominant / experienced or submissive / inexperienced characters:

Dominant / Experienced ☐
Submissive / Inexperienced ☐
Both ☐

5.5 We'd like to include characters close to your ideal lover. What characteristics would your ideal lover have? Tick as many as you want:

Dominant	☐	Caring	☐
Slim	☐	Rugged	☐
Extroverted	☐	Romantic	☐
Bisexual	☐	Old	☐
Working Class	☐	Intellectual	☐
Introverted	☐	Professional	☐
Submissive	☐	Pervy	☐
Cruel	☐	Ordinary	☐
Young	☐	Muscular	☐
Naïve	☐		

Anything else? _____

5.6 Is there one particular setting or subject matter that your ideal erotic novel would contain:

_____

5.7 As you'll have seen, we include safe-sex guidelines in every book. However, while our policy is always to show safe sex in stories with contemporary settings, we don't insist on safe-sex practices in stories with historical settings because it would be anachronistic. What, if anything, would you change about this policy?

_____

_____

SECTION SIX: LAST WORDS

6.1 What do you like best about Idol books?

_____

6.2 What do you most dislike about Idol books?

_____

6.3 In what way, if any, would you like to change Idol covers?

_____

6.4 Here's a space for any other comments:

_____

_____

_____

_____

Thanks for completing this questionnaire. Now either tear it out, or photocopy it, then put it in an envelope and send it to:

Idol
FREEPOST
London
W10 5BR

You don't need a stamp if you're in the UK, but you'll need one if you're posting from overseas.